FIRE
COUNTRY

A Dwellers Saga Sister Novel

Book One of

The Country Saga

David Estes

ISBN-13- 978-1482055986
ISBN-10- 1482055988

Jacket art and design by Regina Wamba at MaeIDesign & Photography

This book is dedicated to my wife, Adele.
Without her, I'd still be in a cubicle.

A Guide to Slang and Terminology in Fire Country

Wooloo- crazy or insane

Baggard- an insult

Tug- a large buffalo-like animal that provides everything from food to clothing to shelter for those who live in the desert

Smoky- attractive

Prickler- cactus

Scorch- hell, or the underworld

Searin'- a mild curse word

Blaze- a somewhat-frowned-upon term for human waste

Killer- large wolfish animals that roam the desert

Burnin'- a stronger curse word

Cotee- Mangy coyote-like animals that hunt in large packs and generally prefer already dead prey

Call- husband or wife previously assigned during a Heater ceremony.

Bundle- diaper

Shilty- slutty or promiscuous

Grizzed- angry

Pointer- arrow

Fire stick- gun

Fire chariot- truck

'Zard- lizard

Totter- a young child, a toddler

Midder- older kids, but not yet teenagers

Youngling- teenager

Shanker- slacker, lazy person

The Fire- the airborne disease caused by long exposure to the toxic air that has lowered life expectancies substantially

THE LAW

*****

In its original form, as approved by the Greynote Council

Article 56

A Bearer shall, upon reaching the appropriate age of sixteen years old, be Called to a man, no younger than eighteen years old, to Bear children, immediately and every three years thereafter.

This is THE LAW.

One

When I'm sixteen and reach the midpoint of my life, I'll have my first child. Not 'cause I want to, or 'cause I made a silly decision with a strapping young boy after sneaking a few sips of my father's fire juice, but 'cause I must. It's the Law of my people, the Heaters; a Law that's kept us alive and thriving for many years. A Law I fear.

I learned all about the ways of the world when I turned seven: the bleeding time, what I would hafta do with a man when I turned sixteen, and how the baby—my baby—would grow inside me for nine full moons. Even though it all seemed like a hundred years distant at the time, I cried for two days. Now that it's less'n a year away, I'm too scared to cry.

Veeva told me all 'bout the pain. She's seventeen, and her baby's five full moons old and "uglier'n one of the hairy ol' warts on the Medicine Man's feet." Or at least that's how she describes Polk. Me, I think he's sorta cute, in a scrunched up, fat-cheeked kind of way. Well, anyway, she said to me, "Siena, you never felt pain so *burnin'* fierce. I screamed and screamed…and then screamed some more. And then this ugly *tug* of a baby comes out all red-faced and oozy. And now I'm stuck with it." I didn't remind her Polk's a *him* not an *it*.

I already knew about her screaming. Everyone in the village knew about Veeva's screaming. She sounded like a three ton tug stuck in a bog hole. Veeva's always cursing, too, throwing around words like *burnin'* and *searin'* and *blaze*—words that'd draw my father's hand across my face like lightning if I ever let them slip out of my mouth like they're nothing more'n common language.

In any case, everything she tells me about turning sixteen just makes me wish I didn't hafta get older, could stay fifteen for the next seventeen or so years, until the Fire takes me.

It's not fair, really, that boys get to wait until they're eighteen 'fore their names get put in the Call. I'd kill for an extra two years of no baby.

Veeva told me something else, too, something they didn't teach us when I was seven. She told me the only good part of it all was when she got to lie with her Call, a guy named Grunt, who everyone thinks is a bit of a shanker. I've personally never seen him do a lick of work, and he's always coming up with some excuse or another to avoid the tug hunts. Well, Veeva told me that he makes up for all of that in the tent. Most of what she told me made my stomach curl, but she swore on the sun goddess that it was the best day of her life. To her, shanky ol' Grunt is a real stallion.

9

But even if there was something good about turning sixteen, there's still no guy in the village that I'd want to be my Call. I mean, most of them are so old and crusty, well on their ways to thirty, and even the youngest eligible men—the eighteen-year-olds—include guys like Grunt, who'll also be eligible for my Call 'cause Veeva hasta wait another two years 'fore she can get child-big again. No matter how much of a stallion Veeva claims Grunt is, I don't wanna get close enough to him to even smell his fire-juice-reekin' breath, much less lie with him in a tent.

"Siena!" a voice whispers in my ear.

I flinch, startled to hear my name, snapping away from my thoughts like a dung beetle scurrying from a scorpion. Laughter crowds around me and I cringe. Not again. My daydreaming's likely cost me another day on Shovel Duty, which we like to call Blaze Craze when our parents ain't listening.

"Youngling Siena," Teacher Mas says, "I asked you a question. Will you please grace us with an answer?" One of the only good things about turning sixteen'll be not getting called "Youngling" anymore.

I feel twenty sets of eyes on me, and suddenly a speck of durt on my tugskin moccasins catches my attention. "Can you please repeat the question, Teacher?" I mumble to my feet, trying to sound as respectful as possible.

"Repeating the question will result in Shovel Duty, Siena, which will bring your total to four days, I believe."

I stare at my feet, lips closed. I wonder if Teacher *not* repeating the question is an option, but I'm smart enough not to ask.

"The question I asked you was: What is the average life expectancy for a male in fire country?"

Stupid, stupid, stupid. It's a question that any four-year-old Totter with half a brain could answer. It's blaze that's been shoveled into all our heads for the last eleven years. "Thirty years old," I say, finally looking up. I keep my eyes trained forward, on Teacher Mas, ignoring the stares and the whispers from the other Younglings.

Teacher's black hair is twisted into two braids, one on either side, hanging in front of his ears. His eyes are dark and slitted and although I can't tell whether he's looking at me, I know he is. "And females?" he asks.

"Thirty two," I answer without hesitation. I take a deep breath and hold it, still feeling the stares and smirks on me, hoping Teacher'll move on to someone else. The fierceness of the fiery noonday sun presses down on my forehead so hard it squeezes sweat out of my pores and into my eyes. It's days like this I wish the Learning house had a roof, and not just three wobbly walls made from the logs of some tree the Greynotes, the elders of our village, bartered from the Icers, who are our closest neighbors. I blink rapidly, flinching when the perspiration burns my eyes like acid. Someone laughs, but I don't know who.

Teacher speaks. "I ask you this not to test your knowledge, for clearly every Youngling in fire country knows this, but to ensure your understanding as to our ways, our traditions, our *Laws*." Thankfully, the heads turn back to Teacher and I can let out the breath I been holding.

"Nice one, Sie," Circ hisses from beside me.

I glance toward him, eyes narrowed. "You coulda helped me out," I whisper back.

His deeply tanned face, darker'n-dark brown eyes, and bronzed lips are full of amusement. I hear what the other

11

Younglings say about him: he's the smokiest guy in the whole village. "I tried to, dreamer. It took me four tries to get your attention."

Teacher Mas drones on. "Living in a world where each breath we take slowly kills us, where the Glass people kill us with their chariots of fire, where the Killers crave our blood, our flesh, where our neighbors, the people of ice country, are bound tenuously by a flimsy trade agreement, requires discipline, order, commitment. Each of you took a pledge when you turned twelve to uphold this order, to obey the Laws of our people. The Laws of fire country."

Ugh—I've heard this all 'fore, so many times that if I hear one more mention of the Laws of fire country, I think I might scream. Nothing against them or anything, considering they were created to help us all survive, but 'tween my father and the Teachers, I've had enough of it.

Watching Teacher, I risk another whisper to Circ. "You coulda told me what question he asked."

"Teacher would've heard—and then we'd both be on Blaze Craze."

He's right, not that I'll admit it. Teacher doesn't miss much. At least not with me. In the last full moon alone, I been caught daydreaming four times. Wait till my father finds out.

"The Wild Ones steal more and more of our precious daughters with each new season." Teacher's words catch my attention. *The Wild Ones.* I've never heard Teacher talk about them 'fore. In fact, I've never heard anyone talk about them, 'cept for us Younglings, with our rumors and gossip—not openly anyway. My head spins as I grapple with his words and my thoughts. The Wild Ones. My sister. The Wild Ones. Skye. Wild. Sis.

12

"It is obvious I have captured the attention of many of you Younglings," Teacher continues. "It's good to know I can still do that after all these years." He laughs softly to himself. "Surely you have all heard rumors of the Wild Ones, descending on our village during the Call, snatching our new Bearers from our huts, our tents, and our campfires." He pauses, looks around, his eyes lingering on mine. "Well, I'm here today to confirm that some of the rumors are true."

I knew it, I think. My sister didn't run away like everyone said. She was taken, against her will, to join the group of feral women who are wreaking havoc across fire country. *The Wild Ones do exist.*

"We hafta do something," I accidentally say out loud, my thoughts spilling from my lips like intestines from a gutted tug's stomach.

Once more, the room turns toward me, and I find myself investigating an odd-shaped rock on the dusty ground. Hawk, a thick-headed guy with more muscles'n brains, says, "What are you gonna do, Scrawny? You can't even carry a full wash bucket." My cheeks burn as I continue to study the rock, which sorta looks like a fist. In my peripheral vision, I see Circ give him a death stare.

"Watch it, Hawk," Teacher says, "or you'll earn your own shovel. In fact, Siena's right." I'm so shocked by his words that I forget about the rock and Hawk, and look up.

"I am?" I say, sinking further into the pit of stupidity I been digging all morning.

"Don't sound so surprised, Siena. We all have a part to play in turning this around. We must be vigilant, must not allow ourselves even a speck of doubt that maintaining the traditions of our fathers is not the best thing for us."

"I think the Wilds sound pretty smoky," Hawk says from the back. There are a few giggles from some of the more shilty girls, and two of Hawk's mates slap him on the back like he's just made the joke of the year.

"What do we do, Teacher?" Farla, a soft-spoken girl, asks earnestly.

Teacher nods. "Now you're asking the right questions. Two things: First, if you hear anything—anything at all—about the Wild Ones, tell your fathers; and second—"

"What about our mothers?" someone asks, interrupting.

"Excuse me?" Teacher Mas says, peering over the tops of the cross-legged Younglings to find the asker of the question.

"The mothers? You said to tell our *fathers* if we hear anything about the Wilds. Shouldn't we tell our *mothers*, too?"

I look around to find who spoke. Lara. I shoulda known. She's always stirring the kettle, both during Learning and Social time, with her radical ideas. She's always saying crazy things about what girls should be allowed to do, like hunt and play feetball. My father's always said she's one to watch, whatever that means. I, for one, kinda like her. At least she's never made fun of me, like most of t'others.

Her black hair is short, like a boy's, buzzed almost to the scalp. Appalling. How she obtained her father's permission for such a haircut is beyond me. But at least she's not a shilt, like so many of the other girls who sneak behind the border tents and swap spit with whichever Youngling they think is the smokiest—although at least they're not following the Law blindly either. I've always admired Lara's blaze-on-me-and-I'll-blaze-on-you attitude, although I'd never admit it for fear of my father finding out. He'd break out his favorite leather snapper for sure, the one that left the scars on my back when I was

14

thirteen and thought skipping Learning to watch the Hunters sounded like a good idea. "Tell your fathers first, and they can tell your mothers," Teacher says quickly. "Where was I? Oh yes, the second thing you can do. If the Wilds, I mean the Wild Ones, approach you, try to convince you to leave, whisper their lies in your ear, resist them. Close your ears to them and run away, screaming your head off. That's the best thing you can do."

Pondering Teacher's words, I look up at the sky, so big and red and monster-like, full of yellow-gray clouds as its claws, creeping down the horizon in streaks, practically scraping against the desert floor. And a single eye, blazing with fire—the eye of the sun goddess. It's no wonder they call this place fire country.

Two

Circ agrees to meet me later on, when it's time to take my punishment for daydreaming in class. But frst, I want to go let my frustrations out to Veeva, who'll understand them better'n most.

I cringe when I hear an eardrum-shattering scream from inside her tent. Her baby's got a set of lungs on him alright.

When I push through the tentflap, Veeva's all in a tizzy, muttering under her breath, rushing about, her hair a mess of curls around her face. She looks like *she's* about to scream, too. All I know is if she does, I'm making a run for it.

She shoots me a look when I enter, but doesn't stop her frantic rushing. "Searin' Polk's been burnin' tossin' his nuggets all day. He'll eat everythin' I got"—as if to illustrate, she stops, shaking her ample breasts wildly—"and more, but then he

16

chucks it all back up no more'n five moments later. Ohhh, yer in fer a real treat, Sie, just wait till it's yer turn. Wc can laugh all the way to the wooloo-hut together!"

'Fore I can respond, Polk lets out another shriek that'd shatter the glass windows in my family's hut. "Shut that vomit-hole of yers, Polk!" Veeva shouts, which only serves to enhance the volume of the squirming baby's cry.

"Lemme take him," I say, dodging puddles of barf to grab Polk, who's rolling around on a tugskin blanket. "You clean up the mess."

Veeva's shoulders drop, and she gives me a grateful half-smile. "Yer one of the good ones, Sie," she says, tucking a blanket between Polk's mouth and me. A precaution against the barfing. Maybe I shouldn't've been so quick to scoop the little bugger up.

Veev goes about mopping up the floor, talking a mile a second. "Ya know, kid," she says, even though she's only a year and a half older'n me, "'sides gettin' to lie every night with my man..." She pauses, looks up at me, licking her lips.

"Eww, gross, Vee!" I exclaim. Polk's surprisingly quiet, staring up at me with big eyes that would almost be cute if he weren't such a little vomit-sprayer.

"What? I ain't gonna lie. Grunt may not look it, but he gits a scorch of a lot smokier when the sun goddess goes to sleep."

I shake my head as a mental image of Grunt's fat belly bounces across my mind. "Agh, too much information, Vee!"

Veeva laughs, goes back to her cleaning. "Well, it's true. Anyway, 'sides the fun parts, this whole baby-makin' business ain't as fun as it sounds." I'm not sure when it ever sounded fun, but ignore it and let her continue. "Gettin' waked up in the middle of the burnin' night, havin' to change his bundle, havin' to feed 'im, havin' to figure out what the scorch he wants when nothin' seems to work."

Ugh. Even with what Veev calls "the fun parts," the whole thing sounds like a whole lot of work. *I still got half a year,* I remind myself, trying not to think about how things'll change when I'm a Bearer.

~~~

"Why would the Wilds whisper lies in my ear if they're going to kidnap me anyway?" I ask Circ the first chance I get after leaving Veev's tent. My voice sounds funny 'cause I've pinched my nose shut with my finger and thumb.

Circ laughs at my voice, and then says, "They're not going to kidnap you, Sie." I snort, 'cause his voice sounds even funnier with his nostrils clamped tight. My fingers come off my nose for a second and I get a whiff of the blaze pit that sits a stone's throw to the side. Screwing up my face, I pinch harder, until it hurts. A little pain is better'n the smell.

"I don't mean *me* me. I mean hypothetically speaking. If the Wilds were to try to kidnap me"—I look at Circ, trying not to laugh at the sight of his squashed nose—"or any other Youngling girl, why wouldn't they just grab her from behind, put a hand over her mouth, and carry her away in a tugskin sack?"

"Maybe they're all out of tugskin?" Circ says, cracking up and losing the grip on his nose. He sticks out his tongue as the foul odor sneaks up his nostrils. The tips of his moccasin-covered feet are touching mine as we sit cross-legged across from each other. We've sat this way since we were Totters.

18

"C'mon," I say, clutching my stomach, "I'm being serious." The only problem: it's hard to be serious when I can't stop laughing.

"I don't know, Sie, maybe it's easier if they can convince you to come with them, rather than having to haul your tiny butt away with you kicking and screaming."

It's a good point, but still...

"Something just doesn't smell right," I say, and we both crack up, but then just as quickly fall over gagging from the thick, putrid latrine air.

"Let's get this over with, then we can talk," Circ says, covering his mouth and nose with a hand.

I smile behind my own hand. "Thanks for helping me with Blaze Craze," I say.

"Just promise me you'll stop daydreaming in class. I don't ever want to have to do this again." He plucks his moccasins off with his spare hand, one at a time, and then pulls his thin white shirt over his head. I've seen him shirtless a thousand times, from Totter to Midder to Youngling, but this time I force myself to look closer, 'cause of what all t'other Youngling girls are saying about him. *Circ is so smoky. What I wouldn't give for five seconds with Circ behind the border tents. You're close with Circ, aren't you, Siena? Could you give him a message for me?* Of course I say I will, but I never do. If they don't have the guts to say whatever they want to right to his face, then they're not good enough for him. Plus, the thought of Circ behind the border tents with some shilty Youngling makes me a bit queasy.

Anyway, I try to see Circ from their perspective, just this once. To call his skin sun-kissed would be the understatement of the year, like calling a tug "Sorta big," or a Killer "Kinda dangerous." It's like the sun is infused in the very pigment of

19

his skin, leaving him golden brown and radiant. He's strong, too. Almost as strong as iron, his stomach flat and hard, his chest and arms cut like stone. But he's always been this way, hasn't he? Still staring at his torso, present-day Circ fades from my vision and is replaced with images of him growing up. Circ as a Totter, five-years-old, small and a bit pudgy in his stomach, arms and face; Circ turning eight and becoming a Midder, less chubby but still awkward-looking, with too-long arms and legs; Circ at twelve, a full-fledged Youngling, much taller and skinnier'n a tent pole, not a bulge of muscle anywhere on him.

The images fade and Circ stares at me. "What?" he says.

"Uh, nothing," I say, shaking my head and wondering when Circ became so smoky. It's weird how when you're around somebody so much you don't seem to notice the changes in them. It's like with every passing year he's become more'n more capable, while I stay just as useless as ever. He's good at everything, from hunting to feetball to Learning. And all I'm good at is daydreaming and getting in trouble. He's smoky, and as my nickname suggests, I'm Scrawny.

"You were daydreaming again, weren't you?" His words are accusing but his tone and expression are as light as the brambleweeds that tumble and bounce across the desert.

"You caught me," I mumble through my hand.

I see his grin creep around the edges of his fingers. He stands up and offers a hand. "Care to shovel some blaze with me, my lady?"

Despite my self-pitying thoughts, he manages to cheer me up, and I take his hand, laughing. He pulls me up, hands me a shovel. While I carry my shovel, Circ wheels a pushbarrow, and we follow our noses toward the stench, which becomes more'n more unbearable with each step. You've done this 'fore, I remind myself. You just hafta get used to the smell again.

If the smell is bad, the heat is unbearable. Although the heart of the summer is four full moons distant, you couldn't tell it by the weather. The air is as thick as 'zard soup, full of so much moisture that your skin bleeds sweat the moment you step from the shade, as if you've just taken a dip in the watering hole. All around us is flat, sandy desert, which radiates the heat like the embers of a dying cook fire. With summer nipping at our heels and winter approaching, almost everything is dead, the long strands of desert wildgrass having been burned away many full moons earlier. A few lonely pricklers continue to thwart death, the usually green, spiky plants turned brown by the sun, but rising stalwart from the desert; we call them the plants of the gods for a reason, bearing milk even in the harshest conditions. Without them, my people might not survive the winter.

We reach the edge of the blaze pit and look down. It's a real mess, as if no one's been here to shovel it for many quarter full moons, maybe even a few full moons. It's gonna be a long afternoon.

"Maybe we can just cover it with durt," I say hopefully.

Circ gives me a look. "Don't be such a shanker—you know it's not full yet."

"I'm not a shanker!" I protest.

"Well, you sure sound like one," Circ says, grinning. Now I know he's trying to get me all riled up.

Determined to prove him wrong, I roll up my dress and tie it off at the side, and then clamber down the side of the pit, feeling the blaze squish under the tread of my bare feet. Gross. Some even slips between my toes. Cockroaches scuttle out of

21

my path. The smell is all around me now, a brownish haze rising up as the collective crap of our entire village cooks under the watchful eye of the hot afternoon sun. Not a pleasant sight.

Gritting my teeth, I start shoveling. The goal is to even it out, move the blaze that's around the edges to the center. You see, people come and dump their family's blaze into this pit, but they're sure as scorch not gonna wade down into the muck and unload it in a good spot; no, they're gonna just run up to the pit as fast as they can, dump their dung around the edges and then take off lickety-split. That causes a problem: the blaze keeps on piling up around the edge, usually the edge of the pit closest to the border tents, until the pit is overflowing despite not being even close to full. Then a lucky shanker like me—not that I'm the least bit shanky—gets punished, and hasta use a shovel and old-fashioned sweat and grit to move the blaze around. Or if the pit is full, you get to cover it with durt so people can start using the next one. That's what I was hoping for earlier.

Anyway, I get right into it, heaping the scoop of my shovel full of stinky muck and tossing it as far toward the center as I can get it. Some of it splatters my clothes, but that's inevitable, so I don't give it another thought. Clothes can be cleaned, but the job's not gonna get done without us doing it.

A moment later Circ's beside me, and within two scoops, his bare chest is glistening with a thin sheen of sweat that reflects the light into my eyes like thousands of sparkling diamonds. Every once in a while, one of us gags, our throats instinctively closing up to prevent any more of the blaze haze from penetrating our lungs. Can a person die of excessive blaze fume inhalation? With three more Shovel Duty afternoons to come, I'm certainly gonna put that question to the test.

Scoop, shovel, gag, repeat.

It goes on like that for a while, neither of us talking, not 'cause we don't want to, but 'cause we can't without choking. At some point I become immune to the smell, but I know it's still there, like an invisible force lying in wait for its next victim. My s'posedly nonexistent muscles are all twisted up, as if a hand is inside my skin, grabbing and squeezing and pounding away. Each shovelful gets smaller and smaller, until there's almost no point in scooping so I stop, try to jab the shovel in the blaze so it stands upright, but I don't do it hard enough and it just falls over.

Circ stops, too, and looks at me, a smile playing on his lips. "You look like blaze," he says, full on laughing now. I *feel* like blaze, too, but I won't say that.

Instead, I get ready to tell him the same thing, but then I notice: although his legs are spattered and dotted with brown gunk, from the knees up he's spotless; he's dripping beads of sweat like the spring rains have come early, but he doesn't look tired; his tanned arms and chest are machine-like in their perfection. He doesn't look like blaze at all, so I can't say it, not without lying, and I won't lie to Circ.

"Sorry, I didn't mean—I was just joking around," Circ says.

My eyes flick to his. How does he know what I'm feeling? Does he know what I see as I look at him, that I see him as perfect? I realize I'm frowning.

"No biggie," I say, my lips fighting their way against gravity and exhaustion into a pathetic smile. "I was joking, too."

Circ studies my face for a moment, as if not convinced, but I look away, scan the pit, try to determine our progress. "Ain't much in it," I say.

I feel Circ's stare leave me, like it's a physical thing touching my cheeks. "We did more than you think. Another thumb of sun movement and we should be nearly there," Circ says.

Another thumb of sun movement? Ugh. Maybe I'm a shanker—but that long might kill me. I think I make a face 'cause Circ says, "Don't worry, we'll do it together. Let's rest for a while and then we'll start again."

Rest: I like the sound of that. There's nowhere to sit in the pit, unless you want to sit in a big ol' pile of blaze, so we climb back out, slipping and sliding on the slope. Once I almost fall, but Circ grabs me by the arm and keeps me upright. My head's down when we near the top and I hear a voice say, "Having fun yet, Scrawny?"

I look up to see three Younglings staring down at me. Hawk's in the middle.

Stopping, I let Circ pull up alongside me. Caught by surprise, I'm tongue-tied, unable to find the right words to send these blaze-eaters packin'. Circ, on the other hand, always seems ready for anything. "Get the scorch out of here, Hawk. We're working."

"Mmm, shovelin' blaze. And from the looks of it doin' a pretty grizz-poor job of it." One of his mates, a guy they call Drag, coughs out a laugh.

"Like you'd know anything about it," Circ says, taking a step forward.

"You're right. I dunno a searin' thing about blaze, other than it comes out from between my cheeks about a day after I eat a load of tug meat. And then you get to shovel it." He laughs. "But the only thing I don't understand, is why you're here, Circ. Wasn't the punishment for Scrawny?" There's a gleam in Hawk's eyes that makes me shiver, despite the oppressive midafternoon heat.

"I don't abandon my friends," Circ says calmly, although I see his fingers curl into fists. "And don't call her that." Another step forward, just one away from the lip. Hawk's friends take a step back, but Hawk doesn't move.

"But that's what she is, right? I mean, look at her. She's skinny, not an ounce of muscle on her—"

"Watch it." Circ's voice is a growl.

"—she's got legs that are wobblier than a newborn tug's—"

"Shut it!"

"—and her chest is flatter than the Cotee Plains."

Circ moves so fast I almost slip again just watching him. I don't even see the step or two he takes before he's on top of Hawk, pounding away with both fists. Hawk's doing his best to block the blows, but he's making a strange high-pitched noise that tells me plenty of Circ's punches are getting through. Drag and the other guy, Looper, seem so stunned at first that they just stand there, but then they finally get their act together and jump on top of Circ, each grabbing one of his arms from behind, pulling him away from Hawk.

Circ struggles, but they've got him so tight he can't get his arms free. I'm frozen, as if the coldness of ice country has suddenly descended from the mountains, gluing my feet to the sludge beneath me.

Hawk stands up.

They're going to hurt him—

Hawk steps forward, wipes a string of blood from his nose, his mouth all screwed up.

—all 'cause of me—

The first punch is below the belt and Circ groans, doubles over, unable to protect himself.

—I hafta do something.

My feet finally move, come unstuck, as if someone else is controlling them. I'm not Scrawny anymore, not a Runt, not Weak, not any of t'other names I been called my entire life. I'm Siena the Brave, and Circ is my friend, and he needs me.

Hawk sees me coming and moves to cut me off, but he's too slow. My muscles ache from the shoveling, but I block it out, block everything out, 'cept for getting to the guys holding Circ's arms; if I can just unloose one of them...

I trip. Maybe on the lip of the blaze pit, maybe on a random rock I don't notice, maybe on my own feet for all I know—it certainly wouldn't be the first time—but regardless, I start tumbling headfirst, out of control, my arms and legs flailing and flopping like an injured bird as I try to regain my balance.

I don't.

I crash into the back of Looper, who feels more like a boulder'n a Youngling boy, my nose crunching off his iron-like elbow, which fires backwards, knocking me off my feet. I'm in a pile in the dust, covered in blaze and durt and a bit of warm blood that trickles from my nose and onto my lips and from the scrape that I feel on my knee.

"Stupid, Runt," Hawk says, looming over me, his shadow providing a much needed reprieve from the relentless sun. "You two ain't even worth the blaze you've been shoveling." He kicks me once in the stomach and I groan, clutching my ribs, which feel like they've cracked in half.

With my cheek against the dust, I see Circ struggling against the boys, bucking and twisting, but they're strong, too, and they have the advantage in numbers and energy. Hawk laughs and saunters back over to Circ. "Don't worry, I won't hurt your girlfriend anymore. She practically knocked herself out anyway." Violence spreads across his face and he slams his fist into Circ's stomach twice, and then, winding up, whips a wild haymaker that glances off Circ's jaw with a vicious thud. Drag and Looper throw him to the ground, where he slumps, unmoving.

All I can think is:

My fault.

Three

Winter is approaching, and with it, the dust storms. Already I can feel a change in the wind, as if it's grown arms and legs and a face with a mouth that howls and cries as it approaches. Every few seconds it reaches its boiling point and sweeps a cloud of dust into the air and into my face. I close my eyes, cover my face with my hands, wait for the tiny pricks of sand to cease. Then I soldier on toward the village watering hole.

It's getting late, the sun having sunk deep on the horizon, where the thickest yellow clouds swirl like a toxic soup, turning the sky darker'n darker brown with each passing moment. Soon the sun goddess's eye'll wink shut completely as she passes into sleep.

I'm glad it's getting late for two reasons: if I run into anyone, it'll be harder for them to see my blaze-, durt-, and blood-covered skin; and it's less likely anyone'll still be at the watering hole. Circ went to his family tent to get cleaned up, but I'm too scared to face my father looking like this. I didn't tell Circ I wasn't going home right away, and he didn't ask, which I'm glad about, 'cause he probably woulda wanted to come with me, which I really can't handle right now.

I'm still muddling through everything that happened. Circ apologized about a thousand times on the way back toward the village, until I finally told him to "Shut it!" He has nothing to apologize about—it's me who messed everything up.

When I reach the watering hole, no one's there.

I sit on the edge and look at the murky brown face in the water. I'm just plain ol' Scrawny again. I been called it a thousand times, probably more times'n Siena, so why shouldn't it be my name? Add it to the number of times I been called Runt, Stickgirl, and Skeleton, and you'll have a number greater'n the total people in the entire village.

Rippling Scrawny looks back at me, Real Scrawny. Her long, black hair is stringy with sweat and durt. Her thin face is dark brown from the sun but featureless, muddled, with chestnut eyes that almost disappear beside her skin. The dress she wears is frayed and torn, soiled from a day spent shoveling crap and scrabbling in the dust. Her bone-thin arms are like the weakest, topmost branches of the trees she's seen sketched by village artists, good for nothing but swaying in the wind. And...

—she's got legs that are wobblier than a newborn tug's—

—and her chest is flatter than the Cotee Plains.

I close my eyes, hating Hawk's words 'cause they're true.

When my bleeding time first arrived I was scared, but also excited. Bleeding meant becoming a woman, finally finding my place in the world. But it never really materialized. I didn't become a woman, just stayed a scrawny girl, the bumps on my chest no more'n mosquito bites, my hips remaining as flat and straight as a pointer shot from a Hunter's bow. The only thing that identifies me as a girl is my long hair. My reflection shatters when the tears drip off my chin.

"It doesn't have to be like this," a voice says from behind, startling me. I go to turn but then remember my tear-streaked face. Cupping a hand in the water, I splash a bit onto my cheeks and then turn around, rivulets of tear-hiding water streaming down my cheeks, neck, and beneath my dress.

Lara. With her scalp-short haircut, she looks more like a boy'n ever under the darkening evening sky. Even more like a boy'n me—but at least she looks like a *strong* boy, her arms tanned and toned, her jaw sticking out a little. Solid—that's the word for her.

"Like what?" I say, remembering what she said.

"Crying because you don't think you're pretty, shoveling other people's blaze, being forced to *breed* when you turn sixteen. The Call. All of it can be avoided."

"I wasn't crying," I say. "And it's not *breeding*." She makes it sound like we're animals, hunks of meat. Look at me—do I look like meat?

She offers a wry smile, her lips barely parted. "Mm-huh. They pick a guy, they pick a girl, stick you together, and nine full moons later out pops a kid. Sounds like breeding to me."

When she says it that way, it almost does sound like breeding. My throat is dry. I haven't had a drink in ages and I really don't have time for no conversating. "Whatever, Lara. Look, thanks for coming by to try to..."—Cheer me up? Be my friend? Scare me?—"...do whatever it is you're doing, but I really need to get cleaned up and get home." I try to stand, but my legs really are as wobbly as a baby tug's, and I put a hand down to steady myself, settling for a crouch.

Lara raises an eyebrow, as if I've said something unexpected. "Just let me know if you want to hear more," she says, and then whirls around and stalks off toward the village.

I watch her go. Weird. I'm not sure what that was all about, but at least it stopped my steep dive into a pit filled with stuff far worse'n blaze. Self-pity.

When I turn back to the watering hole, its face is glassy again, and there I am.

I swipe a hand through the water so I don't hafta look at myself.

~ ~ ~

My skin is clean again, free of blood and durt and worse things. The water even seemed to wash away the self-pity, at least. temporarily. I almost feel refreshed.

My dress, however, is a different story. No matter how hard I scrubbed, I couldn't get all the stains out, and now it looks even worse 'cause it's sopping wet, dragging along below me like a wet blanket.

The moon goddess is out tonight, her eye bright orange in the dark, cloudless sky. Her godlings are scattered all around her, filling the firmament with twinkling red, orange, and yellow lights. I find myself wishing I were one of them.

The watering hole is a short walk to the village, but tonight I wish it was longer. I dread facing my father.

My father ain't Head Greynote, but he's searin' close. At thirty-seven years old, he's already beaten his average life expectancy, and if it wasn't for Greynote Shiva, who's thirty-

31

eight, he'd be at the top. Most men die within a year of turning thirty. Shiva hasn't come out of his tent in a few quarter full moons, and rumor has it he's got a bad case of the Fire, and he'll be dead within the full moon. My father'll take his place.

I pass the first of the border tents, which are inhabited by the village watchmen and their families. The guard ignores me, continues to scan the area beyond the village, his bow tightly strung and in his hand. The attack from three full moons ago has left everyone tense.

As I zigzag my way through the tightly packed tents, I see all the usual nighttime village activities: a woman hanging wet clothes from a line; Totters playing tag, squealing with delight, their mother scolding them for making too much noise, one hand on her hip and the other holding a wooden spoon; a big family praying to the sun goddess before eating dinner—probably 'zard stew or fried pricklers—this one a man with his three Calls and nine children. A Full Family. A rare thing to see these days.

Most of the tents are boxy and upright, a standard collection of ten wooden poles of varying lengths based on size of family, knotted tightly together with cords at each corner. Four of the poles are dug into three-foot-deep holes and form the tent corners, rising up to meet the side and cross beams which run along the upper sides of the tent, as well as through the middle of the ceiling, forming an X, and helping to support the heavy tugskins, which are knitted together and provide the tent covering.

However, some of the tents are half-collapsed, their support poles cracked, bent, or rotted. Anything from strong winds to wild animals to age and decay coulda caused the damage, but the families that live in these tents are forced to make due, as they won't be allotted any further wood unless the sun goddess grants a miracle and trees start growing in the desert, or the contract with the Icers can be renegotiated with more favorable terms.

We used to live in one of those broken down tents. But now, 'cause my father's a top-ten Greynote, we get to live in a sturdy wooden hut.

I reach the end of the eastern tent fields and cut across the eye of the village, which is the quickest path to the western side, where the families of the oldest Greynotes live. I'm not sure why I'm in such a hurry all of a sudden—I think 'cause being alone in the night scares me.

As it has for every night I can remember, a large fire roars in the village center, casting a reddish-orange halo of flickering light in every direction. Men sit on stone benches drinking fire juice and telling boisterous stories and jokes that end with raucous laughter from their mates. There're no women in sight.

A group of Youngling boys sit with the men and try to act grown up by being every bit as loud as their fathers. They even sip out of leather flasks, which are likely filled with cactus milk or perhaps milk from their own mother's teats. I laugh softly at my own joke.

I hurry by, giving the fire a wide berth, keeping my head down so as to not draw any attention to myself. Considering I look like a drowned rat, that's easier said'n done. When I do glance over at the fire to confirm I'm in the clear, one of the Younglings stands up, stares at me. *No*, I think. It's Hawk. Here we go again.

Forcing one foot in front of the other, I keep moving swiftly, not running, not walking, but preparing myself to run like scorch if necessary. But Hawk doesn't move, just watches me, his eyes tracing my path across the village, his lips curled into a smile. He points, says something to his buddies, and they all laugh. I let out a long exhalation when I pass out of their sight and between two of the Greynote huts.

Away from the glow of the fire, it's dark, and I stop in the shadows, panting, trying to force the thud, thud, thudding in my chest to slow down. I lean against the side of one of the sturdy huts, suddenly feeling the need for something to support me. For a few seconds, I just breathe, in and out, in and out, a simple act that my body normally performs automatically, without me even thinking 'bout it, but which now seems so difficult, as if it requires every bit of my energy to make the oxygen fill and then exit my lungs.

Eventually, however, my heartbeat does slow, my breathing does return to normal, and I'm able to move on. My only concern now is what my father'll say when he sees me. Or more accurately, what he'll *do* to me.

Four

The huts flit away on either side. Two, four, six—turn right.

Thud!

I run smack into someone who's moving in the opposite direction. My feet get tangled and I stumble, start to fall backwards, but strong arms grab my thin ones and haul me up, the soles of my moccasins lifting off the ground for a moment 'fore clamping back down. A familiar face stares down at me.

"Where have you been?" Wrapped up in the voice's tone is a question, a threat, and a punishment, all bundled together in one angry snarl. Without waiting for an answer, my father growls, "Get inside!" His fingers are like pincers, cutting into my upper arm and beneath my armpit, as he drags me into the hut on the left. His hut. Although I always called the old, beat up tent we used to live in *our tent,* since moving to the hut, I've never referred to it as *our hut.* It's always been his.

His domain, his palace, his power.

His hut. A king in his castle.

My mom and I are just squatters.

I allow him to pull me inside, 'cause fighting him would just deepen the bruises that I can already feel settling beneath my skin. *You cannot resist!* The phrase pops unrequested into my head. It's what the leader of the Glassies said to us using some sorta device that magnified his voice like a god's. At the time, he was only a speck in the distance, his army of fire chariots and strange, pale-skinned warriors stretched out in front of him, but his voice boomed across the sand-blasted desert plains, over the heads of the men defending us, and into the ears of every woman, child and Fire-afflicted man left behind.

You cannot resist!

The phrase fits so well with my current situation that I accidentally snort. It just slips out, a laugh that I try to stop, to cover with my free hand, which just makes it worse, turning it into a…well, a snort. My father stops just in front of the door, whirls on me, his eyes a black void of anger. "Is something funny?" he says between clenched teeth.

I stare at him, my eyes and mouth wide. When I don't answer, he says, "You show up well past your curfew, smelling like filth, wetter'n a Soaker, and you think something is *funny?*" His mouth is all screwed up like he wants to spit on me, and I know I'd better break my silence soon or things are only gonna get worse.

"What's a Soaker?" I ask 'fore I can stop myself. When I see his face redden, I backtrack. "No—I mean, no, sir. I didn't mean to…I didn't think…"

He releases my arm and pulls his hand back across his body, preparing to strike. I close my eyes, cringe, wait for the blow to come—

Creeaakkk!

A second passes, then two. I open my eyes to find a woman staring at us from the doorway of the hut across the way. Tari—last remaining wife of the Head Greynote. Older'n durt—forty years old!—but tougher'n iron. She'd hafta be to handle her husband.

My father glances at Tari, then back at me. His eyes narrow and for a second I think he'll hit me anyway, but then the tension drops from his arm at the same time as it drops to his side. "Inside. Now," he says.

Just before pushing through the door, my eyes flick to Tari and I try to convey my thanks in the look I give her, but her expression is neutral and I can't tell if she gets the message.

As I move inside, heat radiates off my father. He's royally grizzed this time—more'n I've ever seen before. I wonder if now—in the privacy of our own home—he'll hit me.

While he closes the door, I scan the room. Even without looking, I coulda pictured it. Sari, my newest Call-Mother, sits cross-legged on the floor, making something, probably clothing for one of her kids. Her children, Rafi and Fauna, who are my Call-Brother and Call-Sister, sit next to their mother, playing some game—Rocktop or Tugbug or something. There's an empty chair beyond, where my last Call-Mother used to sit, before a Killer attack two years ago took her and her two children, Jace and Naya. I cried when they died. Father gave me four snappings on my wrist and I shut up; but what he didn't know is that I continued to cry inside, where it counts the most, in my heart. My mother taught me that.

My mother, who's at the table cutting something, fresh prickler probably, looks up when I enter.

"Siena, where in the name of the sun goddess have you been?" she says, standing and navigating past my father.

Seeing my mother's worried face, her eyes every bit as chestnut as mine, free of lines and wrinkles, as if she's still a Youngling, brings hot tears to my eyes. All the fear of my father's wrath slips away in an instant, replaced by the desire to act like a Totter, to make myself smaller'n a burrow mouse, to let my mother hold me and sing me soft lullabies. But I know that's just a child's dream. My father's only getting started.

"I was washing up at the watering hole," I say, blinking away the tears as quickly as they spring up. She puts her arms around me and pulls my head into her chest, which only makes things worse. I'm choking now, sobbing, and I feel the warmth of a tear from each eye roll down my cheeks. It's like the memories of all the awful things that happened today have melted away, dripping from my tear ducts.

"You could have washed up here," she purrs. "We were worried about you." She pauses, seems to think for a second. "*I* was worried about you." I understand her change in word choice. My father worried? Not a chance. If I were dragged away by yellow-eyed Killers in the middle of the night, he'd be thinking about what message to give to the rest of the village to prevent panic, not worrying about my wellbeing. I lick my lips, which taste of salt and well-water. It's like the terrible events of the day are suddenly no more'n pesky springbugs, and I'm able to swat them away using only my mind. All that matters is the fact that my father doesn't give a blaze about me.

"I'm sorry, Mother," I say quietly, pushing her away with both hands.

Her dark brows are creased like a V, her lips a tight line. *Don't*, she mouths.

I ignore her, face my father, whose back is to me. "Want to hear about my day, Father?" I say, scorpion poison in my tone.

His hands, which are clenched at his side, open, and then close again, making fists so tight that his knuckles are blotched with red and white. His shoulders rise and fall with heavy breaths. I don't know what's gotten into me, but I just can't take it anymore. My bones hurt from a day shoveling blaze. My ribs ache in a dozen places, where Hawk kicked me. And my pride? Well, I guess that's the only thing that ain't hurt, 'cause I never had any in the first place.

"Let's see," I say, tapping my teeth with a finger, "where should I start? With getting punished or getting the blaze kicked out of me by another Youngling?"

"I know *all* about your day," Father says, turning sharply. Although I can feel the hot rush of anger coursing through my veins, the look on his face—twisted and gnarled, like he's not thirty-seven, but forty-seven—makes me shrink back. It's as hot as scorch in our hut, but a shiver runs down my spine. This man is but a shadow of the father I once knew: the father who sat me on his knees and bumped them up and down while I squealed with laughter; the father who smiled bigger'n the desert when I came home from Learning holding the Smooth Stone, awarded to the best Midder student; the father who held my hand and confronted Midder Vena when she struck me in the arm. No, the man standing 'fore me ain't the man who did any of those things.

He steps forward and I step back, but my spine bangs against the door, sending needles through my ribs. "Do you know how embarrassing today was for me?" he asks. "First I get called out of a Greynote meeting so Teacher Mas can inform me that you've been given Shovel Duty for the fourth time this full moon. Then Hawk and his father show up at my door to tell me how you and Circ jumped him and broke his nose. These are not small things, Siena!" His voice is the bellow of a tug, and I have the sudden urge to squeeze my eyes shut and curl up into a ball in the corner.

"I didn't...we didn't..." My voice is the squeak of a burrow mouse, barely audible above the echoes of my father's accusations.

"You didn't what?" he spits.

"We were just defending ourselves," I cry.

"I will not have you lie to me, Youngling!" he roars. "I'm on the verge of becoming the Head Greynote. How do you think it looks when I can't even control my own daughter? Do you think the people will trust me to lead them?"

His words must sting my cheeks, 'cause I feel them warming up. "But it wasn't my faul—"

"Excuses! That's all I ever get from you, Siena. You think I give you a hard time to be mean?" *Uh...yeah?* "No! I do it because I want you to be safe, to grow up and have a family. You're less than a year from the Call and you can't even take responsibility for your own actions. How do you expect to raise a child?"

"Maybe I don't want a child!" I scream. I slap a hand over my mouth, right away regretting my words. But the hand is a moment too late 'cause I've already said it, have already admitted what most every Youngling girl thinks. And yet, for some reason, saying it is unforgivable.

At first there's silence, everyone just staring at me, my father's eyes as big as my mother's favorite firepan. His lips open and I dread what he'll say. As if realizing my apprehension, he pauses, runs his tongue along his upper teeth, drawing out the moment, then finally speaks. "No daughter of mine is above the Law. You *will* learn your duties, one way or the other. If I have to throw you in Confinement, I will. It's for your own good."

Confinement? But that's for bad people—people who break the Law. "I haven't done anything wrong," I say. "You wouldn't." I try to say the last bit with as much conviction as I can muster, but even as I speak it I know it's not true. He would. He'd do anything if he thought it'd help maintain our way of life. Even throw his own daughter in prison.

"Try me," he says, his eyes penetrating mine like darts. "Woman, get my snapper."

His last command is to my mother, who's frozen as still as a prickler. She's watching me, her face full of something I can't identify. A hint of sadness, maybe. But there's something else, too, something harder, like stone, noticeable only in her eyes, which don't match up with the rest of her face. *Save me*, I think as hard as I can in her direction.

"My snapper!" my father yells. "Now!"

The steel in her eyes disappears and I know she didn't hear my silent plea. Hidden beneath her dress, her feet carry her across the room and behind the barrier, where my father spends the night with each of his wives on a rotational basis, although lately I've noticed Sari's there at least two out of every three nights. I know it's just the way of my people, but seeing my mother get ignored for Sari, who I barely know, grizzes me off more'n anything.

A moment later she reappears, a black swatch of leather dangling from her hand. At one end is a handle, which wraps

41

around my father's palm for greater grip, and at the other side it splits into ten strips, each of which comes to a knot intended to add a bit of sting to each snap. The teeth of the snapper my father calls them.

Her eyes on the floor, my mother hands it to him.

Five

In Learning they told us about a time when men and women were gods and goddesses, and lived until they were sixty, seventy, even eighty. Some of the kids even said their parents told them people used to live until they were ninety or, in rare cases, a hundred, which I think is a bunch of tugblaze. I draw the line at a hundred.

But that was all before the rogue god, Meteor, attacked us. Going against the sun and moon goddess, Meteor snuck by and gave the earth a real beating, fists and feet and head swirling, knocking over mountains and drying up rivers and wiping out most of the tribes. When Teacher told the story, we were riveted to our seats. It was the first time he had all our attention at once. When he got to the part about how the first Heater crawled out of their hiding spots, in caves and deep pits, we cheered and clapped our hands. They were survivors, just like us. We don't know where the Icers came from, but they musta survived Meteor, too.

Unfortunately, Teacher's lesson today is much less interesting, all about Laws and duty. Although I hate to admit it, the lashing my father gave me taught me a lesson. Since then I been careful in class. No daydreaming, no problem. I keep my head up, try to focus on what Teacher is saying, and try to ignore the nasty comments directed my way by Hawk and his gang.

The snapper scars'll be the worst yet. Worse'n the time I thought it'd be funny to dump a bunch of sand lice under my sister's pillow. My mother spent three days scrubbing them all out of Skye's hair. Father wasn't too happy and gave me what I thought would be the beating of my life. Skye even said she'd never speak to me again, but a quarter full moon later we were best friends again. Until she snuck a handful of dead eight-leggers into my tugtail soup one night. I didn't even realize it until I crunched one in my mouth. Blech! She got a pretty bad whooping for her little revenge prank, too, but even that one was nothing compared to what my father gave me t'other day. I screamed like a banshee as he snapped the leather again and again, across my back, my legs, even my buttocks. He was whipping it so hard I could hear him grunting with exertion. It's times like that I wish I had just a bit more meat on my bones for padding. Or maybe some muscle—that woulda helped. Instead, each blow went straight to my bones, penetrating so deep I thought he'd cut me wide open.

I couldn't see a searin' thing 'cause I was bent over, tears and pain and hair in my eyes, but I did hear my mother scream a few times for him to stop; and she musta come at him, 'cause

I heard him curse and then there was a crash. Sari's kids were crying and she was trying to comfort them, but compared to me, they had nothing to cry about.

It still hurts to sit down, but I manage.

Circ and I haven't talked much. I think he feels embarrassed that he got a beating from Hawk, and I don't really have anything more to say about it all. I thanked him for helping me with the blaze, and for standing up for me, and that was that. I believe our friendship could survive anything.

Life goes on in the village. Late summer gets closer and closer to winter, skipping autumn altogether this year.

There are a lot of lasts this year. The last winter before I'm child-big, my last year of Learning, the last time my father'll be able to call me a Youngling. One good thing about next spring's Call: it'll mean I can move out of my father's hut. I just wish I knew who I'd be living with.

Teacher Mas is going on and on about the history of the human race. Don't get me wrong, some of it's interesting stuff, like how people used to live in these big cities, with tall metal structures where everybody went to work, kind of like the Glassies, I guess, 'cept it was all people, not just one group. I'm not in the mood for it today.

I find myself scanning the room, seeing who else is bored. Everyone seems interested, 'cept for Hawk and his mates, who are passing something under their legs—I can't see what. Finally, my eyes settle on Circ. As though he feels my eyes on him, he turns at that moment and smiles. I can't help but smile back. If I didn't have him as a friend, I don't know what I'd do.

I always get scared for him 'fore a Hunt. The last Hunt of the season is in three days' time, and already I feel a little jittery, like I've got fire ants in my dress or something. In three

45

quarters of a full moon's time the tug hurds'll migrate elsewhere, beyond our reach, off to mate and find food for their new calves. Even Younglings are eligible to participate in the Hunt, if they pass the test, that is. Of course, good-at-everything Circ had to go and pass the skills test the moment he turned twelve, and he's been going with the Hunters ever since. So far he's been lucky, coming back with nothing worse'n a bruised foot from being trod on or a gash from a tug horn. But I've seen men—skilled, capable men—return home with half their head caved in, or missing a limb, or worse.

It would be dangerous enough if the Hunters had only the tugs to contend with. The problem with tugs though, is that they're so full of hunger-satisfying meat that they draw all kinds of attention from predators that are much nastier'n the Hunters.

So, as usual, I'm nervous for Circ, and for myself, too, I guess.

Circ looks back at Teacher, but I keep looking at him, and for just a second, I allow myself a brief daydream, a much needed respite from the real world I live in. What if, in a different world, in a different time, he was my Call? He's the only one under the watchful eye of the sun goddess who really knows me. Would all my problems go away? Would I be just Siena, not Youngling or Scrawny or Tent-Pole? As I gaze at the face of the only person who seems to know exactly what I need and when I need it, I can almost picture what it'd be like. I mean, forget about all the stuff about going to bed with him—he's my friend and I'm no shilt, so I'd rather not think about that—but the rest'd be amazing, right? Waking up and making breakfast with him; playing games with our children; spending the day together, at least when he doesn't hafta go off for another Hunt. A beautiful dream, but then, of course, there'd be another Call, another wife, Call-Children. I know, I know, that's just the way it is, but it'd still suck having to share him. Like my mother's always had to do with my father. Although nowadays I don't think she has any problem sharing, considering how hard he's become, I hated watching before, when she used to laugh, laugh, laugh at things he'd say. And then he'd go off to bed with one of his other Calls and I could see the hurt in my mother's eyes. I hurt for her, wish there was another way.

Breeders.

The word pops into my head like a burrow mouse from its hole. Lara's word, not mine. But it's true, ain't it? Naw, I can't think like that—not when it's only months 'fore my Call.

Something thuds against my shin. I cringe and almost hiss out *Ouch!* 'fore I catch myself and remember where I am. I glance at Circ, who's shaking his head. He's the one who kicked me. I don't know how much time has passed while I was lost in my thoughts, but all t'other Younglings are standing up and leaving our open air Learning hut.

"Try to focus, Siena," Circ says. "I know it's hard, but I don't think either of us wants Blaze Craze again, nor face the wrath of our fathers." By *the wrath of our fathers* he means the wrath of *my* father. He got away with a warning and a secret pat on the back for standing up to three Younglings at the same time, while I got the beating of my life.

I realize Circ's asked me a question, but I didn't hear it, just see his face full of expectation. "Huh?" I say.

"Are you daydreaming about daydreaming now?" he says.

"Was that the original question or a new one?" I ask, trying to keep a straight face but failing miserably.

Circ laughs and it's like we're not Younglings on the verge of major changes in our lives. We're new Younglings again, or maybe Midders, with not a care in the world. Life is fun and I ain't scared of my father and the future holds more possibilities'n living with strangers, a flock of children in tow.

"It was a new question. I asked what you were thinking about when I *snapped* you out of it," he says.

"Ugh. Don't say that word. Just hearing it makes my flesh hurt," I say, reaching a hand over my shoulder to gingerly touch my back. Even through the dress my skin feels raw, like someone's rubbed it with sand, or maybe rope.

"It's not right the way he beats on you," he says.

"Like you've never been snapped," I say.

"Not like you," he says, shaking his head. "A few snaps to the wrist and Father's done. He says it hurts him worse than it hurts us, and I believe him, too. But your father…" He trails off, looking away.

"He likes it as much as I hate it?" I offer.

"Something like that," Circ says.

"Don't worry about it. I can handle him. And saying something to someone'll just make it worse."

Circ looks at me for a long moment, then changes the subject. "Honestly, though, you did look like you had gone far, far away. You were smiling at first, but then frowning."

I scowl at him. "Must you read my expressions when I'm daydreaming?" I say.

"I must," Circ says, laughing again. "But you're dodging the question. What were you thinking about?"

There's heat on my cheeks. "I was just…" My mind races to come up with something. But I don't lie to Circ—never have, never will—and my mind knows it, so it just goes blank.

"Were just what?" he persists. I wish he'd drop it, but that's not the way our friendship works.

I look around. We're alone now—everyone's left, even Teacher Mas. "I was thinking what it'd be like if you were my Call." Dropping my head, I study my feet, noticing how small they look from up here.

"That's not—"

"Hey, Siena!" a voice shouts from the entrance. I turn to see Lara poking her head in. Across the room and out of the glare of the afternoon sun, she really looks like a boy.

"What?" I say, glancing at Circ, who looks surprised that someone else is talking to me.

"Have you thought about what I said to you the other day?" Lara says.

I wince, not because I haven't, but because I have.

"I'll see you at the game," I say to Circ. To Lara, I say, "Walk with me."

~~~

I avoid her question all the way to the feetball match. She prods and pokes and rephrases it a dozen different ways, but I just keep changing the subject. At the game, I'm doing the same, studying the match like it's a strange ten-legged insect with a red tail.

Feetball. Yet another activity I've never been good at. Trying to run around while simultaneously kicking and throwing and catching a ball? Well, let's just say it's about three too many things for my two left feet to handle at once. Not to mention the hordes of defenders trying to do everything in their power to grind you into the unforgiving desert floor. Yeah, violent sports and me don't mix. Scorch, any sport and me don't mix.

I played when I had to as part of the physical activity required during Learning, but never for fun. Thankfully, as a fifteen-year-old female Youngling—also known as a pre-Bearer—I'm exempt from any physical activity that might prevent me from having children in the near future. Which means I get to watch Circ play, which is like watching Greynote Giza paint one of his famous paintings: fluid and natural and graceful. The score is tied and it's already in extra time, which means the next goal'll be the decider.

I'm sitting next to Lara, 'cause, well, 'cause I don't really have many friends at the moment. I don't know if she's my friend exactly, but at least she's not an enemy, and she's never called me any of the not-so-flattering nicknames that I'm used to. So she's okay in my book. Although she is starting to freak me out with all of her cryptic messages.

"You still haven't answered my question," she says, asking for the fourteenth time since the match started.

Circ takes a pass off his left foot and quickly darts past a defender who tries, and fails, to grab him. His movements are faster'n the lightning we get during the winter storms, but not nearly as shocking. So far he's doing nothing I haven't seen him do 'fore. He has three goals and a dozen steals, far more'n any other player.

"I'm trying to watch—"

"Oh, come on. I could see in your eyes that you were intrigued by what I said. That a life of breeding and childrearing and waiting on your Call hand and foot doesn't exactly excite you."

"Shhh, keep it down," I hiss, glaring at her. She might not hate me like most of t'other Younglings, but if she keeps talking like this, using that dirty word—*breeding*, shh!—she *is* gonna get me in trouble. Again. I'm pretty sure my father's threat to chuck me in Confinement is a load of tugwash, but I'm not itching to test him. Especially not so soon after the last time.

"Sorry," she whispers, rolling her eyes.

"Look," I say, as I watch Circ dodge another defender by flicking the ball in the air with his feet, running around them, and then catching it in one hand. "Even if I agreed with you, about the…"

(breeding, shh!)

"…about *everything*, there's nothing we can do about it. The Call is all there is for us. Without it the older generations would die off faster'n the new ones could be created. Without it we wouldn't exist."

"I thought you were different," Lara says, a hint of disappointment in her tone. "You sound just like a Teacher. Or worse, a Greynote."

I grit my teeth. Circ throws the ball over the head of an opponent to one of his teammates, who grabs it and throws it back to him. He catches it in midstride, now streaking down the field faster'n a Cotee, rolls it deftly out in front of his feet and then rips a booming shot at the corner of the rope net. I hold my breath for a second, watching the potential winning shot career just past the outstretched hands of the opposing net guard. I start to stand and raise my hands in celebration, but the ball glances hard off the edge of the wooden netpost and over the boundary line. "No goal!" the judge yells, waving his arms around like he's swatting at sand flies.

Blaze. That was so close, but now t'other team has the ball.

"All I'm asking is that you think about it," Lara says.

I already have. But she doesn't know that. While one of the players chases Circ's errant shot, I study Lara. Her eyes are light brown and flecked with green bits. Really pretty, actually. I've never really looked at her. I mean, I've gawked at her a few times, wondering what she was thinking with her short hair and absence of femininity. Oh and when she started wearing guy's britches to school I almost keeled over with shock. But now, for the first time, I'm really seeing her. Not the masculine girl who doesn't seem to fit in anywhere, but Lara, the person, the individual. To my surprise, her face is really pretty. It's like it was hidden somewhere, like she was wearing a mask, and at just this moment she peeled it away. But that's not it at all. She hasn't changed one smidge. It's me that's changed. I'm giving her a chance, whereas 'fore I wrote her off as some weirdo. I did to her what everyone else does to me.

I look away, unable to bear my own ignorance. I'm as bad as t'others. But I can make up for it now. I can take her seriously, really think about what she's saying to me, which is all she's asking for.

Her words flash back with a vividness that startles me.

It doesn't have to be like this.

Like what?

Crying because you don't think you're pretty, shoveling other people's blaze, being forced to breed when you turn sixteen. The Call. All of it can be avoided.

It's dangerous talk. I've heard 'bout girls who didn't agree with the Call, and they all disappeared. Maybe taken by the

Wild Ones, maybe taken by the Greynotes to be punished forever for breaking the Law.

The ball is back in play, and the opposing team moves swiftly up the field, zipping around like angry bees. Two of them get a good rhythm going: pass, pass back, return. No one can seem to stop them until Circ comes a-flying in and bashes into one just as he releases the ball. Circ lands on top of him in a heap, but now the ball is past him. There's another bone-jarring tackle, this time by one of Circ's teammates, but again, it's too late as the ball's already been launched elsewhere on the field.

The Call. All of it can be avoided.

Breeding.

But why? Why avoid the Call? What's there to gain from it? If enough new Bearers decide to skip out on the Call, then our people'll just die out faster. The very idea is madness! And it's not even possible anyway. The only way to get out of it is to die, which I'm sort of trying to avoid, or get kidnapped by the Wild Ones, which doesn't sound particularly appealing either. And it's not like I can put in a request:

"Dear Wild Ones, on the fifteenth of March I'll turn sixteen, and half a full moon later, will be forced to take place in the Call. If at all possible, I'd appreciate an abduction sometime 'fore then, if you're not too busy, that is. Your friend, Siena (aka Scrawny)."

Yeah, I'm sure that'll fly.

I remember when they took my sister. She'd just turned sixteen. It was the night of her Call. Unlike me, she was so excited. "I'm becoming a woman!" she squealed as I helped her put on her nicest dress. She really did look beautiful, older'n she'd looked only a few days earlier—transformed. I could tell she was nervous 'cause she was babbling on and on, but who ain't nervous for their Call? My father'd already left, so we were walking, my mother, Skye and me, toward the village center, where everyone was gathering. Although it was as hot as scorch, it was a perfect summer night, with every servant of the moon goddess out to watch the event. And the moon goddess herself was full and beautiful, an orange beacon contrasting the dark night sky. That's when it happened. Skye stopped suddenly, said she needed to take a few deep breaths to prepare herself for what was coming. 'Fore my mother or I knew what was happening, she ducked behind a tent. My mother told me to wait and she went after her. That was the last time I ever saw my sister. The Greynotes investigated, found no signs of a struggle, declared her a runaway and a Lawbreaker, said if she was ever caught she'd be forced to bear her first child while in Confinement. There was talk about the Wild Ones, as there was every time another girl went missing, but even that fizzled out after a full moon or two. After all, no one had any proof they even existed.

I realize everyone's standing 'cept me and Lara.

She's looking at me with an eyebrow raised and her head cocked to the side. It's the type of look I tend to get when I been daydreaming. "What'd I miss?" I ask.

"Circ's team lost," she says. "But I think the better question is: What did *I* miss?"

I'm afraid to tell her, 'cause I know now that somehow, some way, she's connected outside of the village. And that scares me more'n anything.

Six

"Please be careful," I say. We're in one of our favorite spots, what we call the Mouth, a pair of sand dunes so large that if you look at their profile from a distance they look like a giant pair of lips. They're far enough away from the village that if we sit with our backs on one of the slopes, no one can see us until they're practically right on top of us. Even then it'd be difficult, 'cause we always burrow a little hole to get a bit of shade. Our shoulders and knees are touching like they always do.

"Don't be such a worrier," Circ says, dropping an arm around my shoulder. I lean into him, feeling a twinge of I-don't-know-what hammering in my chest. He's staring off into nothingness, and I take a moment to study his face. It's a face I don't need to study, 'cause I have every aspect of it memorized. From his sun-chapped lips to the slight cleft in his chin that you can only see from certain angles, to the way his nose casts a shadow in the shape of a ghost on his cheeks, I could draw his face while sleepwalking. I even know the exact depth of the two dimples that burrow so symmetrically in each cheek, regardless of whether he's happy, sad, or something in between. When we were just Totters and first met, I asked him why he had holes in his cheeks. I remember his response as if it were yesterday: "Mama says they're not holes, they're star craters, and they're magic." Ever since that day I still believe there's some magic in those dimples of his—perhaps they're the source of his being so searin' good at everything.

"I'll be watching," I add, as if that'll scare him into being more careful. Regardless, I'm glad the final Hunt of the season falls on a non-Learning day, so I'll get to watch.

I've watched a few Hunts 'fore, and to be honest, the thought of seeing the men shooting pointers and throwing spears into the broad side of a bunch of rampaging beasts curdles my stomach; but the thought of sitting at home worrying about whether Circ'll make it back okay is even worse, so I'm going.

"I'll look for you," Circ says, grinning. "I'll kill my first tug of the day for you."

"How romantic," I say, playing with my bracelet. It's a leather strap, given to me by my parents when I became a Youngling. All Younglings get one. Fastened to it are seven charms, one for me and one for each member of my living family. For me there's a tree, signifying my duty as a Bearer when I turn sixteen, to grow my family. My father's represented by bull horns, for strength and providing for his family, although I think it also means he can be a bit bullheaded sometimes. Okay, *a lot* bullheaded and *all* the time. My mother's

56

got the sun goddess's eye, the sun, to watch over me. My sister, Skye, is a flame, burning brightly as a beacon for me to follow. Kind of hard to follow her when I don't know where she is or if she's even alive. My father's encouraged me to bury her charm now that she's gone, but I just can't. Not yet. Maybe never. For my Call-Mother, Sari, there's a flower for her beauty. My Call-Siblings, Rafi and Fauna, are a footprint and a raindrop, for a road long travelled and new beginnings. I used to have four others, three for my other Call-Family, but when they died, we all buried our charms together, freeing their spirits to the gods. The fourth missing charm is for my other real sister, Jade. She died when she was only seven, taken by a rampaging summer fire. I never saw her body, 'cause the fire was so hot it took every last part of her. 'Cept her soul, which I know is dancing in the land of the gods. When she died, it was the only time I saw my father cry.

I'm not sure how long I been playing with my charms, but when I look up, Circ's holding back a laugh. "Did you just make a joke and then space out on me?" he says, smirking.

"I dunno. Was it funny?" I ask. "The joke, I mean."

He laughs, grabs me under the arms, and lifts me to my feet. "I've got to get ready," he says.

"Me, too," I say, punching him lightly on the arm.

"Hey, watch it! I bruise easily," he says, a twinkle in his eye.

I narrow my eyes. "No you don't."

"Oh, right. That's you I was thinking of." I reach out to punch him again, but he dances away, and my fist wags awkwardly in the air.

"Oh no you don't!" I scream, giving chase.

It's a full two miles to the village and I'm determined to catch him by then. The one thing I'm good at is running, unless of course something gets in the way of my two left feet, in which case I'll probably end up with a mouth full of sand.

He's already at the top of the dune, his head slipping out of sight. I charge after him, stumbling once when I step in a hole, probably left by a burrow mouse, or some other digging critter, but regain my balance and make it to the top.

He's standing just over the crest, watching me. "Good luck," he says, whooping once and racing off toward the village.

I'm after him a split-second later, my legs full of the energy of a day off from Learning, a morning spent with Circ when I was meant to be replenishing our trough from the watering hole, and the anticipation of the afternoon Hunt. Circ's fast—really, really fast—'specially over short distances, but things are much closer the farther we go. Plus, he loves taunting me, letting me get close and then cutting away, almost like he's avoiding a defender on the feetball field. All the time he's laughing, egging me on, trying to get under my skin. But his cries of "Come on, Sie, my grandmother could run faster than you and she's been dead for fourteen years!" or "I think a sand slug just passed you, Sie, how embarrassing!" fall on deaf ears, as I grit my teeth and stay focused. Left foot, left foot. Left foot, left foot. Laughing at my own thoughts, I lose concentration for a moment and miss a rock that's suddenly under my foot, breaking away beneath my tread, rolling my ankle to the outside.

I cry out and go down, wishing the layer of sand were as thick as back at the dunes. Instead, it's like falling on bare rock. My outstretched hands do little to break my fall and probably just make things worse, 'cause they crumple beneath me, roaring with pain. I skid a few feet, my exposed skin scraping against the desert with the force of a winter wind.

I hear a yell from the side, from Circ, but I don't respond, just lay there panting, internally cursing my silly sense of humor, my lack of coordination, and that *burnin'* rock—who put that there anyway?—that all conspired together to trip me up. My shoulder's coursing with heat and I see the hot red outline of blood seeping through my brown dress. The ankle I turned is throbbing and squeezing against my moccasins. And my wrists, well, they're the worst—at least one of them is. My left hand is bent unnaturally, my wrist pulsating with a dizzying level of pain; it almost feels like the king of the tugs is stepping on it over and over again.

"Sie!" Circ yells, right next to me now. "Are you...Oh blaze!"

"I think it's broken," I say, trying to move my wrist. "Holy sun goddess, searin', good for nothin', piece of..." As agony wracks my arm, I let out one of the longest string of obscenities of my life.

"Don't move it," Circ says, positioning his body behind mine so I can lean on him. "What hurts besides your wrist?"

"Everything," I moan, gasping as a wave of nausea-inducing pain shivers through my body.

"We're less than a mile from the village," he says. "I'll go get help."

He starts to get up, but I yell, "No! Don't leave me here. Please." I'm being a baby, I know, but the thought of lying in the middle of the desert—okay, not the middle, middle, but searin' far out—alone, with vultures buzzing around me, waiting for me to die...

Anyway, Circ gets this look of determination on his face where his eyes are like glass, reflecting the rays of the sun in splinters and shards, his jaw sticks out and gets all tight, and his

59

lips push together. I've seen this look many times. It means: I'll win, I cannot be defeated, I am stronger'n faster and more capable'n any other human on the face of the earth. It's always kind of scared me and excited me at the same time.

With a tenderness that surprises me, he scoops me up in his arms and takes off toward the village. I close my eyes 'cause the *bump, bump, bump* of each of Circ's galloping strides sends eruptions through my wrist and arm. By tucking it against my side like a broken wing, I'm able to reduce the shockwaves rolling through it. I concentrate on my breathing, slow and deep, and that keeps my mind off of the pain for a while. The wind's whipping through my hair, so I know Circ's going fast, which, regardless of how little I weigh, is really amazing given he's carrying me in his arms.

Just when my focus on breathing wanes, and the agony of my shattered wrist comes back like a Killer drawn to the fresh scent of blood, Circ begins to slow.

"What's going on?" I hear a voice say. It's his brother, Stix, three years younger'n us, a fresh Youngling.

"Get the Medicine Man!" Circ manages to yell between ragged breaths.

"But the Hunt…"

"Just do it!"

My stomach drops and a fresh wave of nausea rolls through me as he lowers me onto something soft. A bed. When I open my eyes I see Circ's concerned face, his eyes wrinkled at the corners the same way they looked when I burned my hand in the fire when we were only six. Funny how his face has changed so much over the years, losing his baby fat and tiny teeth, but is still the same Circ I've always known.

"Circ," I say, just a whisper.

"Don't speak," he says. "Help will be here soon."

"But the Hunt…" I say, echoing Stix's words.

"I don't care about—"

"They need you, Circ," I say, clenching my jaw as needles stab me in the wrist. Taking a deep breath, I start over. "They need you for the Hunt. Thank you for everything. You've done all you can do for me—the Medicine Man'll take care of the rest. Get ready for the Hunt and make me proud."

In a rare display of uncertainty, Circ stands up, sits back down, stands again, starts to walk away, and then turns back. "Are you sure?" he asks.

"Sure as a searin' Cotee is of tracking a six-day-old scent through a sandstorm," I say, trying to prove to Circ that I'm okay.

He looks at me like I've gone all wooloo on him, but ends up smiling in the end. "I'll see you as soon as it's over. Take care of yourself."

"Be safe," I say.

He grabs my hand—the good one—squeezes for a nice, warm moment, and then spins and is gone, disappearing behind the tent flap.

~~~

As usual, there's steam coming out of my father's ears. I'd try to run away, but it's kind of hard when the Medicine Man is wrapping your broken arm in something brown and tight. Sear my brittle-thin bones! There's no way a simple fall like that woulda broken a normal person's wrist.

"Of all the mousebrained things to do…"

"I'm sorry, Father. We were just knockin' around," I try to explain, cringing when MedMa jerks my arm.

That gets Father's attention and he stops stomping around, his face turning redder'n the noonday sky. Even the Medicine Man stops working on me and looks up. "Watch your mouth, Youngling. I don't care what kind of slang the children use these days, but I will not have my daughter speak to me like that."

"I'm sorry, I just—"

"I DON'T CARE!" my father screams, his face suddenly right next to mine. I flinch back, and MedMa does too, accidentally pulling my injured arm awkwardly again.

"Ouch!" I yelp.

His face is an inch from mine. His breath smells acrid and raunch, like it does when he's been smoking the Pipe of Wisdom with the other Greynotes. He lowers his voice, deepens it too, and says, "Youngling, you are approaching your Call, the most important day of your life. You simply cannot be getting hurt, running around with some guy—"

"It's Circ, Father, not some random guy."

"I don't care if it's a three-headed Cotee with wings," he says, "you will NOT spend time with him anymore."

My heart stops. Well, not really, but it feels like it does. In reality, I can feel it throbbing and pumping away, not only in my chest, but in my wrist and head, too. "You can't do that," I say, my voice just a whisper.

"Yes. I can." All I want to do is jump up, scream at him, flail my arms like a wooloo person, scratch with my nails, do anything—anything—to get my anger out.

But I don't do any of that for two reasons. First, my arm's halfway in a sling so flailing's out of the question. And secondly, I know all too well from experience that doing any of that won't help. It'll just grizz my father off even more and then there won't be any chance of me seeing Circ again. Like he'd probably pull me out of Learning, or throw my bony behind in Confinement like he threatened before.

So I just stare at him, seething inside, thinking, *I hate you I hate you I hate you,* over and over and over again.

"I don't want to keep you apart, Siena, but you leave me no choice," he says, stopping my anger-filled thoughts. I gape at him. *Siena?* When's the last time he called me by my name and not "Youngling" or some variation? It's been years, I reckon. His eyes almost look like they used to, 'fore they became someone else's, a tyrant's. There's a flicker of light in them for just a moment, and then it's gone, maybe forever.

"After the Call you won't be able to be friends with him anyway. It's just not proper." His words sting, but not 'cause he's saying them, but 'cause I know he's right. The Bearers aren't friends with the men, 'cept for their Call. But I can't imagine not being friends with Circ, passing by him with a subtle nod, like we hardly know each other.

"Is that clear, Youngling?" he says.

"Clear as…"—Mud? Sandy water? Tug blood?—"…rain," I say.

Seven

The good news: my wrist is fixed up in time for me to watch the Hunt. The bad news: it's broken in two places and'll take at least a full moon and a half to heal.

There are at least a dozen Hunts taking place today, all around fire country, at the usual and rare spots, where the wildgrass and scrubgrass still flourish, growing in ankle-high clumps. The tug got no choice but to eat right where we expect them to. But that don't mean taking them down'll be easy.

Although Heaters go out on a daily basis to scrounge up 'zard and pricklers and other small animals and plants good for eating, the Hunt is the most important event for our survival. It's where the Hunters will—assuming everything goes well—bring home thousands of pounds of tug meat for the village, which'll get us through the next few full moons.

I'm walking out to one of the Hunts—the one Circ'll be participating in—with a group of other Younglings. Well, not walking *with* them exactly, more like off to the side, but we're all headed in the same direction. My arm's wrapped up as tight as a pink new-faced baby, and strapped to my shoulder, too, using a tugskin sling. As usual, it's hot, exceptionally so for this time of year, and I can feel beads of sweat rolling down my back already.

Out of the corner of my eye I see Hawk break off from a group of his friends and saunter toward me, but I keep my eyes forward, pretending not to notice. When he gets close, he says, "What happened to you, Scrawny? Did the wind blow a little too hard and snap your arm in half?"

My heart starts beating faster, but I'm not in the mood to back down, so I ask him a question of my own. "How come you're not in the Hunt today? Still haven't managed to pass the skills test?" I muster as much confidence in my voice as I can, but it still sounds high-pitched and weak to my ears.

To my surprise, Hawk laughs. "Haven't you heard? I just passed yesterday."

My eyes flash to his. He could be lying, but if he is, it doesn't show on his face. "But then why…?"

"Why ain't I with the other Hunters? Don't you know nothing? First Hunt I get to come in all special-like. They've got me set up on the bluffs with the rest of the spectators."

He's right. Memories of Circ's first Hunt flash through my mind: the other Hunters set up en masse in one area, Circ away from the main body; Circ running up, so much smaller'n them, like a mini-Hunter, the sharp end of his spear showering sparks of reflected light around him; his first kill, a decent-sized tug with long black horns. Typically Younglings don't kill a tug their first time out. But Circ did.

"Took you long enough," I say. Then, staring straight ahead, I think to add, "Don't get yourself killed."

"I'm not the one you should be worried about," Hawk says, but 'fore I have a chance to reply, he veers away, back to his friends, who laugh and pound their fists into his.

What's that s'posed to mean? I'm left wondering. I worry 'bout any of the Hunters getting hurt, but the only one I'm ever really focused on is...

Circ.

"Hey, Sie," Lara says, coming up behind me.

"Sorry, Lara, I'm really not in the mood to talk 'bout—"

"I heard about your wrist. I'm really sorry it happened."

"Uh, thanks. It hurts like a Killer's jaws are sunk in it, but I'll survive. I'm feeling alright after MedMa's herbs."

"It'll get well before the Call though, right?" she asks.

"Yeah, MedMa said it'll only take a little over a full moon to heal. But why do you car—"

"Good," she says. "See you later." And just like that, she's gone too, leaving me scratching my head with my good hand. I want to chase after her, demand some answers to all her cryptic words, but I'm too scared about what she might say. That she's involved with the Wilds, the Icers, or someone even worse. I kick a rock in the direction she left, half hoping it'll hit her.

~~~

The tugs are restless.

They may not be the smartest animals, but they ain't stupid either. As soon as the Hunters come into view they start stomping their cloven feet, bucking their monstrous heads, and milling about like a bunch of Younglings at a Learning social event. They know something's up.

The massive beasts look like hair-covered boulders out on the field, their heads as big and round and wide as the rest of their bodies. The tugs ain't exactly considered sacred animals to my people, but they're not far from it. I mean, without them we'd have died off long ago. Although I don't particularly like the idea of the Hunters killing them, I know it's necessary for our survival. After all, almost everything we have comes from them. At over two thousand pounds each, a single tug can feed an entire family for a year, from boiled liver to spiced jerky to stacks and stack of ribs and rump steaks. It's always a welcome change from the chewiness of 'zard stew or bitterness of prickler salad.

Tug hides are used by the tanners to make leather for our moccasins, dresses for the women, britches for the men (and for Lara, I s'pose), hats, pouches, bedding, and most importantly, tent covers. There're probably 'bout a hundred other uses for tugskin I can't remember.

But it's not just the skin we use. We use everything, which I'd learned by the time I was six. Their sinew, bones and horns are used by the weapon makers to craft bows, pointers, spears, and knives, as well as to make glue and tools. From tug hair we get ropes and stuffing for our pillows. Tails are used for paint brushes—like the one Greynote Giza uses—and decorations. We even use tug blaze. This is pretty raunch, but it works wonders on getting a cook fire started, although I can't say it does much for the flavor of whatever you're cooking.

So, yeah, the Hunt is important, 'specially the last one, 'cause if it don't go well, then we starve.

From high atop the bluffs, I can see for miles and miles, the whole desert spread out 'fore me, like I'm sitting in the sky. I flop down well away from the rest of the Younglings—even Lara keeps her distance today.

A few of the tugs look up our way, toward the spectators, like they know something's up, but they'll have plenty on their minds soon enough to worry about us.

I watch as one of the monstrous tugs circles t'others, as if hurding them, trying to keep them from scattering, where they'll be more vulnerable. Their strength is in their size and numbers. This particular tug must be a leader. With a thick layer of brown shag, a body the size of a boulder and six-inch-long horns that'll impale you quicker'n a mosquito sucks your blood, the male tug can be deadly to even the most experienced Hunter. And this male tug is bigger'n most, a real biggin, with brains to boot.

Stay away from him, Circ, I think. *Stay away from that biggin.*

There are a few baby tug mashed together between a bunch of females who take their motherly duties very seriously, but still, there should be more tug calves. As we've been taught in Learning: the tug numbers are on the decline, which poses a major problem for us and for them.

The Hunters hold their position 'bout half a mile away, maybe a bit less. I see Hawk strapping on his final pieces of gear: thick leather shin and arm blockers, a wicked-sharp curving knife, a sachet of pointers and a tightly strung bow. Lastly, he picks up his spear. He's ready. Like Circ, lack of confidence is foreign to Hawk. Either that or he hides it well. Despite being on the verge of charging into the middle of a bloody battle, the likes of which he ain't never seen before, he manages to crack a joke to one of his friends. A horn sounds and everyone, Hawk included, gazes at the Hunters. My father stands out in front, clad in a stained black leather tunic, a hollowed out tug horn to his lips. The future Head Greynote leads the charge. The horn is Hawk's signal. He takes off.

It seems to me that having the new Hunter run to catch up to t'others is a knocky tradition. I mean, all you do is tire him out 'fore he even gets to the starting line. I haven't heard about many newbs getting killed in their first Hunt, but still... I don't like Hawk, but I don't want him to die.

At first Hawk comes out a bit fast, probably 'cause he's full of adrenaline and excitement and all that first-Hunt stuff, but then he slows a bit, settling into a light gallop. T'others await his arrival patiently, in formation, bangers in the front, shooters in the back, and slashers on the wings. Circ's a slasher and, as usual, I spot him right away. We're maybe a quarter-mile away up here on the bluffs, but I can see him as if he's standing not two feet from me.

After three years, I've memorized everything 'bout him, from the way he stands, to how he holds the slasher-blade when he's anticipating having to use it, to his pre-Hunt rituals, which he starts now, just as I'm watching him. First he squats and scoops up a handful of dust, letting it sift through his fingers until it's just the right amount. He watches the grains of sand fall, gaining valuable information on wind speed and direction which'll be vital in the event he hasta use the bow strapped to his back. The remaining dust is patted onto the handle of his slasher-blade to keep his hands sweat-free. When he regains his feet, Hawk's nearly upon them. But Circ doesn't panic, doesn't rush the rest of his rituals, just calmly goes about them, as if the entire world is waiting for him. A cupped hand over his brow keeps the sun out of his eyes as he scans the tug hurd, looking for weaknesses. Then he checks and rechecks his equipment, making sure he has everything, that nothing's loose. Finally, he assumes a runner's stance, one foot in front of the other, knees slightly bent, head down.

Hawk reaches the Hunters at a dead sprint and the horn sounds again.

~ ~ ~

For me the eeriest part of the Hunt is the beginning. The Hunters charge the hurd, making no sound. Not a war cry, not a yell, not even a hiccup. Their feet barely seem to touch the ground as the hundred or so men and Younglings run on silent tiptoes. The hurd knows they're coming, sure, but the silent approach lulls them into a trance. That is, until the bangers start banging.

Wielding short, stubby hammers and long, pointed spears, the bangers arrive first, prodding at the tugs in the forefront, sneaking in a smash with a hammer where possible. The tugs pretty much go wooloo, which is the point. They lose their cool, start to break off from the hurd, scatter. The only way to defeat a two-thousand-pound foe amongst a pack of two-thousand-pound foes, is to get him away from t'others.

But not all the tugs start running. The biggin does a bit of charging of his own, churning up durt and dust and plowing into the line of bangers, who, realizing they've got a fight on their hands, start to retreat.

Sometimes it's better to be quick than lucky.

70

It's something my father once said that stuck with me. That was back when he wasn't such a baggard. I've always been quick on my feet, even if a bit clumsy, and my father taught me to use that to my advantage. Now, in the midst of the Hunt, being quicker'n the guy next to you is crucial.

Out of fifty or so bangers, about five ain't as quick as t'others. The biggin tosses two in the air like feathers, only they don't come down all floaty and soft-like; they come down like a rockslide, probably breaking half the bones in their bodies. T'other half are broken when the madder'n-scorch tug tramples all over them on the way to his next mark. To take out the third and fourth Hunters, he just lowers his big ol' head and butts them over, leaving nothing but carcasses and guts in his wake. For the fifth one, he has something special planned. To the Hunter's credit, he knows he ain't gonna escape the biggin, and he turns to fight. But it doesn't make one grizz of difference. His spear and hammer just bounce off the tug's hide and he keeps on coming. With a deft flick of his neck, the monster tug gets under the Hunter enough to lift him up on his horns. The guy screams.

I look away when the blood starts spraying.

Stay away from him, Circ, I think again. This time it feels like a prayer.

Well, the shooters start shooting, and their pointers fill the air like a thousand lashes of rain running sideways in a winter wind. At least two dozen pointers pepper the biggin, sprouting out of him at all kinds of angles. He bellows, but I know it's not 'cause he's scared or hurt or surrendering. No, his cry is one of anger and defiance. *Not on my watch*, it says to me.

A banger with a death wish runs up and jabs his spear straight into the tug's side, but it just breaks off before it penetrates more'n an inch. In a move so agile a burrow mouse would be proud, the tug twists itself around and kicks out with his hind leg, which catches the bold (or maybe wooloo) Hunter directly in the face. He goes down harder'n a sack of tug dung and lies still.

Enter Circ.

Somehow I knew he was coming, one way or t'other. It's exactly the type of situation he can't seem to stay away from. One that's impossible. One that'll challenge him to the very end of, or perhaps beyond, his level of ability.

He races in from the side, leaps on the biggin's back with reckless abandon, slashing with his slasher-blade again and again as the tug leader bucks and kicks like he's under attack by a swarm of angry soldier bees. Circ's hanging on with one arm, jerking and cracking around like the business end of my father's snapper. But he's still stabbing, just a flurry of bronzed skin riding a monster tug whose brown coat is slick with red to match the sky.

~ ~ ~

It shouldn't be possible for an animal that large to die, at least not from injury. But die it does, slowly at first, stopping its kicking, still snorting and huffing, but no longer fighting. It's a strange sight: a tug the size of a Glassy fire chariot, walking and stamping his feet, with Circ on his back, like a pesky fly. I know there's all kinds of other stuff happening all around him—like slashers finishing off their kills, a stampede of retreating tugs thundering into the distance, and apprentice healers rushing onto the field to attend to the dead and injured—but I can't seem to pull my eyes from him.

Circ.

I don't know why I worry 'bout him. He's the most capable person I know, always coming out on top. In this case, literally. Flush with the tug's bloody body, he lowers his head to its ear, whispers something. The killing words: *In the name of the sun goddess, I claim your body for the use of my people, the Heaters. You have died with honor, and your passing will save the lives of many. I send you to a better place, Warrior.*

Circ wraps his arm around its neck, and is about to draw his blade across the biggin's throat, when a blur swoops in from the side and smashes into him and the tug.

What the scorch? I think.

Circ loses his balance and topples off the injured tug, which suddenly has a bit of fight in him again, unloosing a bellow that sweeps across the field like a plague. I stand, straining to see who ruined Circ's perfect kill. Hawk comes into view, stalking around the front of the tug, his spear raised to killing height. Beneath the tug, which is stomping and kicking again—not dead yet!—Circ's rolling around, trying to avoid getting trampled. Hawk, the baggard! He's going to get Circ killed!

Hawk thrusts his spear at the tug, but it ducks its head at the last second and the sharp point glances off one of its horns.

Then it charges.

Hawk dives to the side, narrowly avoiding getting gored. Circ's sprawled out form comes into view. He's clutching his stomach, like he mighta caught a glancing blow from a hoof, but clearly he didn't get fully stepped on or kicked, 'cause he wouldn't be able to stand after something like that. Other'n that, he looks okay. Still, I hold my breath until he gets back on his feet.

The tug turns and starts pawing the ground, staring at Hawk and Circ. The two that tried to kill him. Circ yells something, but I'm too far away to hear what. All I know is that Hawk glances back and nods. With three more years of experience— and a scorch of a lot more natural ability—Circ is the one calling the shots.

They run, the two of them, in opposite directions, circling the monstrous red-and-black-splotched tug. It turns one way and then t'other, bucking around like someone's on its back. They're confusing it. Who to attack? Which way to go first? It starts for Circ and then seems to feel Hawk's presence behind it, so it whirls around and makes a move toward him.

The moment the tug turns its back on him, Circ makes a move of his own, a full out sprint toward the creature. He looks so small as he closes in on the girthy tug, 'specially 'cause of how far away I am. From here I can pinch him between my thumb and forefinger.

The tug stops again, as if realizing that the gig is up, that he's been tricked. He twists his head to turn, but he's too late. Circ leaps, lands gracefully on the tug's back as if he's tackling an opponent in feetball, hugging the beast around the neck. There's a gleam of light when the sun goddess's eye is reflected off the broad side of his blade as he slides it across the tug's neck.

A normal tug would drop on the spot after a killing stroke like that, but this ain't no normal tug. It's a behemoth, prepared to fight even as the life drains from him. With Circ still on his back, he charges Hawk, who's standing there dumbly. Now this is the good part.

Hawk runs off like a scared little Midder. On the way, he drops his spear, a couple of knives, and every last bit of his

74

pride in a heap on the desert floor. As it turns out, his hasty retreat probably saved his life, 'cause that final burst was all the tug had left. It slows to a stop, dips its head, and, finally, by the will of the sun goddess and Circ's unmatched ability—collapses, all strength sucked from its legs like venom from a scorpion sting. I sigh.

Circ's safe, and he's killed again.

I know the requirement to kill is necessary for our survival, but I don't hafta like it. The tugs haven't done anything to deserve such a fate. Like us, they're just trying to survive, migrating hundreds of miles each year to find diminishing fields of wildgrass to feed their young. 'Fore we kill them. We only take what we need, yeah, but to them we take everything.

I once asked Circ what it felt like to kill a creature as large and full of life as a tug. "Terrible," he said. "Take the worst feeling in the world and then multiply it by one hundred, and that's how awful it is." A single tear slipped from his eye, the first time I'd seen him cry since he was a Totter.

"Then why do you..." I started to ask, but I never finished the question 'cause I already knew the answer, and he never answered although he knew exactly what I was gonna ask. Why do we do anything we do? Why do girls get Called at sixteen? Why do the Hunters hunt? Why do the Greynotes meet and discuss trade arrangements with the Icers? 'Cause it's the Law, which is our sacred duty to uphold, a requirement for our survival. We don't hafta like it, just to do it.

It doesn't have to be like this. Even after watching the vicious Hunting of the tugs, I can't get Lara's words out of my head. Who does she know? The Icers? It sounds wooloo, but who knows these days? We could potentially avoid the Call by sneaking into ice country. The Wilds? The thieving, sister-grabbing, feral freaks who ruined my life when they took Skye's? I hope not, 'cause I consider Lara a friend and if she's with them I'll never be able to talk to her again.

A horn sounds and my head snaps around. It's not the long blast to start the Hunt, but a short series of tones from somewhere atop the bluffs. A warning, from the watchmen. Not a frequent occurrence, but not unusual either. Sometimes the hunched, wiry Cotees'll hear the initial horn, or smell the blood, and come to investigate. To a lone human, a large group of Cotees can be dangerous, but not to a fully equipped mess of Hunters.

I blink away the daydream and scan the desert, trying to find the gang of furry thieves who drew the alarm. I gasp when I see them. Not a single Cotee flecks the horizon.

Killers.

Eight

Not Cotees, but Killers. It's a big pack, too—I try to count them but keep getting confused 'cause they're moving so fast, flitting in and out of various formations as they rush toward the Hunters. Their movements are practiced. Professional. Twenty is my best guess. A big pack.

Four-legged, with fur as black as night, long, lanky bodies full of muscle and speed, and claws and teeth that can rip and tear through muscle, tendon and bone without discretion, Killers, as their name suggests, are the ultimate killing machines. They're animals, like Cotees, but a whole scorch of a lot bigger and scarier—smarter too, always planning and plotting.

The spectators on the bluff, comprised of women, Younglings, and the few odd men who are too infirm to participate in the Hunt, are jabbering a mile a moment, some screaming, some waving their hands, all on their feet. Scared. Like me.

Circ.

The Hunters can see the Killers now, too, even from their lower vantage point, that's how close they are. My eyes flick to the black death squad and then back to the Hunters, who are reassembling themselves, trying to form their own pack, but it's clear they don't know what to do. Never in broad daylight. Never so many.

My mind racing, I estimate the distance. At their current speed, the Killers are less'n five desert sprints away, as the crow flies, maybe less.

Circ's down there. Will he be killed if I do nothing? I don't know, but I *can't* do nothing, it ain't physically possible for me to sit and watch as he's torn apart by rabid beasts.

I have no time to think, and anyway, thinking's not my skill. Nothing's my skill really, 'cept my speed, and what good's that ever done me?

My broken arm throbs, as if a reminder.

With no other choice, I give myself over to my legs, knowing full well what a stupid decision it is.

As I dart across the bluff, I see a few startled eyes following me, probably thinking I'm headed back to the village to get help. But I know there's no help there. Anyone capable of helping is here, and I'm not seeing any of the other women or Younglings in a hurry to do a searin' thing, so that leaves me. Scrawny. Runty. But fast.

I cut hard to the right, into a narrow passage that slices between the bluff and provides access to the killing fields below. It's the same path Hawk took earlier.

Running with only one arm is harder'n you'd think. Or at least harder'n I thought it'd be. I expected having one bum arm would be no big deal, 'cause when you run it's your legs doing all the work anyway, right?

Wrong.

I'm all off balance, which makes me clumsier'n ever, unable to run in a straight line. First I bash into one wall of the passage, bruising my good arm, and then into the other wall. The second time is my bad arm, which, with the Medicine Man's herbs wearing off, sends scythes of pain through the entire right side of my body.

Knock pain. Burn pain. Pain is nothing when my best friend since I was four is out there.

I've always liked the feeling I get when I run. Wind through my hair and on my arms, drying the beads of sweat that accumulate faster'n they can evaporate. My mind clear, the effort required to pump my legs and arms is enough to clear my head of all the garbage inside. When I'm running is the only time I can think clearly.

Well, this time ain't like that at all.

The wind buffets me, bashing me around like a brambleweed. My skin is hot. I'm sweating but it provides no relief from the heat inside me. And my mind is the worst of all, cluttered beyond belief.

Circ. Killers. Circ. Killers. Hunt. Hunters. Circ. Prey.

The Hunters have become the Prey.

And I'm running into the midst of it all. Clearly when the sun goddess was handing out brains I was last in line. It's one of my favorite jokes, one Circ has heard me tell a hundred times. His response: perhaps the sun goddess had a surplus, and you got all the leftover brains.

I ain't no genius.

With the wooloo thoughts I got going through my head that's so full it's empty, I should be cracking up, rolling on the ground with laughter, but I'm not. I'm just running, running, running. And emerging from the space between the bluffs.

Wow.

From up above, the grazing field looked so small, almost surreal, with little men with tiny weapons fighting fist-sized beasts. As a spectator, no matter how much you care about those on the field of battle, you're still detached from it. Separated.

As I race out onto the field, it all suddenly becomes very real to me. The bluffs loom over me like a dark tower, casting a shadow across the desert, cutting the dead bodies of both men and tugs in half, as if they've been eaten away by vultures and Cotees. The field itself is huge, not just a game board like it appears from above. Hard-packed sand and dirt go on forever, marred only by tiny tufts of wildgrass, which is the only reason the tugs were here at all. The tugs are behemoths, even in death. They lie crumpled in the dirt, dozens of them—surely it woulda been enough to feed the village for the winter.

But that was before the Killers. Now we'll be lucky to get off the field alive.

I skid to a stop and my heart skips a beat when I see them. Black flashes of heat in the distance. Definitely headed our way. There's not much time left. Find Circ.

Frantically, my eyes dart every which way, bouncing around so quickly that there's zero chance of me finding him. I take a deep breath, try to calm my frayed nerves, focus on each thing I see and hear. Men yelling. The Hunters, bandying together, at least eighty strong. I search for anyone I know and spot my father at the same time as he spots me. He's the only Greynote who fights these days. The others are too old and decrepit, many in early stages of the Fire.

His eyes are alight with something. Fear? No. Concern? No. Anger? The snarl on his lips gives away his emotion. "Go!" he yells across the field, his finger pointing back up to the bluffs.

His one word sums up our relationship. Whether his command is to keep me safe or not, I know he'd speak it even if we weren't in mortal danger. Hot tears well up, but I blink them back just as quickly. No time for tears, or fears, or the pain throbbing in my arm. Find Circ.

I ignore my father, continue to scan the desolate field, trying to remember something important, some clue as to where I'll find Circ. Everything looks so different from this vantage point. Up above, I knew exactly how things were laid out, where Circ was in relation to the hurd, to t'other Hunters. Down here it's all one big bloody mess. A man groans nearby, pierced by sharp horns in two spots, round circles of blood.

The black smudges are no longer smudges. They're Killers, so full of detail I wanna scream. I can see their eyes, reflective yellow. They should be staring in a million directions, preparing for the hunt, but I feel as if all their eyes are on me. Their mouths are agape and snapping, two-inch-long fangs the showcase piece in their collection of razor sharp teeth. They're so close now I can see the muscles rippling in their legs as they run. Death on four feet.

Circ must be amongst t'other Hunters. He's nowhere else…

What was I thinking? Why am I here? I have about as much chance of protecting Circ as becoming part of the male-only Greynote club when I turn thirty. If he sees me I'll only distract him from defending himself.

I turn to run back to the bluffs as my father ordered, when I spot the man who groaned earlier. The two spots of blood have widened and his head's lolled to the side, tongue hanging out. He's dead. But there's something about him that means something. Something important. Two spots of blood. Two horn injuries.

The fifth Hunter killed by the biggin! I'm close to where it all went down. Then I see him, the monster-tug himself, a big ol' pile of flesh and fur and bone now. And behind his dead carcass, voices, no more'n whispers, but clear as day now that I know where to listen.

As scared as I am of the Killers, there's no way they'll attack us or the Hunters, right? I mean, why would they? They've got fresh, dead tug meat all over the place, just begging to fill their hungry stomachs, so surely they'll go straight for that.

There are cries to my right from the group of Hunters. The Killers, who looked so much like they were staring at me, heading for me, have veered off toward the larger group, who are shooting volley after volley of pointers at them. What the scorch? They're going straight for them, as if they don't even see the tug feast in front of them. Something's seriously wrong.

Fifty feet away. Feathered pointers stick from their black fur, but it don't stop them.

Thirty feet. More pointers pierce their flesh. One goes down, yelping, as a sharpshooter puts one through its brain.

Ten feet. With a dozen snarls from the Killers and five times that many yells from the Hunters, the battle begins. 'Fore I can return my gaze to the biggin, I see one Hunter get mauled and another stab his slasher-blade through a Killer's throat.

I realize that I've crouched down, instinctively maybe, but more likely 'cause my legs are shaking at the knees. This is no place for a girl with one arm.

I head for the biggin.

~~~

A hand appears over the monster-tug. Then a face. Circ! His expression is grim, determined. Then he sees me and it morphs from eyebrow-raised shock to wide-eyed fear to a decision in the form of a nod: We're getting out of here.

Another face appears. Hawk. The baggard! If we weren't in this searin' life or death situation, I'd have half a mind to march up to him and knock him clear into tomorrow.

Hawk pushes off of the dead tug and hurdles it, landing in a crouch in front of me. Circ moves around the butt end of the biggin, sort of limping, holding onto his gut like he's eaten some undercooked 'zard and is about to spew. The injury from that tug hurt him worse'n I thought. That's why he didn't join the rallying Hunters to face the Killers. Hawk mighta stayed with him to help get him to safety, but more likely he stayed 'cause he's a burnin' coward.

Ignoring Hawk, I head for Circ. Our eyes meet. "We've got to g—" he starts to say, but then we both see it on the edge of our vision. A dark shape, a moving shadow that's not a shadow.

One of the Killers has broken away from the pack and is locked on Circ, probably seeing him as the weakest link, smelling out his injury as if it has a nasty odor, like drying blaze. I'm injured too, of course, with my broken wrist, but I don't have enough meat on my bones to make even a snack for this monster.

I run. Every instinct is telling me to run away, to head in the opposite direction, but they're survival instincts, not life instincts. In life there's only one choice: run to Circ. I keep my eyes ahead, on Circ, try to forget about the Killer, pretend we're just Midders again, playing feetball...and Circ's got the ball.

I'm two steps away and the shadow is all over me. Tackle the guy with the ball.

One step. Blackness everywhere.

I turn my uninjured side toward the front just before I collide with Circ. Even still, it's like running into a hunk of rock at full speed. Circ doesn't have any soft bits on him at all.

At the same time, a burst of air rushes past me. Claws scrape between my shoulder blades. I cry out.

Circ's a fighter. 'Fore today, I already knew it, but I've never really seen him in a situation where death's not only possible, but likely. He's on his feet in an instant, pulling my tangled arms and legs behind him, urging me to "Run, Sie, run!" He pushes me and heads in the other direction at full speed, right for the Killer, as if he doesn't have a set of crushed ribs and who knows what other injuries. I thought I was saving him, but now he's saving me.

'Cause of my momentum, I take at least five steps 'fore I'm able to stop. There's heat all around me, pushing in: on my back, practically tearing through me; on my arm, which, having broken free of the sling, is dangling from my side again; but the worst heat is what I'm now forced to watch: the heat of death and war. Someone hasta die. The Killer or all of us. Running is no longer an option.

Circ's chasing the Killer, and the Killer is chasing Hawk, who's decided to ditch us for the relative safety of the high ground. Circ's fast as scorch, but the Killer's faster and has a headstart. When Hawk looks back his eyes are so wide and white it's almost comical, like a Totter's in a ghost maze when we celebrate the Day of the Dead.

The Killer leaps. At the last second Hawk dives to the side and rolls, rolls, rolls, end over end. The Killer misses again and I think this time it really grizzes him off, 'cause he lets out a growl that sends shivers buzzing up my spine. Unlike Circ, Hawk is slow to his feet, probably a bit dizzy from all the rolling. The Killer stops so fast I'd think it was impossible if I didn't just see it happen. The predator cuts to the right, pounces on Hawk, his teeth bared and dripping clear and red ooze, a mixture of its own drool and the blood of its last victim, one of t'other Hunters. My feet are stone, too heavy to move. After the Killer rips out Hawk's throat, I'll be next.

If my feet are stone, Circ's are clouds, floating across the desert, graceful and light. But these are winter clouds, full of lightning, and right 'fore Circ launches himself at the Killer, his body seems to darken. His slasher-blade—the lightning—flashes against the darkness of his body as he crashes into the beast.

No, no, sun goddess, no!

Take Hawk, take me.

Not Circ.

Not my best friend, not someone so good, so pure, so perfect.

The Killer is on him, shaking and twitching with excitement. I can't see its face but I know why it's excited. Tearing and biting. Clawing and ripping. Feasting on the blood of my world. To me—everything. To the Killer—just a meal.

I've got no sense left in me, if I had any to begin with. I run right at it, determined to kill it 'fore it can take any more of my friend, or more likely die trying. I'm weaponless, but I see the tip of Circ's slasher-blade peeking out from the edge of the Killer's skin. Circ's final gift to me.

I hold my breath, reach for the blade, feel it's warm steel on my fingertips, try to pull it toward me so I can get to the handle. It won't budge. It's trapped under something, Circ's body, or the Killer, or both. I strain against the weight, desperate to get it out before the Killer notices my presence, but I'm not strong enough. Never strong enough.

The Killer's no longer moving. It's frozen. It knows I'm here and is contemplating the best way to turn and rip me to shreds. The blade is my only chance and I'm desperate now. I scrabble at it, try to follow the gleaming metal down to the handle. My fingers only get two inches before brushing against blood-matted fur. The blade almost seems to come from the Killer's skin, like it's hiding it within him, well out of my reach.

It's still not moving.

'Cause it's dead.

Nine

This clinches it: I'm destined to be in trouble for the rest of my life.

I tried my best to save my friend's life—although I think I got more in the way'n anything—nearly dying in the process, and then watched him escape death by a hairsbreadth—and now I'm in trouble for it.

"This is the last grain of sand, Youngling!" my father says, his face red again. He was one of the forty-nine survivors, including Circ and Hawk, of the Killer attack. Evidently their group was the only unlucky one. All of the other hunting parties came back with minimal deaths, all from the horns and hoofs of tugs.

"I have a name!" I spout, surprising even myself. I'm talking back to my father more'n more these days, which is probably stupid, but I can't seem to help myself. He makes me so angry, madder'n a Cotee who watches its dinner get swooped away by a sneaky vulture 'fore it gets even one bite.

"Your name should be Brainless," Father says.

"Roan, go easy," my mother says. I look at her, surprised, but she's expressionless. She's never stood up for me. I always get the feeling that she wants to, but either she's too scared or too smart to do anything.

My father whirls on her, momentarily taking the pressure off of me. "How dare you! I'm trying to save our daughter from herself. She could have been killed today. And you will address me as Greynote, Woman."

In my head I hear it as my father wanting to be called Greynote Woman, or perhaps Greynote the Woman. A snigger escapes my lips, bringing his attention mercilessly back to me, his eyes blazing.

"I have a name, too," my mother says, her voice no more'n a whisper. My initial shock at her interference turns to amazement. What's going on? It's like me and my mother've both had enough of it—all of it. My father's punishments and anger and outbursts. And now we're fighting back as best we can.

My father's head bounces back toward my mother. He takes two strides until he looms over her, at least a head taller and twice as big. For a moment he reminds me of the Killer and I have the urge to rush him from behind.

"Enough!" he snaps. "From both of you. Woman, you will leave this instant or I will make you leave." I admire my mother's nerve as she stares at him, holding it for two moments longer'n I woulda had the guts to do. When she breaks her gaze, her eyes meet mine, flash *I'm sorry*, and then she walks out the hut door.

I'm determined to plead my case 'fore my father turns on me again. "I was only trying to—"

"I said enough, Siena," my father says, surprising me by using my name for the second time in as many days. Averting his eyes, he stalks around the edge of the hut, drawing flaps of tugskin over each of the three windows. Next he'll go for his snapper, I know it.

"Father, I—"

"Stop. You not only put yourself in danger, but the entire village too. We simply cannot have pre-Bearers running around trying to be heroes. If you die, you cannot be in the Call, can you? Siena, you will Bear a child when you turn sixteen, nineteen, and twenty-two, just like all the other girls. You understand?" His voice is lower, less angry, almost petulant.

I nod, even while thinking, *It really is just about breeding, ain't it?*

"I've tried the snapper, I've tried threatening, I've tried everything I can think of. There's only one option left. You'll spend a day in Confinement."

~~~

'Cause my day in Confinement won't begin until tomorrow, I go to find Circ, a final rebellion 'fore Father punishes me. I don't even try to hide where I'm going, but Father doesn't try to stop me either, because there's some big important Greynote meeting he hasta prepare for and I'm suddenly the least of his worries.

Circ's sitting on a pile of sand outside his family's tent, staring into the fire pit, which ain't lit. A gust of wind is sweeping the gray ash in circles, almost hypnotically.

"Some day," I say as I plop down next to him.

Circ keeps staring into the pit. Maybe he's in a trance. "Did steam come out of your father's ears this time?" he asks.

"More like out of his butt," I say, snorting.

Circ laughs, his eyes alight as he finally looks up at me. "What'd you get? More blaze shoveling?"

"Not exactly. Confinement." I don't mention being forbidden to hang out with him.

"What? He can't do that! You're only fifteen." His smile is gone but the holes in his cheeks are deeper'n ever.

"He can do whatever he wants," I say, picking up a stone and chucking it into the fire pit.

"He's not Head Greynote yet," Circ says, throwing his own stone.

"Well, he might as well be. Shiva's in no position to stop him from making all the decisions. It's only a day anyway. He thinks it'll teach me a lesson."

"Will it?" Circ asks, his eyebrows raised.

I look at him and we both laugh. Sun goddess, what would I do without Circ?

"Really, it's nothing I can't handle," I say.

"That's what you always say. But I say he's gone too far. The way he manhandles you and your mother, it just ain't right."

"He's just another Heater man trying to keep control of his Calls," I say.

"Most of the men ain't like him," Circ says. "My father, for one."

"Are your ribs okay?" I ask, changing the subject and motioning to Circ's stomach.

Scowling, he lifts his shirt. Heavy, thick bandages are wrapped tightly around his torso.

"Are those to keep your guts from falling out?" I ask.

"Not just my guts. My organs, bones, the food I eat, everything," Circ says, keeping a straight face, but not frowning anymore.

"Smoky," I say. "You better not take them off then."

Circ's expression suddenly turns serious. "How about you? Are you okay?"

"Nothing a day in Confinement can't cure," I say wryly. When Circ smirks, I say, "Oh, you mean my injuries? I thought you meant my mental problems, tendency toward delinquency, and aversion to being sixteen and big with child."

"You're admitting you have mental problems?" Circ says, raising one side of his lip, which deepens one dimple but not the other.

I punch him lightly on the shoulder. "I'm not admitting anything. MedMa said I didn't do any further damage to my wrist, so I'm still looking at a full moon and a half of healing. He bandaged the four claw marks on my back. Apparently they're deep enough that I'll get some wicked scars, but not deep enough to cause any permanent damage."

"Sounds like the perfect result," Circ says.

We're both silent for a moment, lost in our own thoughts. Me, I'm remembering the day's events in my head, cycling through them as if they're a dream sequence, something that happened while I was sleeping, or perhaps to someone else entirely. I don't know what Circ is thinking, not until he speaks anyway.

91

"Why'd you run down on that field, Sie?" I look up at him, hoping for a clue as to the motivation behind his question, but all I get are curious eyes and flat lips.

I want to tell him everything. How much he means to me, how I'd want to die if he ever got killed, how the thought of losing him is like someone stabbing me repeatedly in the heart. I don't know anything about love, not really, but I know the way I feel when I'm with Circ is the best feeling ever, like the calm after a violent windstorm, like seeing the first prickler buds appear so miraculously after the harshness of winter, like running full-gallop across the plains, wind on my face and skin.

But all I say is, "I didn't have anything better to do and you looked like you could use some help."

He cocks his head to the side, looks at me sideways for a couple of seconds, and then says, "Thanks."

I sense he wants to say more, and might even say whatever it is, but I'm really not in the mood for a serious conversation, so I say, "Did you talk to Hawk?"

Circ laughs, but it's more of a cough-laugh. "Yeah. I talked to him alright. He said, 'Just because you saved my life doesn't mean we're friends.'"

"He burnin' tried to kill you!" I say.

"He claims he didn't see me—that he was just going for the kill."

"Baggard," I say. "You should tell the Greynotes what he did."

"Normally I would, but they've got enough to deal with right now."

"Baggard," I repeat.

"Some people never change."

"What are they saying about the Killer attack?" I ask.

"It's unprecedented," he says. "Everyone knows the Killers are dangerous, but they're also not stupid. They're very clever hunters, attacking only at night when you can barely see them, isolating their prey so they always have the advantage in numbers, going after the weakest link, that sort of thing. But this time was different. They attacked a foe with greater numbers in broad daylight. And they went after the strongest from our village, the Hunters."

"Yeah, but they were only trying to get to the tugs," I point out. "The Hunters just happened to be in the way."

"Maybe," he says. "But it's still strange."

I nod. "Any theories?"

Circ rubs his chin, which has a thin layer of stubble. I guess he didn't have time to shave. "The Greynote Hunters are being especially quiet about the whole thing. Honestly, I feel like they're hiding something. Your father didn't say a word about it after the Hunt, just told us we all did a good job and that we would have to pitch in to bury the dead and secure the tugs before the Cotees and vultures get to them. I'm exempt because of my injuries."

Weird. Everything about the way my father's been acting is weird. "But besides the Greynotes, do any of t'other Hunters have any guesses?" I ask. "There hasta be some reason for the attack."

Circ shrugs. "Some of the guys are saying the Killers must be desperate for food, that they're having difficulty finding it elsewhere."

"Makes sense," I say, closing my eyes.

"Maybe…" Circ says, slowly, drawing out the word like he wants to say more.

"What? What is it?" I ask, opening my eyes to look at him.

"Well, I don't want to scare you, but—"

"That's usually what people say 'fore saying something scary," I interrupt, smirking.

Circ smiles, but it's only half of one. Something's clearly on his mind. "Okay, let me rephrase. I do want to scare you, so I'll tell you what some of the other guys are saying. A few of them think the Killers were targeting us."

"The Hunters?"

"Maybe the Hunters, maybe the Heaters in general."

"But why would they do that?" I ask. "I mean, they killed a bunch of Hunters, but their entire pack died in the process."

Circ throws up his hands. "I know, I know, it sounds crazy. But what if they were out for revenge? And what if that wasn't their whole pack and they only sent a small death squad to kill us? And what if they're not done yet? And what if—"

"Whoa, whoa, hold up, Circ. You're sounding all wooloo. Are the guys really saying all that?"

Circ nods. "They're saying it might be the start of another war with the Killers."

My breath catches in my chest. Another Killer war? "But the Hunters've stayed within the boundaries, right?"

"Of course. We never even get close to the edge of the hunting zone we've used for the last hundred years, since the last Killer war. But what if someone else is?" Another *what if*. Circ's setting some kinda record.

I think back to everything they taught us in Learning. A little over a hundred years ago the Heaters got greedy, started hunting tug outside of their normal area, where the Killers roamed the desert, started taking more meat'n they needed to survive. As Teacher put it, "The balance of nature kicked in." In other words, the Killers started doing what they do best:

killing. They attacked the village every night for days and days, distracting the guards on one side and sneaking in on t'other to drag away women and children, leaving only smears of blood and claw marks in the durt as evidence they'd ever been there. By the time the war was over and the Hunters realized that all they hadta do was reign in their hunting zone, the Killers had wiped out half the village. To replenish our numbers, the frequency of Bearing was increased to every two years for all eligible Bearers. The Bearer age was dropped to fifteen. That lasted for twenty six years 'fore returning to normal. Lucky for me. If it hadn't, I'd already be child-big, my first child on the way, compliments of some unknown guy.

But who else'd be stupid enough to Hunt in Killer territory? The Icers? Not a chance. They never leave the safety of the mountains. The Glassies? It's possible. After we held them off a few full moons back they might be looking to try again. *The Wild Ones.* The words pop into my head and my eyes widen.

I look at Circ, who's watching me, letting me think. "Do you think it's the Wild Ones?" I ask.

Circ shakes his head, but he's not saying no. "I really don't know. Honestly, until Teacher Mas mentioned the Wild Ones I didn't believe they existed."

"Well, who else could it be?"

"A few guys are saying the Marked are behind it."

The Marked. Another fictional group who might just turn out to be real. Growing up, we've always talked about them as if they're real, the same way you talk about the sandmonster as if he's real. You know, just to scare each other. The thing is, I've heard some of the adults talk about the Marked, too, not that that necessarily means anything either. If the stories are right, the Marked is a tribe of all men, covered from head to toe with strange painted markings. Like the Wilds, they're a feral group, eating raw flesh and washing it down with fire juice.

This whole conversation is becoming too confusing.

"I need to think," I say. "I'm going to see Veeva before my father sends me away to prison."

Circ looks at me oddly. "I thought you said it was only a day in Confinement."

"It is. But it's more fun if I'm dramatic about it. Plus, I wanna talk to someone normal for a while."

"What? I'm not normal?" Circ says, his hands out and open.

"You're some kind of freak of nature," I say. "I mean that in the nicest way," I add.

Circ laughs. "I'd say Veeva is anything but normal."

"To me, she's the most normal," I say.

~~~

Sometimes a madhouse is the calmest place of all.

When I enter Veeva's tent, it's chaos, but I feel perfectly at home and more relaxed'n I have all day. You'd think she has a dozen kids, all of them between the ages of zero and three. I know that's physically impossible, not to mention illegal, but still, with the number of bundles strewn about, I wonder if she's not hiding them all somewhere, behind the bed maybe. Her tent is so unlike our hut, where everything hasta be in its place, that it's laughable. Besides the bundles, there are clothes and blankets everywhere, unwashed pots and pans piling up in the center of the tent, and lines of wet laundry drying across most of the small space. I can barely see my friend through the clutter.

When Veeva looks around the edge of one of Grunt's giant shirts and sees me, she says, "Thank the sun goddess yer 'ere, Sie. Grab a bundle and git over 'ere."

I screw up my face. Not the welcome I was hoping for. I've had enough blaze for a lifetime, and although baby blaze is much smaller, it's just as stinky. But Veeva's always been a good friend to me, so, obediently, I grab the first unbundled white cloth I see, and I take it over to her, who's got naked little Polk flat on his back on his tiny bed, his six-full-moon-old arms and legs waving about, grabbing at the air, like he's trying to get his hands on something invisible that only he can see.

Veeva's wearing a shapeless brown frock and a look that could kill. "I tell you, Sie, if there's any way you can avoid the burnin' Call, do it. I swear to you this searin' baby is the spawn of the lord of the underworld, if you believe in that sorta thing."

"Hi to you, too, Veevs," I say, grinning. "What's the little tug-face done now?"

She takes the cloth from me, lies it flat on the bed. Picks up Polk and places his butt in the center. "Oh, you wouldn't believe it, Sie." She looks around, notices how many used bundles there are. "Or maybe you would. He's been lettin' it fly from both ends. Projectile vomit from his mouth, and spewin' blaze from the other end. He's relentless. I think he's tryin' to break me."

With expertness that a year ago woulda seemed impossible, Veeva bundles the cloth around Polk's torso, tying it off perfectly. I guess a little practice goes a long way.

"There's no way to avoid the Call," I say, moving around the tent, grabbing used bundles. I'm careful to keep whatever's inside, well, inside.

"What you sayin'?" Veeva says, Polk now in her arms. She's got her frock pulled way down, her big breasts hanging out as if she's alone and not having a conversation with a friend. Polk knows what to do—he goes right for her teat.

I look away, grab a few more bundles. "You said if there's any way I can avoid the Call, to do it. I'm saying there's no way."

"I wasn't bein' serious, Sie. I know as well as anyone that it can't be skipped. By the sun goddess, you can be so serious sometimes."

I realize then that I was saying it more to convince myself'n Veeva. Lara's words are haunting me even more'n I thought. I need to talk to her once and for all, tell her to quit asking me 'bout what she said, tell her I've thought 'bout it and I don't believe her and I'm going to obey the law from here on out, even if that means breeding. No more getting in trouble for me.

But how can I get her to believe me when I don't even believe myself?

I leave without telling her about Confinement.

Ten

I don't know what to expect from Confinement, 'cause I've never been there 'fore. And most people who have don't really talk 'bout it.

Father doesn't even bother to take me himself, he's too busy snoring away. One of the younger Greynotes draws the short straw and hasta get up 'fore even the butt crack of dawn to make the trek with me. I don't complain, don't say anything, just get on with it. Complaining's never gotten me anywhere so I don't see the point.

The Greynote's name is Luger and he's a real baggard. With dark, slitted eyes so narrow I can hardly tell if they're open or closed, he almost seems excited to drag me into seclusion. He's far too jittery for this early in the morning, always twitching, like every part of his body is moving in unison all the time, every moment of every day. I feel bad for his Calls, the ones that hafta sleep in the same bed with him as he jerks and twitches all night long, even while sleeping.

When he speaks, his mouth reminds me of a burrow mouse, pulled tight in the center, only able to open to a tiny gap, just wide enough to shove a bit of food in it. And his nose is like a vulture's beak, long, narrow, and pointy. He's not an attractive man. But, hey, I'm not one to judge someone based on appearance. It's his attitude that really grizzes me off.

"You're lucky to get just a day," he whines. "I would've given you a quarter full moon for what you did. If your father wasn't the Head Greynote…"

"He's *not* the Head Greynote," I say, staring forward as we trudge across the desert in the dark.

"Two, maybe three days," he says. "The Fire's got Shiva by the balls."

I wince and go silent. Three days and my father'll be the Head Greynote? He's already so full of himself I'd hate to see the power trip he'll go on when he's at the top of the food chain.

Time passes, the sky lightening with each step. My fists are squeezed tight.

The calm of the desert can be eerie sometimes. When the Cotees are howling and the wind is whipping through the dunes, at least you know the world is alive. But now, it's so quiet, with only the sound of our soft treads to break the silence—it's almost like we're walking in a dead land. Which makes us the walking dead, I s'pose.

As we continue on, however, the wastelands gradually begin to awake. First I see a 'zard emerge from a hole. He's a biggin, too, with prickly burs all down his back, starting at his head and going to the tip of his long tail. He's one of those bag-throated ones, with a big ol' sac on his neck that fills with air each time he breathes. It's kinda knocky, if you ask me. He scurries into our path, watches us approach for a few moments, and then wriggles away. He's lucky we're not hungry, or he'd end up in the stew.

Next I see a fire ant hill teeming with activity. Fat, red ants of all shapes and sizes scurry around like their lives depend on their ability to do a bunch of stuff 'fore the sun goes down again; and the sun goddess's eye's not even really up yet—it's just a glow of orange on the horizon.

The fire ants bring my thoughts back to the Marked. One of the stories I heard a lot as a Midder was that if the Marked found someone trespassing on their land, they'd bury you next to a fire ant hill, and let the nasty little biters do the rest. When they'd come back a few days later, you'd be nothin' but a buried pile o' bones. Talk like that always freaked me out, but in a fun, sandmonster kind of way. If something's not real, it's fun to pretend that it is. But now that the Hunters are talking about the Marked like they're real people—prisoner-burying-next-to-fire-ant-hill kind of people—well, now the thought of them ain't so fun.

What if they're the ones disturbing the Killers? How the scorch are we s'posed to stop them? Those are questions my father as Head Greynote'll hafta deal with. For a moment I feel sorry for him. A very quick moment.

After a lot of trudging, and just as the top curve of the sun is peeking above the horizon, the winds pick up. At first it's a nice breeze, more'n welcome under my rather sweaty circumstances, but soon becomes a gale force, swirling the dust and sand around like little miniature tornados, what we call dust devils.

They can be dangerous, but only if there's a whole bunch of them spittin' up sharp rocks and such. These ones are just an annoyance, coating our lips, cheeks and pretty much everything else in a thin layer of dust. The good thing though, is that Luger can't talk to me with weather like this.

When the winds eventually die down, I spot something in the distance, the first real structures we've seen since leaving the village. A line of boxes, like little Greynote huts all in a row, 'cept not covered. Only I know that no Greynotes live all the way out here in the desert. This is Confinement.

Overhead there's a caw and a croak—half a dozen vultures circle lazily overhead, as if they're expecting their next meal to come from Confinement. Perhaps it will. Perhaps they've gotten a lot of meals from this place.

"Welcome to paradise," Luger sneers.

"Thanks," I say, stone-faced. Inside I'm trembling a bit and I've got to grizz. I squeeze hard and hold it—both my fear and my bladder—refusing to let this mouse-mouthed Greynote see my weakness.

He explains everything as we approach. "You've been sentenced to a day. Someone will arrive tomorrow at this time to collect you. You'll receive one meal from the Keeper, and I can tell you, it won't fill even that shrunken belly of yours." He smiles and my stomach rumbles, although I'm not really hungry. Maybe I shoulda nabbed that bag-throated 'zard when I had the chance.

"And water?" I ask hopefully.

Luger laughs. "Let's just say you'll be willing to drink your own grizz by the time the day's over."

I try to swallow, but already my throat seems dry and full of dust. "Anything else?" I croak, sounding more like the circling vultures'n a Youngling girl.

"Yeah. Learn your lesson and you won't end up back here again. Stay away from that trouble-making Youngling until after your Call." At first I think he means Lara, but then I realize it's Circ he's talking about. My father probably put him up to saying all this. Circ is anything but a trouble maker.

"I will," I lie.

"That...I doubt," Luger says. I clench my jaw shut tight to stop it from snapping at him.

When we get to the first "hut" I realize they're nothing like the Greynote huts, which are solid buildings with well-thatched roofs that keep the sun and rain and wind out. What stands 'fore me is a cage, that's the only way to describe it. A series of vertical wooden poles are the bars on both the sides and top. Heavy rope and tug glue lash them together at the corners. Nothing covers the gaps between them, leaving them fully exposed to the elements, as well as prowling animals.

I gulp. "Have the Killers ever...?"

"Only once," Luger says, stopping to face me. "Back during the first Killer war. At that time the Killers were pretty much running unobstructed across all of fire country. There were thirty prisoners in Confinement at the time. When the Hunters went to check on them, every last one of these cages was smashed to pieces." I close my eyes, wishing I hadn't asked the question and hoping he'll stop there. He doesn't. "There were huge paw prints everywhere. They were filled with blood."

My stomach's doing backflips—and not the good kind, like when I see Circ every day at Learning. I think I'm going to throw up. If Circ's right 'bout there being someone hunting in

Killer territory, they might be prowling all around our land right now, sniffing out weaknesses. A bunch of Heaters in cages would undoubtedly be considered a weakness.

"Just get on with it," I say, trying to sound tough. My voice shakes with every word.

We continue past the first cage, which appears to be empty. The second also seems unoccupied, but then I spot him: A curled up blotch of flesh in the corner, no more'n a collection of elbows and knees. If he wasn't staring at me, his eyes blinking every few seconds, I'd think he was dead. His face is gaunt and ageless. His beard long and matted. He's been here a long time. I wonder what he did to deserve such a punishment.

"Welcome to Scorch," he says, his voice whisper-thin.

The next cage is also used, and I'm surprised to recognize the prisoner right away. Bart. A big guy. Well known around the village for starting—and finishing—fights after a night of too much fire juice and fireweed. He also has a reputation for using his hammer-like fists on his Calls. He's prowling around his space like a caged animal, growling and pushing and pounding on the wooden bars every so often. Despite their crotchety appearance, the cages are sturdier'n they appear— they don't so much as quiver under Bart's unceasing assault. When he sees me staring at him, he stops, bares his teeth in what I think is meant to be a smile. "Please, nice Greynote, sir, can I share a cage with her?" He licks his lips.

I look away and we keep going. Luger doesn't say a word.

Behind us, Bart hollers, "Just as well. I'd probably crush her under me anyway." He laughs, a gritty, throaty sound that reminds me of the growl of the Killers that got me here in the first place.

There are at least fifty more cages spread out in front of us, but Luger stops at a real hut, complete with a door, walls, and an inclined roof, one half of a triangle. Above the door is a painted sign: The Keeper. The scraggly words are splotched in a red so bright it could be fresh blood.

"Wakey, wakey, Keep!" Luger shouts, pounding on the door. "I've brought you another gift."

I hear grumbling, a bang, a curse, and then the heavy trod of footsteps on a wooden floor. "Keep yer britches on," an unfriendly voice says through the door just 'fore it opens.

The door rotates open with a bitter creak that makes me think it's as equally annoyed to be awakened as the Keeper. Lit by the bright sunlight, the bare-chested Keeper is as pale white a person as I've ever seen. Some of the Hunters told Circ that some of the Glassies that attacked our village a few full moons back were as white-skinned as the snow. But I ain't seen snow, nor have I seen any Glassies, so that might all be a big load of tugwash. Anyway, this guy looks like he spends most of the day in his windowless hut. He squints his coppery eyes and winces, as if being exposed to the sun gives him physical pain, which maybe it does. His unlined face is barely visible behind a dark mask composed of a thick beard and mustache, bushy eyebrows, and a mop of curly hair that bobs just over his eyes. I guess there's not much point in grooming when you don't see anyone but prisoners.

"A young'un, are ya?" he says, yawning and scratching his hairy chest.

"Pre-Bearer," I say, determined to answer any questions he has with as few words as possible.

"Yer got a name?"

Huh? What kind of question is that? Who doesn't have a name? I've got a few smart responses cooked up, but I settle for just, "Siena."

"She's the Head Greynote's daughter," Luger adds unhelpfully.

"Shiva's kid?"

"Shiva's about two coughs away from kickin' it. She's Roan's," he says, as if my father owns me, like I'm just another piece of his property, like his hut, or bow. It's probably not far from the truth.

"Burnin' scorch!" the Keeper swears. "Bein' out 'ere I'm always out of ter loop. I didn't e'en know Shiva had ter Fire."

"Well he does. Can we get on with it?" Luger says, more a command'n a question. "Some of us would rather not spend the day here." *Like me*, I think.

"Yeah, yeah, don't git yer britches inna knot." The look on Luger's face makes me wanna laugh, but I keep it inside. I'm starting to like this Keeper fellow. He doesn't take crap from anyone, not even a snide Greynote like Luger.

He staggers out, clutches the door to get his balance, and grabs a shovel that's leaning against the side of his hut. "C'mon," he grunts. We follow him to the next row of cages. We skip the first one, which is empty, and stop at the next one. He hands me the shovel, takes a piece of chalk from his pocket and draws an X on the ground in front of the cage. "Start diggin'," he says.

I look at him like he's wooloo, which I'm starting to think he might be. "What?"

"You hard of hearin'?" he says. "Dig!"

Maybe I don't like him after all. With no other choice, one-handed I dip the tip of the metal shovel into the durt, right away feeling the burn of all those blaze-shoveling muscles flare up. As I awkwardly scoop away clump after clump of durt, Luger makes small talk with the Keep.

"How are the other prisoners doing?"

"Eh? As good as can be 'spected considerin'. Most of ter long-stayers ain't gonna last much longer. Ter short-stayers, like Bartie, gimme plenty o' trouble, but nothin' I can't handle."

"Good. And what about the work?"

I glance at the Keeper, who turns away from me, drops his voice to a low rumble. "Them Icies seem happy enough, but we need more lifers cuz they keep dyin' on me."

"I'll see what I can do," Luger says, his voice all heavy and sharp, like the slash of a knife.

"That's deep enough fer a skinny runt like yer," the Keeper says, turning his attention back to me. "Now push it through to ter other side."

As I peer through the bars, I try to figure out what the point of this is. Then I realize: the cage has no door. Getting in and out can only be accomplished by digging. Opposite where the Keep had me dig is another hole, on the inside. I'm s'posed to connect the two. The tiny flywheels in my head start spinning. Is it really that easy to get out? Do you just hafta dig a hole with your hands? Seems crazy none of the other prisoners have escaped.

"I see what yer thinkin'," the Keeper says, "and yer can stop thinkin' it right now." I look at his white face, surprised a man who sounds so dense would be able to guess what I'm thinking. "The bars go down twenty feet, so unless yer a burrow mouse, there's no chance of yer diggin' yer way out. And this front hole, well, I'll take care of that as soon as yer in."

107

I groan inside, but I guess it's good to know there's no way out, so I can stop thinking 'bout it and just settle in for the long haul. Turning my attention back to the hole, I jam the shovel sideways and under the bars, which don't go into the ground at this point like they do all the rest of the way around. I break through the durt easily, creating a narrow crawl space into the cage.

"Get in," the Keep commands, taking the shovel back. As I get down on my stomach, I think how big ol' Bart would hafta dig a hole four times as big to fit through. I guess I've found a benefit of being skinny. Too bad it only applies to when I'm stuck in Confinement, which I'm hoping won't become a regular thing. I wriggle under the bars, using my one free hand to pull myself through the gap and wondering whether I look like the 'zard we saw earlier.

Inside, durty and tired and ready for my little trip to Confinement to be over, I lie on my back and watch as the Keep busies himself filling the hole. But 'fore he gets too far along, he rolls a large stone I hadn't noticed into the hole, stamping it firmly in with his foot. Even if I was able to channel my inner burrow mouse, the boulder's far too big to pull inside the cage, and far too heavy to push through. He fills the gaps around the stone with crumbly durt and throws a final couple of scoops over the top, hiding the barrier. An invisible guardsman.

My day in Confinement begins with a soft whimper that slips from the back of my throat.

Eleven

The worst thing about Confinement: the boredom.

Forget my parched throat and grumbling stomach. I'd trade a tug leg sandwich and a skin of water for a flat rock and piece of chalk to sketch with. I look around at the other cages but there's nothing of interest. The other prisoners know how to pass the time in this sun goddess forsaken place. They sleep.

But I'm not tired, not even after the long hike across the desert to get here. I'm wide awake, partly 'cause I got lots of sleep last night, and partly 'cause of all that's happened over the last couple days.

So, to satiate my growing boredom, I take to writing my thoughts in the durt with a rock. First I list the potential groups involved in the Killer attacks. Glassies. The Wild Ones. The

Marked. Icers. It could even be a group of our own, so I add *The Heaters.*

Next I list out what I know about each group to narrow down the field. I start at the top.

From what they tell us in Learning, Glassies appeared long 'fore I was born, as if the earth itself vomited them up, all pale white and squinting at the bright sun. At that time we didn't have a name for them; the term Glassies would come 'bout later, after they built the Glass City. My people just watched from afar as they tried to build shelters and settle down in fire country. Not long after they appeared, they were all dead. The Fire took them.

But more of them appeared, and they lasted a little bit longer before succumbing to the awful disease that's forever shackled my people. Seems their bodies weren't as well-equipped as ours to handle the air. Eventually though, they built a big ol' glass bubble, sprouting from the ground and shooting way up into the sky, as high as the vultures fly. That's when someone started calling them Glassies, and the name stuck. Well, inside that bubble they built all kinds of crazy structures, the likes of which we ain't never seen 'fore. We still don't know how they did it, but it seems like the bubble protects them from everything that's bad in fire country. They live long now, even longer'n us.

We know it's the air that's doing it, lighting the Fire inside of us, sweating us and cramping us and killing us, but we can't do what the Glassies've done with their big ol' bubble. We're lucky to build our huts and tents and survive the dust storms and wildfires.

For a long while, the Glassies didn't bother us, and we didn't bother them. Then, a few full moons back, they attacked

110

us, out of nowhere, coming with their fire sticks and chariots of fire. It was all the Hunters could do to hold them off, but we lost many in the fight. Circ desperately wanted to fight, but he wasn't eligible. Only Hunters eighteen and up can fight other humans. The younger Hunters hafta stick to the tug.

On the ground next to Glassies, I write "Recent attacks."

The Wild Ones are harder, 'cause I don't know how much of what I've heard is just people being people and making crazy blaze up, and how much is the truth. Now that I know the Wilds exist, the truth is probably somewhere in the middle. So I write "Kidnap Bearers," which is the only thing I really know 'bout them, 'cause of my sister.

The Marked are an enigma. I like that word, and it most certainly applies here. If they do exist, then they very well might be the culprits, whether on purpose or by accident. If they mistakenly crossed into Killer territory to hunt, the Killers mighta thought it was us. I'm sure that to them, humans are humans, just like we can't tell one of their packs from another. Next to Marked I write "Enigma" and "Painted bodies," 'cause that's all I know.

Icers are next to last. I probably know the most about the Icers 'cause they've always been around. I've never actually seen them, but they're our next door neighbors and people talk 'bout them all the time. "Another shipment of timber has just come in from the Icers," or "They say the snow's always falling in ice country." There are trade agreements with the Icers, where we give them tug meat, dried pricklers, and other such fire country delicacies, in exchange for some of their endless supply of wood. My father always says they're a private people, who keep to themselves most of the time. They live in the mountains, where it's cold, or some nonsense like that. I never

111

understood exactly what that means, 'cept Teacher Mas describes it like you take the little shiver you sometimes feel when you get hit with a winter breeze at night, and multiply it by about a million. That's cold. But to feel that shivery seems impossible, what with the sun goddess's eye heating everything up.

I remember something else. When I was digging and Luger and the Keeper were chatting away, Luger asked about how the work was going. Keep replied that the Icies seemed happy, or some blaze like that. He also said his lifers keep dying on him. I don't know what any of it means really, but it seems there's something going on with Confinement and the Icers.

I write "Confinement work" and "Timber trade" next to Icers.

Last is us. The Heaters, getting our name 'cause everything we do is in the hottest of hot under the watchful eye of the sun goddess. Teacher told us one of the forefathers called us that after we crawled from the caves, after twelve moons went by with nothing but heat. We're the long-time residents of fire country. It's our land, and although there are others that live on it, we've never really had to run anyone off. We're a peaceful people, unless provoked of course. Then we fight like dogs to protect ourselves. Like against the Killers. Or the Glassies. Every Midder learns about the Killer war and how there's a strict hunting zone. And the Hunters, they're trained even more. I can't see how any of them would go in the restricted zone to hunt. I don't write anything next to Heaters, just erase them with the back of my hand.

The other four are all in the hunt, so to speak.

~~~

All my thinking and writing has passed the time right along. Lunchtime comes, which I only know 'cause my stomach's trying to eat itself, making all kinds of growling and gurgling noises. And 'cause the sun is directly overhead, trying to burn a hole right through me.

But today, lunchtime don't include food. Or water. Or anything really. Just the same old, same old. Sitting and thinking and trying not to go stir crazy, like I bet most of the prisoners have gone long ago.

Some more time passes, maybe a thumb of sun movement. Finally something happens. I get a visitor!

Lara.

She wouldn't be my first choice, but not my last either. Scorch, I'd take anyone at this point, even Hawk. At least I could give him a piece of my mind. The only ones I'd refuse to talk to would be my father, and maybe Luger.

"Hi, Siena," she says.

"What in the vulture's beak are you doing here?" I say.

"Come to see you," she says.

"What about Learning?"

"I snuck out."

"It's an awful long walk," I say.

"Not that long," she says.

"Sneaking out of Learning…you could get in some nasty trouble for that. Maybe end up in the cage right next to me."

She laughs. "I've done worse." I bet she has. All sheening with sweat from her gallivant across the desert, she looks like a female warrior, her muscles toned and strong. "How's Confinement?"

"Boring as all scorch," I say. "And hungrifying to boot. Not to mention the thirst—I could drink a gallon skin of water in two shakes."

Lara laughs again. "I'd love to offer you some of mine,"—she motions to the skin strapped to her waist—"but that Keeper is watching us like a hungry hawk."

I look past her, and sure enough, Keep's eyes are boring into my skull. "He ain't so bad," I say. "But he ain't so good either. Why are you here?" I ask, watching as Lara frowns. "Not that I don't appreciate it, I'm just wondering," I add quickly.

"I just came to see how you were doing…" I can see the *and* floating around on her tongue, but I keep quiet—she'll tell me if she wants to.

"I'm doing as fine as can be expected," I say, trying to give her time to think.

"And…"—there it is—"…I also came to continue some of our other conversations." Here comes. Skipping out on the Call. Breeding. Woman power. Knock the Laws.

"Look, Lara, I appreciate what you're doing and all, but I'm not sure I wanna get into any more trouble'n I'm already into," I say honestly. I leave the other question on my tongue: *Who are you working with outside the village?*

Lara rises to her tiptoes, grabs the bars with both hands, sticks her face between them. "But what you did yesterday was incredible! I've never seen anything like it. First the Killers are coming, and then you're going, running right into the midst of it."

"Circ was in trouble," I say. I dunno what she's getting at.

"Yeah, and he's your friend. That's my point exactly. You're brave, Sie. And loyal. Just what we're looking for."

Now it's my turn to laugh, so hard I feel like slapping my knees, but I don't go that far. "I been called a lot of things in my fifteen years of life, but never brave. Today is a day of firsts, I s'pose."

"But you *are* brave."

"More like stupid. Almost got myself killed. And Circ almost died anyway."

"But you didn't. And he didn't. So now you have a choice."

I ignore her last few words 'cause I'm thinking about something. Something she said just a moment ago: *Just what we're looking for.* She's just confirmed my suspicions.

I take a deep breath. It's now or never. Just ask. Ask. ASK!

"Who's we?" I ask.

Lara frowns. "What?"

"A second ago you said 'Just what we're looking for.' Who's the 'we'?"

Lara's face gets just a touch of pink on it, starting on her strong cheekbones and expanding to her forehead. "Well, uh, I didn't mean…"

"Spit it out," I say, knowing I hit a soft spot.

"I can't tell you," Lara says, dropping her head to stare at her feet, which scuff around a bit, kicking at the durt and stones.

"Well, why in the scorch not?" Now I'm the one holding the bars, poking my head out to get closer to her.

"I can't until you've agreed to join us." I keep hanging onto the bars, but now it's to keep my balance. My head is chasing circles around my tail, or maybe it's the reverse, I dunno. All I know is I don't know what's going on, 'cept I'm hungry, thirsty, tired, and ready to get back to normal life in the village. I close my eyes and try to think of what to say, what to ask, how to make sense of all my strange conversations with Lara.

"How can I join something I know nothing about?" I say. "Are you with the Icers? Or the Wilds? Or are you some crazy shilt-girl for the Marked?!" I scream the last bit out, losing control.

Lara sighs, looking like she got stung by something big and nasty. "You don't know *nothing*. You just don't know the details. You know it's a way to avoid the Call. You know it's about getting our lives back. You know I'm involved. I'm sorry, Sie, but if that's not enough, I don't know what else to tell you."

"Thanks for stopping by Lara, really," I say. "I'll see you around the village."

~ ~ ~

After my mind-numbing conversation with Lara, I'm exhausted, so I lie down in the durt, being careful not to disturb my notes. The hard-packed ground ain't nearly as comfy as my tugskin rug, but my bones are so worn out that it don't matter. I fall right asleep.

There are Killers in my dream. 'Cept not just twenty. Hundreds. Maybe thousands. They've overrun the camp, flattened our tents and huts into rubble. Everyone's screaming. Everyone's running. Smears of blood and pools of tears swamp up the land. My father's dead, lying there with his eyes staring straight ahead, unblinking, like he's not even real, just some tug-stuffed dummy. For some reason, the Killers don't touch me. They run around and around and around, growling and prowling and mauling and clawing, killing everyone. Everyone

116

but me. I know it's a dream 'cause I'm stuck in Confinement, not in the village. But still, it *feels* so real.

I scan all around me, try to find someone else I know. There. Lara. She's standing a little ways off, watching me. She extends a hand, beckons to me to follow her. Maybe if I go with her I'll be safe. Maybe I'll be happy. But somehow I know that following her means joining her and *we* and *us*. Only I don't know who *we* and *us* are.

I keep searching until I find Circ. He's on t'other side of me, standing atop one edge of the great fire pit in the center of the village. The pointers are flying so fast off the end of his bow that I can't even see his fingers. Every shot is true. Killer after Killer falls, dead. But then one breaks through, the biggest beast of all, bigger'n two men. It dodges Circ's every pointer, slips past them and almost *through* them as if it possesses magical powers. It's right on top of him now, fangs bared, ready to snap, to maim, to *kill*, to satisfy its namesake. I have a choice to make. Go with Lara, save myself, find a better life. Or…run to certain death and Circ, my best friend. Maybe my only friend. I take a step toward Circ, fire in my veins.

I wake up.

The light hurts my eyes so I close them immediately. I don't know what time it is, but it ain't late, still too bright. Maybe still afternoon.

I realize what woke me up. Voices. Keeper's growl and another voice, this one as melodious and familiar as any sound in the entire world, like the tinkle of Miss Merry's glass chimes on a mildly breezy spring morning. My eyes snap open and I shield them from the light with a hand. Using my other hand I push to my feet, feeling every bone and muscle in my body protest, which is strange. It's the ground that's making them sore, and yet, they don't want to leave it.

I gimp my way over to the bars, toward the voices. "This ain't right," Keep says. "Only one visitor 'llowed a day."

The other voice stays low and hard to hear, but I'd know it anywhere. "C'mon. Just...once...kicked by a tug...walked miles...see her?"

"Circ!" I shout.

My one shout is all it takes to win the argument. Whether Keep likes it or not, Circ turns and sees me, sprints over, all smiles and laughs and flashing mahogany eyes. Keep's grumbling something behind him, but I don't care and he goes back inside his hut, slamming the door behind him. I hug Circ through the bars. He's sweaty and warm, but feels so good. Plus, I'm far durtier, covered in a light brown dust and grime, so I can't really complain 'bout a little sweat on him considering he's been walking for the last two thumbs of sun movement.

We pull back but he keeps holding my arms, which feel all tingly, maybe 'cause I been sleeping on them. "You look good," he says, surprising me.

"I do?"

"Yeah, you look like you."

I raise an eyebrow. "So me is all durty and groggy and boreder'n a Totter with no jinglejanglers?"

Circ laughs. "You is you," he says. Now he's talking like Lara too, in riddles.

"If my father knew you were here, he'd kill you and me both," I say.

"But he doesn't." Good point. "How's Confinement?"

"Well, the food ain't bad. It ain't good either. It's neither, 'cause there ain't any."

Circ releases my arms, squeezing one of my hands on the way down. When he let's go, I feel something in my palm. Tug jerky.

"Thanks," I say, grinning. "Though I won't be able to hardly swallow it down without some water."

He looks over his shoulder at Keep's hut. The door's still closed. No windows. "Here," he says, handing me a skin. "I've got another one for my trek home."

"Thanks." Greedily and with shaking hands, I unknot the leather tie and push it to my dry lips. Warm, clear liquid runs down my tongue. I trap it in my mouth, swish it around a few times to let it moisten every nook and cranny, and then swallow it. The first swig burns a little on the way down, but the second is perfect. "Ah," I say, tearing off a piece of jerky and shoving it into my mouth.

"I can't stay long," Circ says. "Learning's over, but Father doesn't know I'm here and he'll be expecting me home for dinner. I'll have to run back."

Mouth full, I garble, "Hard to run with those ribs." I motion to his bandaged torso.

"I'll manage," he says. And then: "I've got news."

I stop chewing. "'Bout the Killer attack?"

He nods, eyes gleaming. "A group of Hunters is being sent out to investigate, day after next."

I swallow the half-chewed jerky in a big gulp. "Whaddya think they'll find?"

"Hopefully we'll find out who's been hunting on Killer land," he says.

A lump forms in my throat, but not from the jerky. "Whaddya mean *we'll find?*"

"I'm going with them," he says.

119

~ ~ ~

"But why you? You're only fifteen," I say. We've been arguing for a while now, pretty much the longest argument we've ever had.

Circ shakes his head. "You know my age has never stopped me before," he says.

"They didn't let you fight against the Glassies," I point out.

Circ sighs. "That was different. That was war. This is an investigation."

"Will you be going on Killer land?"

"Yeah, but—"

"Then it's a war," I say.

"I'll be fine."

"You'll be dead."

"No—I won't," Circ says. He takes my hand through the bars, which I like. He's taking my opinion seriously. "It'll be a quick out and back," he says. "I promise."

I'm about to argue again but his sudden promise stops me. Circ don't make many promises to me. I can probably count them all without even taking off my moccasins. And he's kept every last one of them. Like the time I accidentally kicked the feetball and broke grumpy ol' Greynote Finn's window, Circ promised it would be alright and that I wouldn't get into trouble. He copped the blame and took the punishment for me. Or just before his first ever Hunt and he promised me he'd be safe and kill his first tug. He did, of course. Nope, he never broke a single promise to me. I owe him my trust now.

"Be safe. Please," I say.

"I will." His words are solider'n the stone blocking me from digging my way out. "What's that," he says, motioning past me, toward the durt in my cage.

"What's what?"

"Those scribbles in the durt," he says.

"Just scribbles," I say. "I was trying to pass the time, do a little sleuthing of my own, try to figure out who's behind the Killer attack."

Circ looks impressed. "What'd you come up with?"

"It ain't us," I say. "The Heaters, I mean. No one 'ud be that stupid. Other'n that, I'd say the Glassies are a good bet. They don't know the land as well as us. Mighta done it by accident, or on purpose, to get to us. I don't know much about the Marked, but they coulda done it too, 'cause they were hungry, maybe even starving. I'm still not sure about the Wild Ones, but I hardly think a bunch of Bearers who don't Bear could do much damage. That leaves the Icers, who don't seem the type to come down into the heat of fire country."

Circ looks intently at my scratches in the durt. "I'd say you did pretty well without nothing but your brains and good sense," he says.

"You think it was the Marked or the Glassies, too?" I ask, sitting down cross-legged and sticking my feet through the bars.

"I dunno," Circ says, following my lead. The tips of his moccasins touch mine, just like they should. Only there're bars between us. "But what you said makes sense. Hey, Sie?"

"Yeah?"

"Have you ever wondered what else is out there?" Circ asks.

"More sand, more desert," I say. "What else is there?" I'm not sure where he's going with all this.

"The mountains for one," Circ says.

"Yeah, but that's out of fire country, Circ. We can't go there."

"Why not?"

His question throws me. I never really thought 'bout it. The mountains ain't ours. They're the Icers. We stay on our land, they stay on theirs. We hunt on our land, the Killers hunt on theirs. Everyone's happy. "We just can't. It's the Law."

"Okay. Let me ask you this: Have you ever wondered about *who* else is out there?"

"The Icers" I say automatically. "And I guess the Glassies, too. Other'n that, maybe the Wilds and the Marked, if they're real."

"And beyond them?" Circ says.

"I dunno, no one." This conversation is becoming more mind-whirling'n the one with Lara.

"It's a big world," Circ says, looking up into the sky. I look up, too. The red sky is criss-crossed by thick wooden bars. Not even a single wisp of yellow cloud breaks up the sea of crimson.

~~~

By the time Circ leaves, it's getting late and he's probably gonna get a lashing for missing dinner. I feel bad about it, but I feel worse 'bout him going with the special group of Hunters.

After he's gone, I think about everything he said. I've never heard him talk like that. About the big ol' world outside fire country, that is. He almost sounded like he's ready to run off and try to find it. Well, he ain't going anywhere without me.

The jerky helped, but not a lot. I'm still ravenous—ready to eat a whole tug on my own—when my one meal arrives. It ain't nothing to brag about, just a lump of something thick and bready, and a bit of some overcooked, chewy meat, but after having so little to eat all day, I pretty much swallow it all whole. Wash it down with the three gulps of water Keep provides. Keep goes 'bout his suppertime business without a word, but the rest of the place gets pretty riled up. After a day of everyone keeping silent, sleeping it away, all the prisoners seem to come alive with the food. They're all talking to each other, cracking jokes and laughing, while I sit cross-legged in the corner, counting down the moments till I'm out.

I gobble down my meager ration of food, still unsatisfied, and for the first time all day, I'm glad the cage isn't covered. The heat of the day has melted away to a warm, but pleasant, twilight. The sun goddess's eye is fiery red—even redder'n the sky—and as it splashes on the horizon, deep purple streaks radiate off a clump of yellow clouds that have accumulated low in the sky.

As I watch, the sun disappears, leaving behind only the ever-darkening purples as evidence she'd ever been there at all.

It's the moon goddess's turn to watch the world now. I wonder what she's watching. Whether it's fire country, ice country, or some other country like Circ talked 'bout, so foreign to us that it might as well be on another planet.

I'm 'bout to lie down and do some serious star-gazing, when there's a rap, rap, rap on the wooden bars on my cage. The night is deepening and I hafta peer through the murk to see who's there. Keep. "Yer've got another visitor," he says gruffly. "I'm allowin' it fer special circumstancies, but don't yer think fer one moment yer can git away with this again. If yer ever in Confinement agin, it'll be no visitors fer yer first day."

He stomps away leaving me wondering what special circumstances are giving me a third visitor. And who that visitor'll be.

Twelve

I get up and move to the bars, hearing voices off a ways. Footsteps head my way, so quiet that if my ears weren't listening so hard, I might miss them.

Then she's there. My mother. A soft smile and a warm kiss on my hand.

"Mother? What are you doing all the way out here?" I ask.

"I came to see you," she says.

"Keep said there were special circumstances."

"There are. But I would've come even if there weren't," she says. I believe her. My mother ain't no liar. In the inky black of night her raven hair melts into the air, as if she's become one with the sky. As always, she has my eyes in her head, but they seem brighter'n ever before, shining like an animal's. "Siena, something's happened. Greynote Shiva…" She trails off and she don't need to say the rest. It's obvious.

"Father's Head Greynote," I say. "Head Greynote Shiva's dead."

She nods, barely perceptible in the dark, only visible 'cause her eyes bob and bounce.

"Head Greynote Roan," I say, trying the words out on my tongue. I smack my lips. Cringe. Whether it's an aftertaste from my pitiful meal or the words themselves, I'm left with bitterness on my tongue.

"Yes, Siena. I wanted to tell you first."

"You didn't have to come all the way out here—"

"Yes, I did."

The firmness of her words surprise me. Mother's not usually firm 'bout much. She's always been so wishy-washy. *We'll have to ask your father. Maybe, but let's check with your father. Have you asked your father?* Those are her usual words.

Now, everything 'bout her has changed. She's being firmer with me, firmer with my father. Standing up for herself. Even standing up for me. What the scorch is going on?

"Shiva was…" she says, grasping the bar as if to steady herself. It sounds weird hearing her say Shiva without the Head Greynote part in the front. It's almost disrespectful, but there's no disrespect in her voice. "…a good man. He tried hard, wanted the best for the village. But he's been sick for a long time, longer than most."

I wonder where's she's going with this. Everyone knows how long Shiva's been sick. As soon as someone—anyone— gets the Fire, everyone's always talking 'bout it, making bets on how long they'll last, thanking the sun goddess it wasn't them who caught it.

126

"Your father's been the real Head Greynote for a long time," she continues. "Making important decisions, signing trade agreements with the Icers, deciding the future of the village."

"I already know all that," I say.

Mother nods again. "Your father's a hard man," she says. I already know that, too. My scarred back could tell a thousand tales of my father's hardness. "I think he's doing what he believes is right, but he's way off track."

"Mother, whatever it is, spit it out." I don't usually talk like that to my mother, but she's been beating around the prickler too long and I'm itching to know where she's heading with all this.

Mother half-laughs, half-sobs, once more surprising me. "I'm sorry, Mother, I didn't mean to—"

"No, no, Siena. It's okay," she says. Takes a deep breath. "You say what you mean and you mean what you say." I've never heard that expression before, but right away I like it. "What I'm trying to say is...do you believe in the Laws of fire country?"

It's not at all what I thought would come out of her mouth. I was expecting her to tell me that we both need to be 'specially obedient to my father now that he's the Head Greynote, or something like that. "The Laws?" I say. "Well, uh, yeah. I mean, we all do. We hafta—to survive."

Mother grasps my hand through the bars. Her hand is warm and so is mine, so it's like our warmth combines. "Is that really what you think?" she asks. "Or is it just something they teach you to say in Learning."

Both, right? I'm 'bout to say just that, but she puts a hand to my face and says, "You don't need to answer that now, or even

127

out loud. Just think about it. Think about what you want. And when the time comes, you'll know what decision to make."

She raises my hand, kisses the back of it, and is gone, disappearing into the night as if she was never here at all.

~ ~ ~

What *I* want? Nothing's ever been 'bout what I want. My life's been built with a foundation of duty, a structure of Laws and rules and changes that come with age—a thatched roof of survival. For my people, for me. So my mother's words are buzzing around in my head like flies, and I don't got the swatter to knock them down to where I can look at them.

What she said, it almost sounded like...well, like Lara. All her knocky stuff 'bout it not having to be this way and just think 'bout it. Now my mother's saying I have a choice to make and that I should be thinking 'bout that choice. What choice? It's hard to be thinking about something when you don't really understand what that something is.

Sometimes I miss my sister. This is one of those times. My Call-Siblings are too young to really talk to, and they only share the same father as me, not mother, so it's not the same. Skye is my full sister. Or *was* my full sister. Who knows whether she's still alive, what the Wilds did to her.

We used to share everything with each other. She was going to be my guide for the future, tell me all about what it was like to be a Bearer, let me hold her young'uns so I could practice 'fore I had to do it myself.

I can still picture the dark, bouncing curls in her hair the day she was taken. The day of her Call. The day she was s'posed to become a woman. I wonder if by missing her Call she'll never become a woman, will always be stuck as just a girl, a Youngling. That scares me. Anyway, I remember her curls like it was yesterday. Perfect little circlets of hair, shining with the luster of a fresh washing. When we were little I used to think she had knots in her hair, and that they just needed to be combed out to be nice and straight, like mine. When I'd ask my mother about it, she'd tell me Skye's hair was curly, that she took after our grandmother, but I never believed her, thought she was trying to make my sister feel better when really she had knots in her hair.

I lie flat on my back, thinking about knots and sisters, staring up at what stars I can see. The clearness of the day has given way to a cloudy night, full of black chariots rolling across the sky, blotting out the moon goddess and most of her servants.

Think about what you want. A fly. I swat at it, miss, my anger rising.

You'll know what decision to make. Another buzzing insect. I watch it for a second, and then swing with all my scrawny might. *Whack!* I hit myself in the head, see stars, but not the ones in the sky. Stars so close it's like they're in my skull, or in my eyes maybe. "Urrrr!" I yell, more frustrated'n I've ever been.

I close my eyes, try to sleep. There are too many flies, but I keep trying. Keep trying, trying, swatting, swatting, drifting, drifting, until I hear, "Pssst!"

My eyes flash open. The sound was close. I say nothing. A moment passes, and then a voice hisses, "Hey, you! Youngling."

I freeze, my already still body hardening like tug jerky in the sun. As far as I know, I'm the only Youngling in Confinement. I say nothing.

"I know you can hear me," the voice says. It's brittle and cracking, like a worn piece of leather, ready for replacement. I don't think this voice gets out much.

"So what if I can?" I say to the night.

"What're you in for?"

"Being an idiot," I say. "You?"

He chuckles. "I's framed."

I can't help but to laugh, too. After all my mother's confusing words, and my even more confusing thoughts, this conversation already feels so normal. "I'm sure that's what they all say," I reply, probably a bit too haughtily.

"No, really," he says. "And you're right, a bunch of the guys in here say the same thing. But not because they want people to believe they're innocent, but because they *are* innocent."

Okay, I'll bite. "What exactly did you d—I mean, what did they say you did?" I sit up, scooch over to the bars, try to see the face of the man I'm talking to. At first there's only blackness so black it's like I'm looking into a Killer's eyes. Not black even. The absence of light. But then my eyes start to adjust. I'm always amazed how they can do that. It's like I see nothing, nothing, nothing, and then, Bam! The outline of a face appears, followed by a body, leaning casually against the bars, one leg propped up on t'other.

"You see me now?" he asks.

"Yeah."

"I'm Raja."

"Siena," I say.

"Your daddy's Head Greynote?"

"You been ear-sneaking," I say accusingly.

"Not intentionally," he says. His ghost form shrugs. "When it's quiet like this in here, you can hear most anything."

"So what if I am?" I say. I'm not being nice, but I don't know this guy, least nothing more'n his name.

"No need to get all defensive on me. I got no problem with the Greynotes, generally speaking, although it was one of their kind that framed me, I's sure of it."

"You better watch your mouth with talk like that. It could getcha in trouble," I say.

"You's gonna tell yer daddy on me?" he says.

"I ain't."

"Then I guess there ain't nothin' to worry about. 'Spect things can't git any worse for me anyway."

"How old are you?" I ask, trying to guess. I've always liked guessing ages. Usually I can get pretty close by looking at someone, but this is much harder, as this fellow's sitting in the dark. Based on his voice and mannerisms, I expect he's rather ancient, approaching thirty by now.

"Why's it matter?" he says.

"It don't," I say. "Just curious. You know 'bout how old I am, so it's only fair I know yours." I'm pleased with my logic.

"Eighteen," he says.

My jaw drops, but only for a second. "Liar," I say, letting that mouth of mine get the better of me again. "I mean, that can't be right," I say.

"I got no reason to lie," he says. "I know I don't sound it, but my voice ain't what it used to be. I been in here fer over a year. Lack of food and water and regular speakin' will do that to a voice. Make it sound old, that is."

131

"Okay," I say. "Let's say I believe you about being eighteen. Why've you been in here so long? What did they say you did?"

"I shouldn't e'en tell you," he says.

"Why not?"

"Greynote's daughter and all."

"I told you I won't tell nobody," I say.

He says nothing, playing my silent game now. I can't tell if he's looking at me, or if he's dozed off, as I can't see his eyes. Finally, he says, "There was this little girl who lived next door. She was a real nice Totter, friendly as all get out, always saying hi and pickin' me flowers. She was my little Totter friend. One day, she didn't come home from Learning." Raja's voice catches and his hands move up to grip the bars a little higher.

"Where was she?" I ask.

"Dead," he says. "They found her in the watering hole, sunk to the bottom with a rock tied to her little ankles." I hear a sob escape his throat, and I can barely see his shoulders shaking in the dark.

I wait a few seconds, till he stops shaking and goes all still-like. Stiller'n a stone. "They said you killed her?" I say.

"I didn't," he says, his voice as strong as it's been since we started talking.

"I wasn't saying you did. But that's what they said?"

"Yeah. They had all kinds of proof. Blood on one of my shirts I hadn't worn in a full moon. Footprints near the waterin' hole that matched my feet exactly. Of course, there were a zillion footprints that matched everyone's feet around the waterin' hole, but they picked out just mine. But the clincher was a little doll that this Totter was always carryin' 'round, Josie she called her. Rattier'n hand-me-down socks it was, but she loved it like a real friend, never let it get out of her sight."

"Where was it?"

"Under my tugskin sleeper," he says, metal in his voice.

"Someone put it there." There's conviction in my voice, which surprises me. Why should I believe this convicted murderer's story? I just met him. He probably tells everyone this to get them to like him, when he's really wooloo in the head, getting joy out of watching the life drain out of little girls. But I do believe him. 'Cause of his tears and 'cause I shouldn't be in Confinement either.

"They had to of, 'cause I didn't do nothin' to that little girl. The Greynotes didn't wanna listen to my side of the story, which is why I think at least one of 'em was in on it. They just declared the evidence and gave me life in Confinement. My momma died one full moon after I got in 'ere, and my daddy a full moon after that. I didn't get to see either of them again—they were too sick with the Fire to come visit."

"That's awful," I murmur. "I'm sorry, Raja."

"Thanks for listenin'," he says. "It helps to get it out. When I can't speak it, my past is like a horde of burrow mouses inside my stomach, nibblin' away at me."

"There hasta be something you can do. Someone we can tell. It ain't right, Raja. When I get out I'll tell my father."

"No! Don't do that," Raja says, his voice sharper'n a spear barb. "If you start makin' dunes, they'll lock you up too. There's somethin' dangerous going on here. A dangerous game by dangerous people."

"Whaddya mean? Like a 'spiracy?" I say, shifting to my knees.

"That's exactly what I'm saying, but I won't say no more. Too dangerous for you if you know the rest. They'll kill me and they'll kill you."

"C'mon, Raja. You can't do that. Tell me. No one'll know."

"My lips are sealed with tug-gut glue."

"Fine. Whatever. I'm going to sleep." As sad as Raja's story was, if he don't want to say no more, then I'm done with it. 'Spiracy—bah! The sun's probably gone into his brain.

Thirteen

Although I got a whole swarm of flies buzzing in my head now, I fall right asleep. A day of doing nothing but talking and waiting can make you awful tired. Plus, the sooner I sleep, the sooner I'll awake to a one way trip back to the village. When I do awake I feel like I haven't slept at all. It's still pitch dark, so dark that waving my hand across my face results in nothing but a waft of air on my cheeks. It feels good. The night is hot, as if the ground sucked up all the sunlight and is slowly releasing it, baking me like a 'zard in a firepan.

I'm instinctively aware that I didn't wake up naturally. Something woke me. Some sound, some force, some*one*. "Raja," I say, sticking my ear between the bars to listen for a response. Nothing. I can't even hear breathing, but that don't mean nothing. He might just be a soft night-breather.

"Raja!" I hiss a little louder. No response.

Then I hear it. A clink. Not from Raja's cage, but from further down the row. The clink is followed by a voice, low, but discernible. "Move out, you dogs!" Keep's voice, gruffer'n a Killer's bark.

As my night vision clears, there's more clinking off yonder. This time I can see much better'n earlier. The black cloud army has marched on to another place, and the moon goddess and her star servants are casting a dim glow on everything. A night light.

I see bodies moving about, a thin line of men. They're carrying something. Tools of some kind. Sharp and heavy. Axes. Saws. The type of stuff the hut builders use to construct the Greynote homes. Like ours. I remember watching in awe as what was just a big ol' tree trunk and a patch of dusty land slowly transformed into our house.

I can also see that Raja's cage is empty. A pile of durt sits next to the hole he crawled out of.

~~~

I gotta get out of this cage.

Something's going on and I need to know what. If Raja won't tell me, then I hafta find out on my own.

I could try digging out the hole, pushing the big rock outta my way, but if big guys like Bart can't get out like that, it seems unlikely a scrawny runt like me'll be able to do it. I walk around the cage, tapping on the wooden bars with a rock, checking for weaknesses. Seems pretty solid, but...

It's not made for someone like me. The bars are relatively close together, but not so close that you can't stick your arms and legs through. Like I did earlier with Circ, hugging and touching hands. In fact, some of the gaps are so wide, I might just be able to squeeze through.

They're not made for someone with a child's body, someone so thin and so skeleton-boned that she almost disappears when she turns sideways, as some of the other Younglings like to joke. It's no joke now.

I try a random gap between the bars, try to force myself between the wood, careful to keep my broken arm tucked safely behind me. But this wood is sturdy and has no give. The wood won't budge in either direction and the gap is too small. My hips get stuck 'fore I ever really get started.

Moving on, I try to find a gap that's bigger'n the last one. Most of them are uniform, well measured, but then I find one that seems wider'n t'others. Perhaps it's just an optical illusion, the moon shadows playing tricks on me, or...

I jam myself into the gap with a running start.

Ahhh! The wood stings me, scrapes me, tears my flesh when it rubs, but I'm pushing forward, making progress, nearly through!

And then I'm stuck. Not stuck like I just can't go forward any more, but stuck like I can't go forward or backward or anythingward. Just plain ol' stuck. Like a tug in the mud.

I'm wedged in so tight it's hard to breathe. I suck in quick breaths as I try to think, but none of them fully satisfy my hungry lungs. If I got in, I gotta be able to get out, right? Wrong. I had a lot of momentum coming in, but I got nothing going out. Starting from a stuck position, I can't get enough force going to unstick myself. No matter how much I strain— backwards or forwards—I ain't budging. New tactic required.

Get skinnier.

For me that's difficult since I'm so skinny to begin with. I mean, I could not eat anything for a few days, maybe shed half a pound, slide right on out. But obviously that won't work 'cause then the Keep'll see me stucker'n a 'zard on a skewer. He'll know I tried to escape. He'll tell my father. I'll be sentenced to more time in Confinement. Nope, I gotta get skinnier quicker. Like now.

I count to three. Suck in my breath all the way so all you can see are my ribs. Let out the breath in a groan of effort, straining to squeeze through, my eyes squeezed tight and hard, every pitifully small muscle in my body working together to accomplish the same thing. Inch by torturous inch. And then...

Escape!

It's not like what you'd expect the thrill of escape to be like, all happy and elated and airy. Well, it's airy all right, 'cause a rush of air surrounds me as I go a-flying off into the desert. I was pushing so hard and not going anywhere, but then as soon as I breached the bars, all that energy had no place to go but off into the yonder. I crash land in the durt, practically right on my slinged arm, feel searin', burnin' ripples of pain tear through every nerve on that side of my body. I tumble, not once, not twice, not even thrice, but four times, rolling and bouncing and kneeing myself in the face, which hurts like scorch 'cause my knee is so bony it's sharp like a spearhead. I moan and yell out things that would have my mother blushing, and then settle in a heap at the base of a prickler, which proceeds to jab and poke me in the gut with its barbs, adding injury to injury.

I just lay there. For a long time. I got no idea how long. My wrist's throbbing something awful, and with each *thump, thump, thump*, I feel like I'm going to vomit up my unsatisfying meal and the tug jerky Circ gave me. The pain is so sharp I think I drift in and out of consciousness a little, too, like I'm in a strange fireweed smoker's haze. First I see the stars, shining all perky and happy down on me, and then I'm seeing nothing, just black, as if every natural light in the night sky has been sucked into a void, where only the moon goddess can enjoy them.

When the black turns back to night, and I can see the stars again, I realize I gotta get up or I might never. Then where'll I be? I can just imagine Keep looking in my cage the next day, seeing me sprawled out in the desert, dust on my lips, my arm hanging from my shoulder, limper'n a tug tail.

I'm smart, so I use the prickler to help me to my feet, getting jabbed half a dozen times on the way up. "Thanks, Perry," I whisper to the prickler. He deserves a name for all his trouble. After all, like so many people in my life, he's helped me and hurt me. Either that, or I just like talking to plants.

My sling's a wreck, ripped in at least three places, two holes jabbed in it by Perry, who can't be blamed, 'cause he hasn't moved the entire time. Although I guess it could be argued that if he was really on my side he woulda moved. *Perry, you haggard,* I think, *you shoulda moved!*

MedMa would be appalled at the state of my sling, so I do my best to rewrap it, which hurts worse'n a snap from Father's snapper. But I get it done, let out a breathless sigh, exhausted from the strain of the last…how long's it been anyway? I got no clue. I coulda blacked out for three thumbs of sun movement for all I know. Or just a few moments. More'n likely the real amount is somewhere in between. But which side's it closer to? And what do I do now?

I got a real problem. If I chase after Raja and the other prisoners with the tools, they might already be coming back, done with whatever it is they're doing. But the thought of trying to squeeze back into my cage right now…I shudder. I'm out now so I might as well take advantage.

You're gonna end up back in Confinement, says Perry.

"Shut up," I whisper over my shoulder as I walk away.

~~~

I ain't got further'n a rock's throw away from the edge of the Confinement cages when I see them. The glint of the bright moonlight offa the edges of tools tells me they're coming back already. Either they're real fast workers or I was in a pain-induced stupor for longer'n I thought. Too long.

I grit my teeth and hustle back the way I came, around the edges of the cages, past the sleeping non-lifers. Then I'm back at my cage and I'm staring a torturous reentry right in the face. The gap I escaped from looks even smaller, like the cage has a brain and, upon realizing its flaw, recreated itself. There's gotta be another way.

Back at the front of the cage I stare at the mound where the big rock is covered. The clink of metal tools is carried to my ears on a gust of wind. Hard to tell how far away. Could be a mile. Could be a stone's throw. If they're a mile away, I could maybe dig up the rock, move it, slip through the hole, and pull the rock back into the gap. But the rock would be bare, instead of covered like it's s'posed to be. The Keep would know something knocky was going on.

Voices bounce across the desert like brambleweeds.

They're not a mile away. They're back!

I'm ready to rush 'round to the back, jam myself through the first gap that looks big enough, deal with whatever physical

140

consequences I've got coming, but for some reason I stop to take one more look at my cage. I gaze from side to side, from bottom to top. I freeze.

The top.

It's still got plenty of bars, and up there they're crisscrossed, but each bar appears to be set further away from the one before'n the bars along the sides. Perhaps it's just enough for a skinny lil runt like me to slip through without further shattering my already damaged arm.

Clink!

The sound is so close I could swear it was right next to my ear. I start climbing.

It ain't easy climbing with only one good arm, but I don't weigh no more'n a bundle of vulture feathers. I jam my feet between two of the bars, trying to use the roughness of my moccasin bottoms against the roughness of the wood as a sort of fall stopper. My one good arm does most of the work while my broken one takes the rest of the night off. Well deserved.

Perry's just staring at me, like the shanker that he is. *Thanks for the help, buddy.*

I grab as high as I can, pull with all my might, move my feather-light butt up a few feet, and sort of hop with my feet, almost like a horny toad—don't laugh, that's what they're called—and then rewedge my moccasins to keep from falling. It's slow going.

Grab, pull, move butt, horny toad hop, wedge. Repeat.

The voices get louder. Someone laughs. A gruff voice reprimands. Keep, trying to get control of his prisoners.

I don't stop for the voices, for the clinks, for Perry's catcalls. Slow and steady, I keep moving until I reach the cross bar that means I've made it to the top. The lid on my cage.

One leg over, then t'other. Take a breath.

The voices stop in front of Raja's cage. "You're up next, dog! Get in!" Keep barks, sounding more like a dog himself. I freeze, look down, see Keep with maybe eight other prisoners. Raja drops to the durt, everyone watching him. I'm exposed under the soft glow of the moon goddess. If they look up, I'm knocked! Where are the searin' clouds when I need them?

Raja squirms like a worm underneath the bars. "Lock him in!" Keep growls, handing one of t'other prisoners a shovel. I'm dead-quiet, and to my surprise, Perry is too. Silent schemers. Placid plotters.

When the big rock for Raja's cage is in place and covered, Keep and the rest of them move on. I hold my breath. They walk straight on past my cage, not even giving it a casual look. I'm just a runty girl, couldn't hurt a fly. *'Cept myself*, I think, feeling my arm start to throb again.

When they're past Keep's hut and a few more cages, I breathe again. My heart's beating like the party drums after a successful tug hunt. But I ain't out of the desert yet. Perry agrees, doing his version of a nod, which is basically staying perfectly still and upright. *Stay out of this, Perry!* I think.

Perched on the roof of my cage, I feel precarious. It's not that high, but with holes in the floor, it feels higher'n it really is. There's a certain thrill to it, too, like all my innards are floating inside me, bobbing and bouncing. How to get down?

The smart thing to do, as Perry suggests, would be to slip through one of the square holes and shimmy on down the bars all the way to the ground. Challenging with one arm, but easier'n climbing up here in the first place. Sounds like a plan.

I start to carefully lower myself between the crisscross, keeping one of the bars under my armpit. As I scrabble at the thin air with my feet, Keep shouts, "Cage check!"

Cage check? What'n the scorch? I lose my concentration and my arm slips off the bar. I'm falling! At the last second, I grab and squeeze as hard as I can with my hand, making a fist around the bar. My feet swing underneath me as I hang on for dear life, rocking back and forth in the wind, which has been picking up steadily ever since I started climbing. A morning windstorm. Not unusual for this time of year.

While I hang, there's grumbling and groaning as the whole place seems to come to life. Toward the end of my row of cages, I hear Keep rattling along the cage bars with some instrument, shouting out names and then waiting for a response.

"Koda!"

"Yeah."

Ratatatat along the bars.

"Briggs!"

"Nope."

"Shut yer tug hole! Smartass!"

Ratatatat…

You get the picture. He's getting nearer.

My feet are swinging and I can't reach the side bars. Can't shimmy down. Can't slide down. Can't do anything 'cept hang and swing. My shoulder's aching and I feel my sweaty hand starting to slide off the wood.

"Bart!"

A growl. Big Bart ain't in the mood for talking.

Keep'll pass his hut and then he's to mine.

I got no choice.

143

Outta options.

Perry's chanting, "Do it, do it, do it!"

I do it. I wait until my swing takes me into a more or less vertical position and then I release the bar and drop, trying to keep my legs bent slightly to cushion the fall. For a painfully short moment, I'm weightless, free, untouchable. And then the unforgiving ground touches me. Hard. Like a forearm shiver, but across the whole of my body. My feet hit first, pushing a shockwave up my legs and into my hips, spreading like wildfire from there. My knees give out, sending me rolling—not again!—across my cage. This time it's only one roll though, one big flop, a stomach-jostling smacker that knocks all the air out of me. At least Perry is on the other side of the bars this time, unable to prick me.

Can't breathe.

Can't breathe.

I wheeze and gasp as I roll over to lie on my back.

Ratatatat! "Siena!"

Wheeze. Gasp. No voice. No breath. No way to respond.

"Siena!" Keep repeats.

"Here," I whisper, like I'm back in Learning and Teacher is checking for skippers. But my voice comes out softer'n the rustle of windblown sand. Keep can't hear me.

"I see ya there, Girl. I knows yer ain't used to our ways 'ere, but it's not difficult. I says yer name, and yer respond. Let's try it again."

Wheeze. Gasp. Lips moving but no words coming out.

"Siena!"

"Yeah," I croak, my voice the timbre of a horny toad, my animal of choice for this evening. Perry laughs.

"See, not too hard, eh?" Keep says. He moves on to Raja.

My throat opens and I greedily gulp down the breezy air. My heart slows. My body aches. Perry mocks. Searin' Perry.

"What the scorch are you doing over there?" Raja hisses when Keep's moved on down the line. "I heard a thump." I clench my jaw. "Nothing," I say. "Just sleeping. Or trying to."

"Tugblaze. I heard you thrashing around in the durt like you's fighting something."

"It's too dangerous to tell you, Raja," I say, turning his words back on him. "If I told you, they'd kill you, and they'd kill me."

I slump to the side, grinning in spite of the aches and pains and bumps and bruises. Determined to get a little sleep before Luger comes to collect me. A peaceful end to a very long day in Confinement.

Fourteen

It's nice waking up in my own bed, watching through the window as the sun peeks over the horizon, spraying ribbons of red in every direction. A heavy bank of thick, yellow clouds moves swiftly across the sea of pinkish-reddish sky. It's a very windy day. Through our door, which is open a crack, I can smell the windstorm that's coming. Might even turn into the first sandstorm of the winter season. I can't smell it yet, but if there's a sandstorm coming, my nose'll pick up on it soon enough. I been sniffing out storms my whole life.

Yesterday was a throw-a-way. I was too battered and sore and exhausted to do anything but sleep it off. I coulda just as easily done that in my cage, but I was sure thankful to do it here, on my tugskin sleeper.

I heard Circ come to call on me, but Mother turned him away, said I needed to rest. She was right. Thankfully my father wasn't around when he stopped by—he mighta made a scene.

The crack in the door widens and my father's heavy outline appears in the opening. His eyes are small, no more'n pinpricks. He grunts when he sees me awake. He didn't say a word to me yesterday. I wonder if his grunt means today'll be the same. I can hope, can't I?

Nope.

He strides directly over to me, not even stopping to slip off his dusty moccasins. My Call-Mother'll hafta sweep up the mess later. There's a shadow on my face as he looms over me.

"Youngling," he says.

"Head Greynote," I say, returning his formalness.

"Did you learn anything from your trip to Confinement?"

Scorch, yeah! Heaps! All about how people sent there are treated like animals, caged, poorly fed. About how it's possible to escape if you're all skin and bones, like me. And oh yeah, I found out about some 'spiracy with the Icies, how 'bout that?

At least that's what I think. What I say is, "Yessir. I'll be behaving from now on. Don't want to go back there again. Never."

Although I know I give the right response, he frowns, maybe sensing the deceit in my voice. "Good," he says. "Don't make me send you there again. The next time your stay might not be so short."

As he starts to head for the door, I say, "Congratulations, Father." He turns, looks back at me. "On Head Greynote."

His face is flat. "It's not an award or a celebration. It's a duty. It'll do you well to remember that."

And then he's gone, the flaps of his slitted leather shirt wagging about the moment he steps out the door, the wind whipping them into a frenzy.

It's a very windy day.

I wonder what the wind'll carry into the village.

~~~

"We're leaving soon," Circ says.

Yeah, I'm hanging around Circ still. I guess my father's little lesson in Confinement didn't really take. As long as I don't get caught, right?

I nod. "And you'll be back in three days?" I ask for the tenth time. A burst of sand shivers overhead. It never comes back down, carried along by the ever-strengthening wind. The trip back to the village'll be awful, but for now we're protected in our spot in the Mouth, dug in on the backside of one of the two big dunes.

He looks at me with one dimple. "We've gone over all this. It's an investigation. We're not going to war."

I raise my chin. "Oh, you think I'm worried? No, no, I just know I'm going to be bored stiffer'n a day-old dead burrow mouse with you gone," I say, giving him my best champion's smile. Although I've never been a champion and probably never will, it don't hurt to practice.

He laughs, short and high-pitched, humoring me. "Don't get into any trouble while I'm gone or I won't be there to visit you in Confinement."

"It seems I only get into trouble when you *are* around," I say, ramming my knee against his. "And for your information, I had two other visitors'n you, my mother and Lara. So I think I'm covered there."

His eyes widen. "And you didn't tell me this earlier?" He's turned grumpy on me. "We've only been setting here for one thumb of sun movement, maybe less. And I'm telling you now, ain't I?"

Circ shrugs, bashes his knee against mine and I wince. "Ouch! Sear it all to scorch, Circ, that hurt like a machete blade."

His hands are on my knee in an instant, rubbing and massaging it. "Sorry, Sie, I didn't realize I cracked you that hard." His touch feels warmer'n a hot summer's day.

"No, it wasn't that," I say. "I'm just a tad tender." I keep my eyes down, on my knee where he's rubbing it, but I can feel his frown all over my face.

"Why's it tender?"

I say nothing.

"Sie? What is it you're not telling me?"

Like I always do with Circ, I spill my guts. I hate dropping all these boulders on him just before his mission, but I never could keep anything from him. Nor do I want to. It's nice having someone who knows my every thought. Secrets'll chew you up inside, swish you around, and then spit you in the dust. Maybe even stomp you down a bit. Right away, I feel better after I tell him.

"Holy jumpin' prickler roots, Sie!" Circ exclaims when I finish. "You jumped from the roof?"

I blink. Now that he says it that way, it all sounds pretty wooloo, like maybe something I dreamed, or made up. With a shrug, I say, "Uh, yeah. Seemed like a good idea at the time."

149

"Wow! First the thing with the Killers, and then this. You're getting bolder by the day. Maybe it should be you going on this mission."

Despite the obvious exaggeration in Circ's declaration—females ain't allowed to go on missions as they might get hurt and not be able to Bear—it makes me smile from earlobe to earlobe. "You're just blustering now," I say. "You're full of air and sand, just like the wind."

"We'll see," Circ says, grinning back. "Anyway, whaddya make of it all?"

"All of what?" I ask. Our knees touch again and Circ stops rubbing my leg.

"I dunno. Everything. What Lara said. Your mother. Raja's talk of a 'spiracy." Coming from his mouth, it does sound like a lot. An awful lot. I feel tired again.

I take a moment to think. Then I start slow, taking it piece by piece. "Lara says a lot of stuff, most of which I don't understand. I don't know if I ever will or if I should even take her seriously. I mean, could she really be working with someone outside of the village? How would she even meet someone outside? My mother though, what she said took me by surprise. I never heard her talk like that. I can't help thinking she's losing her mind being Called to my father."

"You think it's the Fire?"

My head jerks toward Circ's, his question taking me by surprise. "What? No. Of course not. She's perfectly healthy."

Circ chews on his lip. "Sorry, it's just, she's getting old. Like both our parents. The Fire's inevitable."

"I—I know that," I say. Keeping it internal, I think *Do I?* My parents have always been there, since the very beginning. It only makes sense that they'll always be there, just like Circ'll always be there. I slam the gate down on those thoughts. It's my heart speaking. Foolishness. My brain knows everybody dies, usually sooner rather'n later. Like Circ said, *the Fire's inevitable*.

Trying not to think about the Fire, or whether my mother is going wooloo, I move on to my next point. "There must be something of a 'spiracy," I say. "Raja had no reason to lie. And I did see them hauling off with all those tools."

"Tell me again what you heard Greynote Luger say to Keep," Circ says.

"Nothing that made sense at the time," I say. "Just asked about how the work was going. Keep said the Icies were happy, but that he needed more lifers to do the work 'cause they were dying on him."

"And what did Luger say?"

"He said he'll see what he can do." I play with a loose strand of hair. Circ kicks at the sand, digging a hole with his foot. We're both thinking real hard.

"So you think the work that Luger was talking about is what the prisoners were doing when they went off in the middle of the night?" Circ asks, jamming his heel into his hole like a pickaxe.

"It'd hafta be, right? What other work would prisoners be doing? And Raja went with them. He was a lifer, Circ. Stuck in Confinement for the rest of his life, all 'cause someone framed him for murder. Or so he says."

"Do you believe him?" Circ looks up from his digging, his eyes big with interest. Beautiful, too, if I'm being honest. So deep and brown and mine to look at all day if I want to. Or at least until he leaves on his mission. "Sie?" I'm staring at him and I look away.

"Uh, yeah. I believe him."

I can tell Circ's eyes are studying my face and I feel my face go warm. A blush. "Siena?" he says.

"Yeah," I say, making eye contact and feeling my face go even redder. There's a look on Circ's face I never seen before. It's hard to describe but it's like fire country after the spring rains. Vibrant, pure, alive. He wants to say something, but his lips are closed. They're so close to me. I guess they always are when we sit here, but I never really noticed 'fore. Now it feels like they're right on top of me, like if I just leaned in a couple of inches, turned my head slightly, I could—

"I'm lucky to have you," Circ says. "You know, as a friend."

I feel a jab to my stomach but no one's hit me. It's his words. I'll take the first part but skip the second if you don't mind. "I'm the lucky one," I whisper.

He leans in, turns his head, his lips closer and closer and closer still, and then brushing past me as he embraces me in a classic Circ hug. Warm and tight. I'm hurting a little inside, but I hug back, 'cause I need it now more'n ever. 'Fore he leaves on his mission. Toward the borders of Killer country.

Fifteen

Three days can be a long time. Longer'n a year if you're missing someone. Longer'n a lifetime if that person is Circ.

First day, I go to Learning, try to ignore the empty spot next to me, daydream the class away without getting caught. I'm lucky. Coulda been shoveling blaze all alone. When I get home I mope around the hut, pretending like I'm helping my mother, but not really doing anything. She lets me.

Neither of us says anything about her visit to Confinement. With my father always lurking, we can't talk openly, even in our own hut. Perhaps that's why she came to see me when I was locked up.

When I go to bed that night, I pray to the sun goddess for Circ. I'm hoping to get a warm feeling in my gut, something to tell me he's okay, but all I get's a big knot. I fall asleep grabbing at that knot with my hands, trying to squeeze it out.

The second day the knot's bigger. Learning again. I try to listen, but my mind refuses to be forced. It dredges up memory after memory of Circ. How every year when the spring rains came we'd sneak out and run, run, run through the wastelands, getting soaked beyond belief. *We're made of water*, we'd say. And then we'd laugh and run some more. It never went over very well with our parents, but we took whatever punishment they'd hand out like champs. It was worth it. There are other memories, too, painful ones, like when Skye was taken on the day of her Call, how I cried. It was the first time Circ'd held me. Really held me. Like I was the only one in the world and we could go on like that forever.

But after all those memories, we're still just friends.

'Cause I'm Scrawny and he…well, he's Circ. Always Circ.

After Learning I don't bother to pretend to help my mother and she don't try to make me. Without saying a word I know she understands. She lets me mope. She lets me shank the day away.

Today's the third day and Circ's s'posed to come home, although he couldn't say whether it'd be morning, afternoon, or night. I hope it's morning so I'm up early even though there's no Learning today. Everyone else's already out and about, doing who-knows-what.

I'm determined to pass the time as quickly as possible, for every second that ticks away is a second closer to Circ returning, safe and where he belongs. I go for a walk, nowhere in particular, just through the village, walking amongst the Greynote huts in my part of the village. The wind is swirling and swirling, working itself up to what'll probably be yet

another winter windstorm. A pair of britches whips past—
someone didn't tie them tight enough to the line. I'm wearing a
white dress, the same one I plan to wear for my Call, a symbol
of purity. Its skirts are snapping in the gale, making a cracking
noise louder'n when Father punishes me. Seems awful silly
women and girls still hafta wear long dresses in weather like
this. But it's the Law.

Most folks have no reason to wander this area of the village,
unless you live here or have business with one of the
Greynotes, so the pathways are empty. A brambleweed buzzes
past, overhead. It's a heavy one, too, with thick roots. It takes a
heavy wind to uproot a weed like that—and keep it in the air
for that long. I sniff the air, trying to pick up any trace of a
sandstorm. Nothing. Just wind as far as I can tell. But surely the
first sandstorm of the season ain't far off. Tomorrow or the day
after, perhaps.

As I ponder the weather, a familiar voice carries through the
thin walls of the Greynote hut I'm passing. "We won't be able
to survive another attack by the newcomers," the voice says.
It's Luger, his whiny voice unmistakable, even through a
wooden wall. Who are they talking about? The Killers? They're
hardly new.

"We need to find out what our Glassy friends to the south
are trying to achieve," a voice replies, sharp and commanding,
like both a crack of thunder and a streak of lightning. My
father. By newcomers Luger meant the Glassies.

Luger responds. "The first team of investigators was certain
an attack was imminent, but gave no indication as to the
motives." Another attack by the Glassies? I need to go tell—

My heart sinks when I remember Circ's not back yet. When
he talked about his mission, he never mentioned there was

155

another team of investigators. Maybe he didn't know. If they're back already, surely he'll be back soon.

"In the absence of information, we have to assume they have only one goal: to wipe us out and steal our land." My father's words hang over my head like a dark cloud, pregnant with rain, unmoving despite the buffeting it's taking at the hands of the wind. Circ, where are you?

~~~

The first Glassy attack was the scariest day of my life, although I didn't really see anything. The women, the children, including all Youngling, and those afflicted with the Fire, were told to stay inside the Greynote huts. I remember how angry my father was with Head Greynote Shiva for making the decision to keep male Younglings away from the fighting. He thought all males aged twelve and older should be out there, defending our village. Shiva wanted them behind, as a last line of defense in case it came to that. Circ got to stay behind.

We huddled together, tighter'n a thousand ants in an anthill. The pre-Totters were crying and carrying on while their mothers shushed and sang to them. Some of the Younglings were bragging about how many Glassies their fathers would kill, like it was a competition or something. I stayed by Circ, always close enough that one part of us or another was touching. Comforting.

The sounds of battle got really close at one point. Men were yelling and metal was shrieking. The crackle and roar and bitter odor of heavy flames and smoke filled the air. I thought they were burning down our village, that they'd broken through, would soon set fire to our hut.

They didn't, although when one of the Hunters came to tell us it was safe to come out, we emerged to find a quarter of the tents burned to no more'n ash and kindling. Evidently the Glassies never set foot in the village, but did shoot a whole heap of fireballs past the Hunters, lighting quite a few tents on fire.

But the Hunters held them off.

And the Glassies haven't come back since.

Until now, if Luger is right.

~~~

I'm the first one to know that the Hunters are back from their investigation. Unable to thwart my anticipation any longer, I take to sitting on the outskirts of the village, watching the desert. Just sitting, waiting, hunger growing in my stomach, thirst growing in my throat, ignoring it all. Sitting and waiting.

They start as dots on the horizon. Could be anything. Killers. Glassies. But I know they're not. They're Hunters. There's a bubble in my gut telling me so. Circ's back.

When he gets close enough where I know without a doubt it's him, I want nothing more'n to rush to him, to throw my arms 'round him, to hold on tight and never let go, but I hold it back, 'cause he looks awful serious with his Hunter friends. Like they've got a story to tell and someone they gotta go tell it to. So I just sit there, watching them march past, thinking how strange it is that everyone always hasta act a certain way, for appearances' sake. Why can't we just be ourselves?

But then, at the last second, Circ glances in my direction and winks, flashes a two-dimpled smile that raises my lips and expands in my chest. He's back, really back.

I follow them through the village, keeping my distance so as to not make it too obvious. When they get to the same hut I heard my father talking to Luger in earlier, they knock and go in. I'm too scared and nervous and excited to eavesdrop, so I just sit a ways off, picking at the sand and waiting for him to come out. He'll tell me everything anyway.

They're not in there long enough for the sun goddess to move an inch in the sky, but it's searin' close to that. I've built two big ol' piles of sand and I'm about to connect the two with a bridge of sorts, when they emerge from the hut. Circ's out first, and he marches right on over to me and grabs my hand, pulls me up, and starts tugging me away. I look back and see my father standing in the doorway, his arms crossed, just watching. I'll most certainly catch it from him later, but my Circ's back, and nothing can stop me from spending some time with him, so I swivel around like I never even saw him giving us the evil eye.

~ ~ ~

We both have stories to tell but I let him go first, 'cause he's practically itching to tell it. He still hasn't let go of my hand after walking all the way to the Mouth holding it. I don't mind at all.

"Sie, we went into Killer territory," he says, squeezing my hand outta excitement.

I frown. "I thought you were just going to the border," I say. My wooloo mind starts conjuring up all sorts of visions of Circ and the Hunters, surrounded by Killers, fighting them off barehanded, bleeding and missing arms and legs. *Stop!* I shout to myself. *You saw as well as I did that none of them looked hurt. Sorry,* my mind says. *Sometimes I can't help myself.*

"Me, too," Circ says. "And that's what we did at first. Surveyed the border, looked for tracks and evidence that anyone might've crossed over from our land to the Killers'."

"Did you find anything?" I ask, prying his fingers offa mine. I don't want to, but his grip is so tight my brittler'n-scrubgrass fingers are starting to ache.

"Sort of," he says. "There were human footprints all right, coming right in from Killer territory to Heater land, as if one of our people had gone over there to cause trouble and then come back. But the strange thing was that there were no prints going in the other direction."

A dull throb starts in my slinged arm. "It's been windy. The tracks mighta just been smoothed over," I say.

"Maybe," he says. "And we thought that too, but some of the tracks coming in were deep. They were made with someone wearing something on their feet that none of us had ever seen before. Not moccasins, that's for sure."

"Not Heaters," I murmur, holding my bad arm gingerly.

He shakes his head. "Someone else. We didn't want to waste the mission, come back empty handed, so we went over the border, not to cause trouble with the Killers, but to see if we could find anything to point us to the cause of their invasion. There were all kinds of tracks over there made by someone else, not Heaters. We found a whole pile of tug bones, too, nice and neat and organized. Someone was hunting."

"Circ, I gotta tell you something too." I tell him what I overheard my father and Luger talking about.

"It makes sense," he says. "If it was the Glassies riling the Killers up, tricking them into thinking we'd come onto their

159

land, then they'd follow it up with an attack of their own. You know, now that we're weakened."

"What about the Icers?" I ask.

"I don't know anything about any of that. We'll probably never know." That might be good enough for Circ, but it's not for me. Call it curiosity or just plain silliness, but if we're 'bout to be invaded by foreigners, I wanna know the whole picture.

"I'm going back to Confinement," I say.

"What? Why would you do that?" Circ turns to face me.

"I gotta know what's going on," I say.

"If you sneak up there and try to follow the prisoners to wherever they're working every night, your father will notice you're gone. There's no way you'll get away with it." Circ's right. I can sneak away for one thumb of sun movement, maybe two, but to carry out a plan like this it'll take more'n five. The snapper'll be waiting when I come back. If I'm lucky that's all that'll be waiting.

"I'm not sneaking there," I say, a plan coming together in my mind. "I'm going back in my cage."

~~~

Circ tries to talk me outta it, but I can be as stubborn as a Totter who won't eat his evening stew. For some reason I get my head set on doing this thing, and I can't think about anything else until I do it.

Before we part ways, he tells me not to do anything stupid until we talk again. I tell him I'll think about it.

When I burst through the door I know I'm in for it. I ain't late for dinner, or shy of my chores, or late on my Learning projects, but something's astir. My mother won't look at me, just stares at the pot of stew she's stirring like it might hold the meaning of life on its bubbling surface.

My Call-Mother and Call-Siblings turn away from me, huddle together and take turns tying knots in a ball of string.

Father glares. "Where've you been?" he demands, 'fore I have a chance to gather my thoughts or figure out what's going on.

"Out," I say. It's not a lie, but it's not what he's looking for either.

"Don't toy with me, Youngling!" he snarls. "I saw you go off with that boy."

"His name's Circ," I say. "You've known him since we was kids." I'm being bolder and feeling bolder'n ever before. Between me and my mother, we're probably really getting on his nerves.

"I know who he is. Playing with him as a Totter and Midder was fine," he says. What's he playing at?

"But now?" I say.

He strides forward, breathing so heavy I can feel it waft off my face. His breath smells like spicy tug jerky. My stomach rumbles. *Shut up!* I tell it. *This is not the time.*

"Listen to me carefully because I'll only say this once more. I will not have my Pre-Bearer daughter running around with some Youngling boy like a little shilt."

My blood's boiling, all bubbly and hot, not too different'n my mother's stew. I'm sweating all over and I know my face is glistening with moisture and heat. No hiding my anger this time. "It's not like that!" I scream, turning to run back outside, away from this place, from this man, from the creature who refuses to call me by the name he gave me when I was born.

161

He grabs my arm, hard enough to bruise, whips me 'round. My eyes are glued to his white-knuckled grip, seeing as much as feeling the strength in him. He might be older'n durt, but he ain't caught the Fire yet, ain't weak in the least. I can't fight him with my runty body.

My only chance is to use my mind.

Sixteen

My father's message was as dark and mottled as the purple-black-blue five-fingered bruise he left in the flesh of my arm: I see Circ again and it's another trip to Confinement for me.

My plan is on track.

I lie in bed thinking. If I can get back to Confinement I'll be able to find out what the scorch is going on. Then maybe me and Circ can come up with a way to stop it. Whatever it is, my father's got his fist clamped on things tighter'n a butcher about to castrate a dead tug. Circ may not approve of my plan, but he'll have no choice but to go along with it once it's in motion.

When my father's breathing from behind his curtain grows heavy and deep, I throw back my tugskin covering and tiptoe for the door, sparing only a second or two to slip on my moccasins. I ease the door open a crack, praying for silence, and then slide through. *Escape!* I think. There's something satisfying and exciting about sneaking out at night. Maybe it's 'cause no one's telling me what to do, or where to go, or what my duty is. Or maybe it's just 'cause I like being a bit rebellious every now and again.

Everything's blacker'n the inside of a tug's stomach, 'cept for the sky, which is aglow with hovering fireflies—the stars. To scare me when I was a Totter, Skye used to tell me that night came when a gigantic monster stood in front of the sun, blocking its light and casting a mammoth shadow over everything. She made me scared of the dark for years, until I was a Midder. Now I'm glad for the big ol' monster's shadow. It hides my movements.

I sneak my way through the Greynote huts, peeking 'round corners and stopping to listen for footsteps or voices every coupla steps. The village is silent. A ghost town. Everyone sleeping, or at least pretending to. When I get to the last row of huts I cut to the right, purposefully avoiding the village center and the fire pit. There're almost always insomniacs there, drinking the night away, stirring the fire up and telling war stories. Hunts gone bad, Hunts gone good, and everything in between.

I'm nearly out of the Greynote block when the last hut's door swings open right in front of my face. I'm behind it, hidden, but whoever opened it is gonna close it any second and they'll surely see me. There's no time to think, to run, to do much of anything, so I drop. Flat on my stomach. Like a worm, 'cept without the wriggling. Just stay still, quiet, not even breathing.

The door shuts and whoever's there makes a sorta groaning noise, but not like he's in pain. Come to think of it, it's more like a sigh, like of relief. I risk a breath and a peek up. Too dark to see anything 'cept the outline of a man, which means he probably won't see me either, unless he happens to look directly down, or trips on me.

There's the scrape of a flint and then a flash of red as he lights a pipe. For that moment I'm completely illuminated, can see my own hands, feet, and everything else, even the tip of my nose. And I can see him too. My breath catches when I recognize the Greynote:

Luger.

But then the light goes out, replaced by just a finger's tip of light at the end of his pipe. A bitter, somewhat fruity aroma settles on the tip of my tongue. It leaves a sour taste in my mouth, like I been drinking stale prickler juice. Luger's not just smoking the pipeweed that so many men around the village like to puff on. It's fireweed. Like I smelled out behind the Learning hut when Youngling Granger got his hands on a whole pouch of it. Half the Younglings were giggling all through class that afternoon. Luger's guilty pleasure, so guilty he can only smoke it in the dead of night.

Luger sighs again and then walks on down the row, skirting behind his own hut.

I move on, first back the way I came to get as far away from Luger as possible, and then up a row of huts to further my distance from him. If he catches me now it might work out okay for my plan, but there're no guarantees. I need to get further.

I edge my way down the row, and once I'm out of the cover of the Greynote huts, I run like I'm being chased by a bloodthirsty pack of Cotees. Tents fly by on both sides, most of them quiet and closed off, but a few of them with late sleepers sitting around cook fires, tent openings wide and flapping lazily in the night breeze. A few of them cry out, but I keep running. All part of the plan.

I get to Circ's neighborhood and slow down, quickly locating his tent, which is half falling over from the recent spat of windstorms we've had. It doesn't look ready to survive the first sandstorm of the season. I'll hafta mention that to him.

Just as I reach the tent opening, a corner of the moon peeks out from the clouds, providing a small measure of much-needed light. Kneeling down in front of the haggard sleeping quarters, I ease open the tentflap, spilling the soft moonglow inside. I pause, take a moment for my eyes to adjust to the inside gloom, and slide in. There are ten bodies inside. Not a Full Family, as Circ, like me, has lost one of his Call-Mothers and two Call-Siblings, but it's not far off. The chorus of peaceful rest-making sounds invites me to join them. My eyes are tired, along with my body, but my mind is still sharp. Not a night for sleep. Least not for me. And in a second not for Circ either.

He's easy to spot amongst the bodies. His bare chest rises and falls more'n anyone else's. He's always been a deep breather and heavy sleeper. Countless times he's drifted away next to me on the dunes, always 'fore I can manage to sleep myself. I watch him sometimes.

One of his Call-Sisters has her foot in his face, and his real brother, Stix, has his head resting on Circ's stomach, rising and falling along with it. For Circ, sneaking out is somewhat harder'n for me.

Don't be clumsy, don't be clumsy, don't be clumsy, I think to myself, placing a hand in an open spot between someone's arm and someone else's head. My other arm is useless, wrapped up in its sling. This'll hafta be a three-legged dance. I move my right foot into another gap, follow it with my left foot. I'm dangling awkwardly and unbalanced above the sleeping bodies, but I only need another few moves and I'll be able to reach him.

Hand, foot, foot. My foot brushes against someone's skin, one of his Call-Brothers, I think, just a Totter. The boy stirs, stretches, nearly clobbering me in the face with his little outstretched fist. Yawns. Turns over and goes back to sleep.

I'm sweating now, the heat of the night and the strain of my muscles bringing my body temperature to a fever pitch. I feel droplets of moisture gathering on my forehead, starting to stream. One drips in my eye and I blink it away, feeling the sting. Another runs down my nose, settles on the tip.

Hand—

The bead of sweat wobbles.

Foot—

The sweat quivers.

Foot—

It drops, splashes someone in the face, another sibling I think—maybe Stix. His eyes drift open but they're still full of sleep. I stare at him as he wipes at his face, feels the moisture there, probably wonders whether a nightmare has made him cry in his sleep. He blinks a few times and I can almost see his vision clearing, zeroing in on yours truly hovering above him.

His eyes widen, his mouth opens.

I pucker my lips and whisper, "Shhh," as soothingly and softly as I can.

He doesn't call out, recognizes me. Nudges Circ.

Circ groans, loud enough to make me cringe. Opens his eyes. Sees me right away. Gives me an as-usual-you're-acting-wooloo look. I nod my head toward the tent flap.

He shakes his head. I give him a look of death. Grudgingly, he nods. Stix watches us curiously as I retrace my hand and foot placements, and Circ pries away the arms, legs, and heads of his siblings and Call-Siblings.

Once outside, Circ ducks his mouth to the side of my head. "Are you wooloo?" he hisses, tickling my ear with his breath.

Shrugging, I look up at the sky, which is clearing faster'n a baby's bundle gets durtied. "I couldn't sleep. Wanna go for a walk?"

He shakes his head, but it's not a no. It's a shake that's part *Why am I your friend again?* and part resignation. He's coming.

~ ~ ~

"Where are we going?" Circ says after a few moments. We're approaching the edge of the village, a point that's the exact middle distance from each of the night watchmen towers. He's only asking to humor me, so I don't answer.

"You were just in Confinement, if your father catches you, he'll..." He stops, understanding dawning in his eyes. "You want to get caught," he says. "Don't you?"

I sigh. "Look, Circ. I hafta know what's going on up at Confinement, with the prisoners. Innocent people are being sent there. It's not fair."

"Since when has life been fair?" Circ says.

"Don't you even care?" I say.

Circ looks at the ground, then at the sky. "You know I do."

"Then help me," I say.

He lets out a sorta growl that's meant to be angry but is kinda cute. "Okay, but we can get caught inside the village. If we try to sneak beyond the borders they'll shoot us deader'n a vulture's breakfast."

"We've done it 'fore," I say.

"Yeah, but not when the guards are on high-alert. What with the Glassies threatening and all the Killer stuff, nothing will be able to get in or out of the village without raising a bunch of alarms."

He's right, although I don't want him to be. I want nothing more'n to escape the bounds of the village tonight, stare up at the moon and the stars like we always used to, away from everything and everyone. "Okay. But can we go somewhere away from things?"

Circ nods. "I know just the place."

~~~

He leads now, along the edge of the village, ducking behind tents whenever we pass a guard tower. Cutting across the village it doesn't seem so big, but going 'round the outer curve, it feels unending. Hundreds of tents stand in rows, like a silent army. And with first sun tomorrow morning, each tent'll open up like a pod, giving birth to six, or eight, or ten people.

We reach the biggest structure in the village and I understand where he's taking me. The Hunter's Lodge.

Standing square and tall like a fortress, the Lodge contains more wood'n anything else we've ever built. I've only ever seen it from the outside, but tonight I'm in for a treat. Circ's taking me inside.

There's a guard at the door, but he's not really paying attention, just sitting there, puffing on pipeweed. Circ motions for me to stay back, behind the corner of the Lodge. He walks up to the guard casually, and I stifle a laugh when the Hunter leaps to his feet, grabbing at his belt for a weapon.

"Whoa, Kiroff, it's just me, Circ," Circ says.

"Jumping 'zards, you gave me a fright," Kiroff says, taking his hand off his belt. "I thought you mighta been one of them Glassies, snuck inside." I remember Kiroff. He was a year ahead of us in Learning. He didn't make Hunter until after finishing Learning, when he turned sixteen, four years behind Circ. Still fresh on the job.

Circ laughs. "Come on, do you really believe all that nonsense?"

Kiroff scratches his head. "The Greynotes seemed pretty searin' serious about it in the briefing. They said all guards had to be extra watchful."

"So you're sitting here smoking pipeweed and letting me sneak up on you?" There's amusement in Circ's tone.

Kiroff kicks at the durt sheepishly. "It was all I could do to stay awake. You won't tell anyone, will you?"

Circ chuckles. "Nah. That's why I'm here. They decided to switch it up, change guards more regularly so everyone stays fresh."

"They didn't tell me that," Kiroff says, eyes narrowing.

"Strange," Circ says. "They must've forgotten. Anyway, I'm here to relieve you of your post. I'm on duty till morning. Get some sleep."

Kiroff seems uncertain at first, his mouth opening and closing, his feet shifting back and forth, but then he shrugs. "Thanks," he says gratefully. Apparently the thought of some extra sleep won out over any sense of duty.

Kiroff trudges off, in the opposite direction, and Circ waves me over. "We're in," he says. Excitement builds in my stomach. Tonight is turning out to be better'n just carrying out my plan.

~~~

I'm not sure how it is during the day, but being inside the Lodge at night is eerie. It's dark and hollow and feels like we're inside the belly of a sleeping beast, wind rushing through the endless passageways.

"Around the edge are the weapons rooms, strategy rooms, commanders' quarters, supply holds and a whole lot of other boring stuff," Circ explains as we walk down a hallway. It's weird, unlike anything I've ever seen. It's almost like all the huts in the village've been joined together, the walls knocked down so that it's one, long hut. We reach a corner and turn right. The next side of the square.

"And all the sides are like this?" I ask.

Circ grins, his teeth gleaming in the light from the torch he lit when we entered the main door. "Yeah, but that's not why I brought you. The real treat is in the middle."

Instead of taking me all the way to the end of the next passage, Circ stops midway, where another path goes off to the right, further into the belly of the beast. I'd expect it to be darker in there, but it's not. The air seems to lighten the further in we get, until I see a square of night sky ahead of us.

"Where does this lead?" I ask.

"You'll see, Circ says, grabbing my hand and pulling me forward, more quickly now.

My heart starts beating faster.

"Close your eyes," Circ says as we approach the soft light.

171

I let my eyelids slip shut. I wanna peek, to squint, to cheat, but I resist the urge. Circ's giving me a treat, after all, he deserves my trust.

I take ten, fifteen, twenty more steps, never stumbling under Circ's guiding hand. He stops me with a firm touch on my hip. Spring butterflies swirl in my stomach. *We're just friends, just friends, just friends,* I think, trying to calm the butterflies. *Duty, honor, the Call.*

Breeding, Lara says in my head.

"Open your eyes," he says softly.

I do, gasping at the sight before me.

~~~

When I open my eyes, what I see is beautiful, but scary too, like the skeleton of a long-dead beast, its skin picked clean long ago by carrion-eaters.

We're in the center of the Hunting Lodge, which is exposed to the night sky. As always, the air is warm, even in the deepest part of the night. The Lodge and its series of rooms and passageways is really just a big, square wall, surrounding the yard we now stand in. Beneath us the dirt is hard-packed, trampled by dozens of Hunter feet, their footprints zigzagging this way and that. Wooden beams and walls and crossbeams rise and jut out and connect in an intricate pattern around the perimeter. Under the pale moonlight, that's what gives the Lodge a skeletal feel, like a mammoth creature has died here, and we're stuck in the middle of its elongated body. Somewhat scary.

But above us, there's only beauty. Although I've seen the moon and the stars countless times, nothing could compare to now. Something about the quiet protection of the fortress around us seems to magnify the brightness and colors and magnificence of the night sky, framing it all like a picture.

"Lie down," Circ says softly, pulling me to the durt.

As we have so many times before, Circ and I lie next to each other, hand in hand, staring up, watching the star servants wink and twinkle, flash in, flash out, *speak* to us.

"Oh," I murmur. Some of the stars are moving, shooting across the sky, born by wings, or by some extra-world power bestowed upon them by the moon goddess. They arc over us, their brightness leaving dazzling tails behind them, and then disappear beyond the Lodge walls.

"Good timing," Circ says, sitting up suddenly.

I sit up, too, across from him, still holding his hand, feeling a flutter in my chest.

Everything about Circ is right. The way I feel when I'm 'round him, safe and happy and excited; his easy-on-the-eyes smile that comes quicker'n a pack of Cotees to a fresh kill; his respect for life and all who live in fire country; his loyalty, above all else.

Releasing his hand, I touch my fingertips against the charms dangling from my tug-leather bracelet. The one for Skye. The one for my mother. The one for me, the tree.

The tree. On the night of my Call, I'll give it to the man I'm Called to be with, to live with, to Bear children with. Not Circ. He's too young, not eligible yet.

Breeding. The thought of lying with some stranger just to bring more children into this world seems to get more revolting the closer I get to my Call. And having more'n one woman do it with each man? Is that right? It's the way it's always been, I know, but that don't make it right, now does it?

I desperately wanna tear off my charm, give it to Circ, his to keep forever and ever, no matter who I end up with, no matter what the consequences. I'll tell my father I lost it, that it musta fallen off during the Killer attack. They'll make me a new one. Circ'll always have a part of me.

"That's not the way," Circ says, touching my finger with his, running it from nail to knuckle to hand, stopping, feeling, exploring. *What's happening? In the name of the sun goddess, how is this possible?*

Circ is strong, graceful, *important.* And I'm...

"Perfect," Circ says.

"What?" I say, my eyes taking in his.

"Don't even think those words about yourself. Don't even joke about them. Not now. Not ever again."

I search his fathomless brown eyes for a clue as to how he's doing this, how he's reading my thoughts as quickly as I think them. The answer's so obvious I've barely scratched the surface of the beauty his gaze hasta offer when I realize it: he knows me better'n I know myself.

I stand up, walk away from him, my mind overworked, practically spinning with Circ's touch, his eyes, his words. Once when I was a Midder, I overheard Skye ask my mother what a Call should be like. My mother smiled, knelt down, and said, "By the time you die, your Call should know you better than you know yourself."

Circ already knows everything about me.

But it's impossible—he can't be my Call. I can't let myself wish it, hope it, want it, not for even one second. For down that path lies only heartbreak.

It doesn't have to be this way.

174

Lara's words crash into me like a heavy wind. What if she's not crazy? What if there's some truth to what she says. What if whoever she's working with really does have something to offer me?

Think about what you want. And when the time comes, you'll know what decision to make.

My mother's words streak across my consciousness like the shooting stars we saw not a moment ago. What'd she mean? How can I possibly have what I want? I don't have a decision. I want Circ, but I can't have him. The Law says I can't.

Warm arms wrap 'round me from behind, startling me. Circ laughs.

"Did I frighten you out of your daydream?" he says.

I was so caught up in my thoughts, in the puzzles with no answers, that I'd almost forgotten he was there. Almost. "It's night," I say, draping my arms over his, pulling them close. How is this happening? He said it himself: We're just friends. Not his exact words, but close enough. Do friends hold each other like this?

"What?" he murmurs, nestling his lips into my hair. Warmth spreads down my spine.

"You said *day*dream. But it's night."

"Okay. *Night*dreams," he says. Keeping one of his hands tight against my stomach, his other drops to my waist, settles on my hip. "What were you *night*dreaming about?"

"How this is impossible," I say, at the same time wondering what *this* is.

Circ sighs. "Siena, when will you see the truth?" His question startles me. *The truth?* I don't even know what the truth is, or where to find it, so how can I see it? So many people are telling me so many different things and none of it

175

makes any searin' sense. "Sometimes I just wish you'd see yourself the way I see you. How strong, how graceful, how pretty. How funny…"

Funny? At least he got that part right, I think. I been known to crack a joke from time to time. But strong? No. Try skinny, barely thicker'n a tent pole. Graceful? More like clutzy. Pretty? I think you just shot your pointer into the durt.

"Circ, no," I say. "Don't kid."

Unexpectedly, he spins me 'round, pulls me in close, leans in—his lips are so close, like they've been so many times before, so close, but different this time, so different, like they're on fire, like they won't stop until they're against mine—

They stop, hovering inches from me. His words come out in hot bursts of breath. "I've wanted to do this for so long, Siena, and I have to before…before you're Called away and I never have another chance."

—and then his lips are against mine, warm and moving and right. Everything I've ever wanted. What *I* want. Not my father, or the Law, or anyone else. Me. My wants. My decisions.

It doesn't have to be like this.

It does.

It doesn't.

I've forgotten to breathe and suddenly I'm gasping for air, pulling away from him, laughing and choking—he's laughing too. A first kiss: inexperienced and somewhat embarrassing, but perfect in every way.

On my tiptoes, I hug him tight. He leans down and I crane my chin over his shoulder, nuzzling my head next to his, my eyes closed. Everything warm. Everything right.

My decision. My wants.

I open my eyes.

My father stands across the yard, fists clenched at his sides, glaring. Always glaring.

Seventeen

"I knew it!" he screams. "You're a little shilt!" Another pot rattles across the floor, ringing out when it stops against the base of the table.

I've seen my father angry a hundred times, but never like this. So angry, so violent. "Father, I didn't plan—"

"I. Don't. Care!" he spouts. "I saw what I saw. I told you to stay away from that—that—that *corrupting* Youngling, but you didn't listen. You disobeyed a direct order from ME! Not only your father but the Head Greynote. How do you think that will look to the rest of the people?"

My mouth opens to answer, but evidently he's not expecting one, 'cause he continues his rant. "I'll tell you how it'll look. It'll look like I can't even keep my own daughter in line. It'll look like I'm weak. They won't trust me."

"I wasn't trying to—"

"Trying?" He takes two giant steps, backing me into a corner in our hut. His veins are popping out of his red forehead. Like snakes they twist and curl across his head, from ear to ear. My head swivels, looking for help, even though I know there's none. Despite it being the middle of the night, when we got home Father woke everyone up, told them to go for a walk. Sari, Fauna, and Rafi scurried out like little ants, without even looking at me. But my mother, she moved slower despite my father's black mood. It was another small act of rebellion on her part. And as she passed me I could swear she smiled and gave a slight nod of her head, like she knew exactly what I did, that I was following what she said, thinking about what I want and acting on it. It felt a scorch of a lot like a nod of approval.

But now it's just my father and me.

I think he might kill me this time.

Even though he's dropped his voice to a whisper, he's so close that it thunders in my ears. "Enlighten me, Youngling. What were you *trying* to do with your face mashed against his?"

I hafta say something, to explain, to make him understand what I'm feeling, what I want. My mind is blank, emptier'n a prickler shell drunk dry. And my throat is dryer'n fire country in summer. My mouth opens but I have no words, and if I did, they couldn't come out anyway.

"'Zard got your tongue?" Father sneers.

A fire roars up my throat and out my mouth. "I wanna be with him, Father!"

Wrong answer.

He grabs me by the throat, hoists me up on the wall, holds me there, choking me. 'Cause I've just spoken the impassioned words I been feeling for so long, I didn't have a chance to take a breath 'fore he grabbed me, so I'm already running out of oxygen, desperately gulping at the air. My airways are closed. Nothing coming in, nothing going out.

"*Be* with him?" my father spits. "That's against the Law, Youngling, not that I should have to remind you."

My vision blurs, my arms go numb, then my legs. This is it. I made my decision and now I'll face the ultimate consequence. My plan failed.

He drops me and I'm too exhausted and confused to brace myself, so I crumple to the ground, banging my broken arm on the wall. Pain rips through me but I barely feel it, 'cause I'm choking, gasping, sucking down throat-burning gulps of life-giving air.

There's a shadow over me but I don't open my eyes.

"Know that I don't do this easily, Youngling. I'm trying to save you from yourself. One quarter full moon in Confinement," my father growls. "This is your last warning."

~~~

As it turns out, my plan worked, but I'm hardly feeling happy about it. I was s'posed to sneak out, meet Circ, get caught, get thrown in Confinement for another day or two. But then everything happened so fast—what in the scorch happened anyway?—with Circ, my muddled thoughts, the kiss, my father.

Everything's all confused now, out of line, with little hope of ever getting back into line. There's not much left to do, 'cept continue on with my plan.

"Hi, Perry," I say to my prickler neighbor when I crawl into my cage, feeling sandblasted from the windy trek across the desert. It wasn't Luger who escorted me this time, but a silent-type named Tod, who I didn't mind much.

"What'd you say?" Raja says from the cage next door.

She wasn't talking to you, Perry says. *Welcome back, Sie.*

"Hi, Raja," I say, crawling over to the side of the cage, too tired to walk upright.

"What're you doin' back here?" Raja looks even skinnier'n the last time I was here, as if everything's been sucked right on out of him, leaving just skin'n bones.

"It's a long story," I say.

"How long?" he asks.

"Too long, but I don't really feel like talking 'bout it."

"No, I mean, how long're you in for?" Raja says.

I hate to tell him. I might sound like I'm complaining, when, compared to his life sentence, a quarter full moon is but a blink and a wink. But he'll find out eventually. "A quarter full moon," I say, keeping my voice flat, trying not to sound either glad or cut up 'bout it.

"Ain't bad," he says. "Ain't good neither. A quarter full moon in here can kill someone as skinny as you."

"Thanks," I say.

"Sorry, I didn't mean to—I been in 'ere so long now I'm not real good at conversating no more. I talk to myself more'n real live humans."

"At least you're not talking to a prickler," I mumble.

"What was that?"

"Nothing," I say.

~ ~ ~

My nerves are coiled tighter'n a rattler ready to strike. Perry seems tense, too, all stiff and silent, so unlike him. The wind's only gotten stronger from earlier in the day.

I slept away the afternoon so I'd be wide awake for tonight. Now that the time's come, I'm considering waiting until tomorrow night. How can I focus on the task at hand with everything that's bouncing 'round in my head?

'Fraidy tug, Perry says unhelpfully.

Now *you've got something to say,* I think. But my wooloo thoughts are just what I need to motivate me to move forward with my plan.

Already the clinks and voices are moving away, soon to be out of earshot. I need to stay close enough to follow them. Relying on adrenaline and chants of *'Fraidy cat! 'Fraidy cat!* from Perry, I grab a bar with one hand, trying to think strong and brave thoughts.

I start climbing, shimmying my way up, one hand grip and foot slide at a time. The horny toad dance. It helps that I've done it once already, during a panicked life-or-death climb. This time is less stressful, more controlled. In less'n the time it takes for my father to lose his temper I'm at the top and squeezing between the bars, the only prisoner small enough to accomplish such a feat.

Lucky me. Skinny me. I blink hard when I remember what Circ said to me last night. *Don't even think those words about yourself. Don't even joke about them. Not now. Not ever again.* I take a deep breath. Okay. No more thoughts about being Runty, or Scrawny, or Skinny. By trying not to think them, I start thinking them more. I pound the heel of my hand against my forehead, trying to dislodge the thoughts, but now they're all I can think. Skinny. Scrawny. Runty. Skinny. Scrawny. Runty.

Perry takes up the chant, adding his own flair. *Skinniest, Scrawniest, Runtiest!*

Time's a-wasting, but how I can I safely climb back down when my mind's full of all this blaze? I gotta replace it with other thoughts, better thoughts. Circ's arms around me, on my hips. His lips pressed against mine. I feel flutters in my stomach and I'm okay again. Ready to move.

Ever so slowly, I ease my way over the edge, the wind battering me, threatening to toss me over the side. Getting up was easy, but I don't want a repeat of the last time when my only option for getting down was a free fall, broken only when my body smashed into the durt. A dull ache throbs through my legs and ribs just thinking 'bout it. Using my hand as a brake, I slide down the side, opening and tightening my fingers to regulate my speed. When my feet hit the bottom, pride surges through me. Even Perry says a few nice words, although I sense a hint of sarcasm in them.

Time's a-wasting.

I move out on footsteps so light a hard-tracking Cotee's ears would have trouble picking them up. The wind is whipping through my hair and I hafta dodge and duck as brambleweeds come a tumbling past, barely visible until the last moment. As cloudless as the previous night was, tonight's cloud*full*. I can't see a single star behind the heavy blanket of black and gray. The only light comes from occasional glances by the moon goddess as she peeks between the roiling clouds. It looks like a spring storm's coming, but it's way too early for that—we ain't even had our first sandstorm of the winter season yet.

I run and run and run, heading in the direction I saw the prisoners taking with their tools. Visibility is poor, good enough to see my own feet and what's just ahead, but not nearly enough to see much further; so I rely on my ears to alert me if I'm getting close, hoping against hope that their march hasn't become a silent one, in which case I might not know I've caught up until I run right into the back of one of them, a clumsy end to my brilliant plan. I'm also praying to the sun goddess that there ain't no packs of Cotees out here. They usually stick well south of the village, where the hurds of tug are plentiful, but you never can tell.

Soon I'm loster'n a blind burrow mouse in a maze of sand tunnels. The wind whips in every direction, starting to pick up bits of sand now, stinging and prickling my skin. If this turns into a sandstorm, I'm knocked. In the morning they'll find my empty cage, but they won't find me buried beneath ten feet of sand.

I'm about to turn back—whichever way back is—when I hear it. A clink, instantly lost on a shriek of wind. Then another. Careless tool carriers. Or carriers who don't care at all.

I make desperately for the sound, covering my eyes against the bursts of sand-filled wind, but craning my ear in what I think is the right direction. My heart leaps when I hear voices. Angry. Mutinous. "This is madness. We're all gonna die out here, you too, Keep." A voice I ain't never heard 'fore. One of the lifers.

"Shut yer mouth and quit yer complainin'!" Keep shouts. "We go back when I say we do."

I see them, finally. A haggard gaggle of prisoners, bent against the wind and sand, trudging at a snail's pace through the desert. No wonder I was able to catch up with them. Just as I spot them they stop. I freeze, drop to the ground, get a mouthful of sand as it splashes up.

There's more grumbling, but no one else is as bold as the last guy. When I peek my sand-crusted face over the dune, I see why. Keep's got a pointer notched, aimed toward the group, keeping his distance. They could rush him, but he'd take out a few of them 'fore they could get to him. And probably none of them are willing to die for t'others.

They start moving again, and almost right away, the wind dies down, the airborne sand drops back to the ground where it belongs, and the clouds part, revealing the bright and full moon. Strange timing.

"See! What'd I tell yer?" Keep barks. "I knew it'd clear. Just a warnin' storm. Nothin' more."

I follow silently.

It's a long hike, and now that I'm not worried about a deadly sandstorm popping up, I keep my distance from the prisoners to ensure I'm not spotted. My mind turns to the slight smile and nod my mother gave me 'fore she left the hut last night. She approved of what I was doing, I'm sure of it. My whole life my mother has been this quiet, weak figure, taking everything my father can dish out without even a word against him. But now…now she's an enigma. She's still mostly subservient, but it's like she's plotting and scheming in the background, delivering cryptic messages to me in prison. I wonder what set her off? Does she know something I don't? Or has she just had enough of his tirades, of his endless displays of power and authority? I might not be the sharpest pointer in the quiver, but I ain't stupid either. I know when something's cooking by the change in the air, the smell. And with my mother, something's definitely in the pot, maybe not boiling yet, but starting to simmer for sure. An enigma.

Something about the landscape changes, catching my attention. I look down at my feet. The sand has disappeared, replaced by hard-packed earth. Not necessarily unusual for the desert, but that's not what caught my attention. Green-stemmed plants poke from cracks in the dry earth, sprouting here and there. I kick at one with my toe and it bends all the way to the ground and then springs back up. Doesn't crack or break like the dried and withered scrubweeds near the village. These are *alive*. Growing.

In fire country, spring brings a hint of green as fireweed, scrubweeds, brambleweeds, and scrubgrass begin to grow with each successive rainfall. But just as quickly as it starts, the growing season ends, chased away by the early summer's heat. The plants turn brown, die, crack and blow away or become kindling for the summer brush fires that give our land its name.

It's still winter and there ain't no rain, least not in the desert. But maybe—

I lift my gaze and scan the country 'fore me. The prisoners are a long way off, but are halted, scattering their axes and picks around them. And towering over them: trees!

—we're not in fire country anymore.

In the dead of the night, lit only by the watchful gaze of the moon goddess and her endless legions of star servants, I get my first ever glimpse of ice country.

~~~

I've never seen live trees 'fore, but I know that's what they are. As endless as the sands of the desert, they rise up like watchtowers. And they don't just go back and back and back. They go up, too. The land rises and rises in an arc, gentle at first, but then steeper and steeper. A mountain! It's green and brown at the base, but quickly turns black as the trees thin out, disappear completely. And higher up, white. It's like the entire top portion of this bigger'n-anything-I-ever-seen mountain is capped with a white cloak. Unbelievable.

My breathing's all tight and heavy. I realize my lips are clamped shut and my nose is doing all the work. I open my mouth, breathe in the cool, night air. Cool? What? But it's the right word, far as I know. The...air...isn't...hot. I've only ever tasted cool air once 'fore. It was late winter and a spring rainstorm came real early, drowning fire country in three days of wet. On the third day, when everything was dripping and crying, it got downright shivery outside. I asked what it meant and my father said the air was cool.

Well, that's what it is now. Cool. Not hot. I shiver.

Ice country is not hot. Just like Teacher always said when we thought he'd been smoking too much fireweed.

For a moment, I try to focus on the trees, thankful for the moonlight. They're exactly like you hear them described. Tall beyond comprehension, they rise like giant spears into the sky, almost disappearing into the few low-altitude clouds drifting overhead. Their—what's that word for the coating of rough brown that protects the wood inside them? Oh yeah, *bark!*— their bark is full of so many shades of brown that I wanna rip off a piece and count them all later. Wooden arms shoot off in a million directions, some thick and heavy enough to hold the weight of a man, and others so spindly and thin they look as if they might break off in the wind. But where are all the leaves? In Learning, Teacher told us of the greenness of trees, of their millions of leaves, sprouting and growing, sprouting and growing, and eventually changing color in the autumn and...*falling off.* That's it. They've fallen off!

That explains the sudden increase in noise. Besides the men's voices, which have picked up again, a deafening sound has been added to the mix. Crunching, like when I munch on the brittle flesh of dried prickler. As the prisoner's pass amongst the trees, each footstep results in a thunderous *crunch!* that a Hunter could track for miles. Scorch, even I could track it.

They're walking on dead leaves, the ground covered in a thick layer of them. In the dark and from a distance, I can't make out the colors, but in my mind I picture them as red and gold and blue and yellow and every other color imaginable. Beautiful, fallen leaves, just like Teacher always described them.

As soon as they get beneath the trees, they start working. Keep's barking orders, pushing them this way and that, shoving one guy—it's Raja!—against a tree. He bounces off of it like it's stronger'n stone, goes to one knee, stands back up. Then he does the strangest thing. He hoists his axe over his shoulder, and slams it into the side of the tree with enough force to knock it clean over!

'Cept it doesn't fall over, doesn't so much as budge one little bit. It just stands there smiling at him, like they're having a good ol' chat. So he chops at it again. And again. And again. I watch in fascination as he keeps it up for a good long while. He stops, moves 'round to the other side, and keeps at it. Meanwhile, all 'round him, the others are doing the same thing. Swinging axes at trees, whacking at them like they got a bone to pick with them, like each tree is their worst enemy.

I've gotta get a closer look at this.

Heading east, I make my way toward the border of ice country in a wide arc, staying low to the ground, watching and listening for any signs that they see me. Everyone keeps working. I see the leaves on the ground, covering every last inch. If I step on them they'll crunch. So I slide my feet slowly along the ground, pushing through them. They make a gentle swishing sound, but it's too soft to draw anyone's attention.

When I reach the tree line, I look up. I've never felt so small in my life. The tree monster stands over me, rattling his branches and laughing. *I could squish you like a bug,* he says in between chortles. My thoughts, getting the better of me, as usual.

Tearing my gaze from the tip-tops of the trees, I touch a hand to the bark. It's rough. Rougher'n chipped and chiseled stone. Not at all like the smooth wood that we use to build our tents and huts.

Although I have the sudden inexplicable urge to stay within the confines of the trees, to walk amongst them, touching them, *learning* them, I wade back through the leaves and step onto the hard earth, which'll ensure my feet don't make any unwanted noises. The *cool* breeze raises strange bumps on my arms and the back of my neck. I shiver again. I feel weird all over.

Shaking it off, I creep along the trees, careful not to step on any of the twisted and curled leaves that've blown off into fire country. Each leaf is my enemy, capable of giving my position away. Step, check for leaves, step, check, step, listen, leaves, step.

I make it within twenty feet of the workers, stop, slide my feet along the ground to avoid crunching any leaves, duck behind a big ol' tree, clinging to the bark. Peek my head out.

That's when the first tree dies.

Eighteen

CRASH!

The tree falls to the ground like thunder, sending tremors through the soles of my moccasins. They killed it. They killed the tree.

CRASH! CRASH! CRASH!

The pure, cool night air is filled with a cacophony of more trees falling, brought low by the axes of the prisoners. Each tree falls perfectly into the desert, as if they prefer to die out in the open, under the gaze of the moon goddess than in the company of their brothers and sisters.

"Good work, tugs!" Keep yells. "One more round and we're done fer ternight."

I see Raja standing over a fallen tree, his elbows on his knees, his face aimed at the ground. He's exhausted. Panting.

Chopping down trees is hard work. The others are in similar positions. These're the lifers. Most of them woulda been in Confinement for quite a while, so they're skinny, underfed, in no condition for heavy labor. But they got no choice—the Keep's waving 'round his bow and pointer again.

"Back ter work!" he roars. I really don't like him anymore, want nothing more'n to take his bow and shove it up his—

One of the prisoner's falls. Not Raja, but a guy near him. Just keels right on over, like he ain't capable of staying on his feet for one second longer.

"Sear it all to scorch!" Keep growls. "We got another diver. Put 'im with ter others."

Raja lifts his head, looks at Keep. "I really think we should—"

"Yer not 'ere to think," Keep says. "Put 'im with ter others, or I put a pointer through yer skull."

Raja just stares at Keep, as if he's considering the offer, but then stumbles over to the guy on the ground. I see him whisper something to him, and the guy's eyes flash open for a moment, but then close again. There's defeat on his face, which is ghostly white under the moonglow. Too tired to fight on. Too tired to chop trees. Too tired to live.

Another prisoner comes over and helps Raja carry him out into the desert. I shrink back, keeping the tree between me and them, unable to tear my gaze away from the prisoner's body. They carry him to an area littered with broken white-painted branches and round sun-bleached rocks. I hadn't noticed them 'fore, but now that I see the strange white objects, they look so familiar, as if I've seen something like them 'fore. "Drop 'im!" Keep orders.

Facing away from Keep, Raja makes a face, ignores the order, lowers the body gently to the earth amongst the sticks and stones, as if it's some sort of altar. Touches the man's face gently. Leaves him there.

Dead under the moonglow.

~~~

The men are chopping again, distracted, and I wanna see what's so familiar 'bout the objects littered around the now-dead prisoner. I got no desire to be near a dead body—nuh uh, no thanks—but something about the white branches and stones draw me to them.

I'm so close to the working men now that each *chop, chop, chop* goes straight into my head, as if they're chopping at me and not the trees. My head starts to hurt.

Keeping my eyes on Keep, who's walking around shouting "encouragement" to the workers—like "Hurry it up or I's fixing ter beat the livin' scorch outta yers!" or "Don't make me put a pointer through yer brain, tugs!"—I reach the body. Fixing one eye on Keep, I aim my other eye at the white objects.

Some of them are strangely curved, while others are stick-straight, with knobs on the ends. The rocks are smooth, almost circular but not quite. Odd. The wind breathes a heavy gust and one of the rocks rolls toward me, clattering slightly on the hard ground. When it turns it's looking at me. Right at me. With sunken, eaten-away eyes.

Not a stone—a skull. Not branches—bones. This ain't no altar, no shrine. This is a graveyard.

Suddenly I'm gasping for air, shaking so hard I can't control it, trying—desperately trying—to turn away from the image of death that stands before me, but I can't, can't, like I'm being sucked in by the hollowed out eyes of the skull picked clean by the vultures and Cotees and whatever other animals might live in the no-man's-land between fire country and ice country.

Grabbing my head with my hand, I force it away from the desert, bury it into the side of a tree, still shaking—might never stop shaking—hot tears springing up and rolling down my cheeks. Silently sobbing. The lifers are sent here to work. And they're sent here to die.

At my feet the leaves look less like dried tree blossoms'n like curled, skeletonized hands chopped off at the wrists.

I shake, shake, shake some more, my fingers like claws, pulling at my hair, wiping away my tears, rubbing moisture on my dress.

A *CRASH!* that's startlingly close pulls me out of the shock caused by the skeletons. The next round of trees is falling. With each one, my mind clears a little and wrests a bit of control from my emotions. What's done is done. These people are dead. I gotta move forward, think of how to help the ones that're still alive.

I gotta think.

I's framed. Raja's words. If he's telling the truth—which I think he is—then this ain't just a 'spiracy. This is murder, plain and simple.

And who's behind it all? Raja says he was framed by a Greynote. And the Head of the Greynotes is…

…my father.

Can't be him. Father's mean and nasty and has a temper a mile wide, but a killer? He's always talking 'bout how it's my

194

duty to Bear, how we need to obey the Laws to ensure the survival of our people, the Heaters. But how're we gonna survive if we're framing and murdering our own? So it's probably some of t'other Greynotes, going behind his back, usurping his authority. Right?

I hear a new voice, unlike the others, both in tone and language. Wiping away a lingering tear, I ease around the tree to check things out.

There's a guy, dressed in heavy white skins, all draped over him like he's wearing blankets. Black, leather boots rise all the way to his knees. He's got a hat on too, furry with a tail on it. Like no one I've ever seen 'fore. His face is shrouded under a beard so thick there could be a whole family of burrow mice living in it. I know right away what he is:

An Icer.

Come from high in the mountains, he's talking to Keep. "Your workers are too freezin' slow," he says, his words clipped and precise. I ain't never heard anyone talk like that. I scan the workers for something to clue me in as to what *freezin'* mean, but don't see anything, so I got no clue what he's going on 'bout.

"They's tired. Hungry," Keep says. "We need more food fer 'em. Our people are starvin'"

"You'll get your food. But tell Roan this: if we don't get more production out of your men, we'll cut off the supply of wood and meat. Mark my words."

"I'll tell 'im," Keep says. "When'll we git ter food?"

The Icer folds his arms across his broad chest. "Tomorrow. It's a sacred day. First day of winter. We'll not have your men working on our land on a sacred day. But they can come to collect the meat and trees."

195

"We'll be 'ere," Keep says.

~~~

It feels like my eyes just closed when I see light on t'other side of their lids.

Morning's come faster'n a wildfire. And with it, a roaring, scattering of thoughts in my overloaded brain, as if the windstorm from last night is inside me. Everything 'bout last night feels like a dream—but I know it ain't. I saw what I saw. I heard what I heard. And now I want what I want. Which is answers.

I gotta talk to Raja, but he won't be too happy if I wake him up on so little sleep. So, instead, I wait patiently for him to awake on his own, enjoying the sunrise.

It's a good one, too, a burst of orange and red over the horizon, casting shimmery beams of light almost *through* the puffy yellow clouds that dot the sky. And just 'fore the outline of the sun goddess's eye appears, there's a burst of color. Not just the usual reds and oranges and yellows, but a flash of blue and green, too, so bright and beautiful that my heart skips a beat as I wonder at the powers that watch over us. The blue in particular reminds me of something Teacher once told us. He said the sky used to be all blue, not red like it is now. The red only came at sunrise and sunset. All us Younglings laughed behind his back after Learning, saying how Teacher'd lost his rocks, gone wooloo. None of us believed him.

But somehow, on this morning and seeing that burst of blue, I can almost picture the sky being all blue. *I'd rather the sky be purple with pink polka dots,* Perry comments.

"I bet you would," I mutter, silently reminding myself how silly it is to be talking to a prickler. But, with Raja sleeping like a pre-Totter, Perry's all I got.

Already I'm tired of waiting for Raja. I was up every bit as late as him, maybe later. I heard him come in, lie down, his breathing get heavy. He was bone-weary and slept right away. Me, I was exhausted, but took ages to doze off, what with all my rambling thoughts and ideas spinning and dancing through my mind.

Bones and skulls. I shiver, although, back in fire country I'm nothing but warm.

Enough. It's time to talk.

"Raja!" I hiss at the sleeping lifer in the cage next to me. "Get your shanky butt up or I'll start throwing rocks!"

"Uhhhh," Raja groans, rolling over. He's looking and acting like Veeva's guy, Grunt, on the morning after one of his fire juice nights.

I don't wanna get a reputation for making empty threats, so I pick up a small stone, find a clear bit of air where our cage bars line up, almost like the sights on a slingshot, and chuck it through.

The rock hits him in the head.

"Ahhh! What the scorch?" he cries, covering his face with his arms.

"Shhh! Keep your voice down or Keep'll hear you."

He mumbles into his arms. "Good. I wanna report a crime. Throwin' rocks at a defenseless, sleep-deprived man."

"Sorry, it's not like I was aiming for your head. I've never been very good at aiming things." I shrug, but Raja can't see it 'cause he's still tucked in his arm-cocoon.

He lifts an arm slowly, peering suspiciously through the bars at me, as if he thinks I'll chuck another rock at him. "You shouldn't be throwin' rocks if you can't aim," he says. Least he's keeping his voice down now.

"I hadta get your attention. I gotta talk to you."

He crawls over, still eyeing me strangely. "About what?"

"Where you and all the lifers went last night," I say firmly.

He rolls his eyes, starts to crawl away. "You must be wooloo. I already told you it's too dangerous to talk about that stuff."

"Wait! I was there."

He stops. Looks back over his shoulder. "Tugblaze," he says.

"I was. I followed you."

"Prove it."

My mind cycles through the memories of last night, as vivid as if I'm reliving them now. Them killing the trees, the dead lifer in the lifer boneyard, the Icer and his thick clothes and strange voice. I shiver again, as if the cold from the edge of ice country followed me all the way back to Confinement.

"We're done here," Raja says, taking my silence for lack of proof.

I keep my voice low, even. "You were chopping down trees, killing them. One of you died. You and another guy hadta carry him and dump him amongst the bones. There was a man. An Icer."

Raja just stares. I swear it's like a whole day passes, him staring, all silent and shocked. Twice I check to see if I've grown a second head, but it's still just the one. "I wanna help you," I finally say when it's clear he ain't gonna speak.

198

He shakes his head, snapping out of his stupor. "You can't help. No one can."

"You don't know that. I ain't a lifer. I'll be heading back to the village soon enough. I can talk to my father, tell him what's happening here."

"Your father?" Raja scoffs. "This is all his idea in the first place."

Now it's my turn to stare. There's no lie in Raja's thin, sun-leathered face. "Explain," I say.

"There's a lot you don't know, Siena."

"Then tell me." My voice is urgent, pleading, but I feel like I'm so close to the truth that I'll do anything to find it.

I'm about to squirm onto my knees and start begging, when Raja says, "Fine. But you didn't hear this from me, none of it. And don't blame me when you start pokin' around and get caught. They'll kill you."

I'm good at poking, Perry says.

Not now, I tell him.

The dead lifer pops into my head. Will that be my fate? Left for dead in a shallow grave? I blink away the thought and manage a nod.

"It's your death ceremony," Raja says, lowering his voice to start his story. "I been 'ere over a year, so I been able to put most of the pieces t'gether. When Shiva was struck with the Fire, your father started makin' his plans. Shiva was still Head Greynote, mind you, but he weren't callin' the shots no more. It was Roan. You with me so far?"

Nothing's surprising about any of this. "Yeah," I say.

"First thing Roan—your father—does is goes and talks to the Icers. Up till then the agreements with 'em were nothin' more than basic trade agreements. You know, like we give them tugskins and tug meat and they give us some wood for our tents and fires and such. But there was something else the Icy ones wanted. Something Shiva never let 'em have."

"What?" I say, leaning forward.

"'Ssurances."

"What kind of 'Ssurances?"

"See, they's scared of us. Not of *us* us, but of our disease. The Fire."

"What about the Fire?" I ask.

"Somethin' you gotta understand, Youngling, is that the Icies are tryin' to survive just like us. They's doin' better at it, too. I heard that they live ten, maybe even fifteen years longer'n us. Anythin' to threat'n their lives scares 'em."

The pieces just ain't making sense. I'm getting all this new information—the answers I been asking for—but I don't feel any better off. Maybe I'm asking the wrong questions. "So…they feel threatened by…the Fire?" I ask slowly.

"'Xactly. A while back a coupla their border guards came down with it. With the Fire. Died miserable deaths like nothin' the Icies'd ever seen before. The guards had had brief interactions with Heaters, so they blamed it on that."

I'm starting to see where this is going. "They wanted 'Ssurances we wouldn't spread the Fire in ice country," I say.

"Now yer gettin' it," Raja says. "Yer father agreed, in exchange fer double the wood, some meat, and help harvestin' the wood."

Ahh. It feels as if the sun just started shining down on my head, even though it's been doing that for our entire conversation. "That's why you and the other lifers hafta go up and chop wood every night." I frown. "But hold on. What's my father really doing for them? How do these 'Ssurances work?"

"Your father—"

Raja clamps up when we hear the scuff of footsteps off yonder. Not just one pair. Several. We give each other a look and Raja points off toward the entrance to Confinement.

Keep's door opens and he staggers out, looking like he's been beaten twice over and then run over by a raging tug bull. "More lifers?" he says to someone we can't see.

A whiny voice answers and I can picture his lips moving like a burrow mouse's. Luger. "They got caught doing all sorts of awful behavior. They won't see the other side of the bars for the rest of their miserable lives."

Luger comes into view, dragging a rope behind him. A guy appears, staggering. He's got bloodstains on his shirt, a black eye, bare feet. Then there's another one, in no better condition. And a third. A fourth. Four new lifers all at one time? Seems hard to believe that many serious crimes were committed overnight.

"Take better care of these ones, will you?" Luger says, handing the rope to Keep. "They weren't as easy to get and we're running out of men who aren't crucial to the village."

"They're criminals!" Keep bellows in one of the lifer's face. The poor guy jumps back. "Whatddya want me ter do? Set down with 'em and have a cup of herby tea?"

To my surprise, Luger grabs Keep by the shirt, shoves him up against his own hut, and holds him there. "Quit killing them," he says. "Head Greynote Roan orders you to feed the lifers three times each and every day. They need to keep their strength up. Are we clear?"

Keep is wide-eyed and blank-faced, but he nods.

Luger releases him, looks at his hand like it's covered in blaze, and wipes it on his britches. "Handle them yourself," he spits, heading back in the direction of the village.

"Handle 'em yerself," Keep grunts when Luger's out of earshot. He shoves one of the prisoners, who barges into another one. "I'll handle 'em alright. Handle 'em right to their graves."

He stalks off, pulling the wobbly-footed prisoners like Totters behind him.

My heart is beating fast and I notice I'm gripping the bar tightly with my good hand, like I might be able to snap it in half. My knuckles are white.

Raja's staring at my hand. "Don't git yerself all riled up. Ain't nothin' none of us can do to stop 'em."

"What were you 'bout to say 'bout my father 'fore they showed up?" I ask.

Raja scratches his head, trying to remember. His eyes light up. "Oh, that's right. The 'Ssurances. Yer father's set up border patrols all along the ice country border, so's the Icers don't have to. No one goes in, no one goes out."

"Is that everything?" I say.

"That's it. The big 'spiracy. Hope you don't git yerself killed over it."

I turn away from him, my back against the bars. I need to think. Luckily, I have another six days to think.

Nineteen

I been thinking for four days, but ain't nothing come to me yet. It doesn't help that Perry's interrupting me constantly with wooloo questions like *What's it like to have legs?* and *You'd never eat a friendly prickler like me, would you?*

Sure to his word, Keep's been feeding the lifers three times a day to our one, but Raja showed me how Keep also cut the portions by a third, so they end up getting the same exact amount of food in the end. Yeah, Keep's a baggard alright, through and through. And every night Raja and t'others get forced to go work the trees. I considered following them again, but it'd be a risk and I already know what they're doing, so I just wait 'round in my cage for them to get back, thinking about everything I know, and worrying about whether Raja's getting dumped with the bones. But every night he comes back and we look at each other. I see the weariness in his eyes, the defeat, the broken will. "Never give up," I tell him, and then we both go to sleep.

Every day the winds swirl faster, along with my thoughts. My father. 'Ssurances. The Fire. Keep us out. More meat. More wood. More lifers. Border patrols. It's all a mess of information and I don't know how to organize it all. Nor do I know what in the scorch to do with it. My instinct is to rush straight to my father when I get home, demand that he stop making innocent men lifers, stop killing them, come clean with the village 'bout his agreement with the Icers.

What'll he do? He'll get out his snapper, add some scars to my skin, and then probably send me back to Confinement until the Call. I need a more subtle approach.

But first there's an even bigger question I need to figure out. Why is my father doing this? A few days back I thought the answer was obvious—'cause we need more food and wood to survive—but now I ain't so sure. Why would he kill off good men who can help hunt and protect the village? Even if we get a little extra food and timber it's still working backwards.

It's almost like he just wants to control us, keep us all in check, away from the rest of the world. Circ's question: *Have you ever wondered what else is out there?* Maybe that's exactly what my father doesn't want us to wonder. If we're too busy struggling to survive, to grow the tribe, to fulfill our duties as Bearers or Hunters or Greynotes or whatever, we won't be thinking 'bout whether there's more to life'n all this. Which means we'll *stay*. In his control. Under his protection.

He's always controlled my life, so why not on a larger scale?

But that can't be it. No matter how lucky he is, the Fire'll get him in the next coupla years, so what's the point?

~~~

It's my last day in Confinement—thank the sun goddess!—and I've decided to start by telling Circ everything I've learned and then we can decide together what to do 'bout it. I already feel relieved that someone else'll know—besides Raja and Perry, who ain't much help.

Circ.

It's weird how I haven't seen him since we kissed. I was marched straight home by my bull-headed father and Circ was told to go home, too. That my father would deal with him later. I wonder what punishment he received. I almost laugh at the thought. Probably shoveling blaze. Or hauling water. Something exhausting and mind-numbing. Sort of like Confinement, but in a physical, rather'n mental way.

In any case, surely he wouldn't be allowed to visit me, so that explains why I been left to my own thoughts with only Perry and Raja to talk to.

It'll be hard to talk to him back in the village without my father finding out, but we'll find a way. We've always got Learning, too. My father can't take that away—it's required for all Younglings.

Yeah, things'll get better as soon as I see Circ again.

I'm glad it's not Luger that arrives to take me back. Just some other Greynote, all serious and bored-like. I don't say a word to him, nor him to me, and we're both okay with that.

I wave to still-sleeping Raja and still-standing Perry as I leave.

Don't let the cage hit your arse on the way out, Perry says.

The hike is long and dark, but at least it's in the right direction. Toward home.

When we crest a dune and the village comes into view, the Greynote extends a hand as if to say, "I've done my duty, now get the scorch out of here." I don't need a second invitation as I'm already running, feeling the wonderful, delicious burn of my underused muscles as they begin to exert themselves. I'm growing more and more comfortable with only having one good arm to swing while I run. When my wrist is finally healed I wonder if it'll throw me off balance again now that I'm used to not having it. Knowing my level of clumsy, the answer's probably yes.

As I pass the tower guards I flash a smile and offer a wave. They just stare at me with heavy eyes, but even they can't break my mood. Not today. I get to see Circ. Things are bad with the 'spiracy I now know all 'bout, but not so bad that me and Circ won't be able to come up with something to fix it. Today I have hope. Today I'm free. Maybe not so free that I can run off to ice country and join the Icies, but I'm not behind bars, and that's good enough for me.

It's still early, the sun barely spreading its light in soft tones across the desert, but I have the urge to run straight to the west tent sector, where Circ's family lives. Just the thought of it sends bubbles bouncing around in my stomach, a lightness filling my chest. Can't. I gotta be strong. Patient. Gotta wait until Learning. I'll see him there and then everything'll be fine.

So I head for home, hoping Father's already left for the day.

He hasn't. He's sitting outside, as if he's waiting for me. Pop. Pop! Popopopopopop! The bubbles of excitement explode in my stomach, leaving me feeling ill. Ill that this is the man who raised me, who's my father, who'd allow innocent men to die for the sake of making 'Ssurances to the Icies. Heat rises in my belly, washing away the sick feeling.

I take a deep breath as I approach. I can't let him know that I know. Not yet.

I stand 'fore him, shifting from side to side, all awkward-like. It's a show. I feel more centered'n I ever have 'fore. More sure of myself. More sure of what's good and what's bad in this world.

"Welcome home, Youngling," he says, standing, towering over me. He's just trying to intimidate me, I say to myself.

"Thank you, Father," I say, fighting the sarcasm out of my voice. Steady. Steady.

"I asked you this after your previous stay in Confinement, and I hope this is the last time I have to ask you. Have you learned your lesson?" I feel like his dark eyes are staring into the very pit of my mind, where the truth lies. But I can't tell him the truth or I'll end up right back in Confinement.

"Yes." A lie, but a necessary one.

His eyes narrow. "I don't believe you. But you *are* going to learn, one way or another." He strides off, leaving me surprised and confused.

~ ~ ~

I try to act natural as I head to Learning, but I know I'm walking way too fast. Most Younglings dawdle, drag their feet, look for anything to distract them. Me, I'm head forward, taking shortcuts, making record time. I'm hoping Circ'll be early too.

When I enter the roofless structure, my head swivels 'round expectantly. Empty. I was so fast I even beat Circ. No matter. I've waited a a quarter full moon—I can wait a while longer.

I sit cross-legged in the back corner, a highly-coveted spot conducive to mischief and whispered conversations.

I hear footfalls and Lara enters. Her hair is even shorter, cut almost to the scalp. Maybe she did shave it all the way to the skin and I missed it, only seeing it now that it's grown while I been away. I expect her to sit next to me, to start talking my ear off and asking questions 'bout Confinement, but she silently takes her normal seat near the front of the room.

Odd.

Silence.

Teacher Mas enters carrying a bundle of scrolls, glances at me, moves to the front.

Where's Circ? It must be getting close to Learning time, but it's still just me and Lara. Dreadfully silent.

The silence is broken when a chorus of voices and scrapes and laughter carry in from outside. Younglings pour into the open-air hut, talking and bumping and shouting. I scan the crowd, my heart leaping as I expect Circ to head for me at any second. I get some curious stares, but no one approaches me until—

"Mind if I sit?" Hawk says.

I curl my lips in disgust. "Keep moving," I say.

"I got a message from Circ," he says, cupping a hand over his mouth, as if someone might be reading his lips.

"You're full of it," I say, refusing to take the bait. I sense there's a punchline coming.

"I ain't lyin'!" he protests. "I owe him, all right?"

Everyone's inside now. Everyone 'cept Circ. Maybe Hawk does know something 'bout where he is. Even though I may be setting myself up for embarrassment, I'm willing to risk it. "Okay. Sit," I say.

"Look, I ain't your friend, or Circ's neither, so don't get the wrong idea," Hawk says.

"Just spit it out, Hawk," I say, refusing to look at him.

"Fine. When you got drug away to Confinement, Circ got sent on another mission."

My heart sinks into my stomach. "What other mission?" I say.

"Like the last one," he says. "A small one. Just a few Hunters."

My eyes narrow and I glance at him. Teacher starts talking so I lean close to his ear, dropping my voice to a whisper. "How do you know 'bout that? It was secret."

"I'm a Hunter, remember?" Right. He might know more'n I give him credit for. "Anyway, it don't matter. Circ left, okay?" I nod. Okay.

"How long ago?" Teacher's attention is on t'other side of the room. Lara's answering whatever question he asked.

"That's the thing. He left the same day you did. The mission was only s'posed to be three days. None of 'em have come back yet."

~~~

My head's hot, but not 'cause I'm sitting in the sun.

I don't have a clue what happened in Learning. It was all a blur. Thankfully, Teacher didn't ask me any questions, 'cause I don't know if I coulda spoken, or even understood them.

209

Circ's been gone seven days on a three-day mission.

Normally, I'd be worried but I wouldn't jump to conclusions, but this time is different. He's in Killer country. And it's my father that sent him there.

Anger curls my toes and boils in my stomach.

"He did this on purpose," I growl under my breath. A group of Youngling girls who're chatting a mile a moment outside the Learning Hut look at me strangely and laugh. I wanna go over and punch them. I stand, seething, consider heading in their direction, but think better of it. Not only would I lose a fight against five other girls, but I'd end up in Confinement again. Now that I know what I know, that's the last place I wanna be.

I'm lost in a sea of nothingness.

Everywhere I look people are going 'bout their business, washing clothes, cooking food, repairing tents. Kids are laughing, playing, running off all the pent up energy from another boring day of Learning. But none of it means anything with Circ missing.

I don't know where to go or what to do when I get there, what to say or who to say it to. I'm empty.

My father.

I could confront him, give him a piece of my mind, but not only would that not bring Circ back, but that's exactly what he wants. He wants to get under my skin, to see that he's not only the controller of my life, but of my mind too. That he can make me angry and sad and upset. I won't give him that pleasure.

There's only one other option then. Something I wouldn't have considered a year ago 'cause I was just a scared little girl. But now I'm desperate, on the verge of becoming a Bearer without my best friend to talk to 'bout it. My best friend who kissed me, who held me, who *changed* me. If my mother says I hafta go after what I want, then that's what I'm gonna do.

I'm going after Circ.

Even as I make my mind up, breathless and scared and excited 'bout the decision, a cry goes up from the tower guards. I'm not that close to the edge of town, but they're yelling pretty loud. I crane my head, waiting to hear it. Waiting, waiting, waiting: for the bells. The guards'll shout 'bout pretty much anything—a harmless burrow mouse scampering across the desert, an increase in the winds, a sneaky shilt and her guy out for a midnight rendezvous outside the border tents—but they'll only ring the bells if there's imminent danger to the village. Like when the Glassies attacked. Or during the Killer War. Sandstorms and wildfires receive a bell-toll too.

Their shouts grow more urgent, but there's no bell. No danger. Not for the village. But they keep shouting. I scan the towers that poke like fingers into the air, high above the village. They're all yelling to each other, trying to get information through the chain, from whichever guard spotted something worth yelling 'bout. Every guard is still in his tower—'cept one. My eyes lock on the empty tower, slide down its ladder, focus on the guard frantically climbing down.

I run in that direction.

~ ~ ~

I don't know what comes over me, but I run like the wind. It's gusting at my back and then it's gone, like I've outdistanced it, leaving me sprinting past surprised villagers in a calm bubble.

It's him. I know it. Circ and t'other men on the mission have returned. Rushing to see Circ'll not go down well with my

211

father, but I hafta. I hafta see his smiling and dimpled face, hafta hear his laugh, hafta smell the dust on his skin.

Reaching the tower at almost the same time as the watchman reaches the bottom rung, I ignore his shout as I fly past him, out into the desert. If we're under attack, I'm rushing straight to death. *There were no bells*, I remind myself. No attack.

I peer across the winter wasteland, feeling the wind catch up to me as I slow my pace, swirling around my feet, swishing my dress back and forth. I see them.

The Hunters coming back from their mission. A small group. Pitifully small considering they might be facing Killers. Five men. Four walking—no, *trudging*, heavy-footed and on the verge of collapse. And one being carried horizontally across another's shoulders. Something bad happened to these Hunters.

I rush forward, squinting to make out the faces. When I get close enough to see details, I realize: none of the four walking are Circ.

An exhausted groan slips from my throat. Not him. *Please, sun goddess, please*, I pray. It's been sunny all day, not a cloud in the sky, but at that moment, just after my silent plea, the world goes dim. I look up, feeling fear and dread in my heart, as a mountain of dark clouds blot out the sun as completely as if it were dusk.

The smell of death lingers on the air, tangy and metallic.

I reach the Hunters, who're too tired to be surprised at the sudden presence of a Youngling in their midst. They're older'n Circ, but not by much, perhaps only on their first Call, or maybe second.

They all have injuries: cuts and scrapes and claw marks. Killer wounds.

212

"I know him," I say, panting, my elbows on my knees. "Please. Is he okay?"

Across the Hunter's shoulders, Circ groans.

He's alive.

Another Hunter helps pull Circ down, lays him in the durt. I hear wheels rattling across the uneven terrain behind me. Help's on the way. I kneel down, lean over him, touch his dust and bloodstained face. "I'm here, Circ," I say softly.

His eyes ease open, and when he sees me he manages a smile. "Sie," he says, his voice barely audible over the sound of the wind whipping through our clothes.

"Yes, it's me," I say, taking in his injuries. His hair is matted with blood, aged and reddish-brown. His brown tugskin shirt is soaked through with blood, concentrated at a point where there's a gnarled and torn hole. I can't see the extent of the damage 'cause there's too much blood. If he can't walk, it must be bad. I've seen Circ leap up after nasty injuries, fight through it. He's not the type to be carried 'round like a dead man.

Tears blur my vision. Circ. Oh, Circ.

"It's gonna be okay," I say. "Everything's gonna be okay." I think I'm saying it more for myself.

"The Killers found us," he murmurs. "We barely..." His voice falters and his eyelids flutter.

"Shhh," I say, fighting back a sob. "We'll get you help. MedMa'll help." A stream is running down my face, dripping on his clothes, mixing with his blood.

Circ sees me, his eyes clear once more. His face twists in agony. The tears start tumbling down his face now, too. I think it's 'cause he's scared to die, but then I see it in the swirls of his deep brown eyes and realize: he's crying for me. Even in this condition, he's focused on *my* pain, *my* anguish, *my* fear that he's gonna die. He's crying for me when he's the one dying.

Shouts behind us. Wheels rattling over stones. A whole village of people—my people—who don't mean a searin' thing without him.

"Sie," Circ says, his voice sounding stronger'n before. "Sie, I need you to know something." I'm holding my breath, furiously blinking back tears. He fumbles at his wrist, almost frantic, like he's fighting against time. His time.

He locates his bracelet, his charms. Snaps the leather, pulls one off. I can't hold my breath any longer so I let it out in a gasp. "Circ, what are you—"

"Shhh," he says, his voice sounding almost normal. Like usual, he's comforting me. Am I the one dying? Did I fall from my cell in Confinement when I was trying to follow the workers? Did I dream everything? Am I dreaming now, in a confused state?

Reality comes rushing back when MedMa's wagon rattles to a stop next to Circ. No, I'm not dreaming. Circ is dying, right 'fore my very eyes. Using his last few breaths to comfort me.

"Circ, I—"

"Take this," he says, stuffing the charm into my hand, closing my fingers over it. MedMa and his apprentice rush 'round the cart. "Please know that someday we'll be together."

He grabs my wrist, squeezes it. MedMa lifts him into the wagon, starts rolling him away. "No!" I cry. "No, Circ, no. Don't leave me. Don't..." I collapse in the dust, mental and physical exhaustion setting in.

I lie still for a moment or two. When I sit up I feel empty, like the butcher's gutted me. No heart. No will. No nothing. My fist is clenched and I feel the bite of cold metal in my skin.

When I peel back my fingers I see it. Circ's charm, a pointer. His gift for his first Call. He's given it to me.

Twenty

Eventually I come to my senses. Chase after MedMa's wagon, catch up just as it reaches the Place of Healing. Circ is unconscious but still alive.

He can't die. He said it himself:

Someday we'll be together.

I hafta wait outside. MedMa has work to do. He makes it sound so ordinary. Work. Like building a tent or chopping down a tree or shoveling blaze. Work, like saving Circ's life.

The sun comes out again. I search the sky but the dark clouds from earlier are gone, vanished. Not moved on. Just gone. I pray it's not a sign for Circ. For us.

I sit in the durt, prop against the Healing hut. Spin Circ's pointer charm through my fingers, watching it catch the light. Under the Law, he's not permitted to give it to me, but he did.

If he survives I don't know what it'll mean. He's too young to be a Call, and anyway, you can't choose. The Greynotes decide. I unfasten my bracelet and slide his charm onto the band, next to mine. The tree and the pointer. Together at last.

For what it's worth, I think healing thoughts for Circ.

He won't die. He won't. Can't. I'm two full moons from my Call, the most important moment of my life, so he hasta be there, right? He's young, strong, invincible. Good at everything. Even surviving. He'll survive, 'cause he never loses.

Everything catches up with me at that moment. The constant name-calling at Learning. The endless fights with my father. Confinement. The boneyard on the edge of ice country. Raja, framed for murder. My broken wrist. Saving Circ from the Killers only to find him on a knife's blade. My body shakes and shudders, my hands trembling as I tuck them 'round my head. Every tear I have left pours from my eyes like a spring rain—the flood of the last few full moons of my shattered and broken life.

Without him, it's over.

MedMa opens the door.

I look up, unable to see, but seeing more clearly'n I've ever seen 'fore.

Circ's dead.

"I'm sorry. I did everything I could," MedMa says. I hate him. Hate his apologies. Hate the Killers. Hate 'spiracies and life sentences and duty and the Law. Hate my father.

As I stand up, my face is full of heat. From the hot, bubbling tears that well up from tear ducts that shoulda been empty long ago. From the anger coursing through every blood-carrying vein in my body. From the sun that's beating—*beating, smashing, pummeling*—down upon me. There's no mercy in the sun goddess's gaze. Not today. I hate her, too.

I run.

~~~

I don't know where I go, or how far, or who I see. There're voices, so many voices, but none of them are alive. Not to me.

Not even I'm alive. I can't be, not if Circ's not.

My legs are already exhausted but I don't notice the way they ache and throb. Just keep running. Through the village at first, I think, and then not. Out into the desert somewhere. Away. Just away.

And then I'm there.

Our place. The Mouth.

Our dunes.

Empty, so empty, without Circ's laughter, his jokes, his knees touching mine, his warmth against me. It doesn't even feel like a real place anymore.

My legs falter and I fall, feeling a twinge of pain in my injured arm as I land on it. The pain helps. I crawl my way to our nook, scrabble in the sand, scooping out shovelfuls till I've made a hole, big enough for only one. Curl up inside it, close my eyes, pretend the sand that's closing in around me is him, holding me, protecting me.

Someday we'll be together.

How could he lie to me like that? Someday'll never come. Never. Even if he'd lived it wouldn't have come. The Law wouldn't allow it. My father wouldn't allow it.

With the wind blowing grains of sand over me and the sky darkening to dusk, I cry myself to sleep, held only by a pocket of sand and memories of Circ.

~~~

Blackness greets me when I wake. The merciless sun goddess is asleep and the moon goddess and her lieges are taking a day off.

For a moment I don't know where I am and I thrash about, as if I'm being attacked. But then I feel it. The sand, soft and warm against my fingertips, tucked 'round me. In a muddled stream of images, everything comes rushing back. Circ's anguished expression as he pushed the charm into my hand. MedMa shaking his head. My run into the desert.

My mother'll be worried 'bout me, but I don't care. It's as much her fault as my father's that this happened. She encouraged me to think 'bout what I want, make my own decisions. Well I did and look where it got me. Look where it got Circ. I killed him. 'Cause I made him sneak out that night, all to grizz off my father, get him to send me back to Confinement so I could play investigator.

A Cotee howls in the distance, perhaps 'cause he's picked up my scent, or maybe for no reason at all. Regardless, it gives me the chills. I roll out, stand up, wipe the salt and sand from my face, and walk numbly back toward the lights of the village. There are still a lot of them, so it's not that late.

With each step the anger builds.

By the time I reach our hut, my body is coiled and ready to strike. I'll fight anyone or anything right now. With my scrawny body, I'll probably lose, but I'll fight. I open the door.

My mother leaps up from where she's sitting, rushes to me, but I stop her with a hand and a look. "Siena," she says, "I'm so sor—"

"Don't," I say through my teeth.

Sari shepherds my Call-Brother and Call-Sister out the door into the night. She knows that whatever's 'bout to go down is not for childrens' eyes.

My father rises behind her, less quickly, at his own measured pace. There's compassion in his eyes, in his tone. False compassion. "Yes, Siena. We're both very sorry. It's a true tragedy for the village."

"For the village?" I say, my voice rising. "This is your fault. Yours alone."

"It's no one's fault, Youngling. Life is fragile, especially for us. We lost another three to the Fire today. All we have is duty, the Law."

I take a step forward. "Don't," my mother warns.

"Why not, Mother? Isn't this what you wanted me to do? To stand up for myself? To be my own woman? To be everything that you're not?"

"Oh-ho! So you've been having secret mother/daughter talks, have you?" my father scoffs. "Women—all talk and no action. It's no wonder you only have a single purpose."

Breeding breeding breeding BREEDING! The unspoken words rampage through my mind, stirring me to life, roaring inside of me. I'm 'bout to let all my anger, all my pent up frustration out when—

My mother whirls on him. She's no longer the timid woman I grew up with. There's a spark in her as she steps into my father's circle, gets into his personal space. "You know nothing!" she says.

My father seems as shocked as I am. He actually leans away from her, as if scared of her rage, of what she might do to him. But his recovery is swift. Rocking on his heel, he launches himself forward and pushes my mother with both hands. She looks like one of my old dolls as she flies across the hut. So small. So weak. So full of nothing but bits of scrubgrass and tug hair. She reminds me of myself.

Her body doesn't stop moving until it slams into the wall, back first, a sickening crack of spine and shoulder blades against wood. Eyes widening in pain and surprise, she slides down the wall, slumping in a pile on the floor, nothing more'n a doll, tossed aside, leaching every last bit of my anger out of me.

My heart is in my throat, for despite my anger toward my mother, I love her. She's the only one who's stuck up for me against my father. "Sun goddess, Father. What've you done?"

He just frowns at me, his mouth contorted in rage. "This is the end of it. Now we get on with our lives," he says 'fore storming out of the hut, slamming the door behind him.

I go to my mother, kneel by her, cradle her head in my arms. She can barely hold herself up, so I do it for her. She cries, and I do, too, more tears for a day that seems built on them. We don't talk about it, but I know we're both crying for Circ, and for my lost sisters, Skye and Jade, and for each other. We don't stop for a long time.

No one returns home that night.

Twenty-One

It don't seem right the way life goes on. Someone that matters to you more'n life itself dies, and yet you go on existing, as if nothing's changed. You still have duties, responsibilities, routines. Things to do, like getting my arm unwrapped 'cause it's healed now. All these things that used to seem so searin' important, that you worried so much about, are meaningless. And yet—yet you go on doing them 'cause you must. Or people'll talk, people'll worry. They'll say, "I'm worried about Siena, I don't think she's ever gotten over Circ's death." Don't they understand? Don't they get it? There's no getting over the death of someone like that, someone who you lived for, laughed for, cared for. No. The most you can hope to do is carry on, get through a day, a full moon, a year, and eventually a lifetime without them. In your every act you hafta try to make them proud just in case they're looking down from somewhere, watching you, a new star in the sky, shining brighter'n t'others. Circ's definitely a star. When I look at the night sky now I see him, bright and beautiful. I thought I'd memorized the heavens, but when I look up now I always see at least one new star. Someone else good has died. Either from our village or from somewhere else. But I know the brightest new star is Circ.

I went to his fire ceremony, watched as his body, covered by a black shroud, was lit atop a pyre and sent back to the land of the gods. I felt like I was being burned too.

Winter is getting on, is almost over, and I still cry some nights when I look at the stars, but with each passing day I'm feeling better, stronger, ready to do what I hafta in this life to make Circ proud. There's a great weight on my shoulders 'cause I live for the both of us now.

When I think about the end of winter and the approach of spring, burrow mice squirm in my stomach. 'Cause this year spring means so much more'n the rains, the Growing, the return of the tug hurds to our area. It means I turn sixteen. It means the Call.

Burrow mice squirm.

Vultures peck.

Pricklers prickle.

All in my gut, squirming and pecking and prickling all at once.

So I try not to think 'bout it. I try to think about other things. I think 'bout how the wind seems to build every day, sometimes raging into horrendous winter windstorms so powerful all we can do is huddle in our huts and tents and wait for it to pass, hoping we don't get blown away. But the wind, no matter how strong, can't seem to pick up enough sand to create the first sandstorm of the waning season. Everyone's talking 'bout it. How we've never had a winter without at least a half dozen major sandstorms. How the sun goddess is blessing us, giving us a break this year 'cause we desperately need it. I don't know if I believe all that. It seems to me the wind is just saving itself for a time when we least expect it.

No one really talks to me anymore. In Learning I'm the same ol' outcast, but it don't really bother me. I don't want to talk to them either. Hawk and his goons pretty much leave me alone now, although I do catch them staring and laughing sometimes. Lara talks to me sometimes, but not the way she used to, 'bout doing things differently and thinking 'bout things. Our chats are much more boring, 'bout the weather, 'bout Learning assignments, that kinda thing. I feel like, in time, we might actually be real friends.

At home things are weird. Sari avoids me like the plague, and I think she's told Rafi and Fauna not to talk to me either, as if she thinks all my bad luck'll rub off on her kids. I've never really liked her anyway. My father keeps up his drivel about duty and the Law, but I've learned not to get so angry about it. I just ignore him. I try not to look at him either, 'cause when I do, I see the bones of the dead lifers from Confinement. Any notions I had of being able to help them went out the window when Circ died. Sorry, Raja. I failed you 'fore I ever really got started helping.

The nice thing is that Mother and I talk more. We've found a common enemy in my father, and it's brought us so much closer. We go for long walks, like the one we're on now, talking about the past, the present, and the future. Mostly it's talk about the goings on in the village, but every once in a while, I'll hear something in her voice, a catch, that makes me think she wants to say something else. But she never does. *Maybe I can draw it outta her*, I think as we circle the village for the third time.

"Mother?" I say.

"Siena?" she says, matching my serious tone and making me laugh.

"Why…" I let the word hang, the anticipation of a question. Should I ask it?

It drops to the durt and I hang my head a little. 'Fraidy tug, I think.

"Why what, Siena?" she nudges.

"I, uh, just been thinking…"

"Dangerous, that," she says with a wink.

"How come we never really stand up to Father?" I blurt out, right away wishing I'd held it back, never thought to say it.

She stops suddenly, her face going whiter than my Call dress, grabs my arm. I think she's mad until she says, "We do, Siena. In our own way. Never think he owns you, you hear me?"

Shaken, I nod slowly. "But when he's hurting me, when he's snapping me, you always walk away."

Mother closes her eyes and she looks sad, so sad, sadder'n she looked when Skye disappeared, sadder'n when Jade died so young. Too sad for what I just said.

"I—I can't stop him," she says. "Not now. I'm so sorry, Siena. I want to—all I want to do is protect you—but we have to wait. We just have to wait for the right time."

The right time? But when is that? And what do we do when we get there? I wanna ask—so burnin' badly, a million and one questions poking all through my mind like prickler stems—but I can't 'cause she pulls me forward hard, as a bunch of Greynotes pass us by.

~~~

No matter how many problems I got, there's always Veeva. Her crazy life keeps me entertained and busy. That's where I am now—in her tent. The winds have been particularly unkind to their tent—which is sagging in the middle, bent and broken, ready to collapse at any second—probably 'cause Grunt did such a poor job constructing it in the first place. Veeva always tells me he's good with his hands, but I don't think she's talking about tent-building.

"Take him, Woman," Grunt grunts, handing a squirming nine-full-moon-old Polk to Veeva.

"Oh no, hot stuff, you ain't gettin' out of bundlin' 'im. Not this time. And if you call me Woman again, I won't lie with you fer a quarter full moon." Veeva's got one arm holding the baby, t'other on her hip, and a third hand figuratively clutching Grunt's manparts.

I'm trying not to crack up.

"Okay, okay," Grunt says, throwing up his tug-sausage fingers. "No need to make them threats of yers, Vee. I'm doin' the best I can. I gotta fix this burnin' tent before it kills us all!"

"I can bundle him," I suggest, trying to be helpful.

Veeva warns me off with a shake of her head. She's got something else up her sleeve. "Mmm, well if you can bundle this beautiful baby of yers *and* fix this here dyin' tent, I got a special surprise fer you." In an act that I find somewhat disgusting, and a whole lot intriguing, she sticks out her chest and shakes her enormous bosoms, which, I might add, are practically falling out of her loose top. Grunt's eyes get bigger'n the moon and Polk grabs at her bouncing breasts like they

226

might be a fun toy to play with. I'm relatively inexperienced in such things—other'n what Veeva's told me—but perhaps to Grunt, Veeva's overly ample chest *is* a fun toy to play with. The way his eyes're bugging out of his head certainly seems to indicate it.

"I'll do it, Woman!" he shouts, his big ol' belly flopping as he raises his fist above his head. He catches himself. "Sorry, I mean, Veeva."

"Mmm, mmm, mmm, I know you will, my stallion," she says licking her lips and holding out the stinky Polk.

Yeah, these are the type of interactions I witness on a daily basis at Veeva's place. Things that would never—EVER—happen in our hut, which I'm somewhat thankful for.

While Grunt gets to putting a fresh bundle on the baby, Veeva fans herself with a hand. "Useless, bugger," she whispers to me. "I gotta threaten 'im like this to get 'im to do any burnin' thing around 'ere. If he wasn't so good in bed, I'd throw 'im out on his arse. The baggard."

I laugh, both at Veeva's insults and 'cause Grunt's got Polk upside down by the foot and is trying to wipe his little butt with an old blanket. Veeva shakes her head. "He's hopeless," she says. Then, her eyes lighting up, she turns to me. You got your Call comin' up soon, don't you?"

I shrug. "Yeah. S'pose so."

She claps. "Who do you got yer eye on?"

"My eye?" I haven't really thought 'bout it, mostly 'cause I'm trying to avoid thinking 'bout the Call at all. "No one," I say lamely.

She puts an arm 'round me. "Still hung up on Circ?"

She says his name so casually, as if he was just an old boyfriend, that it doesn't even sting as much as usual. "I don't know," I lie.

"You know, he couldn'ta been yer Call anyway," she says.

"I know," I say. "But a girl can dream, can't she?"

"Of course!" she says, excited now, her eyes lighting up. "Ooh, before my Call I dreamed of Bearing a million babies with Zerg. You know who I mean?"

I laugh. "Didn't every Bearer in your Call wanna get Zerg?"

She nods. "Yeah, but none so bad as me. That searin' shilt Mariday got 'im. Lucky bugger. And I got stuck with 'im," she says, motioning to Grunt, who's managed to get the bundle wrapped half 'round Polk's leg and half 'round his arm. Grunt's just staring at the baby, all confused-like, as if bundling a baby is the most confusing puzzle in all of fire country.

"Fix it!" Veeva orders, startling Grunt out of his daze. "Or you'll sleep on t'other side of the tent ternight."

At that threat, Grunt pulls at the bundle, desperately trying to untangle it from Polk's wriggling limbs. I'm laughing so hard I hafta hold my stomach. Veeva gives an exasperated sigh and goes to him, puts her arms 'round his shoulders, massaging them slightly. Grunt is sweating like he's been working in the blaze pits. "It's okay, my gorgeous hunk of muscle," she coos. "I'll take care of it. Fix the tent and I won't punish you."

~~~

Tonight I watch the stars. Now that Circ's gone, my father doesn't seem to mind if I go out at night. I don't even hafta sneak out. I just get up, walk out the door. Sometimes I can feel him watching me, other times he doesn't seem to notice. But either way, he never tries to stop me.

I always go to the same place. The Hunters Lodge. The first time I went the guard was hesitant to let me in, particularly after the way we tricked our way in the last time. But after I explained why I wanted to go in and promised not to break or steal anything, the guard let me. Now I'm a regular.

"Not too many clouds tonight, Sie," the guard says when I arrive. "Should be a perfect stargazing night."

"Thanks, Potts," I say, entering through the door he holds for me. I know all the guards' names now.

I don't take the long way anymore, the way Circ took me when he brought me here. I have no desire to walk down the dark, empty Lodge halls. Outside I feel much closer to him. So I go right up the middle, under the wooden struts and girders and pylons that keep the Lodge from getting blasted over by the strong winter winds. Into the open air space in the middle. Here I feel protected, safe, loved. I'm never alone here, not really. It's my special place. A place I'll never bring anyone.

I lie directly in the middle, look up at the sparkling sky. I spot Circ immediately, as I always do, brighter'n t'others. "Hi," I say.

I know he wants to reply, but can't. From up there, he has no voice. But something tells me he's not just a pretty thing to look at. He still has power in him. Power to change things for me, to impact my life. He'll always impact my life.

My discussion with Veeva pops into my head. The Call. Not that far off. Scary close now. If I could choose any of the eligible guys in the village, who would I choose? I know the answer. None of them. None of them are Circ.

But, for the sake of humoring Veeva, I try to think 'bout it seriously. 'Cause I'm going to get one of them whether I like it or not. Grunt pops into my head first and I laugh. Being Veeva's Call-Sister would be incredible, but the thought of lying with Grunt even once makes me wanna throw a handful of rocks in the air and run under them. I'd take thirty rocks to the face over having to touch him any day.

'Cause I'm so anti-social these days, I don't really know anyone. I barely even really know the Younglings I go to Learning with, much less anyone eighteen or older. There're a couple of brothers who seem friendly enough, Graum and Baum. They're Hunters, too, like Circ is—was. Pretty smoky, too. Not Circ smoky, but nice to look at. Either of them would be okay I guess. But there are many more worse options— options I don't wanna think 'bout right now. Not ever.

Circ stares at me. *I'm sorry, Circ*, I say. *I don't wanna, but I don't know what else to do. If there's any other way, please tell me.*

He winks, as if to say, *I understand.*

I cry.

Twenty-Two

The bells are ringing from every watchtower.

The winds have been whipping themselves into a frenzy all morning, dumping grit and sand into the Learning Hut while we sit cross-legged, trying to listen to whatever gibberish Teacher Mas is telling us.

When the bells start clanging wildly, we all suspect there's a full-fledged sandstorm a-coming. I follow the stampede out the door, using my pointy elbows to ward off anyone who tries to jostle me amidst the confusion.

Right away I know it ain't a sandstorm. Hunters are everywhere, rushing 'bout, strapping on thick, leather shirts and carrying blades, spears, and bows. We're under attack. By what or who, I don't know.

Hawk's just finished talking to one of the Hunters, and starts to rush off, but I sprint at an angle, catch up to him, grab his arm. "Let go of me! I gotta get ready!" he says, twisting away.

I squeeze harder, surprised at myself. "Tell me what's going on," I demand.

His eyes are wild. Not with anger, but with urgency. "They're comin'," he says. "The Glassies are comin'." My fingers go numb and he pulls away, sprints off to prepare. Even the Youngling Hunters'll be a part of this fight.

The villagers are everywhere, running amok, parents trying to find their children, brothers trying to find their sisters, Hunters going to wherever they've been commanded to go. The Lodge. Or the guard towers. Or out into the desert to fight.

I race through the village, instinctively veering toward our hut. But then my mind races ahead of my body, pictures what'll happen. My father'll lock us in for our safety, go off to join the Hunters. I'll be stuck inside with my thoughts, the walls closing in 'round me, no way to escape them. Not today.

I stop, head in the opposite direction, toward the edge of the village that faces Confinement and ice country. No one's running in that direction. The Hunters are all going the other way, 'cause that's where the Glassies are attacking from, taking the quickest route possible, direct from the Glass City to here. Soon I'm all alone, rushing past tents that are sealed up tight, full of scared women and children whose lives are dependent on the Hunters' ability to once again hold off the mysterious Glassies, who, for some unknown reason, seem determined to wipe us off the face of fire country.

Even the guard towers on this side are abandoned, the guards called to the front lines with everyone else. I slip out of the village, beyond the border tents. My father'll be grizzing himself right 'bout now. His precious Pre-Bearer is missing. What if I die? What if I get hurt and can't Bear his grandchildren, fulfill my duty under the Law? What then? The thought makes me happier'n anything has in a while.

I skirt along the edge of the village, feeling reckless and dangerous and so out of control that I start to feel *in* control. More in control'n I've felt in a long time. Since Circ's death I've just been bobbing along, like a dead fly in the watering hole, letting the wind and ripples take me wherever they choose.

Not today. Today *I* choose.

As if in anticipation of the impending battle, the wind swirls, so excited that it can't decide on a single direction to blow in. Off in the desert, mini-dust-devils rise up and spin themselves in haphazard circles, flattening the dry pricklers and last remaining stalks of brittle scrubgrass. Despite the dust in the air, I press onward, shielding my eyes with a hand, both from the sun and the sand.

When I'm more'n halfway 'round the village, cries of death rise up.

I pick up my pace, determined to see the battle in all its gruesome glory. I'm full of more energy'n I've had in a long time, and I'm almost scared of what I might do when I get to the other side of the border tents, when I see what's happening. All that pent up energy's gotta find an outlet.

I've done plenty of knocky things 'fore, like jumping into a Killer/Hunter fight or purposely getting sent to Confinement. Maybe I'll just join the fight with the Glassies, I don't know. I feel so alive, like I could do anything, score a goal in feetball

233

without falling over, kill a tug with my bare hands, run to Confinement and break Raja out. Anything.

I'm almost to the front gate of the village, cries of war and mayhem just in front of me, sending shivers and quivers of energy through my whole invincible skeleton-like body—when I trip. I'm not so invincible after all. I'm running so hard that I literally go flying, completely airborne and flapping my arms.

Oh no! Here we go again. I've just recovered from a broken wrist and I'm 'bout to break a whole lot more on the hard, cracked earth.

Powerful arms catch me in midair, pull me down, set me back on my feet.

Oh how I want to believe it—can't believe it—want to—want to—please let it be him. The only one who's ever caught me 'fore—besides my father, who I don't count—so many times 'fore, is Circ. My hero. My friend. Not dead. Just a mistake, a misunderstanding. He's saved me again.

It's not Circ.

Circ burned on the pylon, sent to the stars.

The arms are too thin. Strong, yeah, but thin, too, almost like a girl's. Not *a* girl's. Lara's.

She's looking at me like I'm wooloo, and when I see her I look at her the same way. "What the scorch?" I say. "Lara? What are you doing?"

"I could ask you the same thing," she says.

"I was, uh...I don't know. Thanks for catching me. You're really strong." It's the understatement of the year. With her buzzed head, tightly set jaw, and tight cut-off shirt, she looks exactly the way I was feeling when my two left feet got in the way of my glory. Invincible.

"No problem."

The deep bellows of men at war roar past us, colliding with the wind, which has managed to unite its swirls into a pressing gale force that throws my hair back into my face. I push it away, wondering what I'm doing out here.

I don't know what to say. "We should, uh, get back, right?"

"Wrong," Lara says. "I think you're out here for the same reason I am."

I snap my eyes shut as a smattering of sand whips past. When I reopen them Lara's giving me one of those looks I grew so familiar with a couple full moons ago. "Don't start with all that 'There's another way,' blaze. All we're gonna get out here is a trip to the burner."

"Alright then. I'll see you later." Lara strides off. As I contemplate what she said, a brambleweed flies at my head and glances off my forearm when I throw up my arms to protect myself. One of its gnarled branches slashes my arm, cutting it deep, spilling my blood. The sharp pain of the wound sharpens my thoughts. The answer to the question *Why am I out here?* suddenly seems obvious. 'Cause I want to be. I don't wanna be what everyone thinks I should be, someone's call, a Bearer, a *breeder*. I wanna be more. I wanna stand up and do something. Not huddle helplessly with the women and children while the men give their lives to protect us. The last time I did something this wooloo—with the Killers—it was to protect Circ, which wasn't a choice. This time it's a conscious decision to act. My choice, even if it kills me.

I race after Lara, being careful not to trip again. She's walking slow, almost as if she…

"Knew you'd come," she says as I pull astride. "Like me, it's in your blood to be different." I say nothing, just match the increased speed of her steps.

We're going to fight.

~ ~ ~

Maybe it wasn't such a good decision. We're on the edge of the village, watching men die.

The Glassies are winning, their fire sticks intermittently booming, their chariots blazing in a swarm of fire, moving so fast it's like they have the power of hundreds of Killers' legs inside them. Their skin is as pale as the white sands of southern fire country, bleached, rather'n darkened by the sun. They are a curious people. A curious people who want to kill us. Sun goddess save us all.

I see Hawk amidst a large group of Hunters that've managed to stay organized, shooting pointers as a collective group, killing anything in sight. But they won't last. There are too many Glassies.

"We have to go now or it'll be over before we get there," Lara says.

Which might not be a bad thing, I think. "We don't have any weapons," I point out, hoping I've found a way to change her mind.

She reaches behind her and extracts a pair of twin blades, as long as my forearm and sharper'n a Killer fang. "Take one," she says.

I do, gulping as I feel the sun-heated metal of the hilt against my palm. "Lara, are you sure…?"

"You can do this," she says, gripping my shoulder in one hand and her knife in t'other. She holds it as easily as a Bearer holds her baby. Me, I feel like the blade is as awkward as a tent pole.

I take a deep breath, my legs wobbling like they're made of water. All energy's been sucked from them, from my arms. It's the strongest wind of the season, almost knocking me off my feet with each gust. This is no game, no daydreamed conversation with a prickler named Perry. This is real. The only way I can cope is to pretend.

I picture Circ on the field of battle, majestic and graceful, sweeping his blade like a dance, protecting other Hunters with every swing. The Glassies close in on him, one from the front, one from behind. He's helplessly outnumbered. Only I can save him.

"Let's go," I say, digging my heel into the dust.

Lara smiles. "Now!" she cries. We race off together, two girls in a desert of men. Actually, more like one and a half girls. Guess who's the half.

We're halfway to the battle. It's all happening too fast—too searin' fast—and I can't hold the daydream. Scorch, I can barely hold my blade, which is wavering in my grasp. I'm more likely to impale myself on it than one of the Glassies.

Circ vanishes, gone back to the land of the gods. A fire stick booms and a Hunter drops dead, red all over his chest. The Hunter archers unleash a flurry of pointers and a chariot full of Glassies crashes, pointers sticking out every which way from their skin.

Too fast.

The wind swirls, gusts, unites, threatens.

The sandstorm hits like a tug stampede.

Twenty-Three

If you ain't never seen a winter sandstorm, consider yourself lucky.

Surviving a sandstorm is more luck'n skill. But when your people've been doing it for centuries, you've at least got a fighting chance. The Glassies? Not so much.

Lara grabs my blade, secures it to her leather belt, and in two seconds flat, the air goes from having an occasional burst of sand to being *full* of sand. And in those two seconds, me and Lara do three things, like we've been taught a million times, from Totter to Youngling.

First, we hold our breaths and drop. This is crucial, especially when every instinct is telling you to stay on your feet, to fight through the wind and the sand. To drop is to admit defeat. Not in a sandstorm. Remaining upright just quickens your death. You can't outrun a sandstorm—the sooner you realize that the better.

Second, we curl up in a ball, throw our hands and arms over our faces—which makes me glad Lara took my blade, 'cause I'd probably have impaled myself—continue to hold our breath. To breathe is to die. The sand'll get in every nook and cranny—that's inevitable. But by breathing you're inviting it in. The only issue is that you don't know how long the sandstorm's gonna last. It could be thirty seconds, or way longer. If it's much longer, you hafta do more'n just hold your breath.

So third, we stuff our heads into the top of our dresses. Well, in Lara's case it's a boy's shirt, but you get what I mean. Our clothes are over our heads, which creates a small breathing space. It won't last forever, but it'll keep us going for a few moments, maybe more.

I can't see Lara, 'cause my eyes are closed and my head's stuffed in my dress, but I know she's doing the same. The bare parts of my arms and legs are getting stung over and over again by the hordes of sand that batter us like bee stingers. I can almost feel it chipping away pieces of my skin, shaving it all off until I'll really be Skeleton-Girl, a set of walking, talking bones.

Soon though, the pain subsides 'cause my skin's got a layer of sand so thick it's like tug leather, protecting me from the second wave of sand. I take breath after breath, slow and deep, not panicking. Even so, each breath feels more strained'n the last, like I want more air'n my shirt's got left. Time ain't on my side, that's for sure. If the storm don't end soon, I'm a goner, no better'n the Glassies.

I take a breath, my lungs aching for more. The next breath's even less satisfying. I can still feel the wind lapping against my body, but I can't tell if there's sand in it. My final breath is as deep as I can make it, sucking as much of the life-giving air into my lungs as I can. I hold it, hold it, hold it, start to feel dizzy. If I wasn't already on the ground, I'd probably faint.

I can't hold it, not one second longer. I hold it another second. Then one more. Maybe a third, I don't know, time is moving so slow right now.

I pop my head out of my dress, gasp at the gritty air, take everything in, air and dust and wind, my lungs burning. The storm's over, and although the air's far from clean, it's also far from deadly. Lara's head is still in her boy's shirt. She's not taking any chances and apparently she can hold her breath a lot longer'n me. I tap what I think is her shoulder—she's so covered in sand it's hard to tell—and she comes up, poking her head out like a turtle.

"It's okay," I say.

Together, we look 'round. The sand is uneven, full of human-size mounds of sand. The dead and the living. But which is which? Some of the humps start to rise up, emerging from the sand like a child's monsters, crusted with sand and looking less human'n creature. Although the faces are dusty, the brown sun-kissed skin shows us just who survived the storm. The Hunters. There's not a single pale-white face among the living, not that I can tell, but I'm not 'bout to stick 'round to take a count, and neither is Lara.

"We need to get the burn out of here!" Lara says.

I'm with her there. 'Fore anyone notices our presence, we dash back to the village.

~~~

240

That sandstorm saved a lot of lives. The Hunters. Lara's and mine. Probably everyone's in the village. The first of the season. Short, but a real doozy. It got every last one of those fire-stick-wielding Glassies. They burned their bodies in a separate pile to our dead ones.

I feel Circ's hand in the storm.

Lara and me went straight to the watering hole and got cleaned up, and then snuck into the crowds when people started emerging from their huts. When she saw me, my mother squeezed me like she was a Totter and I was her tug-stuffed doll. I told her I couldn't make it home from Learning fast enough, and ended up hiding out in a different hut with Lara. Her eyes told me she didn't believe me, but she didn't push it.

My father shoulda been thanking the sun goddess for sending that storm, but instead he was mad at me for not getting home in time, and at the Glassies for attacking, and at the dead Hunters for not surviving. Same ol', same ol'.

The Greynotes have been hush hush about the whole thing. The only announcement they made was that we woulda won the battle anyway, if not for the sandstorm, but I saw what I saw. They were dead in the sand. Deader'n dead. Vulture meat. It's as plain as day to me, but to the rest of the folk who were hiding in the huts, they'll believe anything the Greynotes tell them. But the Greynotes can have their secrets.

The only thing that's certain: the Glassies'll be back. And the next time we won't have a sandstorm to save us.

Lara's more excited 'bout the whole thing'n I am. It's been a full moon since it happened and she's still going on and on like it was yesterday.

"It was like fate, Sie," she says.

I got too much on my mind to be excited about much of anything. I turned sixteen yesterday, which is just my luck. If I'd been born a little over a full moon later, I coulda turned sixteen and then waited six full moons 'fore the next Call. Instead, my Call'll be at the next full moon.

"It was stupid, is what it was," I say.

"Come on, you know that's not true. There was a buzz running through your blood just like mine. I saw it in your eyes before you tripped." She laughs.

"Thanks for the reminder," I say.

"Would you have used that knife on one of the Glassies if that storm didn't hit?" she asks.

"I ain't talking 'bout this," I say, scooping a shovelful of blaze. I was daydreaming in Learning again. Lara agreed to keep me company while I sweat it out.

"I would have," she says from the edge of the pit. She's perched like a raven on a prickler bough. "I would've jumped on a chariot, stuck my blade right between one of their ribs."

"They woulda shot you with those fire sticks first," I say.

"I would've been too fast," she says. "Just a blur. Sear that sandstorm for wasting our big chance!"

I drop my shovel in a pile of blaze, glare at her. "You know what? You're wooloo! Completely out of your mind, one hundred percent, grade-A tug wooloo." She stares at me, but I'm not done. I'm too hot, too tired, too searin' broken after Circ. "There's a wooloo farm with your name on it. I think when you got all that muscle you lost half your brain. No, more'n half. Three quarters. You woulda died out there, just like me. That sandstorm saved both of our worthless, Pre-Bearer lives, and you know it!"

When I finally finish my rant, I'm breathing heavy and my muscles are all clenched up. The sun's beating on me like always, but it feels like it's right on top of me, just hammering away at my skull. Lara's mouth is open, shocked. I can almost see the wheels turning in her one-quarter brain, calculating the odds that she'll ever speak to me again. Her mouth closes. The solution? Zero.

Then, in the unlikeliest of responses, she breaks into a huge smile. "Sie, you know what? That was one of the funniest rants I ever heard in my life. We are one and the same, you and I, only I'd figure you're more likely to get yourself in trouble with that mouth of yours than I ever would. Now, what in the scorch is eating you? There's got to be something."

I blink. "Uh."

"Come on, Sie. Out with it. Something's behind that mouth of yours, and I want to know exactly what."

Okay. Here goes. "I turned sixteen," I say, turning away from her, my feet sinking into the mush.

She laughs. "Is that all? I turned sixteen a full moon ago. That's one thing you can't stop, Sie—time. I'd rather jump in front of a hurd of tug than hafta try to halt the days from ticking past."

She's already sixteen. I didn't even realize it. I mean, I was pretty sure we'd be in the same Call, but I'd never confirmed it, never thought to. Why is she not bothered by it? In a full moon we'll both be sitting there, waiting for the name. The name of the guy we'll be Bearing children with. Not in a few years, but like, later that day. Well, not Bearing them exactly, but making them, or creating them, or doing whatever it is we're s'posed to do. And from what Veeva says, there's no way 'round it. You gotta do it and you gotta do it naked. I've confirmed it about

243

ten times with her. Can I keep my clothes on? Do I hafta see his...*prickler?* Her advice: "Wait till it's dark as scorch and make it quick. In and out. You might e'en like it. I did." Thanks, Veeva, that really helps.

"Ain't you scared?" I ask, turning back to face Lara.

She shakes her head. "Sometimes I wonder about you. Have you still not thought about everything I told you? I ain't doing the Call. It ain't for me. It ain't for you neither, but I can't make that decision for you."

I'm flabbergasted. The Call isn't something you skip, like Learning or Shovel Duty. It's the whole point of our lives up to this point. The only way anyone's ever missed the Call is if...

"You think the Wilds are gonna kidnap you?" I say slowly. All of sudden I forget 'bout the Icies, 'bout the Marked. It's gotta be the Wilds she's working with. It's gotta be.

She laughs for the third time, looks up at the sun goddess. "Yeah, they'll kidnap me alright."

Then she gets up and leaves. So much for keeping me company.

~~~

I don't know 'bout a lot of things Lara said, but she was right 'bout one thing: you can't stop time, can't even slow it down. I know, I've tried.

First I tried not sleeping. I figured that sleep is like wasting a third of a day in a blink of an eye. Sleep is skipping time, making it pass faster. So for three days straight I didn't sleep. I snuck out, romped 'round the village, splashed water on my face, held my eyelids open with my fingertips. You know what?

Those days still went right on by like I wasn't even moving. Sure enough, I blinked and they were gone, just like all the rest.

So I filled a jar with stones and whispered a blessing to the sun goddess on each one, which represented the days left till my Call. If I could keep those stones in that jar, the days couldn't pass. I woke up the next day, excited to watch my plan take hold. The sun rose, but I swear it was moving slower'n unusual, which got my hopes up, but by the time I left Learning it was sinking down, down, down, like always. That day went faster'n most.

You can't stop time. It's the most powerful force in the universe. And this time it seems to have taken sides with my father. The Call is coming whether Lara believes it's something we should do or not.

I often wonder whether there are others just like us, living the same lives, but different. Like is there another Siena out there somewhere, not Scrawny but Strong? And a Circ who still lives, having never gone on that mission? Another Lara who doesn't hafta count on the Wilds to kidnap her to escape the Call? I know it's just my imagination creeping up on me in that quick and subtle way that it does, but I still wanna believe it's true.

I hafta believe.

~~~

Three days to the Call. I've asked Lara half a dozen times why she thinks the Wild Ones are gonna kidnap her but she don't have an answer. Or she won't answer. I'm beginning to think she's convinced herself it's true to calm her nerves. Or maybe there's something to it. Could she really know the feral all-girl tribe? At this point anything's possible, I reckon.

Veeva's been giving me tips all quarter full moon, like "Don't let yer Call take control when you lie with 'im. Show 'im who's boss." Like most of what she says, I don't even know what that means.

Father's been extra nice to me, which basically means he hasn't yelled at me or pulled out his good friend, the snapper. That's 'bout as good as it gets with him.

Mother seems happy too, although she's always tired these days. "My little girl is growing up," she says today, while we're sitting together mending a pair of Father's britches. They're from the battle with the Glassies and they got holes in both knees. One of the nice things 'bout being a Pre-Bearer is that I been done with Learning for a quarter full moon. I still gotta go to some Pre-Bearer thing later today and tomorrow, but that's it.

"Do you think Skye's alive?" I ask.

She stops with her needle and thread, turns her tired eyes to me. "Does she feel dead?" she asks, pointing to her heart.

"I—I don't know. I never really thought 'bout it that way. I guess…" I think 'bout Skye, 'bout her raven-black hair, 'bout her contagious laugh, 'bout how she was everything I'm not. Popular, coordinated, pretty. There's no sadness for her in my heart. No. She doesn't feel dead.

I shake my head.

"Well there's your answer," she says matter of factly.

"But Circ doesn't feel dead either," I say, feeling my heart crumble even as I say it.

"Siena," she says, putting down the britches. "You can't do this to yourself. Do you see him sometimes?"

246

I nod. I see him in everything. But I can't tell her that. Instead I say, "Sometimes."

She curls an arm around me, pulls me in. "I still see my first love, too," she whispers. "Sometimes."

My head jerks, eyes widen. "You mean, there was someone else 'sides Father?"

She laughs and it reminds me of Skye. They were always a lot alike. "Your father is my Call." She drops her voice even further, looks 'round as if the hut walls might be listening. "Brev was my true love."

I straighten up, all my attention on my mother and this surprising revelation. "Who was he?"

She stares at me wistfully and I can tell she's looking right through me. "The son of a Greynote. Kind eyes, bluer than the winter rains. Soft hands, but strong, too. Oh, I remember spending too much time kissing him behind the border tents."

"Mother!" I exclaim, shocked. "But that's where the shilts go."

Her grin makes me grin, too. "I wasn't shilty, Siena. I only ever went there with Brev. Besides, people doing what makes them happy ain't shilty." It's funny hearing her saying that 'cause it's what I'm always thinking.

The door slams and Father clomps in. My head is spinning, both 'cause of Brev and how she just said *ain't*, which I ain't never heard her say. In less time'n it takes for a vulture to swallow a burrow mouse I've learned so much 'bout my mother, more'n I ever knew 'fore. I desperately wanna ask her what happened to him, where he is now, whether she ever sees him, but now Father's here, scowling at us like we've just spit on his moccasins.

"You've got Call Class," he says gruffly.

I stand up, meet my mother's eyes for an instant, share our secrets without words, desperately wanting to ask her more. Smiling, I follow my mother's Call outside.

~~~

Call Class. Our chance to ask questions. And we got plenty.

There are 'bout thirty of us. Me, Lara, and a bunch of others who've never really tried to talk to me. The Teacher, a squat woman with laser-sharp eyes, is whacking away the questions with an ease that can only come with experience. She must teach Call Class a lot.

"Can I choose my Call, because there's this guy...?" one girl asks, twirling her hair with one finger. Everyone knows the answer to that question, so it makes half the class crack up. I just stare straight ahead.

Teacher sighs, but answers anyway. "All Calls are at random. An eligible Pre-Bearer's name is selected and then an eligible male name is selected. Listen, Younglings, because this is important. You do not get to choose your Call because it doesn't matter who it is. All that matters is that you Bear children and help our tribe survive. That's it."

"What do I do if I don't like my Call?" a whiny girl asks, apparently not getting Teacher's message.

"Deal with it," says Teacher. "Next."

"How do I know if I'm satisfying my Call?" asks one of the shiltier girls, grinning slyly. "You know, when I lay with him." She's only asking what everyone's thinking.

"I'm sure you know the answer to that already," Teacher says, unblinking. A few Pre-Bearers giggle and the shilty girl blushes and ducks her head. "Next."

248

"What if I miss my Call?" a familiar voice asks from beside me. My heart stops. Every head in the room turns to look at Lara. And 'cause I'm sitting next to her, they look at me too. Guilty by association. There's a speck of durt on one of my feet and I'm determined to stare it away.

"No one misses their Call," Teacher answers, as if it's a perfectly valid question. "Next." I can still feel the eyes on us, but then one by one, they turn back to face the front.

"Why'd you ask that?" I hiss.

"Just for fun," Lara says, grinning.

"You got a funny way of having fun."

"Now it's your turn," she says, winking.

I raise an eyebrow. "What do you mean?"

"Ask a question. A real question. Not something that she's heard a million times, that she expects you to ask. Something else. Try to rattle her. For fun."

I shake my head. "You're wooloo," I say, but immediately start thinking about what question'll surprise the unflappable Teacher.

Another girl asks, "Do I have to have a Call-Sister?"

Stupid girl, I think. This is stuff we've been learning for years. Teacher sighs, but responds, her voice monotone and rehearsed. "A Call-Family is comprised of a man and his three Calls, who Bear his children. Every three years, each Call-Mother is required to become big with child and Bear a new child. They take turns until the family has grown to its maximum sustainable size, which includes three children per Call-Mother, or nine children total. It's at this time only that it will be considered a Full-Family and Bearing shall cease. Next."

The question pops into my mind like most of my random thoughts do. Quickly and vividly. Circ's bloody face wet with tears. His body, still stronger'n most, weakened by injury and blood loss. His voice, urgent and stronger'n expected as he gives me his charm. My charm now. My fingers play on the pointer charm dangling from my bracelet. The question comes out. "What if my Call is dead?" I murmur, almost to myself. The question is rude, uncouth, and inappropriate in a lot of ways. There's a good chance I'll go to Scorch just for asking it.

"Excuse me?" Teacher says.

Lara is tapping her foot with excitement next to me.

"What if my Call is dead?" I say again, louder this time.

Teacher's eyes narrow. "I'm not sure what you're playing at, Youngling, but what you ask is impossible. You haven't received a Call yet, so he can't be dead."

I chose him and he chose me. It's what I want to say, but I know how it'll sound. Like I'm just some lovestruck Youngling. The other girls'll laugh and Teacher'll come down hard on me. Not today. "Thank you, Teacher," I say.

Lara giggles.

Twenty-Four

The Call. Those two words pierce my skull the moment I open my eyes and am blinded by a bright sliver of sunlight. No going back.

I peer out the window, surprised to see the deep red, cloudless sky, and brilliant orange sun emerging from the horizon. It's been raining for two days straight, which is normal for this time of year, but for some reason it's decided to stop for such an important moment in my life.

There's a shout from outside, but I roll over, pull my tugskin blanket over my ears. It's the last morning I'll wake up alone. At least until I hafta share my Call with my first Call-Sister. Or perhaps I'll be the first Call-Sister for someone else, which means I'll hafta share my Call right away. That wouldn't be so bad, not with a guy who's not Circ. Less pressure on me that way.

The door explodes open and I hear heavy boots stomp across the floor. Father. No one else can walk so angrily. "Siena, pretending to sleep won't work. You're going to tell me what you know about Lara immediately."

Lara? Since when does my father even know who Lara is? He's never said a word 'bout her 'fore. Oh sun goddess! I think. He's found out 'bout the things she's been saying to me. About there being another way. 'Bout missing the Call. 'Bout the Wilds.

I roll over, feign ignorance. "Who's Lara?" I ask. He grabs me by the arm, his fingers pressing hard into my skin. "Oww! Father, it's my Call today. Please."

That works and he let's go, backs up a step. "Don't play dumb with me, Youngling," he barks.

"I'm not a Youngling anymore!" I shout, hoping that matching his anger'll get rid of him.

"You are until tonight," he retorts. "Lara's missing, and I want to know exactly what you know about it."

~ ~ ~

I'm still in shock over the whole thing. Lara's missing? What? It's crazy. All this time I thought she was full of hot air, all talk, overcompensating for a future she couldn't control. But now she's on the verge of doing exactly what she said she'd do for many full moons: miss the Call. And she's not the only one missing. There're a bunch of other Pre-Bearers gone, too.

I didn't tell my father a searin' thing. Well, actually, I did, but none of it had a lick of truth. I told him she's been trying to

252

make friends with me, always bothering me, telling me wooloo things. *Well, day 'fore last, she told me she was fixing to run off to ice country just 'fore her Call. Father, I swear I thought it was a bunch of tugblaze or I woulda told you. Please believe me, Father, please!*

He bought the whole thing, which is why I'm smiling now. He wasn't too happy that I hadn't told him earlier, but he didn't give me too much trouble over it 'cause I was so cut up about the whole thing. I don't really know what happened to her, but she seemed to think the Wilds would kidnap her, and maybe that's exactly what happened. Just like with Skye.

So I'm smiling and humming along to myself as I walk back from my last session of Call Class. I mightn't be able to get out of it, but I'm glad Lara did. When I reach our hut, my smile vanishes.

There's one scorch of a commotion outside of our place. A huddle of Greynotes speak in hushed tones. MedMa has his arm on my father's shoulder and is shaking his head and speaking softly. I ignore them all, push past, make my way to the door.

My father sees me. "Siena, don't," he says, but I ignore him, fling open the door.

Evidence of the Fire is everywhere. It's in the wet towels in the wash basin, in the lingering scent of MedMa's healing herbs, in the abject silence that seems to surround the room. And 'specially on my mother's face, which is sheened with sweat, red and white and yellow, sharpened with pain. Her expression is contorted even now, as she tries to smile at me and sit up in bed. "Siena," she murmurs, her loudest voice but a whisper.

"No, Mother. No." Tears well up. I won't go to her. Can't. If I do it'll make it real. The Fire. Come into our home to take the last person I have.

"Shhh," she whispers. "Come to me."

"No...no." Tears in streaks on my cheeks. Numbness all over. Where are you, sun goddess?

"It's going to be fine," my mother says, a stronger woman'n I'll ever be.

I keep my distance even though I know the Fire ain't catching. "Nothing's fine," I say.

A shadow splashes me from behind. I don't turn 'round. "Leave us, Roan," my mother commands. For once in his life, my father obeys my mother, closes the door softly.

"I can't do this," I say, talking 'bout my mother and the Call in one breath.

"You can," she says, extending an arm. An invitation.

Although I don't wanna, I move closer. Closer. Sit on the edge of the bed. Hold her hand, which doesn't hold back. There's already no strength left in it. "So fast," I say, watching a tear drip off my chin and onto her arm.

"I've felt it coming for a while now," she says. "But yes, this Fire is faster than most. Mercifully fast."

"But I'm not ready." Once more I'm talking 'bout her and the Call. Funny how those two things seem so inexplicably linked now, when 'fore they were nothing alike.

She laughs but it comes out as a cough. I calm her with a hand on her forehead. The heat is pouring out of her skin like there really is *fire* in there. There is, I remember. The Fire to end all fires.

I leave her side for a moment, ring out a wet towel in the wash basin, return to her. Dab her face with the towel, wiping away the tears that've begun to spring up. "I've never done right by you, Siena," she says, sadness in her eyes.

"No, Mother, don't say that. You've done right by me. Life is just hard sometimes. Father is hard."

"No excuse," she says. "I'm going to make it right before I go. I have to make it right."

"You don't hafta do anything," I say. "Just rest, Mother. Just rest."

~~~

Jade. Skye. Circ. Lara, earlier today. And now my mother, soon to follow, maybe as soon as three or four days 'cause of how fast-acting her Fire is. It feels like everyone that matters to me is gone. Taken for reasons I don't think I'll ever understand.

It's time. Like my sister did not so long ago, I put on my white dress. There's no one to help me 'cause Sari hates me and mother's too tired to stand. She watches though, her eyes keen with interest. "You look beautiful," she says when I finish.

"Skye was more beautiful," I remember.

"In my eyes, you two will always be the prettiest girls in all of fire country," she says.

I cast my eyes downward. "Will you be able to come to the Call?" I ask, already knowing her answer.

"Siena, I'm too weak. Far too weak. But I'll be there in here." She points to her heart. "And here," she adds, pointing to my hair. I frown in confusion. "In your hair, silly. I want to fix your hair just right."

Tears bubble up but I blink them away. I sit on the ground, not caring if my dress gets durty. It's the only way my mother'll be able to reach me.

She hasn't braided my hair in years, but as soon as her fingers slide along my scalp the memories come flooding back. My sister and me sitting side by side as my mother worked on our hair, poking at each other and giggling. Her expert fingers feel the same now, where I can't see them, almost as if there's nothing wrong with her at all. As if nothing's changed.

The only noticeable difference is the speed at which she works, but I don't know if her slowness is 'cause of the Fire or 'cause she, like me, don't want this moment to end.

But we both know it hasta.

It hasta.

I try to pull our time together out, stretch it, lengthen it, using the only thing I got. A request. "Tell me more 'bout Brev," I say.

My mother doesn't say nothing for a long moment, and I know I surprised her, 'cause her fingers stop working. "What do you want to know?" she asks.

"Everything," I say and she laughs.

"Now that'll take more time'n we have," she says.

"Is that a promise?"

She laughs again and I'm glad. Glad 'cause the Fire ain't taken her laugh away. Not yet. "I'll tell you this," she says, and I lean back against her bed, closing my eyes, trying to picture her at my age. Try as I might, I can't do it. "We were inseparable. We went everywhere and did everything together."

Like me and Circ, I think. "What happened?" I ask.

"The Call," she says and I open my eyes to my future, sitting out in the center of the village, eyes like fire, staring, just staring. I close them again. "We couldn't be together after that. Sun goddess knows we wanted to, but it wasn't right—not by the Law anyway. Your father…he was a good man for a good long while."

But I don't wanna talk 'bout my father—after all, I was there when he started changing—so I ask another question. "Where's Brev now?"

I can't see it, but I can feel my mother's smile, in her fingers, which seem to quicken, working over my strands of hair a beat or two faster. "Somewhere," she says, but that ain't no answer.

"Where's *somewhere*?"

"He couldn't stand it. Neither of us could. I didn't have any choice really, but to stay with your father. Skye was on the way already. I was making a family out of nothing. Brev left."

Left? "But there's nowhere to go," I say, feeling around with my words, trying to work it out. Ice country? The Icers'd never take a Heater on. The Wildes? Far as I know, they're all women and they were only started a few years back. That leaves…

"He started the Marked and I never saw him again," my mother says and I blink, stunned for a moment.

She finishes with my hair, and I absently feel 'round with my hands. Even without gazing into the reflections of the watering hole I know she's done a beautiful job. Several short braids curl delicately 'round my head like a crown, woven so tightly they're like rope. A longer braid falls down the center of my back. Even without the memory that graces my mind at that moment, I'd know it's the same hairstyle she created for my sister just 'fore the Wilds took her.

But I can't think about any of that. 'Cause her true love created the Marked.

There's a knock at the door. The Call. Will I answer?

"Go," my mother says. "You can tell me all about it tomorrow."

I squeeze her hand 'fore I go, saying *And you can tell me 'bout Brev and the Marked.*

~ ~ ~

My feet are heavier'n tug. The march to my Call is full of blazing torchlight marking the way, casting dancing and wriggling shadows along the pathway.

Sari refused to escort me which is fine by me. My father can't 'cause he's overseeing the proceedings and is already there. That means I have no family willing or able to walk with me. It's so different'n my sister's Call, where me and my mother walked with her the whole way—or at least until the point where the Wilds found a way to grab her.

So that leaves Veeva. Sun goddess, bless Veeva. I don't know what I'd do without her.

She's gripping my hand and talking a mile a moment 'bout how proud she is of me and how whoever ends up with me is a lucky baggard. I smile and thank her, but inside I'm quaking like I'm staring down the throat of a hungry Killer. And all that keeps thrumming through my head is:

I'm not ready, I'm not ready, not ready, not ready.

In my heart I know the truth: I'll never really be ready. Maybe once upon a time I coulda been ready, back when things were simpler, when Circ was alive, when my father wasn't Head Greynote, when my mother wasn't dying...

But not now. Now things are so messed up I wanna shake off Veeva's hand, break through the line of Greynotes that are supervising the Call, and run, run, run until my feet fail me and I can't run any more. I could run to Confinement, break the prisoners out, tell everyone what's really happening up there.

258

That's what I'd do if I was brave-Siena, the girl who tried to save Circ. But she died along with him, leaving just me.

We reach the Call so much faster'n I expected we would. My stomach drops 'bout to my feet, like I jumped off something high.

Not ready.

At least half the village is gathered in the center of town, where the bonfire's been churned up to a roaring inferno. Extra seats've been rolled in—shaved tree trunks and boulders mostly—to accommodate all the Greynotes. My father's atop the largest boulder, presiding over the whole thing. His eyes meet mine and a rare smile plays on his lips. This is all he's ever wanted. A daughter of his to make him proud. To Bear. Fulfill a duty, replenish the tribe and all of that blaze. I look away from him.

The rest of the spectators are either family and friends of those participating in the Call, or nosy onlookers who just wanna know all the latest Call news so they're not behind tomorrow when the gossip starts. At the moment, I hate them all.

The eligible men are seated in a cluster on one side of the fire. They're shirtless, as if they wanna be ready to carry their Calls back to their tents as soon as it's over. Grunt's there and Veeva waves to him, making a lewd gesture that draws a grin from her Call. Sorry Veevs, but please, please, please, don't let me get him.

The rest of the Calls, like me, are entering the area from all different directions with their escorts. Some of them wear wide smiles, like they've waited their whole lives for this moment. Maybe they have. Others look as scared as I feel, their faces blank and their eyebrows darting 'round like they might be grabbed and carried off by a man at any moment. Some of the shiltier girls are tossing their hair and wearing dresses so small and tight they leave nothing to imagination. Most of the guys are staring at them, their tongues practically hanging out of their mouths. In a way, I sorta admire those girls' confidence. Least they know who they are and what they want.

Me, I'm a confused mess, all jitters and nerves.

Veeva guides me to a wide, white blanket where several girls are already sitting. She gives me a tight hug and a kiss on the cheek, but I'm so numb I hardly feel it. "Try to enjoy it," she reminds. I blush 'cause I know exactly what she's talking 'bout. And then she's gone and I'm alone.

Lara is off somewhere, maybe being whipped into submission by the Wild Ones, but I know she'll be laughing, too. Laughing that she's not a part of this, like she planned the whole time. I desperately wish she was by my side now.

The remaining girls take their position on the blanket, whispering and giggling. I say nothing, just wait.

It starts. My father stands on his boulder, arms out to keep his balance. "Friends," he says, starting slowly. "It's with a mixture of sadness and gladness that I begin the first Call as Head Greynote. We all wish Shiva could be here, but alas, the Fire has claimed another honorable victim." He pauses, letting everyone take in his words. "He will be missed."

To the villagers, his words probably sound heartfelt. They're probably tearing up, saying silent prayers to the sun goddess. But I know better. Behind his words and tone is the truth. He wanted Shiva to die—couldn't wait for it—so he could take over. For over a year he's been carrying on his own plans and secret trade agreements with the Icies, framing innocent men like Raja to do the grunt work.

I curl my fists at my sides. Right now, anger is good. It chases away the fear.

My father continues. "The Call is an important and magnificent event for us, the Heaters, the people of fire country. It is near and dear to my heart. It is a chance to say to all that threaten us, we will not be defeated! We will carry on, replenish our flock! We are not afraid!" A cheer rises up, but it's deep and heavy—a man's cheer. When I look 'round most of the women are silent.

"It is also when our Youngling girls become women, take on the mantle they've been charged with wearing. They will Bear our next generation, raise them to be future Hunters, Greynotes, and Bearers. One of these Youngling may even Bear your next Head Greynote!" A hardy chuckle from the crowd. My father is working the audience like he's been doing it his whole life. I feel a stone in my stomach, growing bigger with each word.

"Now, without further delay, we begin the spring Call!" Everyone cheers now, either 'cause it's expected or 'cause they're actually excited. I close my eyes.

Someone else takes over from my father, an annoying voice, whiny and high-pitched. My father's right hand man. Luger. "Kaya," he reads and I open my eyes. A girl stands. She's wearing a pretty, flowing white dress that makes her look like how I think a star would look if it fell to the earth—all shimmery and pure. I can see her legs shaking beneath the dress. The village waits.

"Goyer!" Luger shouts. Quite a few people cheer. I don't know him, but apparently Goyer has lots of friends. An older guy, maybe twenty five, stands, smiling. It's a kind smile. He seems like a nice man to have as a father, but as a Call? Uck!

Kaya stands frozen for a moment, takes a deep breath, and then walks to meet Goyer between the two groups. Goyer reaches out and accepts her hand. They walk away, toward whichever tent or hut he's in. There's no time to be wasted—there're children to be a-Bearing!

My stomach is roiling, full of acid and fear.

Luger calls another name, one of the shilty girls. She somehow manages to stand in her skin-tight dress. She pouts her lips at the men, drawing smiles from more'n a few of them. Where's she get that kinda nerve? I wish she'd give me a bit of it.

"Marrick!" Luger shouts. More cheers. A happy, smiling guy stands. His lucky night. The shilt hikes her already short dress up even more so she can strut her way over to him. They walk away holding hands and just 'fore they slink behind the cover of the village, I see her grab his backside. Classy.

Things speed up after the first few as Luger and everyone else involved get into a rhythm. Grunt gets a pretty doe-eyed girl who looks like she might throw up. I watch Veeva's expression, which darkens, as if she may go on a murderous rampage. Things are 'bout to get even more interesting in their already interesting tenthold.

I look 'round. The blanket's already half empty. I'll be Called any second.

Another girl. Another guy. Another happy, baby-making couple.

Luger pauses, looks right at me, eyes narrowed. Smiles. "Siena!" he shouts with greater fervor'n for any of the previous girls.

I shiver when an unexpectedly cold wind gusts through my dress. I feel a raindrop on my face. Then another. Rain or shine, the Call must go on. After sitting cross-legged for so long, my legs are cramped up and I struggle to pull them out from under me. When I do, they're all tingly. In fact, my whole body's tingly, almost like I'm not in it anymore and I'm watching everything unfold from outside of myself. If only it was that easy. If I could separate myself from my body, let it do what it hasta do without me really being there, perhaps I could get through this.

"Siena!" Luger cries again, drawing a laugh from the crowd. I'm taking longer'n the other girls to stand.

I push to my feet, feeling wobbly and like I might faint, my head hot, my palms sweaty, my body cold and shivery. The rain is misting down now, coating my skin with a thin layer of moisture. My dress is quickly becoming saturated, clinging to me like the tight dresses the shilts are wearing. I wait, feeling eyes burning my skin from every direction. But one direction is the hottest and I turn that way. My father's eyes are looking right through me, wide and dark and *ready*. Ready for his daughter to be taken away by a strange man. Not his problem anymore. The best day of his life. 'Sides when I lost Circ, the worst day of mine.

The whole village waits for the name.

"Bart," Luger shouts.

I clench my eyes shut, as tight as my fists at my side.

No, no, no!

I'm dreaming, ain't I?—this ain't happening. I'm back in Call Class, daydreaming, and at any moment a question from Teacher'll snap me out of it. Or, no, I got it, I'm at my Call, but I'm daydreaming *there*. My name hasn't been called, not yet, but I'm dreaming up the craziest, worst-possible Calls I could possibly get, freaking myself out.

I open my eyes, blink, watch huge, muscled Bart stand, his scarred and gnarled face curled into the most vicious grin I've ever laid eyes on. Shirtless, he's huge, easily three of me. The memory of him in his cage in Confinement shudders through my mind:

"Please, nice Greynote, sir, can I share a cage with her?" He licks his lips.

I look away and we keep going. Luger doesn't say a word.

Behind us, Bart hollers, "Just as well. I'd probably crush her under me anyway." He laughs, a gritty, throaty sound that reminds me of the growl of the Killers that got me here in the first place.

My body starts shaking. I clench my miniscule muscles, try to stop it, but I've lost control. I hear laughter from some of the girls behind me. *Crush her...*

Just a dream.

Bart!

Just a dream.

The rain on my face, so wet and soft and *real*. No dream. This is real. All of it. This is my new life.

I realize Bart's walking to where we're meant to meet and I'm still standing there, glued to the blanket. Wind lashing my face. Rain drenching me from head to toe. Considering my options.

Run? How can I run when an entire village is watching me? How far'll I get? Five feet? Ten? No chance. I can go with Bart, try to fight him off in his tent, knee him where the sun goddess's eye don't shine, make a break for it. The chances of that working: near zero. I'm a piece of kindling and he's an entire tree. And fighting'll just make things worse, make him more likely to hurt me.

It's the last thing I want to do, but I'm out of options. I gotta go with him, lay with him, bide my time until I can get away.

I'm still shaking, but I manage to put one foot in front of t'other, start toward him, my eyes on the muddying ground. His hand comes into view, extended, waiting expectantly. "Come, my prize," he growls. I take his hand and he yanks me forward, almost pulling my shoulder out of its socket. But I don't cry out—don't want to give him the satisfaction—just grit my teeth.

When we enter the tent sector, he slides his hand up to my arm, squeezes hard, like my father likes to do. It hurts like scorch but I stay silent. He stops, looms over me, leans his face close, so close I can smell the rancid stench of whatever he ate for dinner—probably raw meat. "You'll do as I say," he says. It's not a question so I assume it doesn't need an answer.

I say nothing.

The back of his hand flashes so quickly I don't have any hope of protecting myself. It lashes the side of my wet cheek with a stinging pain that reminds me of being caught in the sandstorm. Realization comes with more impact'n if the sun crashed into the moon: he'll hurt me no matter what I do. Might even kill me without even trying to. He's three times my size and I manage to break my own bones without much help, just by tripping. Not only is this the worst day of my life, it might also be my last.

The wind goes silent, as if even it cannot bear witness to what's 'bout to unfold. The rain continues pelting down.

I decide quickly. I'm seared if I'll let it happen. Burn him. Burn the Greynotes. Burn the Call. I'll go down fighting; for Circ, for my sister, for Lara, wherever she is, for my mother, for myself. Scrawny? Not anymore.

Today I die Strong.

Twenty-Five

Bart's tent's a mess. Empty fire juice skins lay discarded on the floor. The bitter odor of stale fireweed covers everything like a permanent haze. Durty clothes are strewn 'bout in a way that'd make my mother cringe.

I nearly jump out of my skin when I sense movement to the right. Someone else is here.

Goola. His other Call, a shilty girl who he's always parading 'round like a trophy. When he's not in Confinement, that is. She slinks over.

"Ooh, what have you brought home, Bartie? A new play toy?"

Bart shoves me toward the bed and I stumble on the debris under my feet. I barely manage to keep my balance. "Not tonight, Goo," he says. "Tonight is my time. Get out."

Goola struts over to him, unloosing the top of her dress as she walks. Just 'fore she reaches him it falls away, dropping to her feet like a fallen cloud. She's got nothing on underneath.

I gawk at her as she stands there naked, like it's a perfectly normal thing to do. Whereas I'm all skin and bones, she's full figured with magnificent hips and breasts so full they'd make even Veeva jealous. She puts a hand to Bart's cheek, strokes it, rises up on her tiptoes, kisses him full on the lips, twisting and turning her head wildly. I see flashes of her pink tongue as she rolls it along his lips, slides it into his mouth. I might just get lucky. If Bartie and his trophy Call, Goola, get all tangled up, I might just be able to sneak out of here. I take a step toward the door, my eyes never leaving the lip-locked pair.

Bart grabs her hair from the back, pulls her head away from his, snarls, "I said not tonight! Get out!" He pushes her out the tent opening, still naked as the day she was born. She's shouting obscenities the whole way, both at him and at me. I'm not her favorite person right now.

He leans down, plucks a basket from the corner. To my surprise, it's got a baby in it. I hadn't even thought about the fact that Goola woulda had a child with him already. She ain't exactly the motherly type, and thinking of him as a father is like thinking of a Killer as a pet. "Take Bart Jr. with you, too, Woman," he says, depositing the basket outside. He pulls the tent flap shut, ties it off.

He turns his attention to me. Reflexively I cover my soaked chest with my arms. "See how easy she makes it look," he says, grinning. "If you want it, things will go much smoother."

If he means wanting to kick him in the crotch repeatedly, then yes, I want it. Anything else, not so much. I back away, my mind churning, my eyes roving, trying to come up with any way out of this. Seeing nothing but pain. Go down fighting. Be Strong.

He steps toward me, suffocating me in the tiny space. A baby cries outside. "Get away from me," I say.

Bart laughs. "Can't do that," he says. "You're mine now. And I do what I want with my things."

I take another step back, feel my feet sink into the soft bedding on the ground. He takes a big step forward, closing off any avenue of escape. There's a glow in his eyes, a fire, a red hot desire. For me. To make me another one of his possessions.

I dive back, roll across the bedding, smash into the side of the tent. After the winter winds, a lot of the tents weren't looking so strong, and I doubt if Bart's the type to have rebuilt it from scratch. The tent wall blooms out, but holds, retracts, pushes me back into the center of the bed. Out of the corner of my eye, I see Bart grabbing for me, trying to get hold of my feet. I kick out, catch him in the eye and he lets out a howl, grabbing at his face. "You little shilt, I'll kill you," he snaps.

With every bit of force I can muster, I bash into the tent wall again, hoping it'll cave in, give me a chance to escape in the confusion.

It holds, almost feels stronger'n the previous time, as if Bart's anger is giving strength to his house. His turf. I'm completely knocked.

He grabs my feet and pulls me to him, batting away my flailing arms with ease. Smiling, he's actually smiling, although his version of the happy expression makes me quiver inside. It's too much teeth and not enough lips. And no dimples.

As if he's practiced it his entire life, he swallows my ankles with a massive hand, clamps them together, and then uses his other paw to wrench my arms over my head. Roughly, he throws his weight on top of me and I can feel all of him bearing down on my body. The foul stench of his fire-juice-soaked breath comes in waves, rocking my senses and threatening to knock me out. I'm tempted to give in to the nausea, to hurl or faint or both—that'd put a quick end to all of this—but I won't. Not today. Today I fight.

I throw a knee up hard, trying to catch him in the midsection, but he's in control now and easily holds it down with his powerful legs. He's breathing heavy, almost as if all my fighting and kicking and scratching is exactly what he wants, exactly what he *hoped* for. I shudder when I realize I'm only acting as a stimulant to every perverse fantasy this demon of a man has.

I cry out when he rips at my dress—my purity dress—his fingers like claws, tearing and shredding.

Oh sun goddess, no! Please, no, Circ—where are you?—come back to me.

Please.

Please.

My dress rips away and it's just me underneath, frail and bony and Scrawny, barely covered by the thin fabric of my undergarments. It's like my dress holds whatever strength I have left and when it falls away I'm left with nothing, only fear and exhaustion and weakness.

I feel him, his arousal, on top of me. He's panting now, excited to take me, to take all of me, to take everything I have left. To chew me up and swallow me, making me a part of him forever and ever and ever.

I'm screaming now, crying and yelling things I'll never remember, straining to get him off me, but he won't budge, won't move an inch. I'm his.

The tent door flaps open and a light breeze wafts through, tingling my sweat- and rain-soaked skin. Is it Goola? Come to reclaim her man? I try to look past Bart's thick shoulder, but I can't see anything but his flesh, hot and rough.

"Woman, I told you to leave us!" Bart yells without looking back. His lip is curled in anger and for a moment I think he might take it out on me, hit me in the face.

But then something strange happens. His mouth gasps open and his eyes go wide, like he's been struck by lightning. With a shudder, he collapses on top of me, smothering me like water on the dying embers of a cook fire.

I can't breathe, can't move, and something warm is dribbling onto my skin.

"You're okay now," I hear the voice say, soft and gentle, almost cooing. A voice of comfort, one I've heard a million and a half times growing up, when I was sick or skinned my knee or sad about the things the kids said at Learning.

My mother.

Bart's body is rolled off me and she's there, her face weary and anxious and smiling, her eyes bright despite looking so sunken. "I'm so sorry, Siena, I came as fast as I could, but the Fire, it…"

And then she's crying and I'm crying and we're holding each other, me 'cause she's dying and out of strength and 'cause, despite all that, she came—she *came!*—and 'cause I'm still pure and she saved me and Bart's…

"Is he dead?" I blubber over her shoulder. My eyes flick to Bart's body, which has the handle of a knife sticking from his back, the blade lost in his flesh and inner parts. The handle of the knife is etched with swirls and with the sun goddess's eye, the sun—her symbol, the same one that's on the charm dangling from my bracelet. My mother did it. Not weak like I've always thought. Strong.

She pulls me back, her face a red mess, says, "It matters not. We must hurry."

The perfect crown of hair she created earlier is in shambles, collapsing in broken, wet strands onto my face. I push them away. "Mother, I don't understand. Hurry where? We hafta tell the Greynotes what happened, that you saved me, that Bart's an animal. They'll believe us, they will!"

Mother's eyebrows drop, her soft wrinkles full of compassion. She never had wrinkles until the Fire came. "This was not the life for your sister," she says and I startle.

"Skye?" I say. "Skye was taken."

"No," she says. "I'm sorry, I couldn't tell you, couldn't tell anyone. I sent Skye away from here. To a safe place. She went to live with the Wild Ones."

Her words don't make sense. The Wilds? But they're feral, they're not civilized, they're... "Kidnappers," I say. "They took her."

"Siena, I know this is a lot to take in, but you have to trust me. You have to go now. Your father, he's a monster."

She knows what I know. "Mother, I know, I know, I found out about the agreement with the Icers, how they give us wood and meat and we stay out of ice country, how the prisoners didn't do anything wrong, how they're forced to work, 'bout everything. We can tell the people. We can tell them!"

"You don't know everything," she says. "Your father, he'll never get the Fire."

She's speaking in riddles. "I don't understand, Mother. He's not invincible. The plague'll take him just like everyone else, just like you."

"The Icers give him medicine," she says. "Some kind of herbal drink. It fights the Fire. It's part of the agreement with them. The most secret part. But I watch him, I see what he does—he can't hide his treachery from me. We have to go." She grabs me and pulls me to my feet, hands me a freshly sewn set of Hunter trousers and a shirt. For the first time in my life, I put on something that's not a dress.

~~~

The night is empty. The rain has stopped as suddenly as it started. Although the distant sounds of frolic and laughter hum from the center of the village, the Call party is like another world, something completely foreign to where we are.

Bart lies inside the tent surrounded by his own blood.

We run.

At least it's our best attempt at running. My legs are cramped and tight and sorta tingly, both from Bart crushing them beneath him and 'cause of my mother's words. My father gets a cure for the Fire from the Icers? I have so many questions, like *Why don't the rest of us get the cure?* but I know there's no time. When they find out about Bart, the Greynotes'll come for us and there's only one punishment for murder. Life in Confinement. A knife in the back'll leave no question as to guilt. My mother by actions. Me by association.

My mother's struggling to run, too, 'cause killing Bart and the Fire have sapped the last of her energy. We cling to each other, hold each other up, four legs and four arms and two hearts, all stuck together in one person. I don't know where we're going or what we'll do when we get there, but I'm happy I'm going there with her.

Like me, she knows the best spot for sneaking out of the village—the point furthest from any guard towers. So that's it, we're leaving. Even as I realize it, I know it's for the best. With Circ gone and her soon to be, I have no reason to stay. The village only carries pain for me now.

"Siena," my mother says, stopping, breathing hard, leaning on me. "You have to run like you've never run before. Southwest, where the river lies dead like a snake and the rocks hold hands like lovers. You have to hurry. Your father, the Hunters…they will come after you."

"After me?" I say. My heart skips a beat and tears well up when I realize what's happening. "You're not coming."

"I'm dying, Siena. This is my last act of defiance against your father, my last act of love for you. Tomorrow there is only death."

Rivulets trickle down my cheeks. "No," I sob, "we can get the cure. If he has it, we'll find it. We'll demand he give it to us. I can do it. I can save you." My body shivers with emotion and my mother pulls me close.

"I've tried to find where he keeps it, but it's too well hidden." Her words are strong, almost fierce, a far cry from my own shattered utterances. "It only works to prevent the Fire, but it's useless when you've already got it. Siena—"

"No!" I hiss, louder'n I should. "No, you can come with me. We'll figure out a way."

"I'm too weak…"

"You're the strongest person I know."

"You have to go…"

"I can't leave you." My words are a lie, 'cause I know I can and will leave her. 'Cause if I don't leave, if I don't go and try to make something of my crumbling life, then her sacrifice'll have been for nothing. And I can't live with that.

"Siena, I love you," she says, pushing me away with all her might, falling to her knees.

"I love you," I cry, tear-streaked and stumbling, running toward an unknown world of Wilds who don't kidnap and my sister is one of them.

Twenty-Six

The night paints pictures with the strange strokes of a devilish artist.

Everything's different in the dark. The dunes are rolling humps and heads and tails of gargantuan monsters, asleep and heavy. The pricklers stand firm and tall, like soldiers on guard, ready to fight the dune-monsters the moment they awake. The wind is on the verge of visibility, a silent hand that holds the brush, sweeping it in wide arcs that leave the landscape changed with each stroke.

It dries my tears, too. As I circle 'round the northwestern edge of the village, far enough away that to the guardsmen I'll be little more'n a brambleweed bouncing along the desert, I find my legs. Although I'm scared and sad and bone-weary, I'm not broken. My mother saved me and I won't waste it.

Southwest, where the river lies dead like a snake and the rocks hold hands like lovers.

Vague directions, but enough to get me started. What'll happen when I get there, wherever *there* is? I don't know. All I know is that my sister left by choice, not against her will like I always thought, like they always told me—and my mother helped her do it. The revelation is huge for me. All of Lara's talk about girl's being strong and living the way they want to live was fun and made her who she was, but I never took it that seriously. But knowing my mother and sister were of a similar mind and took real action makes all the difference. It gives me hope.

When I reach the western edge of the village, I stop, look back. Twinkling lights of a raging fire sparkle and dance. I wonder if my mother got caught out or if she made it back to her bed. I wonder if Goola's discovered Bart yet, swimming in his own dark blood. My sixteen years of existence lie in the village. I look up and Circ winks at me between overlapping shrouds of gray cloud cover.

I turn my back on the village, scuffing my moccasins in the durt just enough to scrape off the dust of my old life.

~~~

I'm barely a half mile southwest of the village when the alarm sounds. They've found Bart.

They'll organize quickly, start the Hunt. This time not for tug—for me. With cries and wind behind me, I lengthen my strides, pick up my pace. Run as fast as I'm truly capable of. The britches my mother made me feel weird and restricting against my skin. But at the same time, they make running so much easier. There's nothing to swirl 'round my feet, to trip me. Wearing britches makes me feel alive, somehow.

Something feels heavy in my shirt, glancing against my ribs every few steps. When I rove with my hand I find a wide pocket. And in it: a sheathed knife. I pull it out, feel the swirls of the carved handle against my palm. From touch alone, I know what's carved on the hilt. The sun goddess's eye. The matching knife to the one my mother killed Bart with. Fresh tears swim in my eyes but I blink them away, tuck the knife back into my pocket.

I run for miles and miles, never slowing. For once in my life, my feet manage to keep out of each other's way. At first I navigate by instinct alone, but eventually the night's cloak is tossed aside and the stars show me the way. *Southwest.*

Sometimes the rhythms of the desert whisper songs in my ear. They're 'bout lives long past, 'bout heroes of old whose incredible feats of bravery are destined to be repeated by new heroes.

But not tonight. Tonight I hear different sounds. The sounds of the Hunt. Heavy feet, shouts. They're muffled and perhaps miles back, but they sound like they're on top of me, like Bart was not that long ago. I find myself glancing back more'n more frequently.

When I start running with my head turned perpetually behind me, I run smack into a prickler. No doubt one of Perry's friends. The shock of the barbs piercing my skin, and my head ratcheting off the thick plant focuses me. I'm clumsy. I'm imperfect. But I'm not done yet. I won't be caught tonight. Tomorrow maybe, but not tonight.

I drag myself to my feet and start again, plucking out prickler barbs as I go.

This time, I stop looking back, for I know what's back there. A torn world, a shredded life, those who'd harm me, blame me for the death of a horrible person like Bart. My father, the worst one of all, secure in his knowledge that he'll never hafta suffer the pain of the Fire, 'cause of his agreement with the Icers, etched with the blood and lives of the poor souls of the village, men like Raja.

In a world where there're so many things that can kill us—sandstorms, wildfires, wild beasts, the Fire—where the Law rules all else, I woulda been forced to reproduce steadily from age sixteen till my family was full. My mom didn't want that for me. That knowledge keeps me going.

I gotta tell Circ. The words slip into my mind so casually, like they have for ten years. He's always been the first person I tell anything to. Now that he's gone, I wish I never had anything to tell. The yearning to be near him grows stronger with each crunch of my feet on the brittle desert landscape. To feel his knees against mine, to see his dimpled smile, to talk with him, laugh with him. Oh, Circ.

Circ, Circ, Circ.

Where are you?

Ages later, when the sun casts a reddish smear on the edge of the horizon, I stop. My heart beats firm and fast, but not wildly. My britches and shirt are soaked through with sweat. I'm breathing heavy and tired, but not out of breath. There's fight left in me yet.

With the added light, I finally turn to survey the desert to my back. There are black dots in the distance, but they appear to be miles away. Maybe Hunters, maybe something else, like a pack of Cotees, fresh on the blood trail left by my prickler wounds. I can't stop yet.

Life goes on all 'round me as the desert wakes up. Tiny-nosed burrow mice peek from their holes, snuffling at the wind, darting back inside when I tramp past. Lazy-winged vultures cast shaky shadows across the sand as the sun edges over them. Piles of busy fire ants stream from their anthills, forcing me to zigzag to avoid trampling them under my feet.

I don't run anymore, but walk in long strides. The sun beats on me, but I don't mind, as it's spring, and there are worse things'n sun in spring. After the early spring rains, clumps of scrubgrass and pepperweed poke from the sand, the beginning of the regrowth. Already the pricklers are looking less brown and tired, more green and awake. I wonder how Perry looks now, whether he's changed. Probably not—in my memory he'll always be the brittle-brown wisecracker I knew.

I eat lunch while I walk. When poking around in my shirt and trouser pockets, I found my mother left more'n just a knife with me. Thick strips of tug jerky and crunchy shards of fresh-cut prickler bits were packed in leather skins. The jerky gives me strength, the pricklers give me fluids. They won't last long—maybe a day or two—but at least I can focus on getting as far away from the village as possible, rather'n finding food and water.

Water, as it turns out, ain't a problem. The rains come in the afternoon, and I drink to my fill. With no one 'round, I strip off my shirt and let it catch the rain, and then wring it out into my mouth. Although the prickler moistened my dry tongue and throat, it can't compare to the downpour. I'm drenched and half-naked and excited and more alive'n I been in a long searin' time.

The rain'll cover my tracks, too. The Cotees might be able to stick with me, if that's what was following me back there, but if it was the Hunters, well, they'll hafta turn back, no matter how much my father screams and rants and rages.

I'm free. The thought pops into my head and I wonder what it means. Free of what? Of my father, yeah, I s'pose so. Of my duty under the Call to Bear children to a random guy. Yeah, that too. But am I free really? I guess time'll tell, like it always does.

As I continue on, the rains slow and then stop altogether, but the sky keeps wearing its gray blanket, blotting out any sign of the sun. The break from the heat is much needed.

Darkness falls early, as if the sun goddess has given up the fight against the clouds. As everyone who lives in fire country knows, Mother Nature is a powerful foe. I know I hafta stop sometime, to rest, to gather my wits, to sleep, but the time don't feel right so I don't. Into the night I trudge, stopping only when I hear the hair-raising sound of Cotees howling to the south.

I'm dead on my feet, and I wish I'd stopped two thumbs of sun movement ago, when maybe the Cotees were too far to gather my scent. But now I can't stop, 'cause stopping means they'll catch me. I veer further west, off course, knowing I can get back on track once danger has passed.

For two awful miles I hear nothing 'cept the sound of my own ragged breathing. Then there's another howl. Closer. Much closer. Too searin' close for burnin' comfort.

I break into a sprint, my muscles aching against me, screaming for mercy, getting ignored by my heart and brain which know full well that this is life or death. Out here all alone against a pack o' Cotees, I ain't got a chance.

More howls, different now, not just sounds of interest, but sounds of delight, as they close in on their prey. I can't outrun them—I'll hafta fight. My fingers close over the knife handle in my pocket. When to turn? When to fight? I run a little further, delaying the inevitable.

Something jumps out from the sand, grabs me, bites me on the ankle. I fall, my teeth chattering as my chin slams onto the wet ground. It's got me by the ankle, chomped down so hard I feel like it might tear my foot right off my leg. But what is it? Not a Cotee, that's for sure. It came from the front, almost out of the sand, like a snake from a hole. But the bite on this thing ain't no snake.

I twist my body 'round to get a look at my attacker, crying out as the slight motion sends quivers of pain up my leg. I was right, not a Cotee. Not a snake neither. A searin' trap, set by some baggard Hunter who's too much of a shanker to go out and work for his food. And now he's got me in it, clamped between the metal teeth of a well-anchored mouth.

The pain is nothing compared to the fear. The Cotees are so close I can hear the snuffle of their wet breathing and the trod of their padded paws in the durt. By the time the Hunter finds me I'll be in ten different pieces. Like with Bart, I got no chance. But in honor of my mother, I'll fight anyway.

The first of the Cotees slinks into sight, not running hard, *knowing* by some sixth sense that I'm just setting here waiting for him. His lithe movements remind me of how Goola, in all her nakedness, approached Bart confidently, so sure she'd win his affection. Behind him, six other brown four-legged forms approach. A small pack, but far more'n I can handle on my own.

As they circle me my heart hammers in my chest. I'm scareder'n I ever been 'fore.

I could just let them take me, so I can be with Circ. Find my place in the stars. I can't. I can't 'cause it's not what Circ would want.

My hand aches and I realize with a start that I still got the knife, my fingers biting into it so hard they're hurting. I ease my grip slightly, gritting my teeth at the pain from the trap's teeth in my leg. I ain't a fighter. I'm not built for it.

The first Cotee closes in, snaps at me. I swing hard, put everything I got into it, slashing the knife forward like a spear. The Cotee jumps back, which I realize was always the plan, and I miss, my momentum throwing me facefirst into the durt.

In more pain'n I can swallow down, I know my only chance is to get outta the trap. Stuck like this, I'm 'zard stew. I pull as hard as I can, straining against the metal jaws. "Arrr!" I roar when a red hot burst travels through my nervous system. But I manage to stagger to my feet with the clamp still grabbing my ankle. I'm up, but hobbled, and still unable to move outside of the range of the tether that holds me.

I notice the Cotees are shying away a little, perhaps 'cause of my pain-filled yell a few moments ago. They mighta mistook it for a cry of anger, of violence. Maybe that's what it was. I yell again and they move further away. Once more I release a bellow into the night, but this time they just stare at me. They ain't fooled anymore and my dry throat is growing hoarse.

They close in, blood in their eyes, licking their lips.

"C'mon!" I yell and it doesn't faze them. They just keep moving, padding along, vicious and graceful.

One gets too close. I jab the bugger in the neck with my knife, surprised at how easily the sharp weapon slides through his fur and skin and inside him. Warm liquid flows over my hand and when I pull the blade away it's coated with red. First blood has been spilt.

The Cotee almost looks surprised, it's jaw wagging open, it's eyes bugging out, like it's wondering how the scorch an outnumbered runt of a girl managed to get the best of him. He staggers like he's had too much fire juice, goes down on one knee, and then collapses, tongue hanging from his mouth and eyes rolled back into his head. Dead. 'Cause of me, who ain't the fighter.

The others waste no time. They pounce from all sides, biting and clawing. I hack with my knife, but it's fruitless. There're too many and I'm too weak. I fall to the ground, part of a moving pile of hair and squirming bodies and stars, oh how many stars, peeking in from between cracks in the mass of animal bodies surrounding me. Circ watching. Watching. Watching.

I'm coming, Circ.

The world goes black.

Twenty-Seven

All that's left is darkness.

I expected to see a burst of light, maybe the sun or the moon or the stars, or even all three at once, coming to greet me, to welcome me to t'other side. But all I see is a thick fog of darkness. Dread fills my heart when I realize where I must be: Scorch. The underworld. 'Cause of my actions—disobeying my father, not fulfilling my duty as Bearer, running away—I been sentenced to eternal searnation in Scorch, to live forever with the fire god himself.

No chance of seeing Circ here.

Awareness leaves me and I fall into a deep pit of sleep.

~~~

It's still dark when I awake. Sleep beckons me but I push him away, tell him to pick on someone else. Try a naughty prickler named Perry. He could use some sleep.

Using only my mind, I try to cast away the fog that surrounds me. My hands don't work. Nor my legs. None of my parts, 'cept for my mind. Push, swim, breathe, *thud thud, thud thud, thud thud.* The beat of my heart is like thunder in my head.

Don't make sense.

The dead's hearts don't beat.

Darkness surrounds and I fall away.

~~~

When I awake the third time, the world is one big mess of light. I cringe, shield my face. Maybe darkness was a better option. No! If I'm in the light, then I can see Circ! He'll be here somewhere, wherever stars go when they're off duty.

I remember my beating heart. Musta been a bad dream.

Blink, blink, blink away the haze and the spots.

Blink again.

Blink some more.

The world reappears and I'm not in the land of the gods. I'm in the desert. Still. A hand on my chest reveals my heart: still beating. Not dead. As far from Circ as death from life.

A voice startles me. "You're awake," it says.

Everything comes rushing back in a swarm of memories. My mother's face, red and old and stricken with the Fire; Bart's rank breath on my tongue, his arousal pushed up hard against me; his dead body, limp and bloody at my mother's hand; my flight, the alarms, the Hunt; the Cotees, all over me, tearing my flesh, ripping me away. "The Cotees," I say, my voice whisper-soft.

"Dead," the voice says. A male voice. Old. Maybe twenty. "You killed them."

I'm dizzy and muddled, but I ain't stupid. "Tugblaze," I say. "I killed one, maybe two at the most, but not all." I twist my neck to find the mouth that's connected to the voice but everything's still too bright and spotty.

A laugh, deep and slow. "Well, your mind's recovering," he says. "You'd already killed one when I chanced upon you, and you had your knife buried in another one, so I guess I can give you credit for that one too. The rest were mine."

Violence is sharp and threatening in his tone. Shivers run down my spine. "What are you going to do to me?" Memories flash and dance. Bart grabbing me, holding me down, trying to *use* me.

"You have nothing to worry about. Soon as you're well enough, we'll be going our separate ways." The sharpness is gone from his voice, replaced by a soothing melody that feels like the warmth from one of MedMa's healing salves.

His shadow kneels over me, then the real him. I blink furiously, afraid this might be the last chance I have to glimpse he who saved me from the Cotees. He's blurry at first, but then his image sharpens like a spear point. When it does, I jerk back, try to push to my feet, to run, to escape, to get as far away from him as I can. But my body won't cooperate and all I do is spasm on the ground, feeling hot lashes of pain on my arms, legs, belly, ankle. Fierce, red pain everywhere. But the pain is nothing compared to the fear.

'Fore me stands one of them. The Marked. And all I can think 'bout is what my mother told me 'bout Brev: *He started the Marked and I never saw him again.*

~~~

Apparently I passed out again. My body is in turmoil, fighting against the blood loss and the shock of all the bites and claw scrapes from the Cotees.

When I awake this time I'm ready. "Let me go," I say, not opening my eyes, not wanting to see him again.

"You're not a captive," his voice comes back, clear and warm.

"Then why'd you do it?"

"Do what?"

"Save me."

"Because you were in my trap."

What? The steel-teethed trap is his? "So you owed me?"

"I don't owe you a thing."

"None of this woulda ever happened if not for your searin' trap!" I say, raising my voice to the loudest it's been. Still barely more'n a whisper.

"Not my fault you were stupid enough to step in it," he says, keeping his voice irritatingly calm.

"Stupid? How dare you! I almost died 'cause of your *burnin'* trap!" My eyes flash open and I wince when I see him standing over me. But this time I don't try to run, just stare at him, trying to hide my disbelief at his appearance.

He's practically naked, only a small brown loincloth covering his midsection. Like Circ was, he's muscled from head to toe, but longer and leaner, like one of the trees I saw in ice

288

country on a night that now seems like a million lifetimes ago. His skin is hairless, either shaved or plucked or perhaps never there at all. But that's not what startled me the first time I laid eyes on him. It was the markings. They cover him from head to toe, strange and black and rough, like the textured bark on the trees. Everything 'bout him is so much like the trees I almost expect him to sprout green leaves that'll drop from his arms in the fall.

He sees me staring and smiles. "You like what you see?" he says, rolling each word off his lips.

I crinkle my nose in disgust. "'Bout as much as I like a dead tug carcass," I say, "and I can't help but stare at that just the same, too."

He smirks. "It wasn't my trap that almost killed you. You shouldn't have been wandering the desert alone in the dark. What were you doing out here by yourself?"

"That's my business." I realize I'm still staring at his body, trying to make sense of the markings. I also realize I've barely even looked at his face.

When he replies, my gaze snaps up. "Suit yourself," he says, walking out of my field of vision. But his image remains, burned in my mind, where I can review it as long as I want. Even his head was free of hair, as bald as the day he was born, shaped like a dome. A nice-shaped head, for what it's worth. It's worth nothing. Nobody cares about a nice-shaped head. Even his head had the markings, thick bands and arrowheads, and strange shapes I don't recognize. Only his face is free of them. Which is a good thing 'cause he had a handsome face. Not exactly smoky, like Circ, but pleasing to the eye. Not repulsive, like the rest of him.

Brev. The name pops in my head and although I don't want to talk to the Marked one anymore, I know I hafta. I hafta ask him.

I try to sit up, but a flash of pain bursts in my skull and I'm gone again.

~~~

When I regain consciousness it's night again. The stars are out, but I can't find Circ. He's probably looking for me in the land of the gods, where I'd be if not for the Marked man.

"What's your name?" he asks.

I can't see him, which makes me uncomfortable, so I try to sit up again, taking it slower this time. One elbow up, then the other. Ease higher until I'm sitting. He's sitting across the warm glow of a cook fire. A rusty ol' pot's a-steaming away, filling my nostrils with an aroma that's both tangy and bitter at the same time.

"My name's my bus—"

"Your business, I know," he says, cutting me off. "Well, I'm Feve, in case you'd like to know. My name's not business, far as I know. It's just a name."

Through the crackling fire he almost looks normal. I can't see his markings, just his face. He could be a guy from the village. A potential Call.

"I'm Siena," I say, wondering why I said it.

He smiles, undimpled but warm. Like everything 'bout him. Warm as a spring afternoon. "That wasn't so hard, now was it?"

"You ain't charming nothing else outta me," I say.

"So it was my charm that did it?" he says, his eyes flashing with firelight.

"No, that's not what I meant! I meant…you just twisted my words."

"Twisted?" he says, the amused smile still playing on his lips. "You said it, not me."

I sit back, leaning on my elbows. If that's the way he's gonna play things, I won't say another word, even though I know I hafta.

Brev. A name I'd never heard a few days back—now a name I can't forget.

He rises, bringing his markings back into view. A snake coils around his stony abdomen, disappearing behind him. Three spears cross in such a way that they almost look like the skeleton of a tent. There are many more markings, but my brain goes dizzy from trying to make sense of them all.

"Here, drink this," he says, dipping a skin into the steaming pot. He hands it to me.

"What is it?" I ask, turning up my nose when I taste bitterness in the steam.

"Marked secret," he says, winking. "It'll help with the pain and the healing."

I sit up, accept it, cup the skin in both hands. "What are you, some kind of MedMa?"

"MedMa?" he says, cocking his head at an angle.

"Medicine Man," I elaborate. "We've got one in our village. He heals the sick, treats the wounded."

He laughs, sits down next to me. Too close. I edge away.

"All of my people learn how to heal," he says.

His answer surprises me. All of them? Seems like a lot of wasted time when one person could do the job just fine. As if reading my mind, he says, "You'd be dead if I didn't know the right herbs to use, how to wrap your wounds."

My wounds? The biting, the clawing, the trap. Wounds! Of course I'd have them in plenty. But I've barely been conscious long enough to think 'bout anything, much less my wounds. I chew on his words and then spit them out when I realize what he's done. "What'd you do to me?" I shriek, pulling away from him, clawing at my britches as if I'm one of the Cotees that tried to kill me. When I lift my bloody, torn trousers up high enough, I see the truth. Shreds of cloth are wrapped tightly 'round my ankle, my legs below my knees, my legs *above* my knees—waaaay above my knees.

My hands scrabble at my shirt and lift it too. Heavy cloth covers the skin, spotted with blood. "You touched me?" I accuse.

"You were dying," he says calmly. "I treated you."

The thought of me lying there unconscious while this Marked man did whatever it is he did to me—touched or bandaged or *treated* me—makes me feel sick and I throw down the skin, letting the bitter, tangy liquid bubble out. "How dare you?" I say.

"You'd rather be dead?" he asks evenly.

"No...I mean, yes...I mean, maybe," I say, sputtering. Protectively, I cover my chest with my arms, not dissimiliar to when Bart was looking me up and down.

His voice is devoid of all humor. "What happened to you, Siena?"

When he says my name it fills my heart with warmth, as if it's someone I care 'bout speaking it. But he's no one, a stranger, one of the Marked. "Nothing."

"What do the charms on your bracelet mean?" he asks.

"Nothing.

"What about the one with the pointer? What does that mean?"

I say nothing.

"Who does it belong to?" he asks, and my eyes jerk to his. Does he know? Are his questions all part of an act when really he knows the truth 'bout everything? 'Bout what happened to me, to Circ—what's happening even now to the village?

"What do you know 'bout it?" I say, breaking my silence.

Feve looks at me with an intensity that's almost scary. Almost. "Tell me," I demand.

"I don't know anything, but I'm a good guesser," he says.

"Well so am I," I say. "Does the name Brev mean anything to you?"

His eyes snap to mine and there's a flare of anger, which ain't what I expected. "What did you say?" he says, all warmth stripped from his voice.

I pause, wondering why Feve suddenly seems so hot and bothered. "You heard me," I say.

"That name means nothing," he says. "'Cause he's dead."

~~~

He won't say another word after that, no matter how hard I try to make him. Finally I drink a fresh skin of the healing liquid and it helps with the pain. Warm and confused, I drift off to sleep.

When I awake, Feve is gone.

Twenty-Eight

He left me a skin of herbal tea, enough Cotee meat to last a quarter full moon, and a head so muddled I'm afraid it's full of durt and sand and rocks and maybe a bit of 'zard blaze.

I dunno where he went, and I'm not sure whether to care. I mean, he saved my life but if it wasn't for his searin' trap...the Cotees woulda caught me anyway. The realization sets in hard and fast. I probably shoulda been nicer to him. But still, the thought of him lifting my trousers up, up, up, too far up, reminds me of Bart ripping off my dress—even though I know in my heart they ain't the same thing at all. Bart was taking from me, Feve was giving to me.

I can't believe I met one of the Marked Ones! I almost want to scream it out loud. No one back in the village would ever believe me. They're the people of myths and legends. Not myth. Not legend. Real. Just like my mother said.

The fire's dying so I stir it up, cast a few prickler skins on it, cook up a swatch of meat. I eat slowly, afraid my stomach'll reject the heavy food after going without for so long. It stays down and I cover the fire and smoke with sand 'fore I leave.

Everything hurts, but a few sips of Feve's tea takes away most of the pain—or at least enough of it that I can walk again. Instinctively, I shove a hand in my pocket and feel for my knife. It's there. I pull it out, remove it from its sheath, examine it. Clean and shiny—not one speck of Cotee blood on it. Another gift from Feve. If I ignore the fact that he had to stick his hand in my pocket to put the knife back, I almost feel warm from the gesture.

Everything I've seen from Feve certainly changes my perspective on the Marked Ones, 'specially now that I know my mother's true love was the one who started the tribe in the first place. Maybe they're not so scary and violent and cannibalistic as everyone seems to think. Or maybe I just got lucky 'cause there was plenty of Cotee meat to satisfy his hunger. I shudder at the thought of how different things mighta gone if he'd found just me caught in his trap.

I look 'round, get my bearings, and continue southwest like my mother told me to. The day is hot at first, but then, like most spring days, gives way to a burst of rain that stifles much of the heat. Three days pass with periods of both rain and sun, stutter-stepping at the whims of Mother Nature. I eat Cotee meat every night, drink Feve's tea, get stronger with each passing day.

The fourth day since Feve's departure—which I s'pose is the fifth or perhaps sixth day since I left the village—I spot it, a change in the endless monotony of the desert. From far away it looks like just a small crack in the earth, perhaps a hidey-hole for a 'zard or snake, but as I approach, it grows bigger'n bigger, until it's a gaping crevice, wide and deep and winding off into the distance.

Southwest, where the river lies dead like a snake...

There's no water in the ol' riverbed, save for a few durty puddles from the spring rains. If it ever was a river, it's long dead. And as for the snake part, the way it twists and turns proves I'm in the right place. Although it's winding, there's no doubt it's meandering in the same direction as I wanna go. Southwest.

On and on I follow the Dead Snake River, camping along the edge, hoping that each new day'll bring me to the next landmark—what was it my mother said? *...and the rocks hold hands like lovers.*

I picture two rocks that look exactly like Circ and me, rock arms outstretched, rock hands entwined. Were Circ and I lovers? Does a single kiss make lovers? As I plod along I'm blinded by the tears in my eyes, as blurry as a knock to the head. Whatever Circ and I were, it went beyond the simple labels of humans. Lovers, friends, family...

...soul mates.

That's the only one that feels right when I think it. But Circ's soul's gone far away, where I can't reach it, where maybe I can never reach it. I dry my eyes on my sleeve and keep moving.

~~~

I'm down to the last of my Cotee meat. The herbal tea ran out a coupla days ago but it did its job. Although I'll have scars from the bites, they're all healed over with no infection. 'Cause of Feve and his bandages and Medicine Man training. I'd have died twice over if not for him.

I ain't no Hunter.

The women of the village don't Hunt. They gather and Bear and look after the Totters and wash bloody, filthy clothes. Not Hunt.

But I gotta get food and more'n just prickler skins which leave me feeling unsatisfied. So I take my knife and my speed and both my left feet into the desert to catch me whatever I can catch—a burrow mouse or 'zard or something. I don't venture too far from the dried out river though for fear of getting lost.

I ain't no Hunter.

I know I already said that but after three thumbs of sun movement in the desert I prove it. The 'zards are cleverer'n I ever knew. Here I been thinking they scuttle and scamper 'round aimlessly all day, just waiting for us humans to catch them and skin them. The first one I see is back in its hole the moment I give a funny look in its direction. A moment later it pops outta a different hole on t'other side of me. When I take a step in its direction it jumps back down and outta sight.

The burrow mice are no easier. I find a whole nest of them, but no matter how deep I dig, all I find are more'n more tunnels with no mice. At some point I realize I ain't gonna be killing anything, but it ain't only 'cause I can't seem to get close enough to stick one of them; it's 'cause I don't *wanna* stick one of them. The thought of taking the life of something so small makes me feel sick to my stomach. To save my life from a pack of Cotees, yeah, I'll slash and fight like a wooloo person, but I can't just stab an innocent creature.

I trudge back to the river emptyhanded.

That evening I eat what's left of the Cotee with a side of prickler. Wash it down with a shirt squeeze of rainwater when it starts pouring. Sleep, wet and exhausted next to a fire that's all smoke and wet prickler skins.

~~~

The sun goddess drives Mother Nature and her armies of dark clouds back. By afternoon my clothes are dry, as if they were never soaked through in the first place.

When I get hungry I munch on the tug jerky my mother put in my pockets. Soon I'll have nothing left but the pricklers growing across my path.

Midafternoon, when the sun is long past its apex and starting to sink on down, the Dead Snake River ends. Just ends, like someone filled in the rest of it with durt and sand, made it look like it was never there at all. The tail of the snake—or is it the head?—seems to point off across a wide expanse of flat land. A sure sign as any, so I follow it.

Just as the world is darkening, I spot them. Statuesque soldiers, set out in perfect little rows, directly in my path. Hundreds of them, weather-beaten and proud and probably relatives of Perry. Pricklers. It's a field of pricklers. I ain't never seen anything like it. Most pricklers are loners, wearing their solitude like a badge of honor. Occasionally you'll find a small group of them huddled together—prickler families we call them—but never more'n four in a patch.

298

As I enter their ranks, they seem to close in 'round me, watch me, like they're guarding something. But that's wooloo talk. They ain't no more alive'n Perry was. Yeah, that's right, Perry, you heard me!

Night falls while I'm still amongst the pricklers, and I hafta squint to avoid banging into them—there are that many. Something big'n dark rises up 'fore me, but I can't see what. It's not alive, that much is obvious. It's just something big…and dark. A rocky bluff or black sand dune or something.

I can't see, so I make camp right there within the merry band of pricklers. I'd like to say I don't conversate with them, but a few of the prickly buggers knew Perry from way back when, so I can't help but to do a little reminiscing, tell a few stories and jokes at Perry's expense.

Sleep takes me.

~~~

I awake to lovers holding hands.

It ain't like I pictured it, with two well-cut statues that resemble humans walking hand in hand, but the landmark is clear nonetheless. The big, dark form that I could feel looming in front of me last night is really a rock formation. On either side, pillars of rock rise up, one with a broad, pluming base that narrows at the woman's "waist" 'fore curving back out to give her a nice shape. Her lover's body is bulky and sharp, all angles and edges—no doubt a man. They're connected by a rock bridge that extends from either of them—their "arms"—which meet in a tender embrace in the middle.

A shout rises up in the distance and suddenly the previously barren desert is teeming with human life. Half a dozen forms charge my way. Double that many run in the opposite direction, directly beneath the arch of the giant lovers, hollering as they go. Raising the alarm.

Even from a distance I can see their half-naked, lean, muscular bodies. Their shaved heads. My eyes might be betraying me, but I think I can see their markings, too, dark and twisting on their skin. The Marked. Not just Feve, who might be one of the few civilized ones, but many of them. Racing toward me, carrying sharp sticks.

Uncivilized. Cannibalistic. Bloodthirsty.

Maybe I was wrong. Maybe Feve wasn't acting his usual self.

With their shouts loud and frightening behind me, I run.

Through the ranks of the pricklers I run, stumbling once, regaining my footing, clipping the side of a small bulbous prickler that seems to jump out in front of me; sliding face and chest first in the durt, scrambling, scrambling, scrambling to my feet; heart pumping wildly, urging me on; two left feet moving in tandem once more, but conspiring against me in whispers. To someone watching, my flight is surely comedic and laughable, but to me it's terrifying. These feral men'll catch me, pin me down, and then what? I don't wanna find out.

Out of the pricklers I dash, finally finding my running rhythm out in the open. The shouts are closer and I get the sense that they're not just mindless screams but carrying messages, either for each other or for me. But I'm not 'bout to stop to interpret them.

All of a sudden the earth falls away beneath me as I reach the edge of the Dead Snake River. I teeter over the edge, waving my arms chaotically, but then manage to hold off gravity.

I take a step away from the ledge, feeling the fall that never happened in my gut.

I glance back, see only the blurred forms of my pursuers closing in, much closer'n I expected as if they have superhuman speed, like they're part Cotee or Killer.

I turn to the edge once more. Running'll get me nowhere. I got no choice.

I hafta jump.

My muscles tense, preparing for the twenty-foot drop onto the dry riverbed.

I hold my breath—

"Burnin' wait!" a voice cries. It sounds strange for a Marked voice. So unlike Feve's, which was warm and steady and controlled, this voice is wild and rough and passionate, like a spinning dust storm. And familiar. So familiar, and yet not how I remember it.

Don't trust it—

But I know that voice.

Could be a trick—

How do you trick a voice?

My inner struggle tugs me toward the edge. One foot slides over, sending sand and rocks careening down the nearly vertical slope. But that voice...

I whirl 'round and see her. The voice don't match the body.

"Lara?" I say.

Twenty-Nine

She's too tall to be Lara. And yet she carries herself with the strength and confidence that Lara always had. Also like Lara, her hair is cropped short, like a boy's, not fully bald like the image of the Marked my mind conjured up from a distance, but nearly so. Her body is toned and sheening with sweat from the run, covered only by a swatch of cloth 'round her chest and a flap on the front and back of her torso, leaving her hips exposed. Images are painted on her skin: a sun, a flame, a tree.

I gasp.

The voice, so familiar, but not Lara's...

"Siena, burn it all to scorch, you found us!" my sister says.

It's her, but not her. Skye, but as far from the Skye I remember as possible. I'm frozen to the ground, like a cold breeze has blown in from ice country, cementing my feet. Can it be? Can it really be her?

I'm dreaming, I'm dreaming, I pinch myself, *Ow!* It hurts. It hurts so good. It's real—all of it.

I run to her. She throws down her sharp stick and catches me, her arms so strong and firm and protective, and I feel like I'll never be in danger again as long as I stay near her. Near my sister.

"Sie," she murmurs. "I can't searin' believe it's really burnin' you." It's my sister's voice, but rougher, sharper 'round the sides, like each word is cut all along its edges. And filled with obscenities the likes of which I ain't never heard flying from her mouth.

My tears are swarming but I don't feel ashamed. It's all there, in my eyes, the gashes in my soul laid bare in the streams of moisture on my face. Bart. Mother. Feve. Father. Circ: most of all him.

"Dead," I say, not sure who I'm referring to. Maybe all of them, 'cept Feve. And Father, who I only wish were dead.

"Lara told me," she says, holding me out to look at my face.

"Lara's here?" I say, eyes widening.

"Yeah, she made it, too." Skye looks older'n I remember her, wiser somehow. With her short hair, she should look boyish, but instead it seems to only make her all the more feminine, more beautiful. And yet there's a wildness 'bout her, a freeness, something I ain't never seen in her 'fore.

"What'd she tell you?" I say. She wipes away the tears from half of my face. The side for—

"Circ," she says simply.

I close my eyes.

"I'm so burnin' sorry," she says, thinking I've closed my eyes for Circ. What she don't know is that the tears she hasn't wiped away, the tears on t'other side of my face, are for someone else.

"Mother's got the Fire," I say, scared to say the rest of it, that by now she's dead, that Father has a cure but keeps it for himself, that she saved me from Bart.

She pulls me close and we hold each other for a long time.

~~~

"Siena!" Lara yells as I enter the camp beside Skye.

She runs up and gives me a hug. I hug her back even harder. "You were talking to the Wilds the whole time?" I whisper in her ear.

"Course," she whispers back. "They recruited me long ago. I was never cut out for the Call."

"Why didn't you just tell me?"

"We weren't sure you'd want to come, and your mother—" she says, but then stops, throwing a hand over her mouth.

"My mother what?" I ask, sharper'n I intended.

"You'd better let your sister tell you," she says. "Look, Siena, this was always what I wanted, to get out of the village, to join the Wild Ones, but you..."

"I wasn't a sure thing and you didn't want me to tell anyone," I finish for her.

She nods. "But that doesn't matter now. You're here."

We're still whispering and Skye's watching us suspiciously. I pull away and raise my voice. "I'm here. But where's here?" I ask, scanning the camp.

Dozens of girls are moving 'bout, many of them with short hair like Skye and Lara, carrying on with their business, glancing at us curiously but not outright staring. They're all wearing the same two-piece cloths that leave little to imagination. They're also all lean and muscled and look like they could snap bones with their bare hands.

Skye answers. "We call it Wildtown. It's hidden from all directions 'cause of the canyons, but we can still easily git out the way you came in, 'neath the lover's hands."

Unbelievable. The Wild Ones are real, but they don't look wild at all. On the contrary, they look civilized, with tents and storage sheds and even cook fires that send wisps of smoke curling over the canyon walls. They don't eat raw meat after all.

I scan the canyons, which are pocked with caves. Girls are moving in and out of the caves, carrying bundles of prickler skins and scrubgrass and *weapons*. Spears and daggers, bows and pouches of pointers. Enough weapons to outfit every Hunter back in the village.

"Why do you have so many weapons?" I ask, frowning.

"Fire country's a burnin' dang'rous place," Skye says.

I nod. She don't hafta tell me.

"Are you ready to meet the others?" Lara says, a smile on her lips.

"Meet them?" They don't look too friendly. Other'n their furtive glances, everyone's pretty much ignored me since I arrived. Even the girls who found me with my sister didn't say a word to me, just strode ahead of us, as if I didn't exist. I get the feeling that things won't be any different here'n the village. As usual, I'll be hated for being Scrawny. Always the outsider.

"Searin' right," Skye says, flashing a smile as big as Lara's. What am I missing?

"Uh, sure," I say.

"Can I do it?" Lara says to Skye.

"All yers," Skye replies. I look back and forth between them, trying to figure out why they suddenly seem so cheerful. My eyes settle on Lara, who raises two fingers to her mouth and blows out, letting out a whistle, loud and shrill.

Abruptly, all activity in Wildtown ceases. Prickler skins are discarded, weapons are dropped in the durt, budding cook fires are ignored. Every girl runs toward me, cheering and smiling and whooping and hollering.

Naturally, I shrink back, somewhat afraid, somewhat thrilled by the sudden attention. They close in, the mob surrounding me. Cries of "Welcome, Siena!" and "You did it!" ring out 'round me as they pick me up, clap me on the back, pass me around. Something sparks in me and I can't hold back the laughter. I feel giddy and excited and tearful and *wild*. Completely wild, like I'm already one of them, a long-haired, Scrawny version of them. Tears of joy stream down my cheeks as I laugh harder'n I've laughed in many full moons, years, maybe ever.

For a moment I'm happy. Without a word of question, they've accepted me as one of them.

~~~

After the reception they gave me I'm left breathless. Every girl knows my name 'cause apparently Skye's been talking 'bout me since the moment she arrived. And, although I was introduced to every last one of them, I can't remember a single name.

"You wanna git the scorch outta here?" Skye finally says. I don't want to be rude, but with Skye's invitation comes a chance to get away. Getting attention is much more tiring'n I expected it to be.

I nod, and as she whisks me away I thank as many of the girls as I can, meaning it with every thud of my heart. Lara tags along like my shadow.

Skye takes me to her tent.

Inside, we sit cross-legged in the middle of a wide space, in which a second bed has been added for me to sleep in. Our legs form a triangle, Skye's and Lara's and mine. My head's still buzzing with excitement.

"How're you feelin'?" Skye asks, reaching out to squeeze my hand.

I search my body for the strongest feeling but there are so many. "I—I don't know. Happy and sad and surprised and *everything*."

Skye smiles. "I know exactly whatcha mean. I's the same way when I arrived, more surprised'n a newborn baby tug. Not everyone's been groomed since birth to be a burnin' Wild, like Lara 'ere."

Lara blushes. "I wasn't groomed *from birth*, maybe from a Totter..."

"You were made for this," I say to Lara. Without even trying she fits in with these—these warriors. I'm somewhere between six and sixty miles behind.

"You were too!" Lara protests.

I laugh, hold out my tent-pole arms. "Tell that to my body."

"It's not about that!" she says. "Tell her, Skye."

I look to my sister, once more adjusting to the new her. Everything 'bout her is different. Not just the short hair and her physique, as muscly and lithe as a Killer, but her eyes, too, still brown, but with a steel gray behind her gaze. Also her voice, as cut as her body, as if it's made from stone. It's filled with slang and language so colorful it'd make Mother cringe all

307

the way up in the land of the gods. "She's burnin' right, Sie. It's what's in yer heart that matters. Lara tol' us all 'bout the Killer attack, how you tried to save Circ."

"And about the Glassies," Lara adds.

"The baggards," Skye adds.

I shake my head. "Circ ended up having to save me. And the Glassies? You hadta practically drag me into it, Lara," I say.

"You were already there, remember?" Lara says.

"Tell me everythin'," Skye says. "I wanna hear this blaze from you."

"First tell me 'bout your markings," I say, glancing at her abdomen.

~~~

Her stomach is as flat as the upper parts of the canyon walls, as flat as my stomach even, but like sheetrock, hard and stacked with muscle.

"Hit me," she says. I stare at her strangely. "Go ahead."

"I don't wanna hit you," I say.

"Burnin' hit me!" she repeats, louder this time.

"Just do it," Lara says. "She won't stop asking until you do it."

Tightening my hand into a fist, I aim for the tree marking to the left of her belly button. "Ow!" I grimace when my knuckles connect with her stomach, which might actually be harder'n sheetrock. I pull back my hand, massaging my fingers.

"Father wouldn't recognize me now, eh?" she says proudly.

"*I* don't recognize you," I say. My fingers return to her stomach, graze her skin. A sun. A flame. A tree. No coincidence. "Our charms," I say.

308

"Yeah," she says. "I hadta git rid of the charms, too many bad memories. But I wanted to keep these ones permanently." She nods at her markings.

"Why?" I say, my hand jerking protectively to cover my own bracelet. Circ's charm.

"Burnin' filthy customs and Laws of the Heaters," she says. "First rule: ferget everythin' you learned in that place. Right now."

I frown, think 'bout it, swing the pointer charm back'n forth with the tip of my finger. "If you don't believe in the customs, then why mark the charm symbols on your skin at all?"

She looks away, at the side of the tent. "I hadta keep the three most important people close by. Lara," she says, "can I speak with Sie 'lone for a while?"

Without another word, Lara scoots outta the tent.

~ ~ ~

"What do you know?" Skye asks when Lara's gone.

I stare at her, this imposter that's trying to be my sister. "'Bout what?" I say.

"Ma. How you got here. Any of it."

I shrug. "I don't know much. Mother told me next to nothing till the night of my Call, and then she just said she'd sent you here and she was doing the same for me. And she gave me directions." I shrug again.

Skye pushes out a breath. "Guess she had more time to talk to me," she says. "She tol' me most everythin'."

"She told you about Brev and the Marked?" I say, and as soon as I see Skye's expression, I know she didn't. Least not everything.

"She tol' me 'bout Brev. But what the scorch does he hafta do with the Marked?" Skye asks.

I tell her what little I know, which is next to nothing. How he couldn't hang 'round the village with Mother not being allowed to see him. How he left. That he started the Marked.

"Ain't that interestin'," Skye says, mulling it over for a bit. In my mind is flashing *Feve, Feve, Feve*, like some kind of bright star that can't decide if it wants to shine or not. Should I tell her? Should I tell her that I've met a Marked? I can't. 'Cause then she'll know I was too weak to make it here on my own.

"Have you ever met a Marked?" I probe, snapping her out of her thoughts.

"They come 'round sometimes," she says. "To trade and such. But only their leaders. And they only speak to our leaders."

"Was this Brev guy with them?"

"I dunno. I don't even know their names," she says.

~~~

After getting settled in Skye's tent, we go to meet the Wild leaders. Well, technically I've already met them, but I wouldn't know them from anyone else in the throng.

They set in a large tent, almost as big as our hut back home—well, not *home*, not anymore, and not *our* hut—it was always my father's hut—all in a line. Three girls, three leaders, none older'n twenty. Dim light flickers from torches sticking from the ground, casting an eerie glow over everything. They take turns saying their names.

"Crya," says the one on the left with silky black hair that falls like rain to her waist. Although she hasn't cut her hair like

310

so many of the other girls, her skin is wound with markings, as many as Feve had.

Next, on the right, is, "Brione," with a voice like a hammer, firm and strong. She's built like a tug, with arms the size of my legs and shoulders that could plow through a hut wall. She's gone even further'n the other girls, shaving her hair to the scalp.

The girl in the center, average-looking with brown eyes and standard-length short hair, finishes, her voice as pleasing as tinkling glass. "Wilde," she says. "Welcome to Wildetown."

And with that single introduction, everything clicks into place. Not the *Wild Ones*, but the *Wilde Ones*. Although there is a wildness 'bout all the girls in this place, it's not what gives them their name. This girl, as plain and unspectacular as an old moccasin, started it all when she escaped the Call. I never knew her name but everyone told stories 'bout the first girl who went missing—the first girl who was kidnapped by the Wilde Ones. Really, she left to start the Wilde Ones.

Too engaged in my thoughts, I don't reply. "And we already know your name," she says. "Your sister has told us so much about you."

~~~

I tell them everything. Or at least everything important. I don't tell them 'bout kissing Circ, or 'bout what happened to him, or 'bout my "talks" with Perry. I also thought the bit 'bout almost getting myself killed and being rescued by one of the Marked'll make me look like a Weakling—like they need any more proof of that!—so I skip it, too. I stick to the facts 'bout my father, what he's doing with the prisoners in Confinement, 'bout his agreement with the Icers, 'bout the cure for the Fire. I wanna ask 'bout the Marked leaders, 'bout Brev, but I keep it inside, sealed up tighter'n one of my father's skins of aging fire juice.

When I finish, Crya leans back casually, disinterested; Brione leans forward, plants her elbows firmly on the table in front of her; and Wilde doesn't move at all. None of it seems to surprise her.

"Thank you," Wilde says. "We already knew much of what you told us, but this...*cure*...that is interesting news indeed."

My mouth gapes open. "You already knew most of it?" I say in disbelief. "Then why haven't you done anything about it?" I feel a surge of heat rise up in my chest as I remember Raja and t'other lifers, innocent prisoners.

"Do something?" Crya says, standing, her tone as sharp as a Hunter's blade. "What the scorch is that supposed to mean? You think we give two blazes about the Heaters? Think again."

I shrink back against her stare, sensing a history of violence behind Crya's fierce eyes. She's not one to be trifled with. "Sorry—I—I just—it's all so fresh," I finish lamely.

"It's alright," Wilde says. "Down, Crya."

Gritting her teeth, Crya sits. Brione looks amused by the exchange. "Crya's our Killer," Brione says, and I'm not sure whether she means someone who kills or a real Killer, transformed into a human girl. Perhaps it's both.

Wilde turns back to me. "Unfortunately we can't do much to help the Heaters. The Greynotes have the village by the prickler, so to speak. We're just doing our best to survive. We only monitor what's happening in the village to ensure they don't find us. I'm sorry, Siena, there's not much we can do for those in Confinemement—at least not yet, not until our numbers are greater." Her voice is so steady, so calm, so truthful. I believe every word she says.

"I understand," I say. "How many, uh, Wilde's are there?"

"One hundred and sixty two, including you," Wilde answers.

I raise my eyebrows. "So many," I say. Although there've been plenty of rumors 'bout the number of "kidnapped" girls being on the rise, no one knew the extent. Probably part of the cover up by the Greynotes.

"Seventeen more arrived from yer Call group," Skye adds helpfully.

I scuff the ground with my shoe. There are so many questions I wanna ask, but I'd prefer to talk to Skye 'bout them, so I stay silent.

Thirty

That night there's a welcome party. Apparently they've been delaying it till my arrival—the last from my Call group. All t'others snuck out of the village the day 'fore the Call, but my mother's illness prevented her from helping me to do the same.

When night falls, torches are lit in a circle 'round a massive fire pit, as big as the one in the center of the village. The afternoon was rainy, but tonight the sky is clear; the edge of the moon goddess peeks over the top of the canyon, surrounded by her servants. At first everyone just sits 'round the fire, eating fried prickler and scrubgrass soup, and drinking collected rainwater and prickler juice.

Earlier that afternoon Skye told me how the Wildes don't eat meat. Though they *can* Hunt, they choose not to. Instead they plant and harvest pricklers, scrubgrass, fireweed, and other roots and plants. Most of the year they grow them in the big prickler field I ran into earlier, but during the hot summer days, they dig them up and maintain them within the canyon, so they don't get burnt up by the unforgiving sun. So not only are the Wildes not feral, they don't eat meat. It sickens me how my father and the Greynotes use rumors and lies to spread fear in the hearts of the Heaters.

I'm not sure how I'll feel after a few full moons of eating only plants, but tonight the prickler, which is garnished with some aromatic herb, is delicious. I eat everything on my plate and go back for seconds, which is allowed as part of the celebration. "No burnin' rationin' tonight!" Skye says. "Tonight we dance!"

I laugh, thinking she's had a bit too much of the fireweed she's been puffing on ever since we sat down, but then the music starts. It's just a coupla drums at first, slow and thumping, but soon escalates into a cacophony of entangled sounds including a dozen sand shakers and at least that many reed flutes.

Skye is the first one up, and tries to pull me with her, but I wrench my arm away, embarrassed. She shrugs and starts dancing, moving her hips provocatively, raising her arms above her head and wriggling them like snakes. For a brief moment she's the only one dancing; but soon dozens of other girls clamber to their feet, shrieking and laughing and dancing. Soon Lara, me, and t'other new Wildes are in the minority of non-dancers. Captivated, I watch as the beautifully toned bodies writhe and twist under the firelight. As the music's tempo gains momentum, the girls dance faster'n faster, until their movements are wild and animal, some of them carrying sticks tipped with fire, waving them 'round, painting beautiful fire art

315

in the air. Their shadows wash the canyon walls with gray and black, coursing left and right, pulsing, pulsing.

Although I'm still sitting, there's energy in my veins and my heart's beating wildly. I wanna jump up, join them, be free, but old habits die hard and my father's voice echoes through my head: *Bearers are solemn, controlled, living and dying for their Calls and their children.*

Suddenly, the music stops.

We stare, wide-eyed, as every face turns toward us. Wilde steps out from the crowd to face the new arrivals. "Why do you not dance?" she demands, her voice echoing in the canyon.

None of us answers.

"Tonight you become Wildes," she says. "Tonight you dance and be free!"

As the music starts up again, the Wildes rush forward, pull us to our feet, start moving 'round us. At first I just stand there, awkward and stiff, as Skye shakes and bobs 'round me. But then I spot Lara, the first of the new Wildes to start dancing. She's smiling and laughing and moving. She's got no rhythm, looks completely out of step with the music, but no one seems to care. Skye grabs her hand and twirls her 'round. Excited bubbles churn through my stomach and chest, and my feet lighten.

I start dancing. Just a shake and a shimmy at first, but then more. Lara, me and Skye dance together at first, spinning and twisting and churning, but soon we lose each other in the melee. And then I'm just part of the bodies, sliding and slipping amongst them, feeling more alive'n I've ever felt in my life.

The night is warm and everyone's sweating 'cause of the fire, but no one gives one lick about it. The bodies are so close and so foreign and yet so familiar, somehow. A cry goes up and I watch as Lara's britches are torn above the knee, leaving her muscly legs bare like all t'other Wilde's. Next they shred her shirt, uncovering her stomach, so she only has a strip of cloth 'round her flat chest. Instead of looking shocked and ashamed, she gives me the biggest grin and dances even harder. T'other new Wildes are succumbing to the *clothing adjustment*, too, allowing the others to rip them to pieces.

My heart stutters and I sneak toward the edge of the dancers, planning to slip away when no one's watching. I'm 'bout to make a break for it, when a voice says, "Not so fast."

I look back and it's Wilde, looking anything but ordinary now. Under the firelight her eyes are reddish orange and her hair is streaked with dancing bursts of light. Her skin is warm brown and perfect. She's perfect, like a god fallen from the sky. How I ever thought she looked average is beyond me.

"I'm just, uh, gotta go to the bathroom," I lie.

"Drank too much fire juice?" she says.

"Yeah, way too much."

"You seem fine to me," she says. A beautiful smile flashes across her face and she grabs me by both hands, pulling me back into the spectacular fray. Three other Wildes surround me, pulling at my britches and shirt, tearing the cloth away. *No, no, no, no, no! Stop, no!* In my head I'm screaming, but nothing's coming outta my mouth 'cause I'm on the verge of tears. I know how this'll go down. The laughter, the names, the pointing. When they see my tent-pole arms and scrubgrass legs the music'll stop. Everything'll stop and I'll be run outta the canyon.

Alone and friendless again.

I feel a rush of air against my legs, my torso, my arms.

I close my eyes. It's over. The acceptance, the new friends, the freedom.

Someone grabs my hand, spins me 'round, laughing, laughing, laughing…but not at me. At life, at dancing. I open my eyes.

My legs and arms and stomach are, in fact, bare. It feels weird, being so *exposed* in front of so many people, like a nightmare. But no one's laughing or staring or shouting names at me. They're looking at me, yeah, the same way they're looking at everyone else. Smiles in their eyes and on their cheeks and in their lips.

I dance.

~~~

"Uhhhh," someone groans. My eyes flash open. Skye. She's sprawled out next to me, clutching at her head.

"Skye, what is it? What's the matter?" I say. I scramble to my knees and hover over her.

"Too much burnin' fire juice," she moans.

The laugh springs out of my throat 'fore I can stop it.

"Not searin' funny," she says.

I put a hand over my mouth to stifle another laugh. It kind of is funny. "Why'd you drink so much?" I ask.

"Stupid," she says, rolling over. "I burnin' do it every time there's a welcome party. And every time I say I won't do it the next time."

I shake my head. Again I think how she ain't the sister that disappeared. She's changed and not all in good ways—but not all in bad either. She's independent, making her own decisions, paying for the bad ones with fire juice headaches.

318

"I'm gonna get something to eat," I say.

"Wake me up in a quarter full moon," Skye mumbles.

The camp is already bustling when I crawl outta our tent. Any evidence of the party from the night 'fore's been hauled away, cleaned up. I stand and feel the gentle touch of air on my skin. I gasp, duck back down, hug my knees. I'm practically naked!

It all comes back to me. The ripping of clothes, the shedding of skin, so to speak. In the wildness of the night, of the music and dance, my inhibitions fell away and I almost felt secure in my own Scrawny body. But now, in the stark light of the morning, I feel like a fool for thinking I'll be anything but a Weakling. 'Specially here. 'Specially among these strong girls.

I start to push back into my tent to find something to cover up with, when someone grabs me from behind. "Not so fast," the familiar voice says, using the same words as last night.

Grudgingly, I back out, rise unsteadily to my feet, hug myself. Wilde stands 'fore me, smiling. She's normal again. I mean, she's still strong and has pretty features, but gone is the night magic that made me think of her as a god.

"You look beautiful like that," she says. "Like one of us."

I wait for the punch line. *More like half of one of us!* Or maybe, *As beautiful as a tug leg!* Those I've heard 'fore.

Instead, she says, "C'mon," and grabs my hand. Unprepared for the movement, I stumble, but Wilde holds me up, doesn't laugh, just keeps pulling me along. I don't know what to say so I keep my mouth shut.

She leads me to the central fire pit and I expect her to stop, to sit me amongst t'other new Wildes, who are in a tight cluster, eating and talking, but she pulls me past them. When I see Lara she waves, and I try to flash a confident smile, but I think it comes across crooked and nervous.

When we exit the camp, Wilde releases my hand and slows to let me catch up. The canyon walls narrow and squeeze us closer together. "Do you know why we don't eat meat?" she asks.

I stare forward, wracking my brain. I don't think Skye mentioned why and I didn't think to ask. "'Cause animals are hard to catch?" I guess, remembering back to my pathetic attempts at the 'zards and burrow mice.

She laughs and it reminds me of rain falling at night when I'm trying to sleep, soft and soothing, like a natural lullaby. "Trust me, the Wildes are more than capable of Hunting if we choose to," she says.

"Sorry, I didn't mean—"

"It's okay," she says. "You apologize too much. There's no need for that here. We all make mistakes, but we learn from them." Her words make me relax, my shoulders slumping. For a moment I forget that I've hardly got any clothes on.

"Sorry, I won't apologize anymore," I say. "Sorry, I just did it again."

"And again," she says. Rain falls although the sky is clear. "No, the reason we don't eat meat is because we don't want to rely on it. The village is so reliant on the success of the Hunters, on the ebbs and flows of the tug hurds. One day the Hunters won't find the tug, because they'll be gone. They'll vanish, their numbers decimated by the harshness of fire country or the Killers or by the Hunters' own hands. But we'll survive because we're independent. We grow our own food, more than enough to satisfy every hungry mouth. We're protected from the summer fires in our haven. We build our tents from things that grow, braided plants. Our beds are nests of grass, easily replenished every spring. We're smart. We're capable."

Her words are like a poem that speaks straight to my heart, but right away I see the flaw. "Yeah, but you rely on the village to replenish your numbers. If they die, you die, too." I'm still talking 'bout them as if I'm not one of the Wildes, but I know I am. I have no place else to go.

"You ask a lot of questions," she says, stopping. We're directly below the lovers' hands, the desert framed by the rock formation. The prickler fields beckon to us, green and full of hope.

I look her in the eyes. "That wasn't a question," I say.

She smiles. "We do rely on the Heaters," she says. "One day the Fire will catch up with us and we'll start to die. If there're no Heaters to provide us with runaway girls…" Her voice trails off and her smile vanishes like a snake caught by a vulture out in the open.

"Goodbye Wildes," I say.

"Yes," she admits. "But you've given us hope."

It doesn't take a hut builder to know what she's talking 'bout. "The Cure."

"Exactly."

"My father won't give it up. Even if we tell people 'bout it, they won't believe us. We're outcasts, ferals, freaks." She seems taken aback by my honesty, but I don't stop. "At least that's what the villagers think. And we have no proof 'bout the Cure, 'cept what my mother told me. And she's dead." My voice breaks on the word and I hafta take a deep swallow and blink furiously to keep my composure.

"It's not your father I'm thinking of," Wilde says. "I'm thinking bigger."

I angle my head and frown. It clicks. "You mean…"

She nods. She wants to go straight to the Icies.

"Can I ask you something?" I say, taking advantage of the situation.

She nods. "Hit me," she says, and I almost laugh 'cause I think of Skye saying almost the same thing but in a completely different context.

"You know the Marked leaders, right?"

"Riiight," she says slowly.

"Ever heard of a guy named Brev?"

Her eyebrows lift. "He started the Marked, a long time ago, seventeen, eighteen years I think," she says.

"You know him?"

"Only from what others have said about him. He died in a hunt before I started the Wildes. Before I even knew the Marked were real."

~~~

I'm more nervous'n a new Midder on her first day of Learning. My opponent is another new Wilde named Char, but she's got me in both height and weight. And not by a little. By miles and miles. After this fight the ol' nicknames'll come back for sure.

"You can do it, Sie!" Skye shouts. I wish she wasn't here to watch me get my butt kicked.

Lara pats me on the back and nods encouragingly. I wish she wasn't here either. I just watched her pin her opponent in 'bout three seconds flat. She nudges me into the circle drawn in the sand.

Brione stands in the middle, the instructor for the hand-to-hand combat portion of our training. After my heart to heart with Wilde, I ate breakfast with Skye, who managed to drag her throbbing head out of bed. That's when she sprung it on me. "Training starts immediately," she said.

I wanted to throw up my prickler salad, herb garnish and all.

Brione grabs our hands, pulls them together, forces us to shake. "The only rule is don't kill each other," she says with a gruff laugh, as if she hasn't been making the same joke for every match so far. I'm the last to fight which means my concern has reached a fever pitch. I laugh nervously. The girl across from me just squeezes my hand until it hurts. When she finally releases it, my fingers are mangled and stiff.

Brione backs away. "Fight!" she growls.

Char moves forward and I move back, my legs tangling 'fore I take more'n two steps. I fall backward, landing butt-first in the durt. Not a good start.

She pounces, throws her weight on me, one hand shoving my face into the ground and the other punching at my hopelessly unpadded ribs. I cry out, try to roll away, but she's got me pinned and the count is on. "One," Brione says. "Two!" I squirm and buck and try to roll away, but I'm stuck like a bug trapped under a foot. "Three!"

There are a few claps, a few cheers. Char gets off of me, grinning. She starts to walk away, triumphant, but Brione stops her. "Help her up," she orders. Char stops, looks back, surprised. "Do it!"

Her smile wiped away by Brione's harsh tone, Char offers me a hand. "Thanks," I mumble, taking it. She pulls me up.

"We're in this t'gether," Brione says. "There're no victors, no winners. We're one person, only as strong as she who's weakest." I blush. She's talking 'bout me. I wanna get away, dig a hole, and stick my head in it. "We support each other, help each other. Understand?"

Char nods. "I'm not just talkin' to her," Brione says. "Understand?" she repeats. Murmurs of *yeah* and *yes* and *sure* rumble 'round the edges of the circle. "How 'bout you?" she says to me. I raise my eyebrows. I'm the one who needs the support. Doesn't she know I'm the weakest link? Her hands move to her hips. "Well?"

"Uh, yeah," I say. "Sure."

After it's over, Skye and Lara flank me with words of encouragement, *You'll get them next time*, and *Soon you'll be strong enough to kick the blaze outta burnin' everythin' that moves.* You can guess who said which.

After the first round of fights, Brione explains that the purpose was to see what level we're all at. Now the real training begins, and Skye's not just here to watch me fight and provide obscenity-laden words of encouragement; she's one of the instructors. Although both my ribs and my pride are sore from the first fight, I find waves of excitement coursing through me. When Skye disappeared, she was no fighter either. Now she's teaching others how to fight? Maybe I can learn, too.

They start with the basics: how to block, how to throw a punch, where the good pressure points are to make even the biggest man scream out in agony. Although we're a bunch of girls training, it's all 'bout how to take down a man twice your size. Then they do a demonstration: Brione versus Skye.

We sit cross-legged 'round the circle, chattering with excitement. Most of the girls are betting on Brione and wondering how anyone could match up with her size and brute strength. I'd like to think Skye has a chance, but deep inside I'm thinking the same thing as t'other girls. This'll be over quickly.

Like everyone else, I'm wrong.

They start out circling each other, approaching, backing away, in and out and 'round. "Why doesn't Brione take her out?" I whisper to Lara.

"I don't know," she shrugs.

We soon find out why she's being so cautious. When Brione does make a move closer, Skye's leg flashes out faster'n lightning and snaps across Brione's face. Her head rocks back and she looks stunned. *That's my sister!* I think, my heart leaping.

Brione ain't done yet though, and while she takes more hits'n Skye, eventually she gets within striking distance and starts clobbering Skye with fists the size of tug shanks. Skye tries to escape, lashing out with vicious jabs at Brione's face and head, but it's too late. Brione picks her up and slams her into the durt. Fight over.

Just as she preached earlier, she extends a hand to help my sister up. They're both all smiles. "What's the count?" Brione says.

"Searin' sun goddess, we're dead burnin' even now," Skye says.

Even? They've beat each other the same number of times? My sister has beat the brute who's twice her size as many times as she's lost to her. Incredible! I'm practically giddy with excitement and hope.

"That was amazing," I whisper under my breath when Skye returns to my side.

"I burnin' lost," Skye mutters. But her grin gives away the pride she's feeling. "Anyway, fightin's in our bones. You'll catch on soon enough."

I grin back, hoping she's right.

Thirty-One

I don't catch on that day. By the end of it I've lost sixteen times and I think every bone in my body is broken. For the last two fights I was so tired I couldn't even lift my arms to defend myself.

Skye carries me back to our tent and brings me supper in bed. Lara eats with us, too, chattering on and on about how well I did and how I'll get better and how soon I'll be winning fights. Eventually though, she can't help asking Skye, "So, where do you think I stand in the class?" Lara didn't lose a fight all day, though a few of the girls gave her a real battle.

Skye looks her up and down. "The searin' top," she says. "Tomorrow you'll be fightin' with the class that arrived 'fore the last Call." My heart sinks. Although I know I should be happy for my friend and her rapid advancement, a pit of jealously pops into my stomach, growing and growing until it feels bloated with all the prickler churning 'round in my gut.

Lara's all smiles. "See you tomorrow," she says 'fore she leaves.

"Yeah, tomorrow," I say.

Skye zones in on my mood like a Hunter's pointer on a bird. "You alright?" she asks.

"How am I gonna do this again tomorrow? I can barely move."

"Don't worry. You'll—"

"Catch on?" I say, cutting her off and stealing her words. "That's what you keep saying, but I'm not like you. I'm—"

"Weak? Scrawny? Skinny?" This time she's the word-stealer. "When'll you get it through yer tug-brained head that you ain't any of those things. Stop thinkin' 'em, stop feelin' 'em, and take it one day at a burnin' time!"

The passion in her voice humbles me. So do her words. They're so similar to what Circ told me.

Don't even think those words about yourself. Don't even joke about them. Not now. Not ever again.

My vision blurs. "Sear it, Sie. I'm sorry, I didn't mean to…" Skye hugs me and although it hurts my broken body so bad I wanna cry out, I grit my teeth and bear it. When she releases me there're tears in her eyes, too. "Ma would be proud of you, you know. Her makin' it this far, fer bein' stronger'n you ever give yerself credit fer. You take after her a lot, you know."

"I do?" I say, lifting my chin.

"She's not as weak as we thought. She was always standin' up to Father, just not that we could see. She started talkin' to the Wildes as soon as…well, as soon as Wilde created them. All secret-like, behind Father's back. She had my name at the top of the recruit list. Yers, too, though they weren't sure you'd come."

"I couldn't believe she killed Bart," I say. "I think my eyes were bigger'n Granger's white buttcheeks the day he got his pants pulled down in Learning."

Skye laughs, which scares the scorch out of me. Death ain't no laughing matter. Even with Bart. Then I realize she's laughing about Granger's buttcheeks. "Mother's been hidin' that knife for years," she says, "practicin' with it, stabbing at anythin' she could git her hands on when Father wasn't 'round. I once saw her hack up a tugskin pillow she was plannin' on replacin'."

"But why?" I ask.

"I asked her the same thing when I caught her doin' it, and you know what she said?" I shake my head. "She said you never know when you need to defend yerself or the ones you love, so you've got to be ready. That always stuck with me."

I look at Skye, thinking on what my mother told her, thinking on Skye's words from earlier, about how Mother'd be proud of me. "You know, Skye," I say, "I think Mother'd be proud of you, too."

"Thanks," she says.

And I know I've gotta tell her.

"Brev's dead," I say.

Skye just looks at me, gives a slight nod like she's not surprised, and as tough as Skye seems to be now, she cries with me until we sleep.

Every tear is for Mother and Brev.

~~~

The next day I'm determined not to get down on myself, and though every part of my body urges me to stay in bed, I don't.

Lara's notably absent from the fights, and when some of t'other girls asks where she is, I'm glad to hear pride in my voice when I tell them she advanced a level already.

Again, I don't win a single fight, but I do better. It even takes Char a long while to pin me. I might not have strength in my arms, but I do have strength. My strength, like Skye, is in my speed. I don't have all the right moves, the graceful and tenacious kicks and punches that my sister has, but I can still move. Today I use it to evade my opponents' attacks, to throw them off balance, landing a few blows here'n there. It's not enough to defeat anyone, but at least I'm not completely pathetic.

Latching on to Brione's motto to support even the weakest of the Wildes, t'other girls get behind me whenever I fight, cheering and shouting and urging me on. I might not win a fight, but I do win.

And although I'm sore and tired and wanna just curl up in my tent and let Skye pamper me again, I don't. I set out by the fire with everyone else, eating and listening to everyone's conversations 'bout the day. To my surprise, a measure of love surges through me; not for Skye and Lara only either, but for every last girl setting here, both the ones whose names I remember and the ones I don't. They're family now and I'm glad to have them.

~~~

Although I love it in Wildetown, I been thinking a lot 'bout Circ. What if he was still alive? Would I still've come? Or would he have saved me from Bart, taken me far, far away from the Heaters and the Call and the Law? Or if I *had* still come to Wildetown, could he have come with me? Even Wilde admits the tribe can't survive on its own forever. Would she ever consider adding guys to the mix? Not Calls, but guys that we actually care 'bout, wanna Bear children with. I mean, I'm not in a hurry or anything, but I know if Circ was alive I'd want him to be with me no matter where I was.

I'm just saying.

~ ~ ~

After a quarter full moon I've won twice. After a full moon I'm winning half my fights, not by brute strength but by speed and skill. Skye gives me tips every night 'fore we sleep. And I have muscles! Not big, and kinda hard to see unless you cram your eye right up against my skin, but they're there. My skin feels tight against them.

Some of the girls in my class have cut their hair short, opting to cast away the final reminder of their old life. Others of them have been marked with swirls or artistic designs or images of their own choosing. Lara's got a dozen markings already, and, of course, her hair was already short. She's moved up two more levels, fighting against girls who've been with the Wilde Ones for nearly two years. I'm happy for her. Like me, she belongs here.

My hair is long and my skin unmarked. It's enough for me just to be here. Following Skye's lead, I removed all the charms from my bracelet 'cept for the ones for her, my mother, and Circ. Unlike her, I couldn't bare to part with the bracelet itself. Every night I kiss each charm 'fore I sleep, wishing more of them were alive. Skye's seen me do it a few times but she don't say nothing.

A quarter full moon ago we started learning to use weapons, shooting pointers, throwing spears, fighting with blades. I'm the worst with the spear, improving with the blade, and best with the bow. Even once learning is over, I find myself staying behind, shooting pointer after pointer at the target, until I don't miss.

I've got a long way to go 'fore I can fight like Skye, but at least I'm heading in the right direction. And those awful words that used to occupy every second thought? It's as if they don't exist anymore. I hope Circ, wherever he is, is proud of me.

I hafta blink an awful lot whenever I think 'bout Circ.

As I have been every morning for a while, when I crawl out of my tent I'm excited for another day. However, as soon as I stand I know today'll be different. Wilde's headed in my direction, her face a nest of worry and concern. I've never seen her look scared 'fore, which scares me. "What happened?" I ask, my body tensing up.

"We need to talk," she says. No *good morning...how are you?...did you sleep well?* Not a good sign. "Get your sister," she adds.

I rouse Skye and we follow Wilde to the leader tent, where Brione and Crya are already waiting. Brione's thick lips are pursed and Crya looks like she wants to hit me, her eyes throwing perfectly aimed spears in my direction. There's another girl there, too, small, but with dark, serious eyes that show she's a lot tougher'n she looks. The funny thing about her though, it looks as if she might keel over at any moment, like she's exhausted. Huge, dark bags underline her bloodshot eyes. Her face is red and sweaty, as if she's just run across the entire desert—maybe she has. In my head I'm thinking she should probably sit down.

No one sits.

"Tell them what you told us," Wilde urges the girl.

"I'm Lye," she starts. "I'm the eyes of the Wildes. Every full moon I make a trip to the Heater village, make sure they're not onto us, scope out which Pre-Bearers might make good additions to our group."

I'm surprised but I don't act it, nodding like this is all very expected information. Was it Lye who chose me to join? Or did Skye and my mother have a say in it? But more importantly, why are they telling me this? I'm nobody.

Lye continues. "Just before the last call, I made my trip to the village to make sure all the escapes went off without any problems. I saw you leave the night of the Call." I raise my eyebrows. She actually watched me run off into the desert. "You got away okay. A few Hunters went after you, tracking your footprints, but then the rains made it impossible to stay on your trail." Everything makes sense so far.

"Yeah…" I say, urging her to get to the point.

Wilde says, "Siena, did you see anyone before you got to Wildetown? Did anything happen?"

I stop breathing and my heart skips a beat. The Cotees. Feve. I never told them 'cause I didn't want them to think I was so weak I couldn't even make the trip without help. But what does that hafta do with anything? I let out a slow breath. "Why?" I ask.

Crya charges at me, fists knotted, but Skye bars her path. "You don't get to ask questions!" she screams. "You put us all in mortal danger!"

I shrink back, my face awash with horror. *What?* Danger? But how?

"Back off," Skye growls. "We're all on the same burnin' side 'ere."

"Are we?" Crya says, looking over Skye's shoulder at me. "Because she's keeping something from us. That's what enemies do."

"Crya," Wilde says, her voice as controlled as ever. "This isn't helping."

Crya shoots me one last glare and then casts her eyes downward, backing off. She almost looks embarrassed at her outburst. Skye turns back to me, her eyes almost as sharp as Crya's. "Are you hidin' somethin'?"

I nod. "I didn't think it was important," I plead. "I was embarrassed."

"It's okay, Siena," Wilde says. "Just tell us what happened."

Keeping my eyes fixed on a splotch on the ground, I spill my guts. Tell them 'bout the Cotees, getting caught in the trap, thinking I was dead. Waking up to Feve, the Marked One, his bandages, his herbs, his rapid disappearance. Everything.

"He tricked you," Crya says when I finish.

I glance up, shudder when I see the scowl on Skye's face, and settle on Wilde's gaze, the only one soft enough to bear. "He followed you," Wilde explains.

"What? No! He saved my life!" I protest. There was no lie in his warmth, in his gentle care. I'd be dead if not for him.

"Maybe so," Wilde says, "but he was only there because he was following you. Tell them the rest, Lye."

'Fore I have a chance to consider what Wilde just said, Lye says, "I hung around the village for a few days more, being thorough, making sure your father and the other Greys weren't going to take any further action to track down the runaways. That's when he showed up."

"Who?" I ask.

"The Marked One."

"Feve?" I ask.

"I didn't take the time to ask him his name," she says sarcastically, her eyes narrowing, "but it must've been him." I close my eyes, knowing exactly where this is going. "I knew it was serious though," she continues, "because the Grey's were in one of the hut's all day with the Marked One, with Feve. Under the sunlight I couldn't hope to sneak into the village, but when night fell, I crept in. I arrived just as Feve left the hut—I was searin' lucky he didn't see me when I ducked into the shadows. And then he was gone, like he'd never been there at all."

I feel ill and hungry and angry. How could the man whose very presence was filled with so much warmth betray me like that? Easy—'cause my father probably paid him well, with skins and meat and wood. The baggards!

"The hut walls were thin enough to hear everything if I put my ear up to it," Lye says. "They knew everything. The location of Wildetown, the approximate number of Wildes, the most direct route to get there. It didn't take them long to decide what to do."

"Yeah, hunt us down and kill or capture every last one of us," Crya says, her words clipped and laced with anger."

Lye nods. "They were going to organize the Hunters the next day, take as many men as they could spare."

I count backwards in my head. "But then...shouldn't they already be here?"

Lye sits down, as if her legs won't be able to keep her up as she tells the next part of her story. "I was about to leave the village, to turn a five-day trek across the desert into two days to hopefully warn everyone before it was too late."

"What the scorch happened?" Skye asks.

"The Killers attacked."

~~~

The Killers bought us some time. According to Lye, they came by night, dark shadows with one thing on their mind: satisfy their namesake; kill. Lye had just slipped out of the northern edge of the village, probably through the same gap I escaped from, when the alarm sounded. She thought it was for her, so she ran hard, dove behind the biggest dune she could find.

She heard blood-curdling screams and hair-raising cries, and when she peeked out, the village was in turmoil. The shadows had broken through and were biting, slashing, clawing at anyone in sight. They killed many Heaters 'fore the Hunters were able to maim enough of the beasts to drive the rest away.

Lye waited until it was over, crept back in. No one noticed her. They were too busy carrying the injured to MedMa, dragging the dead to the center of the village where they'd be burned at dawn. Sixty four were killed, including forty six Hunters. In a village as small as the Heaters', losses like that are catastrophic.

When Lye finishes her story about the Killer attack, I let out a deep sigh. Profound sadness rests upon me like a dark cloud. So many innocents killed. However, I realize it's not only a sigh of sadness, it's a sigh of relief at both having not been there when the Killers attacked and at being bailed out. The Heaters won't come for us, not after being decimated like that. Will they?

"The Hunters are on their way," Lye says, and I gasp.

"What? But they've just been slaughtered by the Killers. How can they…?" My voice is high and quivery and draws stares from everyone.

"Your father's hatred for us runs deep," Wilde says. "The Killers may have killed many of his people once, but we take girls every six full moons. And not just girls, *Bearers.* Those who have the ability to add to the population. Without Bearers, the Heaters will wither away to nothing, like a carcass picked clean by scavengers. He's coming to take us back."

"They left three days ago," Lye says. "I managed to get around them as they slept and arrive here ahead of them. We might have two days, but it could be less. They were running hard."

It's all my fault. I led them right to us. I hid the truth of my stupidity from the very people who coulda done something about it. My heart's as hard as stone, cracking and crumbling away. "What do we do?" I ask.

Wilde meets each pair of eyes in the tent. "We fight," she says.

Thirty-Two

Fighting against friends, where the victor extends a hand to help the loser up at the end, is one thing. Fighting to the death is another.

But that's what we'll do. Not just for our freedom from the oppressive Laws that my father stands for, but for each other, for ourselves. For those we've lost: for me, Circ and my mother.

To the death.

With his typical arrogance, my father'll expect to catch us by surprise. That's our advantage. So we'll play into it, pretend to be caught unawares, with our britches down so to speak. Really we'll be ready, with tricks a-plenty up our sleeves.

By Lye's estimation, he only brought fifty Hunters with him, less'n half our numbers. Again, his arrogance playing right into our hands. Either he doesn't realize how many we have, or he thinks he'll crush us like a powder moth under his treads.

Our turf. Ours. We'll let him come to us.

We expect the Hunters to appear at dawn over the horizon, running at full tilt, heavily armored and equipped. Instead, they come at dusk.

After a long day of preparation, we've just sat down to eat, when the scouts run into the camp, preceded only by their shouts. "They're here!" they yell. "The Hunters are here!" A shiver passes through me. The night air is warm.

Silence. First everyone stares at the scouts, who are panting, their elbows on their knees, fear in their eyes. If we look at them long enough maybe they'll disappear like a bad dream. Eventually though, reality sets in. This is happening. All heads turn to Wilde, who stands, her unfinished meal in her hands. "Prepare for war," she says.

Chaos ensues and I find myself walking aimlessly 'round the camp, my legs like lead, my head in the clouds. This can't be happening. So soon after escaping him, my father has hunted me down to bring me back. And not only me—everyone. My fault. Mine alone.

Skye grabs my hand, but I don't respond. "Siena!" she screams, right in my face. I say nothing. She clamps her fingers 'round my cheeks, squeezes, forces me to look into her eyes. My sister's eyes, the same but different. "Do you see the fear?" she asks.

I see only fire. I shake my head.

"Follow me," she says.

She leads me to one of the elevated caves, the one I shoulda gone to as soon as the command was given, with the other archers. I may not be a sharpshooter yet, but Wilde thought I'd be more effective here'n on the ground. The rest of the markswomen already have their satchels of pointers strapped to their backs. Skye helps me with mine.

"I can't do—" I start to say.

"Yes. You can," Skye says. "Do it for Circ."

A cheap shot, but just what I need. If it wasn't for my father Circ wouldn't be dead. He sent him on that mission on purpose, 'cause it was dangerous. 'Cause of me. I won't let him take more of my friends. I won't.

I nod. Skye leaves, gone to join t'other warriors.

~~~

My heart pounds. Sweat pools in the small of my back. My muscles ache from a month of training, but feel stronger'n ever. Revenge burns in my chest.

From my elevated vantage point I can see the entire camp. Skye and t'other warriors sit 'round the still-burning fire, eating and joking and carrying on as if nothing is different. An act for the Hunters.

My eyes dart to the canyon entrance, which dances with flickers from the fire. Shadows play on the walls, making me tense up. I relax when I realize no one's there. *Breathe*, I think, forcing the air in and out of my lungs.

Beside me, a dozen other archers wait as I do.

A Hunter creeps through the entrance, bow drawn, pointer strung. Aimed at the warriors 'round the fire. Aimed at Skye, who, along with t'others, pretends not to see the intruder. I want to let my pointer fly, but when I glance at our lead archer, she don't give the signal. As planned, we hafta wait till more

Hunters are in sight. Skye could be dead by then. My jaw clenches so tightly it hurts.

Six more Hunters flank the first, pointers nocked and at the ready. An almost imperceptible shake of the head from our leader. Not time.

The first Hunter says in a booming voice, "By order of the Greynotes, you are our prisoners!"

Skye and t'others jump up, as if they're caught unawares. They raise their hands above their heads, as if to say, "No threat here!"

"Where are the others?" the Hunter says.

Brione answers. "In the tents, sleepin'. We're early risers 'ere."

Even in the darkening night, I can see the Hunter's smile, lit up by the firelight. An easy victory. He'll be rewarded by my father. He whistles, high and loud. A signal. All clear. Clean up time.

Dozens of Hunters pour into the canyon, wielding spears and blades and bows. I'm surprised to see Hawk stride in with them. He almost looks uncomfortable, his face twisted, like he's got a prickler stuck up his bum. A far cry from the confident new Hunter I saw 'fore.

Then *he* comes. At the back of the pack, protected by five guards. My father, hate-faced and narrow-eyed. After the Killer attack, it'll be a much needed victory for him. At least that's what he's thinking, what he's telling himself. We're thinking something else.

Our lead archer gives the signal.

Magnificently coordinated, the other lead archers tucked in the cave-pocked canyon walls give the signal, too, and suddenly the air is full of pointers. Hunters fall, pierced and bleeding.

Other Hunters, including Hawk, drop to the ground, on their bellies or to one knee, to avoid the pointers flying overhead. "Trap!" one of the Hunters yells, as if someone really needs to point it out.

My pointer is still aimed and I realize I haven't shot it. I've just been watching in morbid fascination as my Wilde sisters do the durty work for me. Sliding my hands, I try to find a target. A pointer zips past, narrowly missing my shoulder and clattering off the stone wall. A group of Hunter archers have spotted us and are shooting into the cave mouth. A girl beside me cries out as she's hit. She slumps over and I can't take my eyes off her. Without checking, I know. She was dead 'fore she hit the ground. Pointer through the heart. There's blood. So much blood. I can't…I can't…my chest is tight and my throat's closing and I can't do this, not any of it.

"Target the archers," the lead cries, and I close my eyes, try to get a grip on myself. Sky's down there. I hafta help her the best I can from up here.

I swivel back, locate an archer, release a pointer. *Twang!* A misfire; my pointer tumbles end over end like an injured bird, dropping harmlessly in front of the archers. A Skye-worthy mouthful of curses tumbles from between my lips as I grab another pointer.

One of my Wilde sisters takes out one of the archers. Three more pointers sail through the cave entrance, two connecting. Not flesh wounds. Death wounds. My sisters are dying 'round me.

I aim and fire. Too high. My muscles are too tense, I can't get a rhythm like I can on the shooting range when there's no one trying to kill me and my friends. When the targets are just targets and not people, not shooting back at you.

342

Don't give up.

Nock another pointer, shoot again—an archer cries out in pain. A leg shot. Another well placed pointer could finish him off.

'Fore I can shoot again, however, Skye is there, swinging her blade like a scythe, cutting down the surprised archers 'fore they have a chance to run. In training she's magnificent, full of speed and grace while kicking the blaze out of someone. She's every bit as magnificent now, but her every move is surrounded by darkness and violence, soaked in blood and anguished cries. 'Fore any of the archers have a chance to throw down their bows and draw the blades at their belts, they're all dead.

There're as many Wilde warriors as Hunters in the Canyon now, fighting hand to hand. An ill-aimed pointer could kill our own, so we lay down our bows, watch the action, safely removed from the carnage. Although we're winning, it's not without significant loss. I cringe as a well-muscled Hunter gut-slashes a Wilde, discarding her in a bloody heap.

Something snaps in me, like 'fore. Like when the Killers attacked the Hunters. Like when the Glassies attacked the village. A force beyond my own takes over, draws my knife, pushes me outta the cave. "Where are you going?" the lead archer shouts.

I shrug and climb down, my knife clamped firmly between my teeth.

~~~

The world swarms, red and black and beyond real. From up above, away from it all, shooting a pointer, trying to kill, felt so

343

easy, a simple act of releasing the tension in a bowstring. Down here, in the thick, to take a life is to lose your soul.

And yet Skye seems to relish it, slashing, hacking, taking a skin-splitting, blood-spilling Hunter's blade across her arm, growling like an animal, half-laughing as if she enjoys the pain, stabbing back, killing another.

Two warriors are struck down by a fearfully large Hunter. I hafta help them 'fore the Hunters finish them off. Moved by the surge of hot blood in my veins, I charge the brute, jam my knife into his back, so close to the dead I can taste it on my tongue. Blood spills over my hand and arm, but he doesn't go down, doesn't die like he's s'posed to. He whirls on me, nearly wrenching my shoulder out of its socket as I hang onto the knife, which is still stuck in his back. Bucking like a cornered tug bull, he wrangles me off, slings me to the ground. Stomps on my chest with a sledgehammer boot. Every last bit of air is expelled from my lungs as stars flash across my vision. His blade glints as it catches the shimmering glow of the fire. A drop of sweat drips from his chin onto my cheek.

This is what I deserve for bringing this scorch upon the Wildes. This is why the unseen force moved me to leave the safety of the cave. To die. To die for my mistakes. His blade flashes down.

The ring of metal on metal shrills in my ear as another blade crosses the Hunter's. Surprised, he's thrown back. Skye stands over me.

"It's burnin' over," she growls. "Retreat while you have the chance."

Through her legs I see the ogre-like Hunter scan the area 'round him, and then, sensing the truth of Sky's words, he lowers his head and runs.

I gasp, suck at the air, come up empty. Fire licks at my chest, splinters of glass pierce my skin. Not really, but that's how it feels.

"Breathe, Sie," Skye says, kneeling over me. I close my eyes, disappear to a place where Hunters and Wildes don't exist.

Thirty-Three

Twenty-six dead Wildes. We dig holes and bury them instead of lighting them on fire, ignoring yet another Heater tradition. Their blood's on my hands. Brione says it's an honest mistake, but I think she only says that outta respect for Skye. Wilde says my father is the only one to blame, and I can tell that she means it. But I know she's wrong. Crya glares at me every time she sees me. She don't say anything, just stares, which feels worse.

No one else knows it was me that brought this on us. 'Cept Lye, and she's gone away again to spy, so that we're ready for when they come back. Which they will. My father doesn't like to lose. And next time it'll be with lots more Hunters, maybe all of them, and they won't be so easily trapped. They'll be ready.

Yeah, my father got away. Skye said he saw her but she's not sure if he recognized her. By the time I scampered into the middle of things he'd already disappeared, the first to retreat when things went sour. Typical.

Hawk wasn't among the dead Hunters either, so I guess he slipped away too. I'm glad for it. If his life was good enough for Circ to save, then there must be something in him worth keeping 'round.

We buried the dead Hunters. Among the lot of us, we were able to identify most of the dead. Skye says she killed eight of them, more'n anyone else by double. The few that were injured we bandaged up and sent packing into the desert. They get to live if they can make it back to the tribe.

There's talk of moving our camp now that the Heaters know where it is, but no one has any ideas as to where. It's unlikely we'll find another spot as perfect. In the end, it's Wilde's decision, so things sorta go back to normal while we wait for her to tell us what to do. We train every day, cultivate the prickler fields, eat, sleep. But no one's heart is in it. Everyone lost a friend, a sister.

Lara survived, although, to her joy, she received several nasty-looking wounds that'll most certainly leave "beautifully jagged scars," as she says.

Char died, as did two of t'others from my Call. I still cry every night for them. I should be the one in the ground, not them. They deserved better.

The only thing that keeps me going is knowing my father'll be back. I don't care if he brings a hundred, or even a thousand, Hunters. I'll get to him one way or another, kill him with the knife my mother gave me. Avenge all the lives he's so ruthlessly taken.

He coulda saved my mother's life.

That statement alone keeps me going.

For the first coupla quarter full moons, everyone's kinda jittery, as if the Heaters might show up at any time, even though we all know the scouts'll let us know in advance. But things settle down as soon as Wilde makes the announcement that we're not leaving. Leaving now would mean abandoning much of the food we've been growing all spring. And doing so just 'fore the fiery heat of the summer sun burns everything away'll mean our certain death anyway. So, no, we'll not flee. We'll stand, fight, defend what's ours.

Her decision suits me just fine.

Another half a full moon passes without word from any of the scouts. The pricklers are full grown. The fields of scrubgrass are thick and high. I train harder'n ever in the mornings, and help to harvest the food in the afternoons. My body is lean and dark and sprouting muscles in places I never knew I had. I'm still the skinniest Wilde, but not by much anymore.

I'm strong. I'm determined. Like Skye, I've changed.

~~~

The first scout appears just as summer does. You can always tell when spring moves to summer 'cause the rains stop. We finished the harvest just in time, too, 'fore the sun goddess's eye could take everything as recompense for the gift of life.

The scout's not Lye, but she looks like her. Small, dark-eyed, and weary. She goes straight into the leaders' tent. This time they don't request my presence. My sister does, however, go with them. She seems to be included in everything, as if she's an unofficial leader.

I wanna stay close, to wait for Skye to come out so I can ask her what's going on, but Lara pulls me away for training. We're back in the same group now, 'cause it's conditioning and agility. Running, jumping, that sorta thing. Although I'm ahead of most of t'others in speed, I'm behind in coordination thanks to my two left feet.

My body is fully engaged in running through the boulder slalom course they've set up for us, but my mind is elsewhere, back at the leaders' tent, trying to figure out what the scorch is going on. What's the scout found out? If it was another Heater attack, wouldn't it've been Lye returning to deliver the news? Where has this road-weary scout been spying?

"What's on your mind?" Lara says, as I trip over the boulder I'm meant to be going 'round. She helps me up.

"There's a scout in camp today," I say.

"There is? Why didn't you tell me?"

It's a good question. It seems ever since the first Heater attack, my relationship with Lara has been fully one-sided. She talks, I listen, offering very little in return. I realize how unfair it's been to her, and how understanding she's been. "I'm sorry," I say. "I'm distracted." A weak explanation. Who's not distracted after everything that's happened?

And yet she nods, her eyes wide with compassion. "Your father has done so much evil," she says. She does understand, which takes me by surprise considering how little I've offered her lately.

"Lara, I know I haven't really been there for you. Char was your good friend. I shoulda…"

"I'm fine," she says quickly. "You've been great actually. It's easier for me not to talk 'bout it." I can't help but laugh. For once one of my screw-ups turned out to be a good thing.

"Thanks, Lara. For everything."

"If your father comes back, we'll get him," she says. The strained look on her face tells me it's not just talk.

~~~

Skye's in our tent when I get back from training. There's a grim look on her face.

"What happened?" I say, unable to hide the tension in my voice.

"There'll be an announcement at supper," she says.

"Skye! Don't make me beg!"

"Okay, okay, keep yer burnin' clothes on!" She repositions herself, curls her legs beneath her, stretches, cracks her neck and knuckles. Her every movement is agonizingly slow.

"Skye, c'mon!"

"Anyone ever tell you yer pushy?" she asks.

"Anyone ever tell you you're irritating?" I return.

She laughs. "All the time. Look, the scout that came in today was watchin' the searin' Glassies. Checkin' that they weren't causin' more problems'n usual. Watchin' 'em buildin' their buildin's, hidin' in their Glass City, that sorta thing."

"And?" I say impatiently.

"And she found out they're fixin' to go after the Heaters again."

My shoulders slump and I sigh. "That's a good thing, right? It'll keep them distracted while they hold the Glassies off like last time."

350

Skye just stares at me, her expression blank.

"Right?" I ask again.

She chews on her lip.

Then I realize. Last time they only survived 'cause of a lucky sandstorm. They were losing 'fore it hit, losing badly, regardless of what the Greynotes say. And now, between the Hunters they lost when the Killers attacked and the ones we killed, their numbers are dreadfully low.

"They won't survive 'nother attack," Skye says, as if to close the loop on my thoughts. "Scout says the burnin' Glassies are bringin' twice as many as last time."

"We hafta warn the Heaters," I say. "Somehow get a message to them. They hafta abandon the village." Although I hate my father, I don't hate the Heaters. Some of them may be like him, but so many ain't.

"They already know," Skye says. "Their scouts found out the same way ours did."

"So they're leaving then."

"No."

"What? Whaddya mean no? They hafta."

"You know, Father. He's the stubbornest, most arrogant man in fire country. He's fixin' to fight."

"What're we gonna do?" I ask.

"Count our lucky stars," Skye says.

I slam a fist in the durt, heat rising in my chest. "We can't do that! We hafta help!"

"Decision's been made."

"Then unmake it."

"They won't listen to me," Skye says. I realize then that's she's already tried to convince them to help the Heaters. I shake my head in disbelief.

"Wilde?" I say.

"Naw. Brione and Crya. Wilde's the leader, but she's no dictator. Majority rules."

"But Brione'll listen," I argue.

"Not this time. Crya's got her on her side."

"Sear it all to burnin' scorch!" I shout. Skye's head bobs back, surprised to hear an outburst like that from me. I lower my voice. "We can't just sit here and do nothing."

"Then do somethin'!" Skye says, 'fore crawling outta the tent.

~~~

Skye's right. It's so easy to fling complaints 'round like rocks, clattering them off the desert floor. But to take action takes guts. After a few full moons in Wildetown, my guts are raring to be used.

I storm up to the leaders' tent, knock on one of the poles, say, "Siena here to see Crya and Brione."

A few seconds later, Brione pokes her head out. "You shouldn't be 'ere," she hisses.

"This is the one place I should be," I retort. "Lemme in." When I arrived in Wildetown, weak and half-starved at the beginning of spring, I never thought I'd talk to someone like Brione like this.

"The decision's made." So she knows why I'm here.

"Yeah, I'm hearing that a lot lately. But that doesn't mean it's true. Lemme in."

She sighs, runs a hand over her bald head. Motions for me to enter.

When I enter I blink away the darkness, letting my eyes adjust gradually. No one's sitting in their normal positions. Crya's way off to one side, against the side of the tent as if she's 'bout to dig her way out. Wilde's on t'other side, sitting calmly, hands clasped. Brione takes a spot between them, so far from either of them she's like a lonely rock in a sea of sand.

"What do *you* want?" Crya demands.

"To talk," I say firmly, not letting myself be intimidated like usual.

"Then talk," Crya says.

"You can't abandon the Heaters," I say. I speak to Brione, 'cause I know Wilde's on our side and Crya won't change her mind, 'specially not if it's me that's asking her to change it.

"They abandoned us when they decided to treat women like slaves, baby machines, *Breeders*," Crya says.

"I ain't no Breeder," Brione says, her fists knotted at her sides. "I ain't ready for kids yet. Might never be."

"I'm not saying you hafta be a Bearer," I plead. "Just that we help them."

"No," Brione says with a humph. "I won't do it." I'm starting to get a feel for what Skye hadta deal with.

"Look, even if we hate what the Heaters are doing, it don't make this right. Their Laws may be all wrong, twisted up, but if we don't help, we'll be just as guilty."

Brione looks uncertain, like I've hit a soft spot, maybe one Skye or Wilde already hit. Another witness to the wrongness of this decision. She squirms, flexes one leg, then t'other.

"Brione!" Crya says, snapping Brione's gaze back to her. "Don't let this Runt tell you what to do!"

I wheel on her, my hands clenched at my side, my jaw set high and tight. The words I've worked so hard to cast out of my life tumble through my mind in a vicious spiral.

Runt, Scrawny, Weakling, Tent-Pole, Scrubgrass.

I am none of those things.

Never was.

Circ saw what I couldn't all along. He knew my heart was stronger'n my body. He saw my potential. "I've made mistakes, but I'm not weak," I say. "And I won't sit back and make more mistakes, even worse ones. Whether you all come with me or not, I'm going back to the village to fight."

"Good riddance," Crya mumbles. "Now get out of my face."

"Brione," Wilde says. "Listen to reason."

Brione's staring at me, just staring, like I've grown a new head that looks like a prickler, green and spiky. "All right," she says, "but I's only helping them this one time. Next time they's on their own."

"This is madness," Crya says. She scrambles to her feet and pushes past me, gone.

Wilde looks at me with interest. "Thank you," she says.

~~~

Skye's waiting for me outside the tent when I return. "You didn't," she says.

"I did," I say.

"I saw Crya storm past and she looked all grizzed off. What the scorch did they say?"

"We're going."

"What?"

354

"We're going," I repeat. "We're going to fight the Glassies."

"You know what? Yer incredible sometimes," she says. Coming from her, it means everything.

"Can you do something for me, Skye?" I ask, biting my lip as I say it.

"Sure. Anythin'."

"Cut my hair," I say.

Thirty-Four

We leave immediately. Well, nearly. Just as soon as we pack up, grab a few weapons, and pause for a moment so Skye can hack off the majority of my long, dark locks. At first I'm horrified, on the verge of tears as I hold the thick hair in my hands. But then I run my fingers over my scalp and I feel...really searin' good. Lighter and more in control. Like a Wilde One. If I see my father, at least he'll know exactly where I stand.

We hold a council 'fore we leave. No one's beng forced to go. Wilde simply states the facts, asks for each and every Wilde's help, and then gives everyone the option to stay or go. "There's no shame in staying behind," she says.

Everyone wants to fight, Crya included, for which I'm glad. We might not get along, but she's one scorch of a fighter and we'll need her. We'll need everyone.

We take enough food and water for two days, 'cause we need to travel light, and 'cause if we don't make it there in that amount of time, there won't be anything left of the village and we'll be able to scavenge all the food and water we want. And if we do make it and manage to help the Hunters defend the village, we'll surely be welcome to partake of whatever meager stores they've got. And if my father don't like it, he'll have my fists and feet to answer to.

We run during the first night, while the air is warm, rather'n hot. Our bows and sheathed blades click and clatter as we trot along, a hundred girls strong, with the Dead Snake River on our left. Surprised 'zards scurry out of our path, diving for their holes. A pack of Cotees prowls nearby, but a well-loosed pointer in their general direction scatters them away. The trip is so different this time.

When the sun comes up we continue on, but slow our pace to that of long walking strides, so as to lessen the effect of the harsh summer sun on our energy levels. We drink and eat without stopping.

The moment the sun reaches its apex in the red, cloudless sky, we stop. No one talks. We simply drop on command, find the softest ground we can, and fall into a restless sleep.

~ ~ ~

The moment the sun's heat falters, we run. Although all the conditioning work we've been doing was miserable and painful at the time, I'm thankful for it now. No one lags, no one crumbles from exhaustion. We're like separate parts of the same creature, moving as one across the desert.

'Fore the sun comes up again we've left the dried up river far behind. Today we run beyond the sun's apex, sacrificing some energy and sleep to gain ground. For all we know, the Glassies are already upon the Heaters.

But eventually we hafta stop, to rest, to sleep.

I'm sweaty and stiff and achy, but as determined as ever. I might be dead tomorrow, but today I'm alive.

~~~

When I awake it's already dark. T'other Wildes are gathering up their things, preparing to leave. I start doing the same.

"Wildes!" Wilde says. Everyone stops what they're doing, cranes their necks in her direction, where she stands on a large flat rock. Crya and Brione are at her sides, loyal now, regardless of previous arguments. I gain a bit of respect for Crya seeing her like that.

"Today we fight for a people who would hunt us down and make us their slaves. A people who we left because we didn't fit in, didn't agree with their customs and Laws. But today isn't about any of that, because they're threatened by others who would destroy them from the face of the earth for reasons we may never know. Just because they can perhaps. We don't do it out of the goodness of our hearts, or because we still have friends and family in the village, but because it's the right thing to do. Today we show them who the Wildes really are!"

A cheer goes up and I find myself joining in, yelling my tired lungs out, relishing the burn in my parched throat. I throw back my head and scream till I can't scream no more, spotting Circ's starry gaze smiling down on me, my silent protector.

For the final night, we run. My legs feel as fresh and light and full of energy as that first night. The miles fall away like the leaves from the trees in ice country.

When day breaks, we see the village.

~ ~ ~

The village reminds me of my mother, of growing up, of Circ. It also reminds me of Bart's hot, foul breath, his weight on me, feeling weak, helpless. I cast away the memories like shards of useless stone. None of that matters now.

We made it in time. From a safe distance away behind the dunes, the village almost looks peaceful. Beyond the guard towers, people emerge from their tents, rubbing their eyes and yawning, starting cook fires and bringing in hanging laundry, like it's just any other day. But one look at the guard towers and we know it's a mirage. At the top they're stuffed with Hunters, looking in every direction, ensuring they spot the Glassies at the earliest moment possible. And below, dozens of Hunters milling about, sharpening blades, testing the tension on their bowstrings, securing leather armor to their bodies. Not a normal day. A day of war.

The rest of the Wildes are hidden away behind the biggest dune in the near vicinity, and I was only allowed to tag along 'cause of Skye. The three leaders are beside us, speaking in whispers. Me, I'm afraid to even breathe, for fear that the village lookouts'll spot me and I'll ruin everything. I'm determined not to do anything stupid today. A couple of pricklers laugh at me. *Perry says hi*, they say. After this is all over

I think I might have MedMa take a look at my brain. (Although I'm not sure how he'd do that—through my ear maybe?)

The sun's rising fast and already it's sweltering; the hottest day yet. With a shock I notice the plentiful amount of scrubgrass growing 'round the village. The stuff is everywhere, practically right up to the border tents. Dangerous. By now, the Heaters would normally have pulled it all out and burned it. Perhaps amongst all their other problems it seemed like a small one. Very dangerous.

I'm continuing to scan the village when I see him. My father, striding from guard tower to guard tower, rallying the troops. I can almost hear his voice. *They're coming. The Glassies are coming.*

As if to confirm what my father seems to already know, there's a shout, and the men in the towers scramble down, waving their arms and pointing to the southeast. Our heads move in a collective swing in that direction.

We see them immediately. A Glassy army. They come tearing over the dunes on their chariots, which growl like animals, spinning dust and durt from the wheels that seem to propel them along. The men are holding glinting fire sticks and waving them in the air like spears. Against the stark whiteness of the desert, their pale skin blends in, making them appear as a strange moving blob, dotted and streaked with black.

Time to move.

"It's burnin' on," Skye says, the first to pull back.

The others follow her, Brione and Crya and Wilde, but I linger, watching the village. The women are screaming and hurding their children toward the huts, while the men—and even the Younglings, some so young-looking they might be Midders—race for the rally point, a guard tower at the southern edge of the border tents, where my father's already assembled a

360

large group of Hunters. Today they fight for their survival, and we fight with them.

"Sie! Come on!" Skye shouts, having realized I didn't follow her.

We run back to t'others, where Wilde is standing 'fore them, speaking. "...and you are all my sisters," she says, firmness and emotion in her clear voice. Despite the pounding of my heart and the shortness of my breath, her voice instantly calms me, like it always does, like spring rains on the desert sand.

"Today we stand for those who can't defend themselves, against a soulless enemy who destroys because it can. We will not remain idle while the freedom of others is threatened. Not when we have the power to do something about it. And we do have the power. As individuals we are strong, as Wildes we are invincible!"

A cheer goes up that surely both the Glassies and Heaters'll hear, but stealth doesn't matter now.

The moment of death is upon us.

~~~

With whoops and hollers, we launch ourselves into the desert.

The battle's already begun and the work of death waits for nobody. Streams of Hunters pour from the village, as volleys of pointers zip like flocks of birds overhead. A Glassy chariot crashes when its driver is killed by a pointer, straight through his chest. It flips, bounces, bashes into another chariot, which spins wildly 'fore crashing against a prickler, toppling it.

Thunderous booms sound across the desert but the sky is clear. It ain't thunder, but the Glassies' fire sticks, exploding and hurting anyone in their path. Hunters drop in waves, but are quickly replaced by a new line. The two forces move steadily closer. My initial exhilaration turns to fear.

What've I done?

Another chariot crashes, filled with pointers and blood.

We're close now and both the Glassies and Hunters seem to simultaneously realize they're not alone. Shouts erupt from both sides of the desert.

The lead archer brings us up short while Skye, Brione, and their warriors—which include Lara—charge ahead. On her signal, we nock our pointers, aim high above the Wilde warriors.

"Now!" she screams.

A chorus of twangs hums in my ears as our pointers are loosed. Dozens of Glassies die, but I can't tell whether my pointer was involved. At least half the Glassy fire sticks turn our way, booming intermittently. Wilde warriors drop like twigs of scrubgrass. I can't tell if Skye or Lara got hit.

A strangled groan gurgles from my throat. So much death. So much. I string another pointer on command. Release it, try to watch its flight. Almost miraculously, it embeds itself in the chest of a Glassy on foot, who was aiming his fire stick toward the Wildes. His legs crumble and his fire stick falls harmlessly aside.

We manage one more deluge of pointers 'fore our warriors get too close to risk hitting them. "Charge!" the lead archer shouts. We take off, carrying our bows in one hand and a pointer in the other.

I glance toward the village, where the number of Hunters is dwindling already. If we didn't arrive when we did...

The thought catches in my throat.

Just then, however, a second wave of Hunters races from the village, clutching bows, like us. The archers.

So much is happening, I can't keep up with it, my head swiveling back and forth. Wilde warriors are dying. Glassies are dying. Hunters are mostly dead. Not Skye or Lara, please not them, I plead with the sun goddess, who's at war, too, her eye beating down upon us with fury at our mindless violence.

There's a raucous shout from the south. Dozens of Glassy chariots growl over the dunes. The second wave.

There're too many.

It's over.

~ ~ ~

A hand grabs me from behind, twists me 'round.

I swing my bow at my attacker, catch him in the face, but still he holds on. "Siena, hold up, it's me." The warmest voice I've ever heard.

Through the tangle of our grappling arms, I see him. The Marked One. Feve.

The last person I expected to see. Or wanted to see.

"You!" I say, dropping my bow and swinging at him with clenched fists.

"Siena, stop," he says, blocking my fists.

But I don't stop, can't stop. If it wasn't for him, the Hunters woulda never found us—so many lives woulda been saved. "This is your fault!" I scream, kicking at him.

Cries of pain and death are all 'round, but I'm trapped in this weird place with a person I'd hoped to never see again. "Sie, I can explain…"

His words are grains of sand and I'm the wind, full of sandstorm fury. I wail on him and he doesn't try to defend himself. "I can fix things!" he screams and I stop.

"Fix things! Look 'round you, Feve." I wave my hand at the battle happening beyond us. "There's no fixing this."

His face seems to crumble when he sees what I mean—

BOOM!

A Hunter drops, his chest red—

A Glassy wanders aimlessly, a Hunter spear protruding from both his stomach and back—

A Wilde warrior strikes down a Glassy with a swift slash of her blade—

I spot Skye, graceful and powerful, hacking at half a dozen Glassies near her, who seem shocked by the intensity of her violence. One of them raises a fire stick.

I dive for my bow, snatching a pointer from my back in one swift motion, perhaps the most graceful moment of my life, my heart hammering outside of me, my eyes held open by determination…

I take aim.

The Glassy fires, a burst of red and black flame shooting from the end. *Noo! No, Skye, no!*

She doesn't drop, doesn't fill with red.

He missed! The searin' Glassy missed!

Flames burst from the ground beyond Skye, as if his shot has rebounded and is coming for her. The flame quickly spreads, rippling orange and red, racing along the desert floor, devouring the scrubgrass and licking at the dead and injured bodies littering the durt. The wind changes, gusting north, and the fire turns with it, roaring toward the village.

A firestorm. Ten times worse'n a sandstorm.

Sun goddess save us all.

Thirty-Five

As I watch in horror at the spreading fire, I see a flash of movement from the corner of my eye. The Glassy, shocked at first by the fire he started, takes aim at Skye, who's slashed down every blade-bearing opponent 'round her.

'Cept for him.

I raise my bow, trying not to quiver. Find my target. Steady, steady. *Twang!*

The sound is crisp and sharp and perfect. The Glassy clutches the shaft of the pointer in his neck as he falls.

Skye jerks 'round, her eyes wide, her face taut, sees me. Frowns when she sees the Marked One beside me. "They'll be here any moment," says the warm voice that I hate.

"They're already here, you idiot!" I scream. "Are you blind!" The air is full of smoke and I cough, choking on the noxious gas. I gasp as the wind changes again and the fire winds a circle 'round us through the scrubgrass.

A horn sounds, surrounding us, as if it's in league with the fire, making it impossible to figure out the direction of its origin. "Not them," Feve says. "*Them*." He motions to the west, where the dunes are suddenly filled with hundreds of brown bodies, their skin marked, a stampede of men and life.

The ground rumbles as they approach and I know I should be scared, 'cause they're charging right toward me, but I can only watch in awe as, like a hurd, they move as one, brandishing strange black-handled weapons with dual blades. They dance 'round and jump through the snaking cords of fire.

The moment they reach us, Feve lets out a guttural cry and melts into them, heading for the Glassies, who have stopped fighting, as stunned as me. The Marked collide with the first of the enemy, cutting them down 'fore they can even consider retreating. A few Glassies start shooting their fire sticks, but it's like throwing a pebble at a watering hole to try to empty it. All you get is a ripple when what you need is a wave.

With renewed vigor the remaining Hunters and Wilde warriors start fighting, chasing after the Glassies, who finally have the sense to retreat. They cut them down, not stopping until they're all dead, badly injured, or racing away on their chariots.

Only then, with my heart pounding, my throat dry, my hands shaking, do I let myself believe that we've won.

I crouch down in a circle of unburnt land, hug my knees, and, amidst a fiery inferno, thank the sun goddess.

~~~

367

"He wants to burnin' talk to you," Skye says. "But I tol' 'im he could shove it up his blaze shooter."

Normally my sister's antics and uncouth way of speaking would make me smile, but not after the blood I've seen spilt today. Brione's dead. Crya, too. Lara pulled through although I'm told I can't see her yet, 'cause she's being attended to by a few of the Marked, whose healing skills are coming in handy considering MedMa's the only one in the village who can help.

So when I hear Skye's words today, I can only sigh.

"I'll talk to him," I say, wondering why I say it. I reach a hand into the smoky air, batting at the wisps of gray as if they're something tangible I can knock away. My fingers go right through the haze. The village was spared, barely, whether by the sun goddess's will or Mother Nature's fickle sense of pity. The wind's changed, pushed the brush fires far, far away, off into the desert. Those who are least injured and not attending to the wounded are busily chopping away the tufts of grass and foliage closest to the village, just in case the fire returns.

"Just let 'im die," she says.

My head jerks up and my eyes meet Skye's. "He's dying?"

"Searin' right."

I hesitate. My stomach feels light as a raft of emotions tumble through it. Relief is definitely there. A tang of celebration for sure. But, to my horror, there's a touch of sadness, too. Why I should be sad 'bout the death of the man who ruined my life—who ruined all our lives—I do not know. I guess 'cause I still have the memories of the good times, 'fore he became a monster, 'fore he turned his back on everyone and everything but himself.

"I'm going," I say. I should be helping the cleanup efforts, but this is something I hafta do.

I hafta.

Skye shrugs. "Yer call. Want some company?"

I shake my head. "I hafta do this on my own."

I feel numb as she leads me through the village, past cries of pain as fire stick pellets are pried outta Hunters' skin with hot pokers, past hobbling Wildes, who are both bleeding and grinning, just like my sisters should. The Marked are everywhere, dark and menacing and serious, and I look for Feve—I'm not sure why—but I don't see him. Questions flash through my mind. Why did he come? Why did he bring his people? Why did they save us?

I shudder when I realize where Skye's taking me. We enter the section of Greynote huts, following a route that's as familiar to me as my own bellybutton. She pushes through the door of our old hut. Inside, darkness awaits.

The first thing I see is my mother's bed, where she lay dying the night of my Call. The bed she dragged herself out of, to help me, to save me, to kill for me. I imagine her still there, not stricken, but healthy, alive. The image vanishes when I hear a groan.

"Go, Skye," I say. She touches my shoulder briefly, and then leaves. Behind his curtain, my father cries out again. A voice murmurs something to him. "Who's there?" I ask.

Feve steps out.

"You!" I say.

"Me," he replies calmly.

"How dare you? Get out!" I have so many questions I wanna ask him, but none of them spring to mind. All I can think of is getting as far away from him as possible.

"Siena, please," he says.

"What are you doing here? Plotting and scheming with my father even on his death bed? You're a real baggard."

"I know," he says. "I screwed up. Your father...he was very convincing. He offered me a lot in return for watching you the night of your Call, following you if you escaped—skins and food and wood—things we desperately needed. We've been working together with the Greynotes for a long time, trading our services in exchange for goods that only your father can get from the Icers."

Although I'm surprised to hear that the Greynotes have a secret agreement with the Marked, I don't wanna hear 'bout it now. "And all you hadta give him was your soul," I say coldly.

"I didn't know, Siena. I swear!"

"Are you so daft as to not realize what he'd do the moment he knew where the Wilde Ones were? He tried to kill us!"

"I thought he just wanted you back. To bring you home. To keep you safe. I believed him."

"Then you're dumber'n a tug stuck in the mud," I say.

"I'll make this right," he says, touching my hand as he passes. I pull away sharply, wiping my hand on my clothes.

"There's nothing you can do to make it right," I say.

Head down, he leaves.

~~~

When I pull the curtain away, I gasp. It's my father on the bed, but not how I remember him. His eyes are closed, hiding his dark and brooding eyes. Dried flecks of blood are crusted on his lips and cheeks. His face is broken with pain.

"Sienaaaah," he murmurs.

"I came here for me, not for you," I say, keeping my distance.

His eyes creep open to slits, and then widen slightly when he sees me. "You've changed," he says. "You look different."

"I'm better for having left this place," I say.

"I've made mistakes," he says, his voice weak and unsteady.

"Name 'em!" I demand, dead set on hearing him admit what he's done.

"I should've listened to you—to what you wanted," he croaks.

"Searin' right," I mutter.

"I thought Bearing was the right path for you, for all the women…" He almost sounds penitent, but I ain't about to let him feel better 'bout himself.

"Bearing's fine," I say, "but you can't force it. And you can't force who we do it with!" My voice is rising.

"I don't know why the Icers are keeping us out," he rasps, his voice fading.

"'Cause they're afraid of catching the Fire," I say.

"Don't make sense," he gasps. "They have a cure. Why would they be scared?"

His question stops me. I'd never really thought 'bout that. Why indeed. But that's a question for another time. Now, he's just ducking all the mistakes he's made.

"You killed Mother," I say.

"No, I didn't help her. There's a difference."

"No there's not!" I scream, rushing forward. I grab him by the throat, squeeze. My hand is shaking, not with fear or uncertainty, but with power, with strength. This is the moment I been waiting for. Vengeance'll be mine.

"Wait," he rasps. "Circ…"

I release him slightly, maintaining a firm grip. "Don't you speak of him. You got no right. You killed him, too." My head's throbbing with rage. This man has taken everything from me.

Everything.

"No. I'm sorry, I never should have..." His voice falters and he gasps.

I let go, my shoulders slumping. I can't kill a man who's already dying. "You never shoulda what?" I say. "I wanna hear you say it."

He licks his chapped lips, wheezes, says, "I never should have fooled you, Siena."

"What? You're not making no sense. You NEVER fooled me. I found out everything, Father, did you know that? I snuck outta my cage in Confinement, saw the lifers—the innocent people you framed—slaving away. All for what? So you could get your precious cure for the Fire and outlive us all? You're disgusting."

"Not...what I...meant," he slurs, fading fast.

"Get to the point then, Father. What the scorch are you trying to say?"

"Circ," he moans. "All fake. Not really dead."

Thirty-Six

I don't know what to believe anymore. Father's dead, and the meaning behind his words with him. If he was trying to give me hope that Circ's out there somewhere, living, breathing, waiting to sweep me off my feet, he failed. There's no hope left for me, 'specially by my father's lies.

Circ would *never* fool me into thinking he's dead. Never. I only know it 'cause I'd never do that to him. It'd be the cruelest act of all. I saw him, watched him dying, pierced and broken. He gave me his searin' charm for tug's sake!

Burn it, burn it, burn it all to searin' scorch!

I'm full of rage so deep and controlling that I don't leave the hut for a long time. At my father. At his lies. At the hope that creeps into me even as I'm denying that it's there.

I break down. Right there on the floor. Curl up into a ball and cry my eyes out.

I don't stop until Skye and Lara arrive and wrap themselves 'round me. The two people who mean the most to me. They don't ask questions, just hold me.

My mind cleansed by my tears, a thought takes hold. At first it's just a wild idea, but then hope and imagination grab onto it, expand it, turn it into something that feels real, more real'n anything else that's happened to me over the last year.

I have no choice.

"I hafta go to Confinement," I say.

~~~

I wanna go alone, but Skye and Lara make the trek with me. It's the first time I've done it as a non-prisoner. If my father was telling the truth, and somehow forced Circ to tell the worst lie of his life to me, the only place he'd be able to hide him away would be in a cage.

"So yer friend Raja'll be 'ere?" Skye says when we're partway there. I told them we were coming to free the prisoners, which we are. They don't need to know what else I'm thinking. Plus, even if I wanted to tell them, I don't think I'll be able to speak what I won't allow my heart to hope.

"Yeah," I say. "If he's still alive." I don't dare to hope that either.

"I still can't believe your father confined innocent people," Lara says.

"He did a lot of wooloo things," I say.

"I'm glad he's dead," Skye says. I am, too, but I won't say it out loud, not after what he told me.

Confinement rears up in the distance, like the skeletons of massive beasts, frozen in time, the moment 'fore they were killed by a monster even bigger'n they. Will I find my heart between the ribs of one of the beasts? Or did my father manage to hurt me again, even with his last breath, giving me hope when there was none? Either way, exhilaration and anticipation swirl through me like the winds from earlier, gusting the fires this way and that.

Without a word, our steps quicken.

When we reach the edge of the prison, I say, "I'm gonna check every cage for survivors, you start digging them out."

Grim-faced, Skye and Lara nod.

Each of the cages contains a body. They look dead, but I can tell they're not, 'cause of the slight rise and fall of chests and shoulders as they sleep the day away. They don't know 'bout the Glassies or the wildfire, nor would they much care. For their lives are forfeit, stripped away by an evil leader who'd cage them to guarantee his own longevity.

I start running, pausing only momentarily at each cage to confirm the body inside ain't his. When I get to my old cage, I stop for an eternity, gazing in every nook and cranny, trying to locate the prisoner. If the world has any sense of irony, he'll be here. My old cage is empty. Perry confirms it. *No one's been here since you*, he says. And then: *Nice haircut.*

I manage to ignore him.

Next to my old cage, Raja lays utterly still, stiller'n my father's body had been when he passed on. Tears bubble up, drip down my cheeks. More blood on my father's hands, even after he's dead. "Oh, Raja," I say through the bars. I start to dig away the stone and rock blocking the cage entrance.

"Siena?" a voice says.

375

My eyes light up and I cry out, as Raja rolls over, his face thin and gaunt and perfect. A smile creases his mouth. "I knew you'd come," he says.

"I thought you were dead," I say, wiping away the tears just as more well up.

"Me? Nah, I'm a fighter. Like you."

I'm blubbering and digging and talking nonstop, telling Raja everything between gasps of air. I probably sound—and look— like a wooloo person, but I don't stop until I've dug through and crawled in. I don't even bother to stand, just squirm over, elbows and knees and hands, fighting my way to a friend I've never touched, never been this close to. When I get to him, I tackle him, forgetting how thin and withered away his malnourished body is.

"Ow—hurts," he groans.

"Sorry, Raja, I'm sorry, I'm just so happy you're here and alive. I've missed you." I kiss his durty forehead, hug him more gently, feel his emaciated ribs poking into me.

"I missed you, too," he says, hugging me back.

I feel so full of emotion I almost wanna go hug Perry. I would, too, if he wasn't so prickly. *You don't look so huggable either,* Perry says, *you're all hard edges and bone.*

I take it as a compliment.

"Yer friend's 'ere," Raja says.

"Yeah, I know," I say. "I came with her. My sister, too." I swivel 'round, looking for where Raja spotted them. There's no one in sight and Raja's looking at me strangely.

"What the scorch are you talkin' 'bout?" he says.

"What are you talking 'bout?"

"Not *what...who,*" he says. "Yer friend with the muscles and dimples."

Tingles zip up and down my body. I'm dreaming. I'm back in Call Class preparing for my Call, daydreaming, and none of this is happening and I'm 'bout to get called on and laughed at and forced to shovel blaze all by myself 'cause Circ's gone, and Lara, too, with my mother to follow soon. All. A. Dream.

"He's 'ere," Raja says.

And I'm gone, running on all fours like a Cotee, diving through the hole, scratching my back on the underside of the cage and my arms on the rocks and debris, but not caring, not hurting, not feeling anything but hope—real, perfect hope— that somehow, some way my father was telling the truth, that something'll go right.

I fight to my feet, dash along the remaining cages, ignoring Raja's cries behind me. Body after random body flashes 'fore my vision and I rush on, all the way to the end of the line, shift to the next line, race along those, too. Hafta find him. Hafta find him now, 'fore my heart explodes and sends me flying every which way. Where is he? Where is Circ? I can speak his name again 'cause he's real—Raja wouldn't lie to me, not after all we've both been through.

The last cage emerges on my right and I practically crash into it, throw myself against the bars, scan the ground. A body, in the corner, stronger'n most of t'others—could be him. "Circ!" I shriek, trying to squeeze between the bars, not wanting to hafta wait to shovel away the entrance.

The body turns, slowly, a face appearing.

I can't breathe, can't will one more breath through my lungs. I'm choking, falling back, curling up, hoping my heart'll stop beating of its own volition.

The face is Hawk's.

Thirty-Seven

"Siena," a voice says. Not close. Not far either. A dream voice. Soft and caring, smooth and gentle. My best friend, the one I love, the one I've always loved. Circ, in a dream.

I got my wish. I've died and joined him. Worth it—so worth it!—just to hear his voice.

I open my eyes to Confinement. Dread washes over me. Not a dream, a nightmare, a haunting voice of torment, sent by my father from Scorch. A voice that may very well drive me insane if I hear it again.

"Siena." The voice again, closer, so heart-warming it's maddening.

I look 'round, see him, so strong and perfect and *real* that I know my dead father's behind it. A cruel, cruel joke. "It's me. Circ," nightmare-Circ says.

I wanna go to him, to pretend he's not a ghost, the walking dead, but I can't. My heart can't take it. "No, Circ. Go away," I say.

He comes closer. Skye and Lara and Raja appear behind him, others, too. The prisoners they've released, skinny and beaten, but not dead. Not like Circ.

"I tried to stop you," Raja says. "Tried to tell you yer friend wasn't in a cage. He was in the hut with Keep. Not a prisoner. Not technically."

I don't know what to think—my head is a sand puddle. I'm exhausted from it all. From the death, the fighting, the searching, the hoping, the losing. My lips taste like salt and my eyes sting.

Finding a strength beyond my own, I stand, take a step forward, then another. When I start running, he does, too. I already know how this ends, how when I go to grab him, to clutch him to me, he disappears—a wraith from a world beyond. But even running *through* Circ is better'n nothing at all, so I keep running, taking in his beautiful skin, his perfect smile, his natural grace through my blurry vision.

Just 'fore I slide through him, I close my eyes.

The collision jars my eyelids open, and then I'm in his arms, and I *am* clutching him, my legs wrapped 'round his waist, my head nestled against his neck, feeling the warmth of his blood, the beat of his heart, the brush of his lips on my cheeks. It's all the proof I need to know—

—Circ's alive.

"Your hair," he murmurs into my neck.

"Skye cut it," I say, worried all of sudden. Perhaps the only thing he thought was pretty 'bout me was my hair. "I'm sorry."

"No," he says. "I love it. You look beautiful."

Thirty-Eight

We laugh loud enough that we can't hear the bad memories.

Sometimes it's at Circ cracking a joke, sometimes it's at me, sometimes it's at nothing at all, just 'cause our knees are touching, our hands are intertwined, our lips keep finding each other's again and again. In our spot, in the crook of the dunes that we call the Mouth, we find happiness.

After being friends for so long, it's strange being like this with Circ. We only had that one kiss 'fore I thought he died, and yet that was enough for us both to know we wanted more. So much more, if it was the sun goddess's will.

Circ kisses me again and then pulls away, looking at me like he always does, like he sees everything—not just what he can see, but what he can't too.

"You're happy," he says. It ain't a question.

"More happy'n ever," I say.

"But your mother…"

My smile fades and I raise my chin to the sky. Tears wanna come, but I won't let them. Not today. "She's up there watching," I say. "Smiling. Like I always knew you were."

Circ nods. "And your father?"

I look down, into the sand. I don't think I'll ever fully understand my father's motivations for his actions. Fear of death, perhaps? Fear of life, too, I think. But none of that matters now. I understand why Circ did what he did, and that's enough. My father threatened to kill me with his own two hands if Circ didn't fake his own death, leave the village forever, spend the rest of his days not as a prisoner, but as an assistant to Keeper, taking over as Keep one day. Circ believed my father would do it—kill me, that is. Circ told me the only reason my father didn't kill him is that he's too talented a Hunter, and he'd be used in that regard only, sent on the Hunts furthest from the village so I'd never see him. I don't know if that's true, but I prefer to hope that maybe my father let him live 'cause of me, 'cause he knew I cared for Circ. Even from the grave, his words haunt me: *I don't want to keep you apart, Siena, but you leave me no choice.*

"I'm sad he died, too," I say, and I think it might be true, if only 'cause of the good memories I still got, the ones that've never faded with time or with what he's done to me.

Circ chews at the inside of his mouth like he's trying to eat through it.

"What?" I say.

More chewing. "And me?" he asks.

I laugh. "Do I hafta spell it out for you?"

381

I don't blame Circ for any of it. I know he did what he thought he needed to do protect me. He did it 'cause he cared 'bout me enough to live without me.

"Could you?" he says, grinning that grin. Sometimes I wish I could just turn it off 'cause it can be a little weird feeling those bubbles in my chest all the time. I punch him, but it don't change nothing.

He won't stop grinning until I answer him. So I do. "I'm glad I'm here with you," I say.

"That all?" he says, those dimples staring me down.

"What the scorch else do you want?"

"I dunno. I thought maybe you'd say something about how you've loved me for a long time, or that you've always loved me, or that you won't never let me go. Something like that." I try to hold it back—my smile, that is—but I can't, not for one moment. 'Cause I know he's not giving me words to say. Nope. He's telling me everything he's wanted to tell me for a long time.

"Yeah," I say. "All that."

He sticks his smile next to mine and I lean into him, feeling all his words in the heat of his body, not saying anything for a while.

Everyone's been so busy for the last few days that this is the first time me and Circ have really been alone. At Wilde's suggestion, we buried, rather'n burned, the dead. The quicker we get away from the old ways the better. Everyone agrees that much. I cried for each'n every Wilde we put in the ground, my friends, my sisters. Several Marked died, too, but not as many due to their late arrival and overwhelming numbers. The Heaters took the most casualties, hundreds. I cried for them, too.

We burned the pale Glassy bodies.

"Do you think the Tri-Tribes will work?" Circ says all of a sudden, like he's just thought to ask.

I close my eyes, remember all that's happened since the battle. After a lot of arguments and plenty of fights, a tenuous decision was made to join forces, at least for now, creating a new tribe, called the Tri-Tribes, comprised of the Marked, the Heaters, and the Wildes, with shared leadership amongst all three groups. I don't know how long it'll last, considering everyone seems to pretty much hate each other right now, but it's nice to have a little peace and stability for a while. Wilde and Skye'll represent the Wildes. Circ's father and Lara's mother'll vote on behalf of the Heaters. Two dark, mysterious Marked men who I don't know stepped forward for them. Not Feve, that's the important thing.

"It could," I say, trying hard to believe it while shooting prayers to the sun goddess.

Circ pushes his foot into mine. "I think it will," he says. "The Heaters seem to be falling into line with it."

"After the beating they took, they better," I grumble. "But it's not them I'm worried about. I don't trust the Marked any further'n I can throw them."

As it turns out, the mysterious Marked weren't so mysterious after all. They've been struggling for a long time, barely surviving the winters, losing numbers every year. Which is why they'd been working with the Greynotes the whole time—to survive. But still, with men like Feve amongst them, I'll be keeping my eyes on every last one of them.

"They decided to move the village," I say, my eyes lighting up all of a sudden, remembering. There're so many *other* things

I like to do with Circ now that I keep forgetting to tell him everything I find out from my sister.

"Really?" Circ says.

"Yeah. Four votes to two. Guess whose representatives voted against."

"The Heaters?" Circ says, raising an eyebrow.

"Of course," I say.

"Stubborn baggards."

"That they are. They'll never learn."

"It's a good move," Circ says. "The further and more hidden we get from the Glassies, the better."

I couldn't agree more. The Glassies'll be back, that's for certain, but we don't hafta make things so easy on them. "They'll announce it tonight," I say. "Now they'll hafta fight 'bout *where* to move it."

"Now *that* could take a while," Circ says, and I laugh. "Anything else you forgot to tell me?"

I think'bout it and then shake my head. "Everything else's up in the air, but Wilde's been hinting that another big decision'll be made soon."

"About what?"

"The Cure," I say.

"What about it?"

"Well, it's all pretty knocky that the Icers don't want us on their land, and they only gave my father such small amounts of the Cure. We wanna know why."

"Guess someone's gotta go pay the Icy King a little visit," Circ says slyly, narrowing his eyes.

"Yeah, someone," I say.

Sounds like another adventure, I think. Another adventure for another day.

"What's with Skye and Feve?" Circ asks and I groan.

"What's with all your burnin' questions?" I snap back.

Circ laughs and the anger drops outta me like a sinkhole. "Just seems like they've been spending an awful lot of time with each other," Circ says.

I wrinkle my nose 'cause he's right. Skye's definitely been talking to Feve, which I both hate and like. I hate it 'cause it's Feve, and he's a low-life baggard who I don't want my sister talking to. But I like it 'cause it means I don't have to talk to him, and Skye can ask him all the questions I been meaning to. Like why the scorch he did what he did, turning us in to my father and then bringing the Marked to save us all. According to Skye, there's been a longstanding agreement with the Marked and the Heaters. Like everything else with the burnin' Greynotes, it was a secret one. They had each other's backs, so to speak. And as for giving up the Wildes, he's sticking to his story that he didn't realize how bad my father really was. As if.

"She's just pushing him for information," I say.

Circ nods but I can tell he don't think that's all there is to it. "I've been talking to some of the Marked too," he says.

My head jerks to the side. "You have? Why?"

"Welcoming them, making friends—you know, the things normal people do."

"And I ain't normal?" I say.

"Not even close," he says, laughing. But 'fore I can even hit him or shoot him a stony stare, he says, "And the guys I've been talking to told me all about where Feve comes from."

"Like I care 'bout where a no-good baggard like him comes from," I say. But then, nonchalantly, I ask, "So what's his story?"

Circ smiles. "It's nice knowing something you don't."

385

"Just spill it."

"You know the story you told me about your mother and Brev?"

I freeze, remembering every word of it. But what's Brev got to do with Feve?

I nod.

"Brev was Feve's father," Circ says.

My head falls back, crunching into the sand. "Of all the stupid, wooloo, good-for-nothing..."

"Not thrilled, eh?" Circ says.

Thrilled? More like disgusted. "It's an insult to my mother and to Brev," I say, squeezing my eyes shut and casting a wish on my mother's star. The wish: that Feve melts into a pile of mush.

I feel Circ grab my hand and I'm pretty sure he knows I'm not happy with the news. He changes the subject again. "Do you think Hawk's a changed man?" he asks.

It's my turn to chew through my mouth. 'Cause it's a tough question. Evidently there was more goodness in Hawk'n I ever knew, although I still can't stand to look at his ugly face. Word is he protested the attack on Wildetown, but my father forced him to go. Afterwards, he spoke out, and was sent to Confinement, ending up in that last cage, when I mistook him for Circ and nearly fainted. He's more'n made up for anything he ever did to wrong me. But still...

"I dunno, but he ain't my friend or nothing," I say.

Circ grins. "Mine either," he says. "But maybe at least we don't have to hate him anymore."

Yeah to that, I think. I been tired of hating for a long time.

But none of that matters to me right now, 'cause I have all I need. I rest my head on Circ's chest, relishing the magnificent sound of his strong heartbeat, as if it might burst from his chest. For this moment I can just be me, Siena, Skinny and Strong, all at the same time.

Circ's hand brushes against my wrist, draws lazy circles on my arm, lingers on my charm bracelet. His pointer charm rocks under a gentle breeze. "You kept it," he says.

"You can't take it back," I say, grinning. "It means you're mine until the sun and the moon and the stars fall from the sky."

"Is that so?"

"Searin' right."

"I wouldn't take it back in a million years," he says, clasping my hand.

"How long can we stay here?" I ask.

"Only for ever," he promises, a lie that's as real as fire country being safe.

~*~

Keep reading for a sneak peak at the action-packed sequel, book two of the Country Saga (a Dwellers sister series), *Ice Country*, coming April 5, 2013!

Acknowledgements

I would be nothing without my readers, who've searin' stuck with me through thick'n thin, who've made all the hours of hard work, of stressing over burnin' deadlines and going wooloo over word count...so now I say, to scorch with all that, 'cause you're awesome and you've made this journey so special and worthwhile and it would mean nothing—*nothing!*—without all of you along for it. So a special thanks to you, my readers, particularly those of you in my Goodreads fan group, which, at the time of writing this, was over 900 members! I never believed it could grow so big, but you all did, and it's all thanks to your efforts, for you forcing your friends and family members to read my books when they probably didn't want to (like *really* didn't want to!). I couldn't do what I love to do on a fulltime basis without all of you.

I also have to give a give a high five and a big hug and kiss to my wife, Adele, who supports me each and every day when I'm lost in other worlds, in other people's (or prickler's named Perry) heads for more than five hours a day, plus another five of tap-tap-tapping on my iPhone, chatting in my fan group and answering reader messages. You are my ultimate beta reader, and our many discussions of plot, the cheesiness of my dialogue, and how much you love my writing helps me in ways I can't even explain. Oh, and your coffee is the most delicious and having you by my side is what keeps me sane. Thank you for changing my life and for believing in me.

To my marketing team at ShareARead, Nicole Passante and Karla Calzada, as usual you never cease to astound me at your unceasing ability to get my books in the right readers' hands.

We started this together, and before our very eyes it's turning into something very special. Thank you for being my partners in all the fun (and for staying up till all hours of the night planning blog tours and giveaways!).

To my cover artist, Regina Wamba, it's my first time working with you but you've simply outdone yourself, taking the smorgasbord of ideas that Adele and I spout at you and piecing it together into something beautiful and a perfect representation of the world I created.

Next, a GINORMOUS thanks to my team of beta readers, some of you who've been around since The Moon Dwellers, and others who've just joined for this book. I love you all. *Fire Country* is at least ten times better because of your insightful and honest feedback. So thanks to Laurie Love, Alexandria Theodosopoulos, Kayleigh-Marie Gore, Kerri Hughes, Terri Thomas, Lolita Verroen, Rachel Schade, Ventura Dennis, Krystle Jones, and Anthony Briggs Jr.

For the first time and certainly not the last time, I'd like to thank my super-secret street team (you know who you are). In the shadows you move like ninjas, penetrating even the toughest of bloggers, slipping my books into their author features and reviews almost without them knowing. I don't know how you do it, but: You. Are. My. Heroes.

I'd also like to offer a very special thanks to one of my readers, Rachel Hanville, for helping me correct a mathematical error in the ages of my characters! Even writers should have a calculator handy!

And last but not least I'd like to thank my friend Teddy (who happens to be a teddy bear), who thinks he's real and helped inspire the character of Perry the Prickler. I know I say bad things about you and throw you against the wall sometimes, but in my heart I love you.

Discover other books by David Estes available through the author's official website: http://davidestesbooks.blogspot.com or through select online retailers including Amazon.

Young-Adult Books by David Estes

The Dwellers Saga:
Book One—The Moon Dwellers
Book Two—The Star Dwellers
Book Three—The Sun Dwellers
Book Four—The Earth Dwellers

The Country Saga (A Dwellers sister series):
Book One—Fire Country
Book Two—Ice Country
Book Three—Water & Storm Country

The Evolution Trilogy:
Book One—Angel Evolution
Book Two—Demon Evolution
Book Three—Archangel Evolution

Children's Books by David Estes

The Nikki Powergloves Adventures:
Nikki Powergloves—A Hero Is Born
Nikki Powergloves and the Power Council
Nikki Powergloves and the Power Trappers
Nikki Powergloves and the Great Adventure
Nikki Powergloves vs. the Power Outlaws (Coming in 2013!)

Connect with David Estes Online

Goodreads Fan Group:
http://www.goodreads.com/group/show/70863-david-estes-fans-and-ya-book-lovers-unite

Facebook:
http://www.facebook.com/pages/David-Estes/130852990343920

Author's blog:
http://davidestesbooks.blogspot.com

Smashwords:
http://www.smashwords.com/profile/view/davidestes100

Goodreads author page:
http://www.goodreads.com/davidestesbooks

Twitter:
https://twitter.com/#!/davidestesbooks

About the Author

After growing up in Pittsburgh, Pennsylvania, David Estes moved to Sydney, Australia, where he met his wife, Adele. Now they travel the world writing and reading and taking photographs.

A SNEAK PEEK
ICE COUNTRY
BOOK 2 OF THE COUNTRY SAGA

Available anywhere e-books are sold April 5, 2013!

Chapter One

It all starts with a girl. Nay, more like a witch. An evil witch, disguised as a princess, complete with a cute button nose, full, red lips, long, dark eyelashes, and deep, mesmerizing baby blues.

Oh yah, and a really good throwing arm. "Get out!" she screams, flinging yet another ceramic vase in my general direction.

I duck and it rebounds off the wall, not shattering until it hits the shiny marble floor. Thousands of vase-crumbles crunch under my feet as I scramble for the door. I fling it open and slip through, slamming it hard behind me. Just in time, too, as I hear the crash of something heavy on the other side. Evidently she's taken to throwing something new, maybe boots or perhaps herself.

Taking a deep breath, I cringe as a spout of obscenities shrieks through the door and whirls around my head, stinging me in a dozen places. You'd think *I* was the one who ran around with a four-toed womanizer named LaRoy—that's LaRoy with a "La", as he likes to say. As it turns out, I think *La*Roy had softer hands than she did.

As I slink away from the witch's upscale residence licking my wounds, I try to figure out where the chill I went wrong. Despite her constant insults, narrow-mindedness, and niggling reminders of how I was nothing more than a lazy, liquid-ice-drinking, no good scoundrel, I think I managed to treat her pretty well. I was faithful, always there for her—not once was I employed while courting her—and known on occasion to show up at her door with gifts, like snowflake flowers or frosty delights from Gobbler's Bakery down the road. She said the flowers made her feel inadequate, on account of them being too beautiful—as if there was such a thing—and the frosty's, well, she said I gave them to her to make her fat. Which, if I'm being honest, was partially true. Now I wish I hadn't wasted my gambling winnings on the likes of her.

In fact it was just yesterday morning when I last stopped by to deliver some sweet treats, only to hear the obvious sounds of passionate lovemaking wafting through the black stone of her elegant front door. Needless to say I was on the wrong side of things, and much to my frustration the door was barred by something heavy.

So I waited. And waited. After about three rounds of the love-noises, soft-hands LaRoy emerged looking more pleased with himself than a young child taking its first step. In much less time than it took for the witch to put the smile on his face, I wiped it off, using a couple of handfuls of ever-present snow and my rougher-than-bark hands. I capped him off with matching black eyes and a slightly crooked, heavily bleeding nose. He screamed like a girl and ran away crying tears that froze on his cheeks well before they made it to his chin.

Hence the bigtime breakup today.

Best of luck, witch, I hope crooked-nosed LaRoy makes you very happy.

Why do I always pick the wrong kinds of women? Answer: because the wrong kinds of women usually pick me.

Walking down the snow-covered street, I mumble curses at the beautiful stone houses on either side. The White District, full of the best and the richest people in ice country. And the witch, too, of course, the latest woman to add to my so-not-worth-the-time-and-effort list.

I pull my collar tight against the icy wind, and head for my other girlfriend's place, Fro-Yo's, a local pub with less atmosphere than booze, where a mug of liquid ice will cost you less than a minute's pay and the rest of your day. Okay, the pub's not really my girlfriend, but sometimes I wish it was.

Although it's barely midmorning, Fro's is open and full of customers. But then again, the pub is always open and full of customers. We might not have jobs, but we'll support Yo, the pub owner, just the same.

Snow is piled up in drifts against the gray block-cut stone of the pubhouse, recently shoveled after last night's dumping. Yo's handiman, Grimes, is hunched against the wind with a shovel, clearing away the last of it along the side, leaving a slip-free path to the outhouse, which will be essential later on, when half the joint gets up at the same time to relieve themselves. There are two things that don't mix: liquid ice and real ice. I've seen more broken bones and near broken necks than I'd like around this place.

"Mornin', Grimes," I say as I pass.

Grimes doesn't look up, his matted gray hair a dangling mess of moisture and grease, but mumbles something that sounds a lot like, "Icin' neverendin' colder'n chill night storms..." I think there's more but I stop listening when he starts swearing. I've had enough of that for one day. And yet, I push through the door of the obscenity capital of ice country.

"Dazz! I was wondering when you'd freezin' show up," my best friend says when I enter. Following protocol, I stamp the snow off my boots on the mat that says *Stamp Here*, and tromp across the liquid-ice-stained floorboards. Buff kicks out a stool at the bar as I approach. He's grinning like an icin' fool.

For a moment the place goes silent, as half the patrons stare at me, but as soon as they recognize me as one of the regulars, the dull drone of conversation continues, mixing with the clink of tin jugs and gulps of amber liquid ice.

"Get a 'quiddy for Dazz," Buff shouts to Yo above the din. The grizzled pub owner and bartender sloshes the contents of a dirty, old pitcher into a tinny and slides it along the bar. Well practiced bar sitters dodge the frothing jug as it skates to a stop directly in front of me. As always, Yo's aim is perfect.

"Thanks," I shout. Yo nods his pockmarked forehead in my direction and strokes his gray-streaked brown beard thoughtfully, as if I've just said something filled with wisdom, before heading off to refill another customer's jug. He doesn't get many thanks around this place.

"Out with it," Buff says, slapping me on the shoulder. His sharp green eyes are reflecting even the miniscule shreds of daylight that manage to sneak through the dirt-smudged windows.

"Out with what?"

Shaking his head, he runs a hand through his dirty-blonde hair. "Uh, the big breakup with her highness, Queen Witch-Bitch herself. It's all everyone's been talking about all morning. Where've you been? I've been dying to get all the the details."

Elbows on the bar, I lean my head against my fist. "It just happened! How the chill do you know already?"

Buff laughs. "You know as well as anyone that word travels freezin' fast in this town."

I do. Normally, though, the gossip's about me getting broken up with after having done something freeze-brained, not the other way around. "What are they saying?" I ask, taking a sip of 'quiddy and relishing the warmth in my throat and chest.

Buff's excitement seems to wane. He stares at his half-empty mug. "You don't wanna know," he says, and then finishes off the last half of his tinny in a series of throat-bobbing gulps.

"Tell me," I push.

"Look, Dazz…" Buff lowers his voice, a deep rumble that only I can hear. "…the thing about women is, when you want 'em they're scarcer than a ray of sunshine in ice country, and when you don't, they're on you like a double-wide fleece blanket." Now I'm the one looking at my unfinished drink, because, for once, one of Buff's snowballs of wisdom is spot on. I thought I wanted the witch—because of her looks—but as soon as I got to know her I wanted to toss her out with the mud on my boots.

Using my knuckles, I knock myself in the head three times, exactly like I rapped on the witch's door this morning before it all went down. *Don't ask, don't ask, don't ask,* I mentally command myself. "What are they saying?" I ask, repeating myself. Having not listened to my own internal advice, I feel like knocking my skull against the heavy, wooden bar a few dozen more times, but I manage to restrain myself as I wait for Buff's response.

"Well...some of them are saying good sticks for you, she got what she deserved, Brown District pride and all that bullshiver. You know the shiv I mean, right?"

All too well. I nod. "And the others?"

Buff chews on his lip, as if deciding how to break something to me lightly.

"Give it to me straight," I say.

He sighs. "You know tomorrow they'll move onto the next freezin' bit of juicy gossip, right?"

"Buff," I say, a warning in my voice. I know what's coming, so I tilt my tinny back, draining every last drop in a single burning gulp.

"If I tell you, promise me you won't start anything—I'm not in the mood."

Looking directly into his black pupils, I say, "I promise."

He rolls his eyes, knowing full well I just lied to him. Then he tells me anyway. "Coker's been saying the witch was too good for you, that she shoulda dumped your mountain-fearin' arse a long time ag—"

I'm on my feet and breaking my false promise before Buff can even finish telling me. My stool clatters to the floor behind me, but I barely notice it. I get a bead on Coker, who's between two of his stone cutting mates, laughing about something. Regardless of what it is, and even though they've probably moved on from discussing me and the witch already, I pretend it's about me. About how I'm not good enough for someone in the White District. About how I'm lazy and good for nothing.

My fists clench and my jaw hardens as heat rises in my chest. Always aware of what's happening in his pub, Yo says, "Now, Dazz, don't start nuthin', remember the last time..."

399

"Dazz, hold up," Buff says, his feet scuffling along behind me.

I ignore them both.

When I reach Coker he's already half-turned around, as if sensing me coming. I spin him the rest of the way and slam my fist right between his eyes. A two for one special, like down at the market. Two black eyes for the price of one. His head snaps back and thuds gruesomely off the bar, but, like any stone cutter, he's tougher than dried goat meat, and rebounds with a heay punch of his own, which glances off my shoulder, sending shivers through my arm.

And his friends aren't gonna sit back and watch things unfold either; they jump on me in less time than it took for the White District witch to cheat on me, swinging fists of iron at my head. One catches my chin and the other my cheek. I jerk backwards, seeing red, blue, and yellow stars against a black backdrop, and feel my tailbone slam into something hard and flat. The wooden table collapses, sending splinters and legs in every direction—both table legs and people legs. I'm still not seeing much, other than stars, but based on the tangle of limbs I'd say the table I crashed into was occupied by at least three Icers, maybe four.

I shake my head and furiously try to blink away the dark cloud obscuring my sight, feeling a dull ache spreading through the whole of my backside. When my vision returns, the first thing I see is Buff hammering rapid-fire rabbit punches into one of the stone cutter's, sending him sprawling. The area's clearing out, with patrons scampering for the door, which is a good thing, because Coker gets ahold of Buff and throws him into another table, which topples over and skids into the wall.

Me and Buff spring to our feet simultaneously, cocking out fists side by side like we've done so many times growing up in the rugged Brown District. Buff takes Coker's friend and I take Coker. We circle each other a few times and then all chill breaks loose, as the fists start flying. After taking a hit in the ribs, I land a solid blow to Coker's jaw that has him reeling back, off balance and stunned. I follow it up with a hook that sends a jolt of pain through my hand, which is likely not even a quarter of the pain that I just sent through his face. He drops faster than a morning turd in the outhouse.

I whirl around to find Buff in a similar position, standing over his guy and shaking his hand like he's just punched a wall. The guy he was fighting was so thick it probably was like hitting a wall. We stand over our fallen foes, grinning like the seventeen-year-old unemployed idiots that we are, enjoying the aliveness that always comes with winning a good, old-fashioned fair fight.

Yo's glaring at us, one hand on his hip and the other holding an empty pitcher. I shrug just as his eyes flick to the side, looking past us. The last thing I hear is a well-muffled scuffle.

Everything goes black for good when the wooden stool slams into the back of my head.

Ice Country by David Estes, available now!

Made in the USA
Coppell, TX
14 January 2021